Winds of Change

Sundowners
A Division of
Treble Heart Books
1284 Overlook Dr.
Sierra Vista, AZ 85635-5512

Published and Printed in the U.S.A.

ISBN: 978-1-932695-87-8

3 1969 01958 0264

What reviewers are saying...

Winds of Change brings alive the West before the Civil War, moving from bison hooves shaking the earth and traditional, horse-rich Arapaho villages to Army forts with their rigid society and trappers' rough encampments in the Cascade Mountains, and finally to the wind-blasted prairie of Kansas Territory, where farmers begin to slice into the black prairie sod. Although rich in historical detail, this saga of a family broken and re-formed is timeless, a journey through the lives of ordinary people who must come to terms with who they are in order to walk the path they are given with love.

—Susan J. Tweit, author of *Walking Nature Home: A Life's Journey*, forthcoming from Univ. of Texas Press

With an easy, unpretentious writing style, Gwyn Ramsey keeps her novel moving at a brisk space. *WINDS OF CHANGE* blends the best elements of historical, romance and Western fiction, and reminds us of why Americans like to read a good, strong story about our country.

— Johnny D. Boggs, Three-time Spur Award-winning author of *Camp Ford* and *Northfield,* Dorchester Publishing Co, Inc.

The characters in *Winds of Change* are so real that it is evident Gwyn Ramsey did in-depth research. The way she weaves the different character's lives together is intriguing and exciting, and kept me wanting more. The incite into the lives of the American Indians and how they survived off the land is extremely vivid. These native people had so many good qualities but the violence among the different tribes is an eye opener. By our standards, even in that time, they lived a very hard life even before the Whites encroached upon them. This story is a fascinating read.

—Martha Kowalski, Reader

Gwyn Ramsey's series about the American West features well-developed characters, well-researched history, and well-crafted stories. As you read her novels, step back in time and enjoy the ride!

— Joyce B. Lohse, award-winning author, "Now You Know Bios"

"In this historical family saga, WINDS OF CHANGE, Ms. Ramsey has captured the human spirit and the human heart."
— Loretta C. Rogers, Author of *ISABELLE AND THE OUTLAW,* The Wild Rose Press

Other Books by Gwyn Ramsey

Journey to Tracer's Point

Acknowledgements

I'd like to thank my friends Marilyn Russell and Nan Brown who diligently edited each chapter with a critical eye. And to Candace Peterson who was always on the lookout for that one special book to add to my reference library.

My special thanks goes to all of my friends who read the many drafts and contributed to the finalization of this story, a story of my heart.

Dedication

To my parents Geraldine and William Koetterheinrich who would have been proud to know that my book was finally published.

And to my children, Mark Ramsey, Steve Ramsey, Dana Clemons, Jeff Ramsey, Jim Marcrum, and Glen Morris. May they remember age is not a deterrent and that reaching for the stars is a wonderful adventure.

Winds of Change

Gwyn Ramsey

Sundowners

a Division of

Treble Heart Books

Prologue

Spring of 1852, St. Charles, Missouri

Crossing his arms over his wide chest, Patrick O'Brien leaned against the log wall in his older brother's workshop. Watching John pull the drawing knife over the raw piece of maple, he toed the shavings that littered the floor. The smell of fresh cut wood was intoxicating. Pat envied his brother's woodworking talent, especially since he had trouble nailing up a sign.

John was a gifted man who turned timber into beautiful pieces of furniture. He bent his thin five-foot-eleven-inch frame over his worktable. Strands of bright red, wavy hair straggled across his freckled forehead.

"You make that look so easy," Patrick said. Moving away from the wall, he ambled over to the shaving horse and ran his fingers over the smooth surface.

"With a little more training, you'd be able to do this." John stood up and stretched his arms over his head.

Patrick laughed. "I don't think so. Don't you remember what happened when you asked me to help with that chest top a couple of months ago? Never saw so many grooves and waves except in the Mississippi River."

John grinned and nodded. "You could be right. On the other hand, you have a sure hand with horses."

"Yes. Your wood smells better and the shavings are easier to clean up."

John chuckled. "There are times I believe you take after Da more than I do with your gift of gab." Then he grew serious. "Are you still thinking about heading west?"

"Yes." Patrick sauntered to the open door and watched the wagons making their way, heading up the Boone's Lick Trail. "I have to try to find Sarah. She's out there somewhere and my only hope is she hasn't found someone to turn her head."

"Do you think you can find the Andersons? They've been gone three years."

Patrick turned to face his brother. "I don't know, but I've got to try. They were headed to California."

"That's a lot of territory to cover."

"I know." He paused for a moment. "I can't get her out of my mind. All I do is think about her, remembering that beautiful face, the auburn hair, and her wonderful smile. When I left her the day of Da's funeral, my heart hurt and my stomach lurched." He kicked at the shavings on the floor, feeling a bit foolish. "I gave her a cross that day made out of grass, promising someday to find her. I plan on keeping my promise."

John arched one eyebrow and grinned. "I didn't realize you were smitten with her."

Dismissing his brother's remark, Patrick continued. "I wonder if she still has the cross I made for her."

John put down his drawing knife. "I remember Sarah watching us leave the inn that terrible day." He gazed at his brother. "Well, maybe it's supposed to happen for you two. Maybe you'll find her waiting for you."

"I'll find her!"

"If you don't, remember you can always come home. You can stay with me."

"I know that," said Patrick. "I'm just not suited for this city life. Hell, by the time I'd get back, you'll be married, what with the attentions you're paying Charlotte Sue Evans."

John looked down at the floor, his face flushed. "You're probably right."

The two brothers stood in deep thought, reflecting the changes in their lives over the past few years.

Finally, John spoke. "You know, Ma's gonna be upset with your leaving."

"Why? She has Mr. Blackwell sitting in the parlor this very minute, drinking tea. From the looks of things, they'll be married before the year's up."

John laughed. "I guess you're right about that, too. How do you feel about having a step-father?"

"It's all right by me. Ma needs someone. Soon Elizabeth and Joshua will be leaving and then she'd be alone."

"Yes."

"Look after Elizabeth and Joshua while I'm gone. Especially our little brother. He keeps getting into all kinds of trouble."

"You know I will." John grasped Patrick by the shoulders. "Take care of yourself." Then he threw his arms around his younger brother and hugged him.

Embarrassed by the unexpected show of affection, all Patrick could do was clear his throat.

John stepped back. "Remember, it's wicked and hard out there."

"I'll be okay. I'm traveling with a wagon train. Got most of my stuff packed and ready to go."

"You want to take my black stallion?"

Patrick shook his head. "No, but thanks for the offer. My Bay will get me there. Besides, I'd hate to part with Sparrow. She's kinda like family."

"Well, at least drop us a letter when you get a chance."

Patrick smiled. "I'll do that."

"Do you need money?"

"No, I have enough."

"So, how long have you been planning this trip?"

Patrick grinned. "Oh, a couple of months, give or take a few."

John laughed as he slapped his brother's back. "And you didn't even tell me about this little scheme? When are you gonna leave?"

"Tomorrow morning." Patrick hesitated for a moment. "I gotta get going. Still have things to finish up."

John reached over and hugged his brother. "Take care of yourself and bring Sarah back here, at least for a visit before you settle somewhere."

As his younger brother strolled out into the street, John watched him cross the road and head south. He'd miss Patrick, but he knew his brother had to travel down a different road. *God be with you. Hope you find Sarah Anderson.*

Chapter One

Arapaho Camp, 1853

Dog lay outside the teepee door, growling in the back of his throat. The hair on the back of Vision Seeker's neck prickled as she slid from beneath the warm buffalo robes.

"Husband. Something is wrong. Listen." She pulled on her moccasins. Then she quickly slipped her soft doeskin dress over her head and secured the belt at her waist.

Running Swift sat up. He jumped to his feet and grabbed his loincloth. Once it was in place, he pulled on his moccasins and headed for the lodge opening. After grabbing his bow and quiver from the pole by the doorway, he flipped the buffalo skin aside and stepped out into the brisk morning air. Darkness still covered the valley floor as the rose colors of early dawn crept across the mountain ridge.

Running Swift hurriedly scratched on his brother's teepee flap. "Deer Hunter. Trouble comes," he whispered. Then he went to his cousin's teepee. "Hands So High. Enemy here. Tell others."

Running Swift and Deer Hunter moved quietly in the shadows of the lodges, avoiding the open areas, using hand signs to communicate.

Deer Hunter nodded in the direction of the horses and motioned to Running Swift, letting him know he saw movement among the herd.

Running Swift silently dropped to the ground, inching his way through the brush. Raising his fingers, he indicated six men, two to the south and four to the north of the animals. He raised his two fingers and pointed to the south. He waved his hand in a circle then walked his fingers in the air.

Deer Hunter signaled. The hand signs continued. He would circle the south end of the corral to surprise the two men hiding there. Meanwhile Running Swift would edge around the north side.

Four braves and Hands So High joined Running Swift on the ground, while five braves crawled in behind Deer Hunter.

Running Swift crept slowly along the gully to keep from spooking the horses. He was determined not to lose any of the animals, especially his warhorse he kept tied near his lodge.

As he closed in on one of the Blackfeet busy cutting the hobbling tether on a small mustang, the attacker raised his head. Alerted by a movement in the grass, the warrior screeched, "Aiyeeeeeee." The wail warned his companions and panicked the animals.

Running Swift sprang into action. "Send the horses back into the Blackfeet," he yelled.

The Deer Hunter and the other Arapahos tried to drive the frightened horses forward, but the Blackfeet jumped onto the backs of their waiting mounts. The raiding party shook their weapons over their heads and yelled wildly, as they broke away into different directions, trying to avoid Running Swift and the other braves.

"Stop them!" shouted Hands So High as he grabbed at a passing Blackfoot, but the brave maneuvered his horse to the side and swung his club at the head of the Arapaho.

The braves chased after the mounted warriors, firing arrows and throwing spears, but their targets were soon out of range.

The thunderous hoof beats of the horses reverberated through the village. Men scrambled from their lodges, many of them still naked. They ran and waved their arms to divert the spooked horses. Running Swift and Hands So High dashed through the village.

Some of the women with small children ran for cover of the woods while others stood ready for an attack as the enemy rode past, raising their clubs in the air. Young boys ran among the enemy, firing arrows from their small bows. Many of the villagers scrambled between teepees to seek safety from tomahawks and pounding hooves, all the while swinging knives and clubs to defend themselves.

The Blackfeet galloped into the center of the campsite, shooting arrows wildly into the crowd of attacking Arapahos. One warrior slashed a teepee pole, causing the covering to collapse and catch fire from the pit inside.

"Stop the horses!" shouted Running Swift. Quickly, he ducked a wild thrust by an attacker, which barely scratched his shoulder. He nocked his arrow and took aim. The feathered shaft pierced the rider's chest. The brave died on his way to the ground. Running Swift grabbed a handful of mane and swung into the empty pad saddle.

As he rode into the melee, he yelled, "Push them to the lake."

Deer Hunter ran toward the water, trying to keep the

raiders in front of him. With his quiver empty, he threw his spear at one of the Blackfeet, missing by two feet. His arrows would have found their mark.

Hearing the thunderous hooves pound the campsite ground, Vision Seeker darted from the path of the panicked animals. She held her son, Little Feather, in one arm and waved the other, trying to divert the frantic horses.

A woman in front of her stood terror stricken by the battle raging around her.

"Move," Vision said as she dodged a Blackfoot's tomahawk. She grabbed the woman by the shoulder and pulled her between two teepees. A young boy bumped into Vision, knocking her off her feet as he sprinted after the enemy with his bow and arrows.

Clutching Little Feather to her chest, Vision raced toward the shelter of several trees to hide her son. She hung his baby bag safely from a branch.

From the tree line, Vision saw Many Faces pick up her small daughter, Little Fawn. She yelled, "Many Faces, behind you!"

The woman swung a club at a brave on horseback. An arrow struck her in the stomach. As she crumpled to the ground, she dropped her daughter.

Overcome with anger, Vision screamed, "Kill them. Kill them." She watched Deer Hunter and other braves scramble to get to the other side of the village before the enemy disappeared. "Kill the Blackfeet."

As she looked around for Little Fawn, Vision spied another woman protecting her.

Vision picked up a stone club outside the tree line.

A Blackfoot brave saw her emerge from the trees. He charged his horse toward her. She dodged the horse and swung the club into the animal's front legs with all her might. The horse went down. The man rolled over, leaped to his feet, and lunged at her, tomahawk raised over his head. He collapsed in front of her, an arrow protruding from his back.

Her husband's cousin, Hands So High, jumped over the body. Just as he started to turn, an arrow dug into his arm. Falling to his knees, he dropped his bow. Vision picked it up and shot the oncoming enemy squarely in the chest.

Hands So High got to his feet and yanked the bow from her hands. "Do not touch!" he screamed at her. Breaking off the arrow shaft, he charged back into the fight.

She knew she brought bad luck to Hands So High by touching his bow, but her club just would not do.

She pulled her knife from its sheath and headed toward the center of the village to revenge her people.

Arrows hissed overhead, one stabbed the ground next to a small child to her left. She shoved him aside. "Hide in the woods!" she yelled. He scurried away.

When she reached the center of the campsite, the Blackfeet separated into two groups. Four of the enemy fought the attacking Arapahos while two braves from her village chased the rest of the enemy through the village, riding directly in Vision's path. She ducked behind a teepee to keep from being trampled.

Suddenly, the raid was over as the enemy galloped across the ridge after the horses.

Thick smoke from the teepee fires and dust from the hooves of the animals saturated the air. The desecration of her village overwhelmed Vision. Six lodges were destroyed. Many injured villagers huddled on the ground, as others hurried to tend them. Seven Arapahos lay dead among the debris. A sad beginning for a spring day.

She stooped and picked up a small crying girl, her face covered with blood. White Doe lay dead several feet away. Vision carefully cradled the small one in her arms and stepped over the mother's body.

All because of horses. Stealing them from other tribes was an ongoing battle. The wealth of a warrior was how many ponies he owned. Was it worth the death of her people?

She straddled a dead man and ripped a piece from his torn striped shirt. Gently, she wiped the blood from Pretty Flower's face. Her small arm hung twisted. Carefully, Vision wrapped it with the red stained cloth.

The child's grandmother, Bending Woman staggered toward her with her arms held out. "Give her to me."

"The small one is hurt, grandmother," Vision said, "but alive."

Gently clasping the child to her breast, the old woman asked, "My daughter? Have you seen her?"

Vision turned her head and nodded toward White Doe lying on the ground.

The grandmother ran and fell to her knees next to the body, her loud grieving wail spiraled like smoke to the heavens.

Weaving her way through the campsite, Vision searched for her husband among the wounded. He was nowhere in sight, neither was his brother.

"They chase after the Blackfeet. Maybe get some horses back," said Hands So High, walking up behind her. "My woman is tending our lodge."

"I will help her as soon as I get my son." Vision Seeker ran toward the woods, relieved that Running Swift was alive. Grasping Little Feather, she slipped his bag from the branch and clasped him to her breast as he cooed softly.

"You are a brave little warrior," said Vision. "Strong

of heart, my small one. I'm afraid your morning bath will have to wait." She kissed him lightly on his forehead. He nuzzled his mouth against her chin and cheek, as he searched for his breakfast.

"Be patient, hungry one." Sitting down on the grass with her back to the tree, she slid open her deerskin dress for the baby to suckle. She held him close to her breast, watching the village people sifting through the debris to attend to the bodies of their loved ones.

Life was a complicated struggle with wars and death never far away. She wondered when it would ever get easier. There were moments of happiness. In spring and fall, thousands of massive furry buffalo grazed across the plains, cloaking the sky with dust when they ran. The hunt kept everyone busy from sunup to sundown, filling Arapaho bellies, working the kill. Life in the village was good.

As her son tugged at her breast, memories of her past brought sadness to her heart. She shut her eyes and thought about a redheaded woman and another little boy with brown eyes. A different life, with cabins, wagons, and cotton dresses.

"Little one, life is strange and changes can be so challenging. I have a secret to tell you, my son. Once, a long time ago, before I came to live among The People, I was a *ho:xu'_wu:ne'n*, a white woman named Sarah Anderson. Somewhere across this beautiful prairie and high mountain range lives a woman I once called mother. How I miss her sweet voice and loving arms, but I can never go back. I would not be accepted as I am today. And, my small brave son, you would be an outcast forever. So here we stay, where we belong."

Vision slipped back into the village and headed for Hands So High's lodge.

"Where have you been?" asked Dark Moon, her mother-in-law, standing with Plenty Hoops Woman. "You are never around when you are needed, you ugly *ho:xu' wu:ne'n*. I do not know why my son married you. You are helpless and lazy. I watched you walk around like you own the world."

Dark Moon swung at her, but she dodged the blow. "Get to work. After we get Plenty Hoops Woman's lodge up, we will put up mine. My son would want it so. Now go and put that half-breed down. He'll survive."

Vision hung Little Feather on the stretching frame, away from the work area. Under the scathing supervision of Dark Moon, Vision and Plenty tied three long poles together and raised the tripod. Then they laid seventeen poles carefully into place between the main poles. Once the women pulled the hide covering around the pole, they fastened the teepee front with lacing pins and put up the smoke flap poles.

True to her nature, after the lodge stood tall and ready, Dark Moon left to stir up more mischief. The two younger women were relieved to be free of her biting tongue.

"It looks like I only have to make two small repairs to the back hides. No poles were broken. We are very lucky," said Plenty.

"Yes. Not many can say that today," Vision replied.

She picked up two horn scoops, a skin flesher, and small kettle, ready to hand them through the opening to Plenty, who entered her lodge with several buffalo skins.

"Hurry," said Vision, "we need to get my mother-in-law's teepee up before she returns to snap our heads off again." She picked up her son, cuddling him in her arms.

Plenty stepped through the opening of her lodge. "Her hatred of you is great."

"Yes, and I am sure she would kill me or have me killed. But, she is afraid of her son, my husband."

"Be careful. She might poison you."

Vision smiled. "I am very careful when we eat together. Since she has her own teepee, there isn't much danger in that."

Vision and Plenty walked toward Dark Moon's lodge. They found her standing in front of smoldering hides. Nothing was left to salvage. Anger etched the old woman's face.

"I go to live with my son," she spat, venomously. "I am now the woman of his lodge."

As she stalked off toward Vision's teepee, Dark Moon shouted over her shoulder, "Hurry, you lazy white girl. I want my son's teepee up immediately."

The two younger women hustled some distance behind the marching woman.

"The great spirit must watch over you now," Plenty whispered. "I fear for your life, if she is to live with you."

"She cannot be the owner of my teepee. That she will learn soon. But, do not worry, I will be careful and pray to the Great Spirit for his guidance." She tried to sound sincere, but failed miserably. Doubt crept into her voice. Life had just taken a dangerous turn for her. Knowing her husband would control his mother, she must pray for his safe return.

"We better hurry," she said. "There is much to do. Worry will have to wait. I need to get food prepared. When Running Swift returns, his hunger will be great."

Plenty nodded. "Tonight, the council will have to decide what steps to take against the Blackfeet."

"Yes. We will punish them with a raid of our own. But first, the dead must be honored and their spirits sent to their ancestors."

They rounded a teepee and stopped short. In front of Vision's lodge stood Dark Moon, arms folded, tapping her foot. An expression of loathing curled her lips. Hatred shot from her eyes.

"But first," Vision whispered, "I must tackle a more dangerous problem."

Chapter Two

Early in the gray foggy mist, Vision Seeker knelt on the grassy river shore as she unwrapped Little Feather from his bundle. He squirmed to be free. "Easy, little one. The water will be cold for your bath this morning. But it is necessary to be clean, for the spirits do not like dirty people."

She smiled down at him as she removed his shirt and the dirty moss from the bottom of his sleeping bag. Dipping into the water with a piece of softened doeskin, she rubbed the homemade buffalo soap onto the skin and began his bath, much to his displeasure. Once she cleaned and dried her son, she powdered him with finely pounded buffalo dung.

Comfortably wrapped in his pouch, she held her son in her lap and cuddled him close. As she gazed out over the river, her mind went back to the early days. She could remember the wagon she traveled in with her family, but the faces were dim as was her memory of her kidnapping. Sometimes her dreams woke her, her skin glisten with sweat. A cold chill danced down her spine.

The horrible ordeal of living as a slave with the Crow caused pain to her body. Civil treatment among the Crow tribe was nonexistent. Hunger gnawed at her belly every day she lived with the tribe. She remembered feeling her backbone against her ribs. Most of the food she ate was riddled with maggots and smelt rancid.

She remembered the way several other girls were brutally beaten and dragged through the village for the least infraction or error. Two girls escaped one night, only to be brought back to camp. The Indian women slashed the girls' feet so they could not walk or escape again. She shuddered involuntarily thinking about the horrors she saw. Infection set in to the girls' feet and their toes swelled. They did not survive the winter.

After the Crows traded her to the Arapahos, life did not become easier. Yet, there was hope as she learned to survive living among the Indians.

She kissed the top of her son's head. "At first I lived tied to a stake in The People's village, but there was food and warmth at night in the teepee of Heavy Foot. Slowly I became familiar with their language. At thirteen, I was a wild woman, threatening everyone. Many of the women were afraid of my rantings. By fourteen, I took to sitting quietly outside Heavy Foot's teepee, my mind drifting. Images floated around like ghosts riding the winds. I spoke of them to The People, told them what I saw. That was how I received my name, Vision. This gave me prestige in the village.

"A young brave, named Running Swift caught my eye. He was tall and handsome, wide of shoulder, slim of hip. His deeds were the talk of the village and I knew I would be his wife one day. My heart ached to talk with him, but he ignored me. When I spied him, he would turn his head and walk on the other side of the path. One day, when I sat near Heavy

Foot's teepee, my eyes closed, deep in meditation, he came to me. Startled with his body so close mine, I jumped to my feet."

"You have changed since you joined Our People," he said.

"Yes. They are kind to me."

He reached forward and lifted a red braid that hung over my shoulder. Then he turned and left.

I stood there watching him walk away, puzzled as to why he singled me out now after two years. Before he acted as if I was poison, now he touched my hair.

By the end of the year, he asked Heavy Foot if he could court me. When Heavy Foot told me why Running Swift had visited, I purchased love charms to be sure he continued to look my way.

One day he arrived with his red blanket trimmed in blue and white.

"Will you join me under my blanket and walk with me in the village."

Shyly, I raised my head and smiled. "Yes. It would honor me.

"Enveloping his blanket around me, we paraded in quiet conversation so all The People would know what his intent was. I smiled knowing soon I would be his wife.

"Running Swift brought many horses to Heavy Foot to show he was a true and honorable man. Dark Moon, his mother, did not want me as his wife. But we married four months later."

Picking up the soap, doeskin, and her son, Vision got to her feet and headed back toward the village. "Your father is a brave man, my son. He is a man of the Spear Men Lodge. He rides into danger, fighting other tribes, not afraid of death. Most important, he stands up to Dark Moon for both our sakes. He is indeed very brave and strong."

Later, Vision stood in front of the lodge, gazing across the campsite, lost in solemn thought over the events of the last three days.

The heavy hearts of her people cried and mourned for their dead. Families dug graves and chanted to the Great Spirit. The funeral procession wound through the village, as they sent their loved ones onto their spirit journey. Each body received painted sacred red circles on their cheeks and foreheads, so the Great Spirit would recognize them.

She watched one mother place her son's moccasins and blue-beaded breastplate on the buffalo robe, covering his body. A grandmother rent her clothing and cut her hair, while another mother chopped off a finger, wailing loud enough for her ancestors to hear.

Four nights later, a ceremony and feast was prepared for the spirits. The Arapahos gathered in a circle, swaying and chanting. Vision listened to the rhythmic beat of the drums, thump, thump. Howling Dog, the medicine man, shook his feathered rattles in the four directions, chanting praises for the dead to the Great Mystery above.

Howling Dog raised his arms to the sky, and then turned. "We send our dead to the spirit world before their walking ghosts stir up mischief. It is so."

Vision was touched to the depth of her soul by the rhythmic cadence, keeping perfect time with her heartbeat. Grieving consumed her as she worried about Running Swift's safe return.

"Why do you stand here doing nothing? Go and look after that whiny child of yours." Dark Moon stalked off to join the dancers and add her voice to the chanting.

Vision Seeker stood stone still. Her cold blue eyes drilled holes into the old woman's back. Revenge would be hers, but now was not the time.

She left the circle and moved to the low branch where she hung Little Feather in his baby sack. Gathering him in her arms, she hummed his favorite lullaby until his heavy eyes closed once more.

Much later, she entered the teepee, laid her son on a fur robe, then added a few more buffalo chips to the small fire to chase the chill away. Gently, she unwrapped him, held him in her arms and stroked his chubby cheek, placing small kisses on his nose and forehead. Waking, his tiny hand grasped her braid, tugging like a bird pulling a worm from its hole.

"Ah, little one. Soon your father will be here to hold you. He won't be much longer."

She stared across the room at the buffalo robes she shared with Running Swift. Waiting made her anxious to feel his muscular body against hers, to feel his strong arms holding her close. His dark, oak-colored eyes, with their hint of mischief, melted her heart. He was a good husband.

Smiling at her son, she said, "Your father will come riding into the village, victoriously leading the horses. You will see. He will not fail."

Standing among the Thorkelberry bushes, Vision picked the plump fruit, placing it into the small basket. Little Feather, fast asleep, hung in his cradleboard from a tree limb.

Plenty threw a berry at her and giggled.

"Missed," teased Vision. "You were never good at hitting your mark." She moved quickly to the side, dodging another attempt.

"Stand still, then I can hit you." She laughed as she tossed another.

"Do you think me silly?" questioned Vision.

"Don't waste the berries," whispered Snow Bird, Deer Hunter's wife. "Our mother-in-law is close and you know how nasty she can be."

"You speak so softly, sister-in-law. Speak up. I can't hear you," teased Vision. Then she lowered her voice. "Let's see you stand up to her."

"Look," said Plenty. "The crier runs through the village. Something is happening."

"Hurry," shouted Snow Bird, waving one hand over her head, carefully balancing her basket as she descended the slope.

Vision slid the cradleboard onto her shoulders and cupped the bottom with one hand, holding the small basket of berries with the other. She used her elbow to push aside the branches. Traveling down the hill was slower for her, but Plenty stayed close by, assisting with the bushes.

The tribe gathered quickly, filling the center of the camp. Voices rose to meet the clouds overhead, for no one wanted to miss the news. Excitement built as the crier shouted, "Listen people of the Arapahos. I have marvelous things to tell you. Coming over the ridge are two brave men of our village. They come with honor. Through courage and bravery, they bring our horses back to us. Hear me. You will see with your own eyes."

He continued dancing, waving his feathered spear, and shouting the accolades of the men. The herd crested the ridge, galloping freely, making their way into the campsite.

Behind the animals, Running Swift and Deer Hunter rode, whooping and hollering to the villagers. Fresh scalps dangled from their spears.

Hands So High and several other braves ran to meet them. They carried ropes in their hands to round up the horses, driving them to the repaired corral.

Vision pushed through the crowd, making her way to the front. She grasped her husband's leg as he walked his horse among the excited people.

Cheers erupted around her, echoing through the campsite, "Tell us. Tell us." People pushed closer to touch the two returning riders, making it impossible to move.

Chief Black Bear reached the center and raised his arms. "The Great Spirit has protected our young braves and has returned them to The People. Our ancestors are pleased. We will gather at the fire tonight and listen to their stories. Let us make room for them now."

As a pathway opened for the riders, Vision and Snow Bird followed behind their husbands, along with Dark Moon.

Once they reached their teepee, Vision left her husband to tend his warhorse. She flipped the skin covering and stepped inside. Gently, Vision put Little Feather down, knelt beside him, and began to undo the cradleboard lacings.

Standing stiff and looking down her nose at Vision, Dark Moon crossed her arms. "Why do you not have my son's meal prepared?"

"The soup is warming."

"You are never prepared as a good Indian wife should be"

Vision leaped to her feet, both hands fisted tightly. "Leave me be, you sad old woman."

"You will not talk to me that way."

"Enough," shouted Running Swift, entering the teepee. "I will not have this quarreling." He turned to his mother. "This is my wife's teepee. If you wish to remain with us, you will be more willing to help Vision, not criticize. Otherwise, you may move in with my brother and his three children."

Dark Moon clamped her mouth shut. She sat down on her buffalo robe, stiff and straight. Scorn etched her face.

Running Swift then turned to his wife. "You will respect my mother, for she is the grandmother of our child."

He squared his broad shoulders, stalked to the opening, and lifted the flap. "Both of you will learn to work together and not argue so much. When I return, I expect a warm meal and peace in this lodge."

Averting her eyes, Vision stirred the liquid in the small black kettle, hanging on a tripod over the fire. She felt her mother-in-law's cold stare. A deadly silence settled around them. Neither of them moved.

Finally, Dark Moon rose to her feet and pulled her blanket around her shoulders. "I go to join my son."

Vision watched the woman step outside, relieved to see her go. Sadness filled her heart. She had angered her husband by talking back to his mother, causing contention instead of paying respect and tribute to his return. She must beware of the disdain the old woman held for her, a hatred growing ever more dangerous between them.

Hastily, she set about finishing the meal before Running Swift returned.

A scratching on the teepee flap startled her for a moment.

Snow Bird stuck her head through the opening. She knew it was impolite to enter without being invited.

Vision smiled and motioned her to come in. She masked her discomfort, knowing everyone in the village must have heard the quarreling from their lodge.

"We will gather soon," said Snow Bird, taking a seat. "I am eager to hear Running Swift's story about recapturing the horses."

Vision nodded. "He is anxious to attend the gathering tonight. I like the way he tells his stories."

"He can't outtalk his brother," Snow Bird taunted.

"Our people will sit for hours to hear him. They will ask him to retell the tales all night until he can no longer speak."

"That is true," said Snow Bird, with a giggle. "Deer Hunter will never be a grand speaker like Running Swift." Then she placed her hand on Vision's arm. Out of respect, she had waited to ask what concerned her the most. "Does our mother-in-law cause more trouble?"

"Yes. I lost my temper. It was not a good night to do such a thing. I should be grateful my husband has returned home safe and with honor."

"Our mother-in-law is an unhappy person. I have come to ask you to try to settle your differences. If you do not, she will be living with me. With three small children and one ugly old woman, my life would be miserable."

Vision's heart felt heavy but she knew Snow Bird was right. Her twins were still in cradleboards and her small boy kept her busy. There was no room for an angry woman with intent to cause trouble in Snow Bird's lodge.

"I will work it out so you will not be bothered by her."

Suddenly, the teepee flap slid open and Snow Bird jumped to her feet. "I need to get back." She quickly darted outside.

"What did she want?" asked Dark Moon, crossing to her bedding.

"It does not matter. Snow is always welcome here. It is my wife's lodge." Standing behind his mother, Running Swift's sober stare silenced her. He sat down in the place of honor. "Now, we eat. The drums will beat soon and we will gather for the stories."

The huge celebration carried over well into the wee hours of the morning as Running Swift and Deer Hunter repeated their stories about their brave deeds. The two men displayed the scalps for all to see, shaking their spears as they talked. Finally, the younger people danced to the beat of the drums, dipping and swaying their bodies, casting long shadows across the campsite ceremonial ground.

* * *

Vision opened one eye and snuggled closer to the warm naked body of her husband. She loved the early morning hours. The smell of her husband's manliness was intoxicating as he encircled his arms around her. He nuzzled her hair with his cheek and kissed her nose. Gently he removed one arm and moved his fingers under her face, trailing them down her check, to her neck, and across her chest. Being sure the buffalo robe covered their nakedness, he cupped one breast.

A spastic coughing caught their attention. Dark Moon removed her covering and adjusted her dress as she stood. "We need fresh water."

Running Swift raised his head. "Water can wait." Then he whispered, "And so can our son. His father has needs. It has been too long."

Dark Moon grabbed her blanket and stomped out of the lodge, dropping the flap.

Vision grasped her husband's face between her hands and peppered him with tiny kisses. Then she wrapped her arms under his armpits, as he gently swept her away.

Running Swift gave his wife one last hug before grabbing his breechcloth and belt. Standing, he adjusted the cloth, and then left the teepee to relieve himself.

Vision picked up her dress, pulling it over her head. She tied the belt around her waist, checked to be sure Little Feather was still asleep, then headed outside, carrying two water pouches. It was still early for only a few people wandered about. She loved this time of day. The morning dew glistened on the ground, as the sun peeked lazily from behind the trees.

Setting down the water containers, she stretched to work some of the soreness out of her muscles. Vision shifted her weight from one leg to the other. After raising her arms over her head, she picked up the pouches and strolled down the trail to the river. The birds chattered and swooped through the trees, eager to find breakfast for their young.

Behind her, Plenty Hoops Woman called her name. She slowed her pace and waited.

Small wisps of hair escaped Plenty's braids. "Morning is so beautiful. So cool and refreshing. Soon the buffalo will come."

"That means work until the sun sets."

Plenty rolled her eyes and rubbed her stomach. "That means lots of food."

Vision laughed. Plenty's appetite saw no end.

Tilting her head, Plenty smirked, "You do well this morning?"

"Yes," said Vision. "My buffalo robe was warm."

"How long do you think your mother-in-law will stay?"

Vision stared at Plenty. "Not forever. Maybe we will marry her off to Short Eagle."

"Oh. He is ugly with bowed legs and no teeth."

"And she deserves better?"

Laughter filled the sky as they made their way toward the river.

After climbing the small rise back toward the village, Vision and Plenty jostled their way through the gathering mass of excited people running about the campsite. Men shouted commands above the din as women and children moved about gathering their possessions.

"What is happening?" asked Plenty, stopping a passing woman.

"Buffalo. The Buffalo are back. We leave. Hurry."

Chapter Three

Fort Laramie, Late May, 1853

Dashing toward the flagpole, a soldier shouted, "Patrol's coming in!"

Patrick O'Brien stopped working on a split-eared bridle and glanced up to watch the dust-covered mounted troop ride past the stable doors. Returning from patrolling the mountain range southwest of the fort, the tired dusty unit crossed the hard-packed parade grounds in an orderly formation.

Small Indian skirmishes cropped up weekly, keeping the Army on its toes. Squelching the encounters was a nuisance and sometimes a deadly chore.

Anxiously, Patrick stretched his neck to see if any white captives rode with the group. They came back empty handed, as usual. Disappointment gripped him, but he refused to give up. *One day they'll find Sarah Anderson. Until they do, I won't budge from this fort.*

As the sergeant shouted a barrage of orders, Patrick

watched the soldiers dismount to the sound of squeaking leather saddles. Hordes of curious people, Indians and settlers alike, congested the parade ground, watching the troop form rank.

Patrick's mind drifted back to last year when the wagon train he was traveling with stopped at the fort to take on supplies. By a strange coincidence, he ran into Jim Castor, an Army scout, at the post sutler's store. After striking up a conversation with the man and befriending him, Castor invited Patrick to share a couple of drinks at the saloon.

Slightly inebriated, Castor told a story that personally haunted him, about Indians kidnapping a young girl named Sarah Anderson. He told Patrick how he stood in the commander's office the day Mrs. Anderson reported her daughter missing.

As Patrick relived the story, cold chills danced down his spine, the hair on the back of his neck prickled, and his hands turned to ice. Breathing became difficult. The dreams he cherished of finding Sarah in California evaporated into wisps of smoke. His destination changed forever that one day. Now, time hovered as he waited, waited for news of the girl he loved.

Castor rode over to the stables and dismounted. "See you're still here." He clapped the boy on the shoulder. "You daydreamin' again? Got to admire ya, son. You got that stick-to-itiveness. Like that in a young fella."

"You know I'll stay here as long as she's out there," said Patrick, frowning. "This civilian job doesn't pay much, but repairing tack keeps me busy. How did it go this time? Much fighting?"

"Nah. By the time we got there, the Indians had disappeared into the hills. We chased them until we lost the trail. They're sneaky buggers."

"Did you see anything of a white girl with red hair?"

"No, Pat. If I do, believe me, I'll bring her in. Has Mrs. Anderson been around?"

"Nah. The commander says she's due to ride in soon. Seems she heads to the fort once a year, asking the same questions I do."

"You missed seeing her last year by a couple of days," said Castor, walking his horse into the stables.

Patrick followed behind him, hanging the repaired bridle on a nail. "Well, when she gets here, it'll be a pleasure to see Mrs. Anderson again. Have a lot to ask her."

"Son, I don't want to disappoint you, but Miz Anderson's not exactly like you remember her. Ridin' over this territory with that bunch she's with makes a woman a little rough around the edges. She doesn't stay in one place very long.

"Doesn't matter." Patrick stuck his hands into his pockets and looked at the ground.

"Don't get me wrong, she's still a good lookin' woman." Castor glanced at him. The lad was ebbing low again.

"Hey, we'll keep searchin' for Sarah. One day, I'll bring her in and deliver her right at your feet."

"Yes, I know you will." Patrick poked his toe into the dirt. "I'm not gonna leave here until someone finds her. I've got nowhere to go. Nothing else is important."

"I know that." Castor glanced at the young man. He cleared his throat and changed the subject. "You still livin' in the shanty over behind the magazine?"

Patrick grinned. "It's not much to look at and it needs some repairs, but at least it's a roof over my head. Keeps the rain and snow out."

"A bit crowded, I'd say, with five men sleepin' in that hovel." Castor unsaddled his horse. "Doesn't give you much space. I'll keep my eyes and ears open. See if we can't find you better accommodations."

Patrick strolled to the open door and stared across the grounds. Beyond, the flooded Laramie River lapped at its banks as the murky water flowed in a serpentine course past the fort.

"The Post's blacksmith been keepin' you busy?" asked Castor, siding up to Patrick.

"He's over at the other stable firing up. These wagon trains are keeping him busy fixing and repairing broken wheels. I only do the tack and saddle repairs here. Kinda quiet a good portion of the time."

Castor nodded in the direction of a small man strutting toward headquarters with a journal under his arm. "I see the Officer of the Day is keepin' a detailed report on the migrants headin' west. Who's that on duty today?"

"Henry Rogers," said Patrick. "The man talks more than he writes. I hear his reports not only total all the people passing through here, but also include the animals and wagons. Pretty detailed, if you ask me."

"Glad he's doin' the countin'." Castor walked out into the open area just in time to see the sun disappear behind the mountain peaks. "Love to watch that ball of fire dip out of sight. That reminds me, it's time for a swig of Jake's whiskey."

Facing the scout, Patrick took a broad stance and placed his hands on his hips. "You know, it's a shame peace can't be settled so that the farmers and Indians can live quietly together. But, I guess the Indians do have some complaints: losing their land, game killed off, treaty broken a dozen times. Jeez, I'd get mad, too."

Castor turned and adjusted his gun belt. "To tell you the

truth, if the Army ever gets their act together and honors that treaty they signed with the Indians back in '51, we wouldn't be havin' these raids."

"Castor," yelled the sergeant from across the parade ground. "Commander wants you to report. Now!"

"Be there in a minute." Turning to Patrick, he asked, "Can you take care of my horse for me?"

"Sure." He watched the scout swagger toward headquarters.

Feeling the crisp mountain breeze blowing out of the west, Patrick headed inside to brush down Castor's horse. The day was ending and he didn't want to miss his evening meal at Miz Trudy's. He needed to hurry or there wouldn't be any grub left.

Patrick fed and stabled the horse, and then pulled the large wooden doors closed and locked up. Trudging across the open desolate area with head bent, he bucked the cold cutting winds. Loneliness enveloped him.

Maybe tomorrow Sarah will find her way to Fort Laramie. Maybe a future existed for the two of them. Maybe. Maybe was the only hopeful word that kept him living day-to-day.

Chapter Four

Snow Bird perched on the makeshift scaffolding post, sliding the wooden lodge pins from the holes in the teepee covering. Below, Vision Seeker steadied the rough supports.

One by one, the pegs dropped at Vision's feet. "How many more?" she asked.

"One more." Snow Bird stretched her hand over her head. "I can't reach it."

The framework shook.

"Be careful." Vision ducked as the pin hit her shoulder. The covering collapsed to the ground around the lodge poles, stirring the dust about her feet.

Snow climbed down and gathered the wooden pins, placing them into a deerskin bag, along with the cover stakes and the anchor peg. "Ah, the ground feels good to my feet." Jokingly, she said, "I don't believe I'd make a good bird."

Vision chuckled as she coiled up the rawhide tie and handed it to her sister-in-law. "Here, we need to hurry."

"Are you packed?" asked Snow.

"After I attach Little Feather's cradleboard to the saddle, I am ready to follow the trail."

"And our mother-in-law?"

"She helps Many Suns pack. The woman is old and her daughter's too lazy to help her."

"Once we get this covering folded and put on the travois, I'll be ready," said Snow. "I look forward to moving on."

"Enjoy it while you can. Hard work waits for us. I wonder how many buffalo my husband will get."

The women took the tripod frame down, untied it and laid the poles with the others in a bundle on the ground. They continued to talk about the buffalo, working quickly, tying the poles to the side of Snow's horse.

Whispering to Vision, Snow nodded toward the next teepee. "Our cousin looks like she needs help. You know she is with child."

"I hope it goes better for Plenty Hoops Woman this time," said Vision. "The little girl born last year only lived two days." She raised her head and shouted, "Plenty. We will help you."

Snow tossed the deerskin bag onto the travois. "I'll climb the scaffolding, seeing that I've had more practice."

"Like a bird?"

Both women laughed as they made their way to Plenty's lodge.

Silence settled over the deserted village. Only two skeleton teepees stood, neither inhabited since the death of their owners. Single file, the line of people stretched a mile on the trail behind the braves, who scouted two miles ahead of the tribe checking for trouble that might await them in ambush.

The women led their horses through the tall grass, while small children rode on the travois or scurried along beside their mothers. Some of the elders walked, and others rode their horses on the long and exhausting journey. Behind the procession trotted the extra animals surrounded by the horse-keepers.

Two days later, they reached the campsite. Vision quickly erected her teepee with Dark Moon's help. She fed Little Feather and then prepared a stew for their meal as the gray night blanketed the sky. A quarter moon rested high above, stars spilled across the horizon.

Running Swift sat outside the lodge, playing a haunting tune on his cane flute. The trilling melody floated through the teepee opening, soothing the tension within Vision's body. Closing her eyes, she stirred the soup to the rhythm of the song, slowly swaying her head from side to side.

Rising to her feet, she went to join her husband, sitting cross-legged next to him. Leaning her head against his shoulder, she said, "Your song tonight is soft and gentle. It tugs at my heart."

Running Swift cupped her cheek with his calloused hand and gently turned her face to him, placing a kiss on her small nose. "You are my woman for as long as stars shine above."

"It is so."

"I sit thinking about the first day I saw you enter the village. My heart hurt, for there was much pain in your eyes. Remember when you spread your arms wide and told the village women the Great Spirit would punish them for beating you? A week later, one woman broke her arm. Another almost died from eating a poison root. I knew you were different. A Vision Seeker."

Brushing a stray hair from her forehead that escaped from her braid, he smiled. "I did not know you, but I knew we were to be one. Not until you spit on me did I realize I would have to tame a wolverine."

"You tease me, when I feel I need your warmth."

"Ah. It is only because my love for you is wider than the sky, stronger than the mountain." He paused for a moment. "My mother never approved of our marriage, but it does not matter. You are my woman, my life."

"Your mother was not happy to see me adopted by one I cannot name."

"It is so," he replied. "We must not speak of those who have gone to the spirit world."

They sat together quietly for a moment, soaking in the emotion between them. Finally, Vision said, "Your meal is ready."

Slipping one arm around his wife, Running Swift held her close. "Yes, and I am ready. The meal can wait."

She nestled into his chest, placing her forehead into the softness of his neck, loving the sensuous musky scent of her husband.

In the distance toward the center of the campsite, a rhythmic thump, thump from the large drum called The People to gather at the big fire.

"Tonight, their prayers and songs will rise toward the heavens, seeking approval of the animal spirits and the four winds for a successful hunt," he said.

With an impudent grin, Vision placed her hand on his chest. "You will have to wait a little longer. We must join the others."

He helped her up and held her close one more time before entering their teepee. "Tonight we will dance into the night to celebrate the news of the buffalo."

* * *

With Little Feather left safely behind at the village with the aged grandmothers, Vision secured the travois behind her horse and placed her knife into the sheath at her waist.

As she climbed into the saddle, Dark Moon rode up next to her. "You are slow. We go now." She turned a cold shoulder to Vision and rode off to join the other women in line, headed toward the hunting fields.

Cresting the ridge, Vision shielded her eyes, looking down onto the blackened prairie of dusty moving bodies interspersed with naked figures of men on horseback, darting around and through the thunderous herd. The deafening noise excited the women.

Several dead buffalo already lay waiting. Dark Moon pointed and mumbled, then nudged the horse forward. Reaching the valley, the two women searched for the marked arrows of Running Swift.

"There, to the right," shouted Dark Moon.

They quickly dismounted, tethered their horses, and hurried toward the dead animal. Once on their knees, the two women said a prayer to the spirit, thanking him for the nourishment of the big hairy beast that lay on the ground. They tackled the butchering, carefully skinning the buffalo, taking care not to mangle the hide. Then they wrapped the liver for the feast that night.

Vision laid the skin across the travois, hair side down. They cut the meat into large hunks, placed it on the hide, bundled it up, and secured the sinew thongs. Next, they placed the animal head and bones on another old hide and secured it. Vision removed the entrails and heart, putting them in a skin bag hanging from the horse's side. Once the two women finished, they found a second bison and repeated the procedure, before returning to the village.

Dark Moon, impatient to begin working, unwrapped the first hide, and then grabbed the entrails bag. She watched Vision return with Little Feather and hang the cradleboard on a tree limb.

"Humph! A true Arapaho would be ready when her husband arrives and not play around with that half-breed."

Vision stared at her. "I am ready." She removed her knife from her belted sheath, knelt on the ground next to the travois, and began cutting the large hunks of meat into sizable pieces.

"A true Arapaho would listen to her husband's mother for advice on preparing the hide," said Dark Moon

"I will listen when I begin to work the hide."

"When do you plan to prepare your husband's meal?"

Vision leaped to her feet and entered the teepee to stir up the embers. When she came back to her place, she thrust her knife into a large piece of buffalo rump, stabbing it to the hilt. Placing it in front of her, she removed her knife and cut off a sizable chunk. Piercing the meat dead center, she rose to her feet and carried the hunk, dropping it into the kettle that hung over a small fire. Next, she added spices and a few wild turnips to the water.

As she returned and knelt to work again, Dark Moon ducked her head, but warily glanced sideways at her daughter-in-law.

The two women continued to work in silence. Vision cut the meat into smaller hunks for soup, and long thin strips for pemmican. She laid the strips over the drying pole frame. Next, she scraped the bones and removed the marrow.

Sweat soaked her blood stained dress. The tedious chores of skinning, scraping, and butchering numbed her fingers. She continued to work the meat, one large hunk at a time. Tomorrow she needed to tackle the hide before it dried out and became too stiff to stretch.

Running Swift returned to the village and stood proudly watching the women in his family as they worked. He left to tend to his horse, and then went to the river to clean his body of dirt, sweat, and blood. When he returned, he ladled a bowl of soup from the kettle, knifed a chunk of meat, and sat down to eat. Pushing his empty bowl to one side, he lazily stretched his legs. Exhausted, his head nodded. Rising to his feet, he entered the teepee to rest a few hours.

Vision and Dark Moon continued working until the sun dropped behind the trees. Taking the strips from the drying frame, they covered all the meat with a robe for the night and set aside the scrapers and knives.

With Snow Bird standing beside her, Plenty Hoops Woman shouted, "We go to the river."

Tired and exhausted, the four women trudged toward the water to clean themselves. Reaching the rocky water edge, they removed their bloodstained dresses and plunged them into the water, rubbing and thumping them against the rocks to clean the doeskin garments. After wringing the clothing by hand, they laid each article flat across the rocky ground and bushes.

Snow stepped into the chilly river, splashing water over her naked body. Slowly, she edged her bottom onto the pebbled bed, letting the current caress her arms and legs, easing her aches and pains.

Plenty joined the women, thrashing through the cold stream. Skirting her hands across the top of the water, she sprayed Vision who sat quietly moving her arms and hands through the water, feeling the gentle movement.

Plenty flopped down next to Snow.

Vision scooped the water with her hands, wetting Plenty's hair and face. A water fight developed, laughter filled the valley and the echo followed the moving current down stream.

"How many buffalo did Running Swift get today?" asked Plenty.

"Two," answered Vision.

"That is good. We have only one. The Buffalo are not many this year, but there is much work to do."

"There is always work," said Vision. "Remember when I came to live with The People? So young and scared, I didn't know what to expect."

"I remember," said Snow. "You were lazy."

"Humph. Still is," remarked Dark Moon. The three women ignored her.

"You wore that old dress. Not good for much: dirty and torn." Plenty wrinkled up her nose and shook her head. "You yelled at everyone. So disagreeable."

"You cannot blame me. I was taken from my family to live with strange people and so far from home. I did not know how to do the chores the way The People did them. I could not even speak your language."

"I thought you were funny," said Snow.

"I was terrified. How would you like to be traded for blankets and a kettle. Three years of fear and anguish. So much to get used to." Vision sat staring ahead, remembering her horrible experience of slavery. "When I was brought to your village and given to Heavy Hand, he tied me to a post outside of his teepee for days. After the buffalo came, I sat scraping hides for everyone until my fingers bled. Even his dogs ate better than me."

"You were disagreeable and mean," spoke up Dark Moon. "Didn't deserve any better. Still don't."

Vision bit her tongue to keep from hurling a sharp reply. "Even though I was treated harshly, no one beat me."

Plenty swirled the water around her body and rubbed sand across her legs. "You were a crazy person, especially that one day you got angry at Heavy Hand. You jumped up and down, and then ran around the camp, raising your arms in the air and screaming. Everyone was afraid of you."

Dark Moon's muttering did not escape Vision's ears.

"Remember when she ran through the village naked?" asked Snow, sarcastically "You screeched and waved your hands at us, shouting 'I see it. Beware.' Everyone in the village thought you had lost your mind, including me."

Plenty raised her arms in the air, pointing her fingers to the sky, in mocking motions. "I see it! I see it!"

"I was hungry and thirsty, half out of my mind. I actually do not remember too much about that day. I know I screamed at two women who taunted me. I only recall Chief Black Bear naming me Vision and placing me with the woman-we-cannot-name. She treated me like a daughter until she went to the spirit world."

"Do not speak of the dead," said Plenty.

"As a white girl, I never realized how spoiled I was," said Vision "Here among the people, work begins at sunrise and continues through the day, never wasting anything, yet life in our village is so peaceful."

"It gets late. We better head back." Snow stood and rubbed her backside. "Besides, my bottom feels numb from the cold water."

"I agree. Tomorrow, we must scrape all the hair from the hides, and then soften them before stretching them on the frames." Plenty splashed her way toward the bank.

"Hear the big drum? We must hurry," said Vision, following the other women towards the bank. "I do not want to miss the buffalo tongue ritual or the thanksgiving feast ceremony. It is good to hear Howling Dog chant the praises to the buffalo spirits for supplying us with meat."

The women donned their clean doeskin dresses, rolled up their wet washed clothes, tucked them under their arms, and dashed toward the village.

Chapter Five

South of Platte River, 1853

In the center of the large lodge, Chief Black Bear sat in council with three sub chiefs and thirty leaders representing the six societies in the Arapaho Tribe.

Jumping Goat, the keeper of the pipe, removed it from the ceremonial bundle and lit it. Then he raised it over his head. "This pipe is our people. The striped stem is our tribe's backbone. The red bowl is our head, the color of our blood." He passed it to Chief Black Bear who put it to his lips before passing it on to the next warrior until all had taken a puff.

After Jumping Goat placed the pipe back into its protective bag, the medicine man asked the spirits for guidance for the council and the Arapaho people. Raising both arms in the air, he silenced the warriors. No one spoke. All eyes turned to Chief Black Bear.

"We have come to talk, for much has taken place in the last two years that is not good." He looked at the men surrounding him as he spoke. They all nodded their heads in response to his statement. "I wish to hear what needs to be said."

"The white man does not hold true to his word." Deer Hunter slapped one fist into the other palm. "We signed a treaty in good faith. The soldiers smile, shake our hands. But, nothing comes from the white man."

"Yes," shouted a brave. "The white man puts lodges on our hunting grounds. The soldiers do nothing to stop them. Soon there will be no buffalo, elk, or deer to hunt."

Running Swift, of the Spear Men Society, jumped to his feet. "Our children will go hungry. Our old will have no robes to cover their bodies to keep them warm. We must make a stand. This is our land. They do not belong here."

Chief Swooping Bird rose slowly to his feet. "We must be sure that once we decide to war on the whites, we are ready to stand and fight, for the soldiers will come looking for our warriors. Our women and children will be in danger"

Chief Two Horses nodded. "It is so."

This statement caused a rapid discussion among the warriors. One man in the back, from the Tomahawk group, stood proudly. "I am ready to make war *now*," he said and pounded his chest.

Another warrior raised his arms over his head. "Are all of you afraid of the soldiers? Are we not strong and fierce? We can call the other three bands together and attack the fort."

Chief Broken Arrow quickly rose to his feet, waving his arms to quiet the group. "Wait. You are too anxious to war. Have you forgotten the cannons that sleep at the fort?"

A man from the Dog Men Society stood. "Chief Broken Arrow speaks true. They have more guns than we do. More soldiers arrive every day."

Strong Bow shouted, "Then we should attack the white

wagons that cross our hunting grounds and the hunters who run off our buffalo. The soldiers have not honored the treaty signed by our chiefs. The paper we hold is useless. Maybe we should burn it."

An old warrior from the Sweat Lodge shook one hand and spoke. "At the fort, our people are treated with hatred. The white people look down on us and call us names. They do not respect us. How can we live in peace with the white man if he does not respect us as a people?"

Chief Black Bear listened to all who would speak, weighing each statement. The heated discussion continued and grew louder. Finally, he raised his hand for silence.

Gazing about the lodge, he looked at each of his chiefs and warriors around him. "Yes," he said. "I have seen the hatred in the white eyes. They are jealous and want our land. It is true. The soldiers have not stood by their word to protect our land or us. The treaty we made at Fort Laramie two years ago is not good. More people come every day looking for the yellow stones they call gold.

"We must be patient a little longer for the time is approaching for our Sun Dance. We, the Long Beaver Band, are not strong enough to wage war on the white people. We need the Long Leg Antelope People to join us, for they have many warriors. Once we all come together with the Greasy Face and Quick to Temper Bands, we will talk as one and decide what we must do. Then our force will be mighty and the white man will fear us."

He paused for a moment. Grumbling could be heard among the men. "Until that time, we must watch carefully. More and more wagons cross the river each day. We must not attack them for then the soldiers will come to our village with guns. They will kill our women and children. Have patience. Soon we will right the wrong done to us. This I promise you."

The other chiefs nodded their heads in agreement with Black Bear, but Running Swift and Deer Hunter sat stone still, as did several other members of the Spear Men Lodge. They were eager to resolve the hurt and embarrassment against their people.

Later that evening, Running Swift and Deer Hunter met with ten other braves from their society. They gathered down near the lake in the high grass, discussing the council meeting.

"We are the warriors of our people. We must fight," said Crooked Nose.

Hands So High looked around at the men. "The white man accuses us of stealing their horses, yet many of the animals are lost on the prairie when we find them."

Deer Hunter lifted an eyebrow. "We do steal their horses. I admit that. But, it is what we do with the Crow and Blackfeet. It is what we do best."

"The white man does not understand our way of life and does not wish to know us." Strong Bow crossed his arms and lifted his head. "They will never live and share with us. All they want is our land and for us to leave."

"Hear me," said Running Swift, trying to keep his voice low and steady. "We can attack and burn their wagons. If we are like the eagle and swoop down on them quickly, we can stop them from taking our land. How many of you are with me?"

Slowly each man nodded his head.

"Good. We ride before the sun wakes. Make ready tonight, but do not show what you are doing. We will meet over the hill and ride our war horses across the prairie."

Hands So High raised his head. "I stay here for I do not agree we must do this now."

"You are part of our war lodge and it is your duty to war on our enemies," shouted one brave.

"Running Swift, raise your notched club and we will be ready," said Deer Hunter. "I will follow you."

Running Swift waved his hands in front of him. "Keep your voices down or the others will know what we do. There is no shame in Hands So High not wanting to go. He may choose as each of you may do. Those of you who do not wish to ride with us, stay and protect The People."

Sitting in a circle, they discussed their plan of attack on the white man and his wagons. Finally, Running Swift said, "It is time to gather everything you will need. Go now and make ready." He rose and headed toward his teepee.

Vision Seeker woke when Running Swift slipped from beneath the robes. She rose up on one elbow and watched him dress quickly. When he picked up his war club, her skin turned cold. She knew he was going to battle. He was the leader of his lodge. It was his duty to rush ahead of the warriors into the fighting, strike the enemy first, and escape quickly back to the charging warriors. The danger of his death was imminent. She was afraid for him.

He turned at the lodge opening, glancing about the teepee for one final look. The smoldering coals from the pit cast shadows on the lodge skins. Their eyes met and fear clasped her heart in a cold fist. Knowing she might never see him again, she rose and moved quietly toward him. She wrapped her arms around her husband's waist. He circled one arm around her shoulder, pulling her tightly against his chest, gently placing a kiss on top of her head.

"I will return," he whispered. Releasing her, he ran his

finger down the ridge of her nose, and smiled. He took one more glance at his wife, turned, and stepped outside.

She waited a moment to steady herself before pushing the flap aside and stepping through the opening to join him. Running Swift had disappeared into the darkness with the other men. Only the lazy stars lit the sky as they spread across the horizon to greet her. Even the dogs missed seeing the warriors leave.

Dark Moon walked up behind her. "You shame my son with your worry, sending him off to claim his rights as a warrior."

"I do not shame him." She turned to face her husband's mother. "I love him and fear he will not return this time."

Dark Moon drew in her breath. "Do not speak so. You are no vision maker, only an ugly white girl."

"I know what I speak. My heart tells me and my mind knows, he will not return this day. Neither will many of the others. It is not good. More will happen to our people, many will die."

Dark Moon raised her hand and slapped her daughter-in-law across the face. "Be quiet, you stupid girl. Do not speak like that. The evil spirits will hear you."

Vision Seeker placed a hand on her hot, aching cheek and glared at her mother-in-law. Stiffening her back and pursing her lips, she turned and entered the teepee to care for Little Feather, leaving Dark Moon behind in the night shadows. This was not a good day. She needed to prepare for whatever was to happen.

As the morning progressed, news of the Spear Men warriors' departure spread quickly among the villagers. Vision Seeker set about preparing a stew and then sat outside beading a pair of moccasins for her husband. She was careful not to use too many blue beads for they were hard to trade for. She wanted to make Running Swift a shirt, decorated with the round shiny beads.

She concentrated on her work, trying to keep her mind and hands busy. She did not want to think about her husband and his journey. Fear grew in her heart like a prairie dog's mound, a few grains at a time, rising ever so high to meet the sky, spreading across the horizon. She also said prayers to the Man-Above, the ever-watching spirit, to be with her husband.

Snow Bird sat down beside her. "Our men are brave to make this journey and punish the white man for his cruelty to our people."

Vision kept sewing. She did not want to think about the raid. She kept her answer simple. "Yes."

"Why are you so sad and quiet? You should be proud of your husband. He is a great leader and will bring honor to your teepee today."

Vision stopped beading, put down her work, and faced her sister-in-law. "Today is not a good day. I feel evil around our people and death stalks our warriors. Something is wrong." She looked at Snow. "Something is terribly wrong."

Snow rose to her feet and stared at her. "Do not speak so," she whispered. "It is bad. So very bad." She scurried away, never looking back.

Dark Moon haughtily exited the lodge behind Vision. "Look what I found, a strange white man's symbol. This is why my son's life is in danger." In her hand, dangled a dried grass cross on a piece of rawhide.

Vision jumped to her feet and grasped at the cross. "Give it to me. It is mine. You've been in my parfleche again, where you don't belong."

Dark Moon stepped back out of her reach. Clasping the cross in her hand, she began to crush it.

Vision leaped at her, shoving her over and landing on top of Dark Moon. The cross fluttered to the ground as the two women battled each other, swinging fists and pulling hair. Vision's anger exploded as she pounded Dark Moon, bashing her large prominent nose. People gathered around as the two women fought, rolling across the ground, knocking over stretching frames and other items in their way.

Finally, Hands So High stepped in. "Enough," he shouted. "You should be working together with Running Swift away, not fighting like dogs after a bone." He yanked Vision to her feet and then helped Dark Moon up, as Vision made one more swipe at her mother-in-law.

Plenty Hoops Woman grabbed Vision and pulled her aside. "She has had enough. Here," she said, "this belongs to you."

Placing the crumbled grass cross into Vision's hand, Plenty pulled her away from the teepee and began wiping the blood from her face with her hand. "You have shown her you are not afraid. Now it is time to clean up and look in on your son. Do not worry about Dark Moon. Many Suns will take care of her."

Plenty followed her into the teepee. Little Feather was still asleep.

"Why do you fight over this white man's symbol? What does it do?" Plenty asked, eyeing the cross with skepticism.

Cupping her hands, Vision splashed her face with water left standing in the bowl. Then she wiped it with a small cloth. "Before I came to live with The People, a friend made the cross for me. His family stayed behind in a large city because of a terrible sickness. It was his way of saying goodbye."

"Did he want you for a wife?"

Vision smiled. "I was too young to think that way. I suppose it could have been."

"Was he handsome and brave?"

"He was...Irish," replied Vision.

"What is Irish?" Plenty asked.

"You ask too many questions. It happened so long ago."

Plenty eyed the cross warily as Vision laid it on a piece of soft doeskin and very gently flattened the crumbled pieces as smoothly as possible. Then she wrapped it up and placed it back into her parfleche for safekeeping.

Vision turned to Plenty. "I remember something he told me before he left to follow his family's wagon."

With her curiosity piqued, Plenty edged closer. "What?"

"He said 'I promise I will come'."

The two women stood facing each other in silence until Plenty could stand it no more. "So. What did he mean by that?"

"That he would find me."

"Running Swift will not like him coming here. Do you think he will come to find you?"

"No. It has been too long. I cannot remember what he looks like. Besides I have a husband and a son that I love."

Little Feather squirmed in his bag. Vision untied him, moved the buffalo robe, and placed him on his stomach on her bed. He rolled over onto his back and looked at her with his dark shining eyes. His sweet round face warmed her heart. Smiling, he moved his hands and feet in jerky motions. She swept his straggly black hair back away from his face as he cooed.

"I would never leave my home or my family behind. My husband is good to me and treats me with kindness. This child is of my body. Our bond is great. There is no need for me to look for another."

Vision sat down next to him, untied her bodice, and suckled him. "One day we will have another baby. Maybe in three years."

Plenty smiled at her. "I am with child."

Vision feigned surprise. "What wonderful news. When?"

"When the buffalo become shaggy. Will you help me when the time comes?"

Vision took her hand. "Yes."

When Dark Moon returned to the lodge that night, her face was swollen and several hunks of hair were missing from her head. She crawled onto her pallet, turned to face the teepee wall, and covered her body with her buffalo robe. Silence filled the teepee.

Vision was grateful she did not speak, for anger still hid within her heart. She lay warmed by her robe and tried to sleep, but her loneliness for Running Swift was great and her fear for his life strong. Sleep did not come easy.

Chapter Six

Stretched on his stomach in the high prairie grass upon a small ridge, Running Swift watched the early morning activity around the wagons below.

Overhead, ribbons of light blue and rose gradually replaced the gray shrouded blanket of night, blotting out the twinkling stars gracing the sky. Soon the sun would greet the morning.

He signaled to the warriors near him to crawl back into the ravine and make ready for battle. Running Swift first stripped his saddle and personal gear from his horse. Next, he laid his weapons in a straight line, being careful not to step over them. Finally, he removed his shirt, laying it aside. From a doeskin bag, he extracted an eagle feather his spirit helper gave him many years ago, and stuck it into his hair. This was his personal medicine and supernatural power that would protect him, with the help of the Spirit World. Hunkering down, he opened his beaded paint pouch and prepared to mark his face.

Running Swift rummaged through his bag and stopped abruptly. His magical red color was missing. How could this be? He looked at Deer Hunter.

"What bothers you, brother?"

Running Swift stared at him for a moment. "Red not here. Spirits will be angry. We must pray to Wakan Tanka, the Great Mystery above for help." He looked down and shook his pouch one more time. Two other men, who knelt next to him, looked at each other then averted their eyes, mumbling a small chant.

He realized there was nothing he could do. To borrow another's color would only bring evil spirits to the group. His destiny cast, Running Swift dipped into the blue color. Starting at his hairline, he ran two fingers down across his eyelid, on the right side of his face, stopping at his chin. Then he dabbed black from burnt wood onto his left cheek. Putting everything away, he knelt and chanted softly, raising his arms above his head, looking up into the sky.

"Oh, Great Spirit above. Hear my prayer. Today I go into battle. Let me ride straight as an arrow and strike swiftly, bringing honor to our people, for my bravery is great."

When he finished, he motioned to the warriors to gather in a sacred circle, crouching close together.

"It is early," he whispered. "Many still sleep. We attack now. Ride with the wind." Grabbing his club, Running Swift jumped to his feet, and leaped onto the back of his powerful warhorse. The other braves mounted their steeds, riding a distance behind Running Swift as he galloped out of the ravine toward the wagons, holding his club above his head.

"Aiyeeeeee!" he yelled at the top of his voice, followed by shrill whoops. He urged his horse forward in a full gallop, straight at the wagons. He wanted the enemy to know he was here to slay those who took their land and killed the buffalo, defiling their hunting grounds. Anger rose up within his chest. Hatred filled his heart. Exhilarated, he rode wildly across the prairie with the wind caressing his face.

"Death to the white man," he shouted, as he made the four sacred passes around the wagons.

Disoriented and confused by the lone rider's circling attack, the pioneers scurried from beneath their wagons. Pulling up suspenders and grabbing their boots, they struggled to locate their weapons. Some fired randomly while others secured their families. Women screamed as they gathered their crying children to safety.

"Kill the bastard," shouted one white man.

"There are more coming. Fire. Fire!" yelled the wagon master.

By the time Running Swift's horse jumped over a wagon tongue and into the campsite, all hell had broken loose.

A white man aimed his rifle at Running Swift. The Indian swung his club, bashing in the man's head.

"Die," howled Running Swift at the top of his lungs, clubbing another man who hit the dirt, bleeding profusely. Three braves joined Running Swift as they dodged bullets, all the while circling the inner camp area, making a shambles of everything in their way, trampling one child under the hooves of their horses.

Leaving behind several dead bodies lying in the dust, Running Swift headed back outside the wagon circle, urging his powerful steed across the prairie toward the last of the charging warriors as bullets zinged overhead.

The stinging power of a direct hit threw him forward onto the animal's neck. Pain shot up his back and into his head. Running Swift dropped his war club and grabbed for the horse's mane, trying to keep his seat. The world twisted around him. He lost his grip and hit the ground with a thud.

Lying on his back in the prairie dust, pain surged through his twitching body. He felt the powerful horses' hooves pound the earth past him. Unable to move, he watched the haloed sun peak over the horizon. An eagle squawked and swooped down toward him, gliding on the gentle breeze, bringing the soft whistle of his ancestors who came to carry him to the spirit world.

The sun slowly sank behind the forest to sleep. Long shadows crept across the land like grasping fingers. Vision Seeker sat on the ground cloth outside the lodge, rocking back and forth, keeping time with each beat of her heart. She gritted her teeth and nervously wrung her hands. Her head throbbed. Something was not right. Where was her husband? Why was he not back? The men left over two weeks ago. The raid should not have taken this long

Every night since Running Swift left, she kept vigilance, searching the ridge for returning riders. Raising her head, she stared through the gray shadows. Was that movement or just her imagination again? Straining her eyes, she observed a man on horseback cresting the hill above the lake. Behind him trailed several horses. Then another man appeared on top the ridge.

Vision jumped to her feet, screaming. "The men come!" Excitement escalated as men and women left their teepees and meals, gathering into the center of the campsite. Voices filled the air with enthusiasm. Then a subtle hush settled around the area like a blanket of doom. Only two riders approached the village. They did not sing their victory song nor dress in their best-fringed shirt. No scalps hung from their spears. No crier ran through the village, announcing their arrival.

The beaten men, with heads bent and shoulders hunched, rode silently into camp, bringing back their dead. Wolf Slayer led four horses with bodies draped across the saddles. Women screamed and cried as they rushed to touch their dead husbands and sons.

Vision spied Snow Bird wailing and renting her dress as she staggered toward her husband's body.

Dark Moon dashed to Deer Hunter's steed, grasping her son's head while his wife held his arm. "My youngest son. No. No. It cannot be. Oh, Great Spirit, no."

One by one the horses clomped passed Vision. She strained her eyes in search of Running Swift. "He must be safe," she chanted. "He must be safe."

Then Strong Bow rounded the lodges, leading her husband's warhorse and three other animals.

Dashing to him, her heart heavy with pain and unable to breathe, she screamed, "No! No! *Ne:s,* my husband."

Darting behind Vision, Dark Moon shoved her aside. "Away, devil woman." She grasped onto the saddle and clung to her son's body, screaming, "My son. My beautiful son. How can this be? Two sons gone. Oh, Great Spirit, you have deserted me."

Vision reached toward Running Swift, but Dark Moon shoved her away again. "Get away from my son."

Struggling to keep her footing, Vision ran to the opposite side of the horse. She reached out and clasped her arms around her husband's leg, stumbling as the horse proceeded into the inner circle of the campsite.

The next day, Vision sent Little Feather with Many Suns so she could prepare her husband's body for burial. She joined

Plenty Hoops Woman and Dark Moon. As they worked in unison, they sang the death song.

First, they washed Running Swift, and then dressed him in his best clothes. Next, they painted red sacred circles on his cheeks and forehead so the Great Spirit would recognize him. Taking Running Swift's best woolen blanket of red and blue, they wrapped his body, tucked in his favorite pipe and other small personal items from his parfleche, before closely sewing up the robe.

Once they finished, they entered Snow Bird's lodge and helped to prepare Deer Hunter for burial, dressing him in his best. Snow Bird's two small children huddled together on their buffalo robe, crying and holding each other. Propped up against a pole, Little Feather slept in his cradleboard.

Snow knelt over her husband, grief-stricken. She wailed. "What will my children do without a father?"

Plenty placed her hand on Snow's shoulder. "He was brave. He travels the great road with his father and brother. One day we will join them."

Dark Moon moaned and painted red circles on her youngest son's face. "Today I bury my only two sons. Without them and my husband, my life is nothing. What will become of me? I have no one to care for me in my old age."

The three younger women continued to work in silence, not heeding her lamenting and self-pity. Death lay all around them. They did not care to worry about her.

Dark Moon looked up. "I go to live with my brother's son, Hands So High. He will care for me."

Plenty's head jerked up. She stiffened as she faced the old woman, not saying a word, then glanced toward Vision with a pleading look. Vision continued to wash Deer Hunter's arm. Plenty rose to her feet and stormed out of the teepee.

"Besides," said Dark Moon, "Plenty will need help with the baby's coming. I will be there when it arrives."

The dead silence filled the teepee as the women waited.

Wolf Slayer entered the teepee. "It is time." He lifted the teepee side and slid Deer Hunter under to Strong Bow who waited outside. Then a warrior cut a braid from the dead man and handed it to Dark Moon who placed it in the ceremonial bundle with his father's hair and Running Swift's.

Calling the women together, the families began their funeral trek toward the burial grounds. Hands So High and the other warriors stayed as far as possible from the dead. The Medicine Man walked between the lodges, shaking rattles and chanting to the Great Spirit.

In her lodge, Vision pulled the flap aside and motioned to Plenty Hoops Woman, Snow Bird, and two other women relatives to enter her teepee.

"The grave has been dug. It is ready," Plenty said.

The women wound through the village, walking the difficult path behind their dead, wailing the funeral dirges about each warrior's deeds of valor.

Vision Seeker led the procession, carrying her husband's bow and arrows, medicine bag, and bear claw necklace, wrapped in his favorite pouch. His mother walked behind her holding a clean set of clothing and a few more of his personal belongings. Another woman followed behind, leading Running Swift's saddled warhorse.

When they reached the burial site, Vision reached over to touch Running Swift's shoulder. A farewell gesture of love. Slowly they lowered his body on straps into his final resting place.

Dark Moon swung and backhanded Vision, knocking her to the ground. "Do not touch my son. It is forbidden."

Vision jumped to her feet, grabbed Dark Moon by her braids and twirled her around in circles, finally flinging her several feet away. "He is my husband," she yelled, throwing her arms in the air. "You do not command me anymore, you vile snake."

Dark Moon staggered to her feet, lunging for Vision's face with her nails. Quickly the younger woman dodged to one side, booting the older woman in the behind, causing her to stumble and fall flat on her stomach.

Vision stood ready to defend herself, one hand on the hilt of her knife at her waist. "Do not ever attack me or death will come swiftly."

Blocking another attack on Vision, Plenty shouted at Dark Moon, grabbing her by the back of her dress, "Enough. Your fighting angers your son. You two must work together. He would want it so."

Dark Moon glared at her daughter-in-law, hatred etched her face. Finally, she threw her hands in the air and relented. Regaining her dignity, she placed her son's personal items into the hole and began wailing in mournful tones.

Vision Seeker hurriedly picked up Running Swift's scattered items off the ground and laid them on top of her husband's body. All except his bear claw necklace, which she secretly stuffed into her dress. She would keep it for her son. Little Feather would need its good medicine.

Vision dropped to the ground, wailing with grief, asking the Great Spirit to care for her husband, all the while pushing the earth back into the hole with her hands to cover him. Dark Moon knelt on the opposite side, shoving the dirt forward. She chanted and cried wildly, collapsing onto the ground. Once they mounded the gravesite, the two women piled large stones to cover the loose dirt to keep the animals from digging him up.

A woman relative led Running Swift's warhorse up to the eight by four feet grave and slit the animal's throat. Now he would not have to walk in the Spirit World.

Nearby, one mother placed her son's moccasins and blue beaded breastplate on the buffalo robe that covered his body. Another woman rent her clothing and cut her face.

Snow knelt, wailing and pounding the ground on her husband's grave. Taking her knife, she hacked off her braids, stood and tossed them onto the dirt. Stepping back, she slashed her arms and face. Wielding her bloody knife in savage circles, she threatened those around her, shouting, "Oh, Great Spirit. You take my man. I give you others."

Half crazed from grief, Snow collapsed onto her hands and knees, and crawled toward Vision. With her knife still grasped in her hand, she hissed, "You must join our men. You she-devil! You brought this evil thing upon us. You must die to appease the Great Spirit."

Dark Moon jumped to her feet and danced about as if she lost her mind, urging on. "Kill her. Kill her quick. She does not deserve to live. I will help you."

Snow quickly pushed up from the ground, moving the knife back and forth in front of her. "Yes, I'll slice her heart out. We will eat it."

Weapon in hand, Vision leaped up and dodged Snow's slashing knife. She kicked her sister-in-law over and shoved Dark Moon aside.

Plenty dashed forward and grabbed Dark Moon around the waist, separating the two women. "Enough. You defile the memory of a great man. Let there be peace. No more fighting."

Then Plenty grabbed Snow, trying to soothe and quiet her. She removed the knife from Snow's fist.

The grieved woman stumbled back to her husband's grave, wailing and crying.

Dirty and pained with grief, Vision turned and spied Running Swift's bear necklace wedged between two rocks. She picked it up and stuffed it back into her dress.

When she reached her teepee, she gathered all of Running Swift's last remaining belongings and carried them outside. As the Arapaho custom dictated, Vision distributed all of his personal items to each member of the tribe, a headband, arrows, leggings, an old shirt, and other items once owned by the man she loved. All she had left were memories of her life with a kind husband.

Reentering the teepee, Vision put together her personal items. Then she threw Dark Moon's belongings onto a Buffalo robe, rolled it up, and tossed it outside, through the teepee opening.

Glancing about her lodge, she thought about the short span of time she shared with Running Swift. His kindness. His tenderness toward her. Their hours of intimacy. His gentle touch. The earthy smell of his body. But most of all, she would miss the feel of his strong and loving arms enveloping her body.

Plenty stuck her head through the opening. "Vision. We must go. It is time."

Vision strolled toward the opening carrying her belongings, glancing back one more time before leaving.

Outside, Snow Bird's teepee and six other lodges were already afire, flames leaping high into the sky. Hands So High touched the lighted torch to the hide covering. The flames caught quickly and licked the sides, girding the structure and spreading upward.

With Little Feather's cradleboard strapped to her back, she stepped back to watch for a moment.

"Goodbye, Running Swift. One day, we will meet again." Then she turned away.

"Snow is going to live with her brother." Plenty chattered on, guiding Vision toward her lodge. "They welcome her and the children. She needs care. Her mind is not good since Deer Hunter died."

Vision only nodded as she watched Dark Moon slip into Plenty's lodge with her Buffalo bundle.

Seeing the look of disgust on her face, Plenty Hoops Woman said, "We will marry your mother-in-law off quickly. She is too much trouble and needs a man to tame her."

Vision heard the crackling behind her and felt the heat. She refused to watch the fire eat away at her teepee. She lowered her eyes and bowed her head. "Thank you for taking us in," she whispered.

Plenty hugged her. "You are family. I need you. Dark Moon is vile and hateful."

She paused for a moment and then continued. "You are strong and have Little Feather to help you. Mourning will only last one year, then Hands So High will help you select someone to marry."

"Who will take in a half-breed child and a white woman?"

"Now is not time to worry. You will see." Plenty lifted the hide flap of her teepee. "There will always be someone

Chapter Seven

"Soldiers come! Soldiers come!" Pandemonium spread through the village as they fled their lodges, grabbing babies and weapons, while the other children scrambled to hide in the woods. The villagers scurried to find a place of safety and prepared to defend themselves against the onslaught of the bluecoats' bullets and horses.

Thunderous hooves pounded the ground as the soldiers galloped down the ridge and into the Arapaho village, firing a few shots into the midst of the fleeing natives to get their attention.

"Burn their lodges," ordered Sergeant Prescott. "We'll show these devils a thing or two. Maybe they won't be so ready to attack another wagon train."

"Watch those two braves on your right," came a warning.

A volley of arrows ripped through the air. Soldiers sprayed the area with bullets, striking men, women and children, killing them where they stood. A soldier slipped from his horse with an arrow in his leg.

Two teepees caught fire. Smoke swirled skyward.

"Behind you." Jim Castor pointed his rifle and fired at a brave climbing onto the back of Private Pickering's horse.

"Kill that squaw," someone yelled, pointing at Vision Seeker.

She dashed toward her Plenty's lodge, stumbling over a body as a bullet whizzed overhead and struck a warrior standing to her left. *My baby. I must reach my baby.* Heart beating rapidly, unable to breathe, Vision dodged horses, shoving people out of her way.

Dark Moon stepped out of the teepee, holding Little Feather over her head, swinging his cradleboard from side to side. "This is what you come for?" she yelled.

"Put him down," screamed Vision, clambering to reach her son.

"My sons are dead. Yours does not deserve to live, demon woman." A high cackle escaped from Dark Moon's lips as she tossed the papoose into the path of an approaching horse.

A soldier swung his rifle toward the old woman and fired. The bullet struck Dark Moon in the chest, flinging her against the teepee. Sucking in air, she sank to the ground with a thud, leaving a trail of smeared blood down the side of the hide covering.

Vision ran forward waving her hands to scare the animal. "Stop. Stop. Baby. Baby." Falling onto the ground, she covered her son's cradleboard with her body.

Castor's horse reared up, forelegs whipping the air as it danced about the ground, trying to avoid trampling the huddled woman in the dirt. Jumping from his horse, knife in his hand, he grabbed her braids and yanked her to her feet. With her head forced back, scorn and hatred etched her face as she clasped her son to her breast.

"Kill her, Castor. Kill the bitch." A soldier leveled his rifle at Vision.

Castor jerked her to one side, keeping her off balance, and then shoved the soldier's rifle barrel upward, sending the shot skyward. "Wait. This one has red hair. She's white."

"Shoot her anyway," said Private Pickering, standing behind Castor. "She's no good anymore after bearing that bastard. Who'd want her now?"

Releasing her braids and afraid she might bolt, the scout's large rough hands gripped her shoulders, making her wince. "Shut up, Private, and see to helping that injured soldier."

Fearing the worse, Vision twisted and turned, kicking at his legs, trying to extricate herself from his hold. *What did he want from her? Would he cut her throat? Kill Little Feather? Rape her?* Holding the cradleboard in one arm, she tried to reach her knife in the back of her waistband.

Wrapping his arms around her body, sandwiching the child between them, Castor diverted her attempts to escape by shaking her like a rag doll. "Be still. Don't be afraid. I won't hurt you. What's your name?"

Vision only stared at him, fear written across her face.

She started to spit in his face, when Castor spoke in Arapaho. "What are you called?"

Startled for a moment, she answered, "Vision Seeker."

"What was your name before you came to this village?"

Vision stiffened and did not answer.

"What is your child's name?" Castor was losing his patience. Maybe he should take her back to Fort Laramie and let the commander question her. Yet, there was something familiar about the young woman. "Is your name Sarah?"

Vision was startled to hear her white name. Forgotten faces flitted through her mind. Images of a beautiful woman with a soft voice and a gentle touch unnerved her.

"Are you Sarah Anderson?" shouted the scout, shaking her again, trying to get her attention.

Private Pickering sided up to Castor. "You think this is Miz Anderson's daughter? She looks a little crazy to me."

"I say she is. She's about the right age. Look at the auburn hair and blue eyes."

Vision nodded. "Yes, Sarah...Anderson."

"Well, I'll be. If that don't beat all," whispered Pickering. "After three years, we run across her all because of an Indian raid on a small group of wagons." Then he yelled, "Hey, sergeant. Castor's found the Anderson girl."

From the far side of the open area, Sergeant Prescott shouted, "Get her on a horse."

"The Indians have all scattered into the woods, sir," yelled a private.

"Good. We'll leave them to what's left. Mount up men. We're moving out."

Castor smiled. "Well, Miss Anderson. I've come to bring you back to the fort. You mamma's been alookin' for ya. Private Jensen, bring this lady a horse. Can't have her walkin' back to Fort Laramie. It's not proper."

The private gave him a sour look but led a stray horse toward the scout. "We taking her back to the fort dressed like that?"

Castor turned on the two men, standing near him. "Yes, and I don't want any comments from either of you. You hear me?"

They nodded, but their faces showed their hatred for a white girl in Indian clothes.

The scout released Vision and grasped her elbow to assist her. "Here, Miz Anderson. Let me help you up."

She handed the cradleboard to him and then held up her hand, making a sign. Dashing to her lodge, she stepped over the body of Dark Moon and entered.

"She's getting away," yelled Pickering, moving forward, rifle in hand.

Castor raised his arm to block the private. "Hold it, soldier. She's not escaping. She's after something."

Vision returned with a parfleche under her arm and tied it on the back of the saddle. Holding her head high, she smiled at Castor, and mounted the horse with ease. Reaching for her son, she secured his cradleboard to the pommel. Sitting straight and proud, she watched the scout climb onto his horse.

Sergeant Prescott shouted orders and the troop trotted forward in formation with Vision riding next to Castor.

Passing the teepee, Vision looked down at Dark Moon slumped against the partially destroyed lodge. The dead woman's wide eyes stared into a void, her mouth gaped open. No venomous words would escape her lips anymore. She looked as though she were about to sing but forgot the words. Vision did not feel even the tiniest bit of remorse for her.

Turning away from the devastation and urging her horse forward, Vision whispered, "I live here no more."

Chapter Eight

April, 1853—Crossing the Cascade Mountains

Caroline Anderson trudged through knee-deep snow, trying to keep her balance. She led her exhausted horse, pulling on the lead rope. Tired and worn out, she was ready to fall and didn't care whether she froze to death. The cutting wind dug at her face, the brim of her hat barely protecting her from the thousands of freezing needles that stung like maddened bees.

She lifted her knees high with each step only to plunge deeper into another snowdrift. The effort was draining her quickly. For the past hour, she had followed her brother-in-law, John, along the narrow ridge. The drifts grew taller as the wind whipped the snow in a frenzied blizzard, unrelentingly, pushing her back every third step.

Caroline knew they had waited too long to cross the pass and head back down the other side of the Cascade Mountains. With the trail buried, she knew they were lost. No one would know where to find them. If only John had stuck to the original plan to follow the river valley back instead of taking a short cut through the mountain pass.

"Can you find the trail?" she yelled.

No answer. The man in front of her was only a blur. Was she getting snow blindness? Was he leaving her? Was he even there?

John Anderson, yelled back, "Close up the space. You're getting too far behind."

But the wind caught his words. She couldn't make them out. *Did he say close up or stay behind?*

She tried to push harder to close the gap, struggling to reach the rear end of the supply horse in front of her. With her energy and willpower, she shouted, "I can't go...any further. Too tired."

She collapsed into the powdery snow, sinking into its bitter cold arms, unaware of the glacial air around her.

Snowflakes kissed her cheeks and numbness enveloped her body. She knew death wasn't too far behind. The snow crunched around her and a dark shadow blotted out the gray-covered sun. As she drifted into another world, a lifting power seized her. She rode on the freezing breath of the winter wind. *This must be what it is like to die.* The earth circled around her. The floating sensation was peaceful. She did not feel the sting of the biting cold anymore.

Slowly she opened her eyes, half expecting to see angels standing around, waiting to give her wings. The warmth was intoxicating. A light flickered and beckoned to her. She reached forward to touch the glowing light. Instead, a grisly icicled beard and cold breath brought her to her senses.

"You'll be all right. Just lie there and warm yourself. I'll see to the horses."

John opened the cabin door and struggled to pull it shut. Snow drifted in, leaving small clumps on the floor.

Where did the dilapidated cabin come from? Did he know it was here?

Blurry eyed, Caroline looked at her surroundings. She lay curled up, on the dirt floor, her knees to her chest. The door was askew, held on by one leather hinge. The windows were nailed shut, except for a frosted dirty glass near the door. In the middle of the room, a fire swirled and spit as tiny gusts of wind snaked through holes between the log walls, fanning the flames. There was no furniture. Bits and pieces of wood lay strewn about the room. She stretched toward a long board, but her arms wouldn't cooperate.

She moved her hands together, clapping them, trying to bring life back into her fingers. Her legs felt useless, asleep. She rubbed them. A stinging sensation made each leg jump. Her hat was frozen to her head, ice stuck to her hair. As the snow began to melt, the water dripped down her jacket collar, chilling her to the bone. She needed to get undressed and into dry clothes, but that was impossible. Everything was in the saddlebags on the horses outside in the blizzard.

Her stomach growled and rumbled. She couldn't remember the last time she ate. Even a few crumbs would taste good right now. Working her frozen hat off her head, she removed her gloves and pressed closer to the fire. A little bit at a time, the warmth brought life back into her body. Shivering, she realized she needed to get out of her wet trousers and shirt, but to do so she would have to remove her heavy, antelope-hide coat. She struggled, pulling at one wet sleeve.

"Why did we wait so long? Once we crossed the peak, John was sure the pass would still be open." She removed her boots and pulled off her wet socks. "The Indians tried to warn us but, no, he said we had time to hunt a few more days, and then cross through with plenty of time to spare.

"Men!

"I've lived with this man for four years and still don't understand him."

Caroline continued to talk to herself as she struggled to get out of her cold, wet coat. "As a young girl, he left me pregnant back in Pennsylvania. He loved adventure more than me. So, I married his brother.

"Now that my husband has died, here I am, following behind John again.

"Do I really want to marry this man?

"I don't know."

John pushed open the broken door, then leaned against it, letting snow blow into the room, almost extinguishing the fire. He dumped the saddlebags on the floor along with the three empty canteens. Collapsing on the dirt floor, he rested on his hands and knees, breathing heavily.

"Shut the door," she yelled.

He kicked it closed, sat down and leaned his head against the log wall. "Need to go back. Get the saddles." Closing his eyes, he drifted to sleep, his head lolling to one side.

Caroline crawled to him and gave him a good shake. "John. John! Wake up. You need to get the saddles."

He jolted upright and stumbled to his feet, using the cabin wall. "Be back." The door flew open with a gust of wind and he fell into the snow outside.

She leaned on the heavy wooden door, trying to close it, fighting the wind. If the hinge broke, they would be in trouble.

On his return, John tossed a saddle onto the floor and then left again. The snow was piling up a good three feet in the entryway. Each time he entered, snow blew in, covering more of the dirt floor.

"What are you going to do about the horses?"

"I put them up into the thicket behind the cabin. They're

on their own. They'll strip the bark for food. We can't worry about them. We're hardly able to take care of ourselves."

"Where are the furs?"

"I set the cache behind some brush. They'll be safe outside."

He left for one more trip outside. When he didn't come right back, she worried. *Maybe I should go look for him.* Suddenly the door flew open. John and the saddle collapsed into the room. He lay there exhausted, caked in snow from head to foot, ice clumped on his beard, mustache, and eyebrows.

She righted the door to fit the opening, and shoved it closed. Grabbing a board off the floor, she wedged it against the panel to keep it from flying open.

"What happened? Why were you so long?"

John curled up in a ball, shaking fitfully. "I lost...my way back. Blizzard's worse. We're snowed in."

Stooping over John, she pulled off his outer garments and laid them to one side. She added another piece of wood to the fire. Opening a saddlebag, she retrieved two metal cups, packed them with snow off the floor, and heated them. Using her hat, she removed the cups from the hot embers, opened a hide bag of coffee, and dumped a pinch in each cup, stirring with a small stick she retrieved from the floor.

Caroline lifted his head and held the cup close to his lips. "John. Wake up and drink this." At first, he didn't respond. She shook him and blew in his ear. *That should get him stirred up,* she thought, smirking a tiny bit.

Nothing.

She shook him hard and he moaned. "Here, take a sip. It'll warm your insides."

He touched his lips to the rim and moved his face to one side. "Hot."

She blew into the container, trying to cool it down. Then she held it to his lips again. "Sip a little at a time."

The aroma and warmth enticed him to take several sips.

"That's...good." Some of the coffee grounds stuck to his wet lips.

She wiped the dregs away with the sleeve of her shirt, scooped out a few floaters with her fingers, and set the cup down so that she could help him sit up.

"Here, drink some more." She handed him the cup. Then she took several sips from a cup she prepared for herself.

Reaching for a pair of saddlebags behind her, she rummaged through them, pulling out a dry shirt, some socks, and a pair of trousers.

John leaned forward, wobbled, and fell over backwards, passing out cold, spilling the coffee on the floor.

She stared at him. Undressing him was going to be a chore.

Vexed and tired, she jostled his body. "Some cooperation would be appreciated here, John."

He woke as she struggled with his trousers. "No undergarments."

"I see that. Aren't you the brave one?" She smiled. "It's not the first time that view's been displayed. Now raise your butt." With his help, she pulled the trousers up and buttoned them. Next, she attempted to put on his socks. After struggling for a few minutes, she finally left them barely covering his heels. "That will have to do."

Once he was dressed, she rolled him closer to the fire without singeing his beard or clothing. Reaching into the bags again, she found a dry shirt and one sock, but no trousers. She removed her wet clothes and pulled on the shirt and sock. Her behind would have to remain bare, unless...inside another bag, she found a bandana and a piece of cloth. Tying them together, she fashioned a cover for her bottom. With a few more sips of coffee, she relaxed, relishing the warmth that spread through her chest as it slid down her throat. It hit rock bottom in her gut, but she was too tired to think of food. Pulling John's buffalo coat over her, with the hair inside, she snuggled close to him for body heat, tucking her bare foot under his legs. The hide side of the coat was wet, but the fur inside was only damp from perspiration. It was better than freezing to death.

When Caroline woke, the fire was almost out. Hurriedly, she put two more pieces of wood onto the hot embers. On her hands and knees, she gently blew into the fire. The wood caught and flared. Slowly she got to her feet, her whole body ached. Picking up the wet clothing, she laid them flat on the floor to dry. She reached into the saddlebags and found one biscuit and a piece of jerky to share between them.

"John, wake up. You have to eat some food and drink some more warm coffee."

He tried to sit up, but failed. "Can't feel my toes."

"Here, eat this." Handing him half a biscuit and a small piece of jerky, she lifted the coat off his legs and massaged each toe, and then the whole foot.

He squinted at her, trying to adjust his eyes. "What are you wearing?"

"A shirt."

"I mean around your bottom half."

She looked down at her long, bare legs, embarrassed at being so exposed. "I have one of your bandanas and a piece of cloth tied together. I couldn't find any dry trousers."

"Mighty good view to warm a man's blood."

She pushed the cloth lower between her legs. "Don't get any funny ideas. Now eat your biscuit." She grabbed his other foot and forcefully rubbed it.

"Easy, woman. Don't rip off my toes."

"If you don't behave, that won't be the only body part you'll be missing," she warned.

For two days, the wind blew hard and the snow fell steadily against the dark gray clouds. Caroline rubbed the windowpane with her fist to see outside, but they were plastered with blown snow and frost.

The cabin was bitterly cold and the firewood was almost gone.

She turned the clothes over to the other side and pulled them closer to the fire. The shirts were dry, but the woolen trousers were still slightly damp. She handed John another dry shirt. Then she put on the additional one. Her feet were numb, as were her fingers and nose. Even her ears felt frost bitten.

John stooped over, checking the saddlebags. "Here's the last biscuit. There's no more jerky."

They sat down to eat their meager meal. "Tomorrow we need to leave, if the snow stops. We can push hard and get down the mountain in two or three days."

Caroline concentrated on the biscuit in her hand, pinching off a few crumbs and sticking them into her mouth. "We don't have anything else to eat. Can we make it to the bottom without any food?"

"The land further down the trail won't have as much snow. Maybe I can shoot some game."

She looked at John. "I don't want to die up here. I want to get to Fort Laramie to find our daughter. You promised me." Tears filled her eyes as she choked back a sob. "John! We have to find Sarah. Who knows, she might be out in this blizzard with nothing to eat, freezing to death like us."

"Quit! You'll only make yourself sick."

He took her into his arms and clutched her to his chest. "I know I made you a promise, and we will make Fort Laramie. But, right now, we have to get out of this blizzard and off this mountain. Now eat slowly and rest."

The next morning John opened the door a few inches. The snow had stopped falling and the sun was out. The temperature was cold enough to freeze your blood.

Pushing the door closed, he announced, "We're leaving this morning so let's get things packed up."

They dressed in the driest clothing and then threw all the damp clothes into the saddlebags. John reached into one near-empty bag. His hand touched something hard at the bottom. Pulling it out, he smiled. "Look what I found."

He held up a four-inch piece of dried meat. Caroline grabbed her cup, stuck her hand through a small opening by the doorway, and packed the cup with snow. Then she set the last piece of wood on the fire, blew on the embers, and placed the cup near the heat. As the snow melted, she placed the piece of meat into the hot water. "We'll soften it and heat it at the same time. I do believe we have breakfast."

She sat on the floor, waiting impatiently. She was famished. Every so often, she turned the meat to soften the opposite end. It smelled tainted, but it was food. They ate the meager meal, chewing slowly.

He kissed her forehead. "We'll have a good meal soon as we get out of this snow. There's bound to be game further down the trail."

John made two trips to saddle the horses. He recovered the furs from under a blanket of snow and loaded them on the supply horse. Returning to the cabin, he hoisted the saddlebags. "Did you get the canteens packed with snow?"

"Yes, I have them ready. It took a while. I broke off a stick inside one of them."

"That's all right. You ready?" he asked.

She nodded.

"Let's go." He pulled opened the door and tramped down the path.

Caroline fastened the last two buttons on her coat, stirred the fire with her boot and followed him out the door into the blinding sun. The landscape sparkled like millions of diamonds. Icicles hung from snow-laden limbs, causing the branches to bend toward the ground, resembling a mother hen protecting her chicks.

Mounting her horse, she rode south following John along the tree line. The sure-footed animals plunged belly deep through the snow Hungry and tired, Caroline swayed from side to side with each step the horse made.

Later that morning, John spied a weasel. Taking careful aim, he leveled his rifle and shot. The animal popped into the air, then laid still.

"I do believe we have supper." He slipped from his saddle, landing crotch high in snow. Handing Caroline the lead rope to the supply horse, he headed toward his prey.

She dismounted and stood watching him trudge away, pushing himself through the high snowdrifts. She was starving but leery about eating a weasel. *What did it taste like...rat...snake... possum? Was the texture stringy, oily, strong? Weasel! What else would this man eat?*

Chapter Nine

Leaving the worst of the snowy terrain behind, Caroline followed John into the rocky Cascade foothills. They passed a lake nestled in a protective area, surrounded by massive towering hemlock and fir trees, blotting out much of the sun. She tried to rid the taste of the weasel from her mouth, but the flavor lingered on her teeth and gums.

"We'll stop here and make camp. The branches of the fir tree should protect us from the wind," said John.

Caroline dismounted. Unable to take her left foot out of the stirrup, she hopped on one foot, trying to dislodge her wedged boot.

John strolled over, grasped her by the buttocks, squeezing lightly with both hands. He lifted her high until she managed to wiggle her boot free. "Nice feel, soft yet firm."

She slapped his arm with her hat. "You are so ornery, enjoying this at my expense."

He laughed and sauntered away.

She leaned her head against the horse's belly, holding onto the saddle.

He knew she was exhausted. "I'll take care of the horses," he said. "You get a fire going. We'll warm the rest of the meat from this morning and then get some sleep."

Once the horses were tethered and left to graze, John found a spot to settle in for the night. Pulling some brush together and adding a few cut branches, he built a snug shelter.

With a warm meal in her belly, Caroline curled up in her heavy coat and blanket from her bedroll inside the brush. Sleep came easy that night.

The next morning, John stood outside the shelter and shouted, "Wake up sleepy head. Breakfast has arrived."

She pushed aside a branch and stared at him.

In his hands, strung on a long stick were two fish. "I'll have these two gutted and ready to eat faster than lightening. So, get everything together. We need to ride after we eat."

"Where did you get them?" she asked, stretching her arms over her head.

"There's a stream on the other side of those trees and down a ways."

She struggled to her feet, brushing the dirt from her clothes. Yawning wide, she moved her shoulders to work out the kinks, then gazed around the area.

"John, come here," she yelled.

He rushed to her side with rifle in hand. "What!"

"Look," she pointed seven feet above her head. "Claw marks."

"That's why we have to eat and ride. The smell of food might bring that grizzly back and I don't want to be around when he shows up. A nine-foot hungry bear weighing over a couple hundred pounds is not my kind of morning entertainment. Everything ready?"

"Almost." She crawled into the brush to gather their belongings.

He returned to attend to the fish.

After they ate, John put out the fire and got the horses ready. Climbing into the saddle, he said, "We have about two more days of riding before we make our camp down below."

Caroline sighed with relief. "I know Ben and Sadie are probably worried sick about us. They most likely gave us up for dead."

He grimaced. "I guess I'll never hear the end of this story."

A mischievous smile spread across her face. "It'll be a good one to tell around the fire, over and over and over."

"I get the point."

"Two things about getting back. It'll be good to sleep in our tent again and I look forward to Sadie's cooking."

John rolled his eyes and nodded as he led the way forward.

Wading in Pogo Creek, Standing Tall speared another fish and flipped it onto shore behind him. Glancing up, he spotted two riders off in the distance. He stretched his neck and focused on them heading his way at a slow trot. "They come back," he whispered.

He picked up his catch from the bank, strung them on a rawhide string, and made tracks toward the campsite. "Riders come," he shouted.

Sadie Tedder shuffled out of the tent and raised her hand to shield her eyes from the sun. "Well, I'll be." She flipped the tent flap. "Ben Wilson. Get your sweet body out here. We got company comin' in."

Ben grumbled as he joined her. "What's all the ruckus about? Who's comin' in?"

Sadie pointed to the riders. "What'd I tell you? Didn't I say they'd make it back just fine?"

"Well, I'll be. I hate a *told-you-so* woman. Look a bit ragged to me. Standing Tall, get those fish cleaned. Micah, your father's back. Better stir up that fire. Believe those two wandering misfits finally found their way home. Sadie, we need to get that rabbit cooked and those fish a fryin'. We're eatin' tonight." He did a quick jig, then grabbed his back

"You old fool. You should know better than to start high steppin'. What's the matter with your brain? Go sit down."

He patted Sadie on the behind. "I'll just sit in over here and watch you cook."

She lifted one eyebrow and sniffed. "Don't get too friendly there old man. We ain't married yet."

Micah Anderson grabbed some wood and added it to the fire, stirring up the embers. Nudging Standing Tall, he asked, "Do you think those two will ever get along?"

"Sadie and Ben?" asked the Indian boy. "They bad talk each other. Not mean anything by it."

The mulatto lad, with tightly curled hair, ginned. "I think she'd toss him out on his ear if she didn't like him."

The two boys ran to the edge of camp to greet Caroline and John.

"How's everything here?" asked John. "Sadie and Ben doing okay?"

"About the same. Always grumbling at each other," answered Micah.

"What took so long?" asked Standing Tall. "Mountains hold you for ransom."

"We took a short cut through the pass," said Caroline.

"A short cut?" both boys asked in unison, then stared dubiously at John.

"Even I have better sense not to cut through those mountains this time of the year," Micah said, eying his father.

"Quiet. I don't want to hear any remarks right now," he said. "Help get these furs off the pack horse. Put them with the others."

Standing Tall grabbed the reins of the extra horse and led the animal away. Micah followed him.

Sadie rushed toward them, arms raised, ready to hug whichever one reached her first.

"My, my. I see you two finally decided to come home. What were you doing so long away from camp, anyway?"

"Don't ask," said John. "Just don't ask."

Ben joined the others. "Don't ask what?"

"Never mind," quipped John. "We'll tell you later. Right now we're hungry, dirty and tired."

Ben grabbed the reins of both horses. "These horses look plumb wore out. I'll see to them while you get yourself ready for some good vittles. Sadie's cooking tonight." He took a couple of steps backward, looked over his shoulder, and shouted, "Micah, come get these horses, rub them down, and feed 'em."

Ben sat down by the fire next to John. "Well, you talkin' yet?"

Caroline gave him a mischievous smile. "I can't wait to hear his version. I'll just listen to be sure he gets the story straight."

John glowered at her.

"We're waitin'," Sadie said. "What took you so blasted long?"

John put his plate down and took a deep breath. "We were visiting an Indian camp up in the Cascade mountains. We spent a good two weeks hunting with them."

Ben shuffled his foot. "I should have been along, doggone it."

"Not the way you were feeling. You being sick and riding that distance. Why you probably would still be up there, six feet under," said John.

Sadie slapped Ben on the arm. "See, I told you. You were better off here with me, you stupid old goat."

"Hmm," replied Ben. "Ain't gonna get better with you beatin' on me all the time." He turned back to John. "Anyway what happened?"

"Yes, what happened John?" echoed Caroline.

The caustic sound of her question set John on edge. He poured himself a cup of coffee. "I made a wrong decision."

"Only one?" asked Caroline.

"Don't get pushy, woman. No, I made two bad decisions."

John knew everyone was waiting to hear the rest of the story. He hated to own up to his mistakes, especially when he'd put Caroline's life in danger.

"First, I decided to stay a week longer. The hunting was great and the Indians enjoyed getting most of the meat."

"So, what was wrong with that?" asked Micah.

"Indians like to eat good," said Standing Tall.

"We ate good," replied Caroline, "we just started too late to travel back his way."

"What way was that John?" asked Ben. "You took the river valley back, didn't ya?"

"No." John sat there staring at his folded hands, clenching his teeth.

"NO!" shouted Ben. "I knew it. You took the mountain pass, didn't ya? Can't believe you'd do somethin' that stupid this time of the year."

John screwed up his mouth and stared into the fire.

"Yes. I took the pass."

Sadie gasped. "Oh, John, you know better."

"The snows were over with and the pass was beginning to clear some. I thought we could get through, but then we hit that stupid blizzard." He took a drink from his cup. "We were lucky and found a cabin to ride out the worst of the storm."

Sadie stood up. "Well, what's done is done. We need to get this mess cleaned up. Mornin' will come soon enough." She grabbed all the tin plates and chucked them into a big wash pan. A pan of hot rinse water sat next to the fire. "I'll tend to these dishes."

Ben stretched his legs in front of him. He filled his pipe, grabbed a small glowing stick from the fire, and lit it. "I'm gonna sit here and enjoy a smoke."

"When did you take up smoking a pipe?" asked John. He tossed the last of the coffee in his cup on the ground, before handing it to Sadie.

"A while back. Don't smoke it much." He waved it toward John. "Want a puff?"

"No thanks."

"What do ya think we oughta do, now that you're back?"

"We should spend two more days here getting things together. We shouldn't wait too much longer, though, before heading out."

"Yep, I agree with that. Been watching the mountaintops. Sure is a lot of snow on 'em."

"Been there," said John.

"Oh, I forgot." Ben took another puff from his pipe. "Where we gonna go from here."

John looked in Caroline's direction. She was helping Sadie with the dishes. "We'll head to Fort Laramie. Have a little unfinished business to attend to there."

"Hoping you would say that."

"Hey, we're going to Fort Laramie," shouted Micah.

Sadie raised her head and smiled at Caroline. "We're headin' back to the fort, honey. Maybe this time she'll be waitin' for ya."

Tears welled up in Caroline's eyes. She bit her lip to hold back a sob. "Fort Laramie," she whispered, "to find Sarah."

Chapter Ten

Late June, 1853, Fort Laramie

T he sound of horses sloshing through the mud made Patrick O'Brien look up from his work. Laying the bridle across his lap, he watched the haggard troops file by, two by two, as they headed toward the flagpole.

"It's always the same every time they return. Nothing. This waiting is driving me crazy." The desolate surroundings of the stable were depressing. He'd never felt so alone.

Wiping his hands on his leather apron, he picked up the needle and waxed linen thread, and returned to repairing the bridle buckle. The gray overcast clouds shoved his spirits into a new low. The cold brisk breeze from the drizzling rain chilled him, as it whistled through the open doors. He needed a good stiff drink to warm his bones. Lowering his head, he turned his back to block out the pathetic view. Without being told, he knew the soldiers would have no news of white captives among the Indians.

Maybe he should give up his dream of finding Sarah and move on. After a year at the fort, he had accomplished absolutely nothing...except heartache, sore hands, and an empty pocket. His brother was right. This territory was too blamed big to find one person, one beautiful girl who held his heart captive. But, if he returned to St. Charles, he would feel like a failure. He couldn't live with that. He never failed, never. He shoved the needle through the hole. Just once, he wanted to touch Sarah's face and look into those beautiful blue eyes again. Was that too much to ask?

Disgusted with his work, Patrick dropped the tack onto the dirt floor. He propped his elbows on his knees, holding his throbbing head between his hands. His anger built as he thought about Sarah being out in the territory alone among the savages. He hated to think about the atrocities that she had to endure. Trying to block out the shouting and noise outside, Patrick closed his eyes and clenched his fists. He wanted to yell, scream, or knuckle-blast someone.

"What in the hell am I supposed to do?" he yelled. "Just sit here and wait? Wait for what? That's all I've done since I got here."

Grabbing up the bridle, he flung it across the room. He jumped to his feet and kicked the bucket, watching it bang into the wall and ricochet into the stall. The rebounding noise caused the horses to whinny and kick up their heels.

A private dashed through the doorway, wet and out of breath. "Mr. O'Brien."

Patrick jerked his head around to face the soldier and bellowed, "What?"

The private backed up, eyes wide, afraid of the menacing face confronting him. "They found her."

Patrick couldn't believe his ears. He rushed forward, grabbing a fistful of the small man's collar, shaking him like a rag doll. "What did you say?"

"They found Sarah Anderson. She's in the commander's office."

Patrick shoved the private aside, knocking him against the stall post. Bolting out the door, he ran outside into the rain, before the soldier could finish his sentence. Tearing across the muddy parade ground, he reached the commander's doorway, barred by two sentries.

"Sorry, sir. No one can enter," said one private.

"Listen, you dense-headed peon. Let me in or I'll bash your teeth down your miserable throat." He raised his fist and drew back his arm. Both sentries pointed their rifles at him in unison.

"Patrick!" yelled Jim Castor, jumping onto the porch behind him. "Hold on there. No need to fight and end up in the stockade."

Patrick pivoted toward his friend, his face livid with rage. "Sarah's in there and I want to see her, *now*!"

Lowering his voice, Castor tried to pacify the irate young man. "You have every right. Let the commander talk with her first. It'll take a while. Why don't you join me for a drink or two? We have time and it'll warm your innards."

He eased up to Patrick and placed his arm across the young man's shoulders, pulling him off the porch, steering him toward the pub. "Let's go talk. I have an interesting story to tell you."

Tearing off his work apron, Patrick threw it over his shoulder, allowing the scout to lead him away from Headquarters. Rain peppered both men, as they made their way across the open area.

* * *

Rapping his knuckles on the counter, Castor yelled, "Barkeep. Give me a bottle of your good whiskey and two clean glasses."

Murphy grabbed the glass container off the shelf behind him. "How ya been, Jim?"

"Doin' fine. You remember Patrick O'Brien."

Patrick nodded.

"Good ta see ya again, young fella. Seen ya around some. Enjoy your whiskey." With that said, Murphy picked up the coins that Castor tossed onto the bar and moved on.

The scout scooped up the glasses and bottle. "Let's go sit over in the corner so we can have some privacy."

Patrick followed him to a small, round wooden table near the window and took a seat in the open-backed chair facing outside. He kept one eye peeled on the doorway of the headquarters across the way. Stretching his legs under the table, Patrick slid his heels on the grungy floor, leaving marks.

Murphy lit two ceiling oil lamps, brightening the dark room. The smell of wet, dirty bodies, musty wood, and whiskey mingled with the stale smoky odor.

Castor poured two fingers of whiskey into each glass. "Bottoms up." He threw back his head as he gulped down his drink and then belched. "Ah, feels good. Nothing like a burn deep in your gut."

Patrick belted down his drink and set his glass on the table. He stared at the scout. "Where did you find her?"

Castor poured another round. "We rode out to the Arapaho village northeast of here. Had a tip we'd find the Indians that raided the Becker party. Anyway, we went to arrest the braves and bring them in. Unfortunately, the villagers refused to cooperate. All hell broke loose. A couple of Indians got killed and one soldier was injured."

Patrick sat forward and stretched his arms out, grasping the table's edge. His eyes narrowed. "You didn't answer my question."

"I'm gettin' to it. Don't hurry me, boy. Where's your manners? Anyway, some old Indian woman darts out of a teepee and flings a papoose in front of my horse. I had a hell of a time keepin' from tramplin' the baby. Out of nowhere, this Indian mother throws herself over the baby to protect it."

"Jeez, Castor. What in the hell's that got to do with Sarah?"

The scout took another drink and eyed Patrick. "You ain't listenin' very close. That mother protectin' her baby was Sarah."

Dropping his arms to his side, Patrick slumped back in his chair. Dumbfounded, he sat with his mouth open, eyes wide. "Sonofabitch," was all he could manage to say. Slowly he reached for a second glass and downed it.

Castor watched him for a moment, and then continued to clarify his last statement in more detail. "She was married to a brave that got himself killed. The papoose was his son."

Patrick gritted his teeth and shoved his glass forward. "Fill it."

Castor tipped the bottle. "Gettin' drunk ain't the answer. What ya got to do is decide what steps you're gonna take. How you're gonna talk with her? Set up some plans."

Tipping his chair back, leaning against the clapboard wall, Castor said, "Dang-nabit, Pat. You've been waitin' for this gal for over a year. Constantly bellyachin' because we never brung her in. Now that we find her, you act like the devil stole your soul. Or is it, you're too good for her now?"

The two men sat in silence, each fighting his own demon with a glass of whiskey. Hostile, Patrick scowled and kept his eye on the headquarters door. "Is she wild and uncontrollable? Is she Indian?"

"Nah," said Castor, realizing the young man was torn between relief and anguish. "She kinda struggles with being able to speak her mind, but she gathered her stuff up and rode with the troops, quiet and ladylike. Look, it's gonna be harder on her than you. She's a white gal that's been livin' with an Indian, has a baby to show for it. What do you think people are gonna say about her? You think they're gonna be polite and accept her? She needs you now more than ever. So, pull up your boot straps and quit actin' like some easterner who don't know his head from his ass."

Patrick chuckled. "You always had a way with words, Castor. Good book learning."

"Yep. I should be elected president or something."

"What's the commander going to do with Sarah? Her mother hasn't arrived yet. She has no money. Where's she gonna live?"

Castor swirled the liquor in his glass. "Well, I'd say our good leader's gonna have her livin' at Bedlam House for a while. There's extra rooms there and the commander's wife will probably take her under her wing. Miz Garnett's a gentle woman, always helping those less fortunate."

Patrick closed his eyes, propped his arms on the table in front of him, and leaned forward. "All I wanted when I came out here was to find her and ask her to marry me."

"Yep." Castor poured himself another drink, sipping this one slowly.

"It was a simple plan. I didn't ask for all these complications. Nothing's going like I anticipated. I've got some serious thinking to do."

Castor nodded toward the window. "Looks like you don't have much time to do any of that. She's leavin' headquarters right now. You better get yourself in line. That's if you're still interested in that pretty young thing."

"What does she call herself now?" asked Patrick.

"Let me see. I believe it's Vision Seeker."

"Vision Seeker." Patrick repeated. He took one more gulp from his glass, stood up, and left the bar.

Castor sat there, watching him saunter across the open area, heading for headquarters. "Good luck, kid. Think you're gonna need it."

He poured himself another three-fingered drink and gulped it down. Raising the bottle in the air, he squinted to see how much was left. "Hell, no use in wasting good liquor." He finished off the last of the bottle and then plunked it down on the table.

Castor stood in the saloon doorway watching the two young people as they faced each other in the drizzling rain. A girl dressed in doeskin with a cradleboard strapped to her back and a boy in buckskin with muddy boots and not much else to offer, trying to bridge the gap of time to find their destiny.

"Those two have a long journey to travel. God help `em. Nobody else will."

Chapter Eleven

Vision Seeker watched the tall man hastened toward her in the rain, each step sure and decisive. His features and bearing seemed familiar. He had long, dark brown hair. A wet cotton shirt clung to his body, accentuating wide shoulders. Sleeves rolled up to his forearms, revealed thick wrists above strong wide hands. Buckskin trousers hugged his lower body, emphasizing his muscular thighs. Worn muddy boots covered his calves. He was extremely handsome...for a white man.

He stopped short of the porch. "Sarah?" Searching her face for some kind of recognition, he asked, "Are you Sarah Anderson?"

Vision scrunched her brows together as she listened to the words. *Who was this man? Should she answer him?* Pursing her lips together, she lowered her head and looked at her moccasins.

The stranger took two steps toward her. Quickly, she lifted her head and stepped back. "Yes. Sarah Anderson."

A smile crept across the man's face as his penetrating gaze scrutinized her from head to toe. Nervously, she watched him and then raised one hand to halt his approach.

"You are?" she asked, pointing at him.

"I'm Patrick O'Brien from St. Charles, Missoura. Don't you recognize me?"

Her mouth fell open, unable to fathom the change of the boy she once knew into the man that now stood before her. She clutched her hands nervously at her waist. "Patrick?"

He nodded. "I've been here for over a year, waiting for word that you were alive. I can't believe you're standing in front of me. All these months, waiting. Never sure if you were dead or alive."

The haunted look in his eyes pierced her heart.

"Well," said First Lieutenant Richard B. Garnett, stepping through the doorway, pulling on his glove. "I see you've met Miss Anderson. Now if you'll excuse us, we are heading to Bedlam House where she will be living. I see my dear wife is waiting for us on the porch." Taking Sarah's elbow, the lieutenant proceeded to escort her down the steps.

"Oh, by the by, Mr. O'Brien. If you wish to call on Miss Anderson, please contact my aide first."

Patrick stepped into his path, blocking the lieutenant. "Stop. I want to talk with her. I've waited at this fort for over a year to see her. At least give me a few minutes. I deserve that much."

The commander raised one eyebrow, scowled at the young man, and stared him down. "Get out of my way, Mr. O'Brien."

Patrick grabbed the lieutenant's jacket, jerking him to one side. "Look, commander—"

"Unhand me, Mr. O'Brien," Lieutenant Garnett exclaimed. He grasped Patrick's wrist, yanking the young man's hand away. Summoning the soldiers from the porch with a wave, the commander brushed his crumpled sleeve and straightening his jacket with several tugs.

With two rifles aimed at his midsection, Patrick raised his arms to indicate that all was well. "I was only asking for a few minutes with Sarah. That's all." He stared at each soldier and repeated, "That's all."

"There'll be plenty of time for you to socialize." Garnett dismissed the two privates with the nod. "Right now my main concern is to get Miss Anderson and her son out of this damp weather. I'm sure you are as worried about their health as I am."

Sarah gazed at Patrick. "Please," she whispered, fear in her voice.

Patrick lowered his arms and stepped aside. He stood watching the lieutenant spirit away his dream. "I'll call on you, soon," he shouted.

Mixed feelings danced through his mind as he watched her walk away in her doeskin dress and leggings, with the papoose strapped to her back. Was there a way to bridge the gap in their past? He was emotionally drained and having trouble dealing with Sarah living with an Indian. And, there was the baby. He gritted his teeth, hating the thoughts that played through his mind. People will call her soiled. He didn't want to think that way. She was still his Sarah. Fighting back bitter tears, he hung his head. The need to be near her was eating at him. Looking up, he stared at the saloon. Maybe Castor could answer a few more questions, talk about what was bothering him. If anyone could understand his feelings, Jim could.

Wiping the rain from his face with his forearm, he watched her climb the stairs to Garnett's quarters. Hunching his shoulders, he buried his hands in his pockets and headed back to the stables.

Vision quickly glanced over her shoulder at the man one more time before following Lieutenant Garnett toward the big building.

Mixed emotions filled her heart and head. Even though her body hurt for her husband, Patrick O'Brien had traveled far, searching for her. He came from her past, looking for a future. With her.

There are those who will call me ruined, but I'm not. I was a good wife, a kind mother. Will people understand my life with the Indians?

Confused and disillusioned, she turned to watch Patrick walk away in the rain, all alone.

A lady in a dark burgundy dress, with a shawl across her shoulders, stood waiting on the second floor veranda, watching their approach. As Vision stepped up the last painted step, the woman reached out and grasped her hand.

"Oh, my dear, we are so happy to finally find you. When the sergeant came and told me you had been found, I couldn't believe it."

The commander stepped onto the porch and hesitated for a moment. "I'm going to let you two ladies get acquainted. I have paperwork to do." Then he touched the tip of his hat and left.

Mrs. Garnett gave a small smile to her husband and then turned to Sarah. "Come in, you are soaked to the bone. Bring that sweet baby inside where it is dry. My name is Jane Garnett."

The woman pushed the wooden door open and ushered Vision into a large room. The terra cotta painted walls made the room drab. Bronze green drapes from ceiling to floor shielded the sun from entering the small room. The furnishing consisted of two mahogany chairs upholstered in deep red velour, a large walnut desk, and a rosewood sofa covered in green brocade.

Vision removed the cradleboard and propped it against the wall. Checking first to be sure Little Feather was still asleep, she stood in front of the strange green piece of furniture, poking the softness with her finger. She sat down and bounced a couple of times, smiling at the delightful feel on her bottom.

Mrs. Garnett stiffened as she watched the Indian woman in wet clothes, bounce on her prized sofa. "That's a sofa. Would you rather sit in a chair? I can have my maid bring one from the dining room."

"No, it is good to sit on something so soft and pretty."

Mrs. Garnett rubbed her hand lovingly across the material. "We purchased it in Alexandria, Virginia, and brought it out by wagon. Isn't it beautiful?"

"Sofa," repeated Vision. "Yes, it is nice." Across the room, a round glass bordered by an ornate wooden frame, hung on the wall. Crossing the room, she stood in front of the mirror and stared into it. A woman stared back at her.

"We call that a mirror."

"Yes, I remember." Vision cocked her head from side to side. How different she looked. She patted her hair and slid her hands down her braids. Then she ran the back of one hand upward across her cheek. "Like my mother."

Stepping up behind Vision, Mrs. Garnett whispered in her ear, "You do look like your mother. She returns to the Fort every year searching for information on your whereabouts. Each time she leaves, her heart is saddened because there was never any word of you."

Jane Garnett grabbed Vision's shoulders, turning her around. "But, now is the time to be happy. Come with me, Sarah. I'll show you to your room where you can freshen up and attend to your little one. Our evening meal will be served in one hour so we need to hurry."

Vision picked up the cradleboard. Her son still slept, but she knew he wouldn't for long. He would be hungry. She followed the commander's wife through the house, feeling stifled by the surrounding walls. They did not breathe like her beloved teepee.

"We have a nice room in the back that will give you privacy. Our daughter used it when she lived with us. It is small but comfortable."

The door opened into a tiny, drab room with few furnishings. An iron-railed bed covered by a plain brown coverlet rested against one wall. A marble-topped dry sink with a blue and white ceramic pitcher and basin hugged the same wall. Across the room was a wooden chair with a cane seat and a large clothespress, reaching from the floor to above a man's height and two arms wide. To the right of the bed, a tiny window faced the mountains.

Vision placed her son on the bed and unlaced the cradleboard bindings. He opened his round black eyes, waving his freed arms and legs, making cooing noises. Sitting next to him, she bounced, testing the softness of the bed. The springs squeaked. She laughed as he tried to roll over on the uneven surface.

"That, my dear, is a lovely bed where you will sleep tonight."

Her thoughts drifted. She wished for her beautiful Buffalo robe placed by a warm fire. She missed the freedom of her village, the spaciousness of her teepee, and the loving arms of her husband. What was to become of her and her son? Who truly cared about them? She fit in neither world now.

Mrs. Garnett continued. "This is your room until you decide to leave. If you should need anything, please let me know." She opened the door and called out, "Ladesha, please bring some water for Miss Anderson."

Facing the clothespress, Jane Garnett opened both doors. She brought out a light green dress with a white bodice. "This is a dress that belonged to my daughter. You're about her size. I am sure it will fit you. If not, we'll alter it. There are underthings here for you, also. Now, get yourself settled and freshened up." She replaced the garment and closed the doors.

Vision nodded her head and picked up her son, sitting him on her lap.

A stout Negro woman sashayed into the room carrying a small bucket of water. She wore a brown dress covered by a plain white apron. Her hair was starting to gray around the temples. She filled the basin.

"This is my maid, Ladesha." Jane turned to her maid. "This is Mrs. Anderson's daughter, Sarah. She will be staying with us for a while."

"Yes, ma'am," Ladesha said. She picked up the bucket, and vanished down the hallway.

"I will call when the meal is ready. In the meantime, I will try to obtain some clothing for your son." Jane exited the room, shutting the door behind her.

Standing up with Little Feather in her arms, Vision rounded the bed, laying the baby next to the big bowl. First, she removed his clothing and the damp moss from his bottom, dropping it on the floor. Then she picked up a small cloth and began to wash him. Grabbing a towel from the tabletop, she dried and wrapped him up, hugging him to her chest. Sitting down on the bed, she suckled him until he was full and content.

She glanced about the room. The small glass window brought back memories of the cabin she once lived in, only there was never any cloth hanging from it. Placing her son on the floor, she edged toward the curtain, grasping the gauze material between two fingers. She sniffed it, rubbed it across her cheek, and then covered her face. *How strange. It is so soft and thin. I can see through it.* Outside, the distant mountains beckoned her to freedom. This would be her road to escape when she was ready. Where would she go? Who would she go to?

Turning to her right, the big box against the wall intrigued her. Pulling on the large wooden handles, the two doors fell open. Inside hung the green and white dress, so full it spilled out over the wooden edge. She gathered the material in her arms, crushing it to her body. The dress came loose from the hanger and Vision fell onto the floor, the garment still in her arms. Her naked son crawled toward her, grabbing one of her braids. Laughingly, she kissed him on his forehead. Getting to her feet, she spread the dress out on the floor and walked around it, straightening the edges. Little Feather pulled the edge of a sleeve into his mouth and sucked on it.

"No, that is not food, little one." Laughing at her son's antics, Sarah picked him up. She swung him back and forth in her arms as she stepped lightly around the room in circles. Hearing his giggles gladdened her heart.

Stopping in front of the garment, she stared down at it. "Never have I seen such clothing. So much stitched together for one person to wear."

A knock at the door startled her. Jane Garnett stuck her head through the opening. "I thought I would check to see if you need help in getting dressed."

Vision motioned her in.

"Here, I have some clothes for your son."

Putting Little Feather down, Vision accepted the garments.

"My goodness, I see you have the dress ready. Here, let me help you undress." Jane grasped the bottom of doeskin dress.

Vision clutched the sides of her outfit, forcing it downward. "No, I can do it."

"Oh, don't be so shy, you silly girl. It will take two of us to get you dressed." The Jane yanked the doeskin up over Vision's head. Her undergarments consisted of leggings gartered at the knee.

"My, my," was all Jane uttered. "Those will have to come off," pointing to the leggings.

Sarah untied the garters and stepped out of the leggings, pushing them to one side with her foot.

"Now aren't these lovely." Jane passed Sarah the white knee length stockings from the clothespress.

Vision pulled the stockings on, and stared down at her naked body with white legs and feet. Placing her hands on her hips, she broke out in a grin.

Jane tried to suppress a giggle as she handed the young woman the long underdrawers.

Once the pantalets were in place and tied, Jane picked up a long shirt. "Now raise both of your arms over your head." She pulled the long skirted chemise over the Sarah's head. "Now you are looking more presentable."

Holding the crinoline out, she said, "Step into the opening and I will secure it for you."

Vision stepped back, pushing the fluffy thing to one side. "What is it?"

"It's a petticoat to make your dress stand out. You'll see. Back east, the crinolines are seven or ten feet circles. But, we'll do with this small one."

Jane secured the garment, placed her hands on her hips and said, "Now, twirl around a little."

Vision felt like a stuffed Buffalo stomach, trussed up. Spreading her arms out from her sides, she stiffly turned around, avoiding the dress that lay on the floor. Her son lay on his back making gurgling noises and playing with the petticoat as she stepped over him. His eyes followed her as she moved about the room.

"Now we'll put on the dress." Jane bunched the material up in her hands, slowly lowering it over Vision's head. "Here, put your arm through this hole." Pulling the strings in the back of the bodice, Jane tightened the dress snuggly to Sarah's body.

It fit perfectly. She stood back and admired the young woman with long auburn hair. "Oh, how lovely you look. Green is a good color on you. Now, we must unbraid your hair. I do believe I have an extra hairclip somewhere in my room. I'll be right back." She dashed out the door.

Vision sat on the bed. The skirt flared up in front. It spread from the foot rail to the pillow. Little Feather crawled to his mother and grasped her leg. She reached down and scooped him up in her arms. "Dress and underthings, very uncomfortable. Too much to wear and it's hard to breathe," she said in Arapaho.

Lying back onto the bed, she tossed her son gently into the air and listened to his laughter, spittle stringing from his mouth. Then she clutched him to her breast and shut her eyes.

Rising from the bed, she strolled to the window. "See my son, there are the Spirit Mountains. The clouds caress their pointed tops. There is our freedom to fly with eagles. To feel the wind in our face." She stared out the window, lost in thought.

Chapter Twelve

Jane Garnett led Sarah toward the dining room, chatting incessantly and waving her hands about. "You must think of yourself as Sarah from now on, not Vision, whatever. You need to select a new name for your son, too. We'll think about that tomorrow."

"Sarah," Vision repeated. It had been such a long time since anyone had called her by that name. Her tongue felt strange as she mouthed the word, but with practice, it would come.

She smiled as she looked down at her feet. Her moccasins peeked out with each step. The heeled boots in the clothespress just would not do. There was no way she was going to tie her toes in those. Moccasins suited her better.

With each footfall, the garments she wore made her waddle like a large pregnant buffalo looking for a place to rest. Her son gurgled and squirmed in her arms. He grasped his shirt, pulling it up and exposing his belly. Suppressing a giggle, she whispered, "Patience, little one. We will put these clothes away when we get back to our room."

Three soldiers stood in the dining room, drinking brandy and talking with the commander. "Ah, the women have arrived," announced Lieutenant Garnett. "Gentlemen, I would like to present Miss Sarah Anderson and her son."

The three sergeants nodded.

With a flip of his hand, Garnett continued, "Miss Sarah, may I present Sergeant Prescott. And over here are Sergeants Williams and Morrissey."

Sarah timidly smiled and cast her eyes toward the floor.

"Ladies, please be seated. Our meal is ready," Garnett announced. "Ladesha!"

She smiled as she entered the room from the kitchen. "Yes, sir?"

"You may begin serving the meal. Gentlemen, please take your seats." The lieutenant sat at the head of the table and Mrs. Garnett sat opposite him. Prescott and Williams sat on the bench to the left of their commander, Sarah and Morrissey occupied the bench on the right.

The commander's wife leaned over toward Sarah. "Ladesha will take your son into the kitchen and feed him."

Sarah's protective senses took charge. "No, I feed him."

Mrs. Garnett patted her hand. "Now, now, the child will be much more comfortable with our servant. He will be well cared for while we eat."

Ladesha enter the room. Sarah watched her place a steaming platter of prairie chicken covered in brown gravy on the table. She quickly returned to the kitchen and brought out two more dishes.

Sergeant Williams sat up straight. The savory smell brought a smile to his face as he checked out the food.

Noting the sergeant's expression, Ladesha pointed at Williams and said, "Now don't you touch that food until I puts down these taters and squash."

"You better mind your manners," warned the commander, grinning up at her, "or she'll slap your hands."

The black woman gave a soft snort as she placed the bowls in the center of the table. Then she reached over and took Little Feather from Sarah. "My, my, he sure is a sweet one. Just look at those big black eyes. You come with me, Sugarberry. I'm gonna take good care of you. We'll leave these white folks to their eatin'." She snuggled him close, wrapping her nutmeg-colored arms around him, all the while talking to him as she walked away.

Sarah's gaze followed the servant's swaying backside until the woman disappeared into the next room.

Jane passed the homemade rolls to Prescott on her right. "She was our daughter's nanny. I suppose Ladesha will always be part of our family. My parents gave her to us as a wedding present. You know..." she continued to babble on.

Lost in remembering what it was like to be a servant, Sarah bit her lower lip. Thoughts, about those terrible times working in the Crow village from sunup to sundown with very little to eat, flitted through her mind. Looking down at her left hand, she envisioned bleeding fingers as she knelt, scrapping hides all day long during the buffalo hunts. She never knew from one minute to the next what would come her way. The villagers spat on her, never giving a kind word or gesture. Finally, tiring of her whining and having to feed her, the Crow traded her to the Arapahos. Again, she found herself tied to a post, working in the dirt.

She raised her head and looked around the table. All the men were dressed in their nice clean uniforms, not a hair out of place, everything formal and in order. Jane's dress lay in soft clean folds, without a speck of dirt. Everyone sat smiling, enjoying the meal. *I wonder how hard their lives have been. No one here looks as if they ever had to fight dogs for a scrap of food to survive.*

She remembered the day of reckoning in the Indian village when she obtained her freedom. People were afraid of her and no one wanted to take her in, except for Heavy Foot who treated her with indifference.

Salvation and sanity did not come until she married Running Swift. *Oh my husband, how I miss you.* Tears welled up in her eyes. She quickly blinked them away and sat tall in her chair.

Jane placed a piece of meat on Sarah's plate. "...and then we moved to my husband's new command at Fort Laramie."

Startled, Sarah realized Mrs. Garnett had been talking to her. She nodded and looked down at her food.

"Here, let me help you," said Jane, handing her a napkin.

Sarah held the cloth in one hand not sure what to do with it or where to put it.

Jane whispered, "Put it on your lap. It is used to wipe your hands and face."

She watched Jane pick up her fork, sticking the prongs into the squash and placing the vegetable into her mouth. Sarah imitated her. "It is strange to my hand, but I do remember." After a few attempts, she began to master the fork.

Lieutenant Garnett talked to his officers, averting the attention from Sarah's struggles. The soldiers suppressed their smiles. When one of the men looked as though he were about to laugh, the lieutenant cleared his throat.

"How do you find Fort Laramie, Miss Anderson?" asked Sergeant Prescott.

"Nice," replied Sarah.

"I'm sure she is happy to be back in civilization," the commander said. The tone of his voice chilled her to the bone.

"Oh, my. I'm sure she is delighted to be here. Aren't you, Sarah?" asked Jane.

"Yes." Sarah said, before taking a bite of squash.

As the last morsel of gravy-covered prairie chicken disappeared from the platter, Ladesha entered the room, carrying a chocolate cake for dessert. She placed it in front of Sergeant Morrissey.

His eyes grew large as he stared at the delicious morsel. "Would you look at that!" he exclaimed.

Leaning forward, Prescott examined the chocolate confection. "Reminds me of my grandmother's baking."

Jane clapped her hands to her bosom. "My goodness, Ladesha. You've outdone yourself this time. How marvelous. Please, let the commander serve."

Lieutenant Garnett picked up a large knife and sliced into the four-layer cake. He placed a piece on each small plate and passed it down the line to his guests.

After the dessert, Ladesha brought Little Feather back to his mother. Sarah followed Jane and the men into the parlor. The soldiers kept their conversation directed to their senior officer, obviously uncomfortable with two women and a baby in the room.

Eventually, Williams asked, "Miss Anderson, how did you come to live with the Arapahos?"

Sitting forward on the sofa, Sarah answered, "I was traded by the Crows for blankets and a kettle."

"Why didn't you run away?" asked Morrissey.

"Gentlemen," said Mrs. Garnett, rising to her feet. "I do believe we should save our questions for another time. I am sure Miss Anderson is extremely tired and ready to retire after a long day."

Sarah nodded her head. "Yes, I am tired." She looked down at Little Feather, asleep in her lap. "I must put my son to bed. Good night."

The men taking their cue, headed for the front door. They

said good night to the ladies and their commander before closing the door behind them.

Cradling the baby in her arms, Sarah rose from the sofa and headed toward her room. Thoughts rambled through her head as she looked back over the events of the day. Life took strange paths and only He Who Knows can predict the future.

After the door shut behind her, Sarah felt sudden relief. She placed her son on the bed and undressed him, freeing his body. He lazily opened his eyes and then fell back asleep. She smiled, leaned over, and kissed his forehead. *My little one, son of my husband, how I love you.* Her chest felt tight and her throat was closing up. She needed to breathe.

Standing in the center of the room, she yanked the dress over her head, disrobing one garment at a time until she stood naked and free. Stepping across the clothing, she raised her arms over her head and took a deep breath. She picked up the dress, stuffed all the clothing into the bottom of the clothespress, and shoved the doors closed. *No more will I wear such things.*

She laid Little Feather on the floor and stripped the bed of all the linens, including the blankets, making a pallet for them. "We will sleep better down here," she said, as she covered him. "There is much to teach you, and much I have to learn myself. But freedom we must have. I will keep you safe from the evil and hatred that surround us because of who we are. I see their eyes stare at us. But, I will not let the ugliness touch you."

She walked toward the window and raised the sash halfway to let in some air. Then she sat cross-legged on the floor, chanting and singing in Arapaho. She lifted her face upward, her arms raised overhead, her hands stretched toward the window. "Ahhhhh, yi. Ahhhhhhh, yi, ya. Oh, my husband, my heart is pained by your death, and sorrow fills my body.

Touch me with your love through the evening breezes. Rain upon me with the leaves from the cottonwood trees. Great Spirit, hear me now. Let Running Swift ride through your fields as a warrior, for he is brave and strong. Tell me of things I must do. Ease my heart so that I may go forward."

"What is that noise," asked Commander Garnett, sitting up in bed.

"I believe it is Sarah. How sad she sounds." Jane grabbed the blanket, pulling it up to her chin. "Tomorrow, I will talk with her."

"Well, I hope she doesn't do that every night." He lay back down. "She needs to realize how fortunate she is that we rescued her and that she has a warm place to stay."

"Yes, dear. Now try and get some sleep."

Patrick walked among the small adobe buildings, arguing with himself. *All of my plans shattered. I'm not sure how to proceed anymore. Nothing's the same. I need to find Castor and have that talk with him.*

He kicked a post. *Why did Sarah sleep with that Indian? I could understand if he forced her. She gave him a son. She's white, not a savage whore.* As Patrick rounded one of the smaller structures, he stood behind Bedlam House.

Hands in his pockets, he stopped in his tracks, listening to a melancholy song drifting his way from a partially opened window of the post commander's house. He couldn't make out the words, but the sad tune touched his soul. Suddenly, he realized it was Sarah. The hairs on the back of his neck prickled. There was so much pain in her voice.

Heavy hearted and dispirited, Patrick stayed in the shadows, eavesdropping, unable to leave as the sorrowful-sounding melody floated away into the night.

Chapter Thirteen

Early the next morning, Patrick trudged through across the damp parade grounds toward the stables. The sun peeked over the mountain range, warming the still air. He loved this time of the day, but this morning his mind was on Sarah. His thoughts were divided between what he wanted and what he needed to do.

Soldiers rushed from every direction to make the call to reveille. In front of Bedlam House, officers stood adjusting their hats, pulling on their gloves, or straightening their belts, waiting for First Lieutenant Richard B. Garnett to make his appearance.

Patrick hesitated for a moment, scanning the porch, hoping to see Sarah, but she was nowhere in sight.

"Hey, Patrick, hold up a minute," shouted Jim Castor, as he sidled up and joined Patrick's stride. "You headed to the stables?"

"Yes," he answered.

"Care if I join ya? Got a few things to talk over with ya. Been thinkin' about Miss Sarah and you."

Patrick shot him a sideways glance, not uttering a word.

"The story's goin' round that Garnett's wife pushed a little too fast last night, dressin' that sweet gal up in a big dress and all. Could scare her. Cause her to run. If that happens, she's gonna be out in that open territory by herself with no one to protect her and that baby. So, as a suggestion to ya, you might want to call on her *real* soon, to put her mind at ease. Take it slow. Get her confidence before you start anything serious. Treat her like a wild mustang. You know, gentle her down a bit at a time. But be in command."

Patrick narrowed his brows and chewed on the side of his lower lip as he slowed his stride. "I understand. I don't think Lieutenant Garnett wants me hanging around his house. He wasn't too cordial yesterday. In fact he went out of his way to tell me as much, without so many words."

"Ya gonna let that stop you?" Castor spit sideways into the dirt. "I thought you were serious about this little gal."

Patrick stopped dead in his tracks and shouted, "I am! It's just there's so darn much that keeps getting in the way. When I think I have a plan all set, something else rears its ugly head."

"Well, boy, you better step right over those rattlesnakes. Attack the enemy before they attack you, if you understand what I'm sayin'."

Patrick threw his arms in the air and stalked off.

Castor caught up with him, grabbed Patrick's shoulder, and spun him around. "All I'm tryin' to say is—"

"What are you trying to say?" Patrick swung his arm, knocking his hand away.

Castor grimaced and shook his head. "Whew. Are we a bit ornery this mornin'? Look, all I'm tryin' to tell you is take your time with the little lady. Just get her out of Bedlam House as soon as possible."

"How in the hell am I going to do that?"

"You figure it out. Don't wait too long. Next thing you know, they'll have her spirited off somewhere and she'll be gone. The lieutenant won't keep her around too long. He hates Indians." Castor paused for a moment. "Worst than that, he hates white women who sleep with Indians. He's ugly enough to send her away before her mother arrives."

Patrick yanked the stable doors open, banging them against the outside wall. After yesterday's rain, the musty building reeked of horse manure and urine. He stood in the doorway, head down and hands on his hips, wrestling with his thoughts.

Castor pulled an old cigar stub from his pocket, struck a match on his soiled leather pants, and lit it.

Patrick faced the scout. "I'll drop by Lieutenant Garnett's place around noon and see if I can get a visit with Sarah this evening. That should give her time to settle in."

"Good. Gotta go. My only suggestion for you is to start settin' about another plan, one that might work for both of ya. Things are gonna get real ugly here once the rest of these highfalutin women begin pickin' at your gal. They ain't too friendly in bunches, ya know. She's gonna need a lot of protection."

"Jim," Patrick called.

Castor stopped, took a draw from his cigar, and then exhaled. "What?"

"How do you know what's gonna happen?"

Castor tossed the cigar into a puddle and then removed his hat. Punching the inside crown several times, he placed it back on his head. "Boy, I was married one time to a Shoshoni. Prettiest woman you'd ever want to see. Smart, too." He pushed some straw around on the ground with the toe of his boot. "Well, I brought her into town and left her there for a few days, thinkin' she'd be safe. Those ugly white women turned their backs on her, spit on her, and threw things at her, calling her all kinds of names."

He stopped, drew a breath, and shook his head. "Never saw her so depressed in my life. I vowed I'd never take her into a white town again. She never got over being treated so badly."

Patrick watched the expression on his friend's face, seeing the hurt and pain. "Where's your wife now?"

"She died givin' birth to our son. I buried them both up in the hills."

Patrick started to apologize.

Castor ran his hand over his face and stared at the sky. "That's all right. I miss her, but I learned to keep livin'. Life goes on. Remember that."

"Thanks for the advice."

Castor mumbled a response and turned to leave.

"Jim, can we talk when you get back?" Patrick hesitated for a moment. "I need some questions answered."

Castor smiled. "See ya at Murphy's? You buy the drinks this time."

"That's fine. Where are you headed this morning?"

"The rumor is Yellow Bear and some of his followers are stirrin' up trouble north of here. From what the lieutenant says, we'll be gone most of the day." Then, like a man on a mission, he heeled and toed it at a fast clip, making his way toward the flagpole.

"Well, I guess I better get Sergeant Prescott's horse ready," Patrick muttered to himself. "He'll be here soon, moaning and groaning about the patrol."

* * *

Later that afternoon, with hat in hand, Patrick climbed the stairs to Lieutenant Garnett's quarters on the second floor of Bedlam House. He rolled his shoulders a couple of times to loosen up, waiting a few minutes before knocking, trying to get his confidence up. He raised his hand to knock.

The Negro servant threw open the door. "What you want?" she asked, cocking her head from side to side, scrutinizing him.

"I'd like to speak to Miss Sarah, please." He crumpled the brim of his hat in his hand, feeling like a schoolboy waiting to be reprimanded.

"Just you wait right here. Don't want them muddy boots traipsin' across my clean floors." She shut the door in his face.

Nervous and anxious, Patrick paced back and forth on the veranda. He ran his fingers through his hair. What was he going to say to Sarah? Did she even care he was here? Questions buzzed through his head.

Suddenly, the door opened and Mrs. Garnett extended her hand. "Please, won't you come in, Mr. O'Brien? How can I help you?"

"I'd like to call on Sarah this evening."

"Won't you be seated while I inquire if she is available?"

Patrick eased onto the red velour upholstery. He placed even weight on the fragile chair, hoping it wouldn't collapse from under him. When he heard Mrs. Garnett returning, he jumped to his feet, stretching his neck to see if Sarah was walking behind her. The commander's wife clasped her hands together as she stood in front of him.

"Miss Anderson will see you this evening around seven."

Patrick grinned and nodded, crunching his hat between his hands. "Thank you, ma'am."

Descending the stairs, he swaggered to the stables with a rhythm to his step and a smile on his face.

Patrick closed up the stables earlier than usual and headed toward his sleeping quarters. He washed up and put on his only extra set of clean clothes. Dashing to Miss Trudy's for a quick bite to eat, he grabbed a couple of pieces of meat off the platter in the kitchen and a piece of bread.

"Where are you going in such a hurry," asked Sam, the cook. "You goin' courtin' or somethin'?"

He punched Sam's shoulder. "Yes, something like that."

"Oh, I get it. It's that Anderson gal you been waitin' on for a year. You tread careful-like over at the commander's. You upset him and you'll never see her again. He's a bear for protocol."

"I already got permission to see her, but thanks for the advice. Gotta go." Patrick rushed out the door, across the parade ground, stopping short of the Bedlam House staircase. He removed his hat and pushed the stray hairs behind his ears. Then he checked to be sure his shirt was tucked in properly, before rubbing the toes of his boots on the back of his pant's legs. After fastening his collar button to make himself presentable, he clutched his hat in his hand, took three long breaths, and climbed the stairs two at a time.

His knock sounded louder than he anticipated.

Lieutenant Garnett yanked the door open.

"Well, I see you've found your way. Come in. Miss Anderson will be here shortly."

Patrick stepped through the doorway and followed Lieutenant Garnett.

"Have a seat."

"No, sir. I prefer to stand."

"Suit yourself. You want a drink? Brandy? Whiskey?"

"No, thank you, sir." Patrick shifted his weight from one foot to the other, crushing his dilapidated hat in his hands.

"So, exactly what do you have planned for your future, Mr. O'Brien?" asked Garnett, pouring himself a shot of whiskey. "Are you going to continue repairing tack in the stables?" He looked at Patrick from under his eyebrows with a sneer on his face.

"No, sir. I plan to farm."

The lieutenant stopped drinking, hesitating with his glass in hand. "Around here?"

"No, sir, out in Kansas territory. I hear the land there is fertile and there's talk that one day soon, they'll be opening up the area for homesteading."

"Humph. Farming, huh." The lieutenant took his pipe off the side table, stuffed tobacco into the bowl. "What if Miss Anderson doesn't take to farming? Have you given that some thought?"

"Well, sir, that's something Sarah and I need to talk over. That's why I am here to find out what her plans are."

The commander struck a match on the bottom of his boot, lit his pipe, and drew on the stem. He blew the match out, and then took a long pull. "I believe you might be rushing things a little. I'd suggest you wait until she has time to reacquaint herself to living as a white woman again." His eyes met Sarah's as she stood on the other side of the sofa in her native doeskin dress and leggings.

Patrick turned, crushing his hat in his hands. The look on her face told him she must have been watching them for a while.

"You come to talk." She nodded to Patrick and gestured toward the sofa, ignoring the lieutenant. "Sit." She joined him, leaving a space between them.

The commander stood watching the young couple as he smoked his pipe.

Mrs. Garnett entered the room. "Richard, dear. Would you help me in the dining room?"

Lieutenant Garnett lifted an eyebrow, took one more draw on his pipe, then left the room.

Patrick was tongue-tied. There was so much to talk about and nothing came to mind. "Ah, how are you?" *That was a stupid question.*

"We are fine." Sarah sat straight and stared at him.

Patrick began to sweat. "Would you care to take a walk in the fresh air? I could show you the area, what there is to see."

She sensed that he was nervous, but his deep brown eyes gave her a strange sensation in the pit of her stomach. "Yes, let us walk."

Opening the door, Sarah slipped passed him and stepped out into the night air. Together they descended the stairs to the parade ground.

"The stars watch us, to see what we say to each other."

Patrick stopped and tilted his head upward. "Sometimes I think I can touch them."

Sarah glanced at him, enjoying the smile that crept across his face. "They are ancestors who watch over us."

He turned his head to look at her. "Maybe one of them is my father."

"What is it you want to talk about?"

Totally taken off guard by her question, he felt unprepared to discuss the future. Struggling to regain his thoughts, he bit his lip. "What do you want to do now that you are back?"

Sarah turned and walked ahead. "I know not what I will do. My son and I do not fit in this world or with your people."

"They're your people, too." He hesitated for a moment. "Sarah, would you consider coming with me to—"

"I must mourn one year for my dead husband."

Patrick stopped, cut to the heart with her words.

She turned and faced him, sensing that what she said was not what he wanted to hear. "I see my words hurt you. I am sorry, but it must be."

"Does that mean that you will stay at Bedlam House for a year?"

"I do not know."

They walked toward the Post's store, neither talking. Her silence scared him. What was he to say? Would she understand how he felt about her?

Sarah gazed into the darkness beyond the fort. "I must wait for my mother. She comes soon. Jane tells me it is almost time."

"I guess I can wait." Disappointment registered in his voice. *Patience, she isn't ready for any future.* "Only promise you will talk with me when you are ready."

Sarah looked into his eyes. "Yes, I will do so."

They turned and headed back. "By the way," said Patrick. "Do you still have the cross I gave you in St. Charles?"

She did not look at him and kept her back straight. "Yes. It is with me."

His heart leaped. *Maybe there was still hope for a future with her. Otherwise, why would she hold onto my homemade grass cross, if she didn't still think of me?*

When they reached the house, they climbed the steep stairs up to the veranda. Patrick removed his hat, the words would not come. "I would like to call on you again, if that's okay."

She nodded. "It would be good."

"Maybe we could ride out toward the mountains."

She smiled. "Yes, I would like that."

He touched her shoulder for a moment. She didn't pull

away, but stared at him with her sad eyes. He wanted to take her into his arms and ease her pain, but could not bridge the gap that lay between them. "Good night, Sarah."

"Good night." She turned and reached for the doorknob.

He plopped his hat on his head. Heavy-hearted, he trudged down the stairs, listening to the door shut behind him. Rounding the back of Bedlam House, heading toward his quarters, he thought about tomorrow and their future. Was there a future?

He would call on her after breakfast and they would ride west into the mountains on neutral ground. He needed to take one day at a time, as Castor told him. But hurry.

Chapter Fourteen

Lieutenant Garnett faced his wife, chest puffed up, face blood red. "Don't argue with me, woman. The fact that she had a child with an Indian makes her unacceptable. She has to go. The quicker the better. I already arranged a seat for Miss Anderson and her son on Mr. Schultz's wagon train. She's heading back east to Independence. Once she's on her way, I don't care what she does as long as she doesn't return. I'm sure she'll find some place to live in the city, maybe even get some reasonable employment."

"Richard, you can't do this," Jane Garnett pleaded. "It's wrong. You have no right."

"Don't tell me about my rights. I command this post. She's going."

"But her mother is due to arrive any day now."

"Her mother. Ha." He shook his head. "That woman is as bad as that Indian squaw down the hallway."

"Richard, hush. She'll hear you."

"I don't care. It's time she realizes what a disgrace she

is, allowing an Indian to, well, you know." Flustered, he grabbed his gloves and belt from the table near the door. "I have work to do at headquarters. See that she is packed and ready to go in the next couple of days. I'll explain to her about her journey. Now, I don't want to hear any excuses. When I return tonight, I want things to be in place." He stormed out, slamming the door behind him.

Jane threw her hands up in disgust. Sometimes, her husband was an insufferable ass. She needed a plan. There was no way she was going to send Sarah off with no one to look after her, especially when her mother might arrive sometime soon. "How can he be so insensitive?"

Looking up, she spied Ladesha standing in the doorway, arms crossed over her chest, shaking her head.

"Mmmm, mmm, mmm. What's we to do, Miz Jane? He's sure all fired up riddin' this here house of her. Sure is a shame to push her out with baby Sugarberry."

"Well, we can't let that happen. I need to think." Jane paced back and forth in the parlor, wringing her hands, stopping every so often, placing her fingers to her forehead.

"You's gonna wear out that there floor, traipzin' like that. Why don't you come sit and drink yourself a cup of tea? "

"Yes, I would like that," Jane said, dropping onto the sofa.

Ladesha bustled into the kitchen, muttering to herself, "Worry, worry, worry. She's gonna put herself in an early grave, she is. Oh, that man, what's we to do with him."

Oh, Richard, Jane thought as she sat clasping her hands in her lap. *Why are you so hardheaded and stubborn? Your hatred is going to consume you one of these days.*

* * *

Patrick stood in front of the Garnett's door and knocked twice.

Ladesha opened the door, a scowl on her face. "You again. What's you want this time?"

"I would like to speak to Sarah."

"Humph. Wipe your feet and come on in." She turned and walked away, leaving him standing in the entryway.

Patrick strolled toward the sofa and sat down. He felt a little more secure sitting there than taking the fancy red chair. Hat in hand, he ran his fingers through his hair, tucking a few strands behind his ears. He needed to get a haircut. Then he ran his hand across his chin. Maybe a shave, too.

Jane Garnett entered the room. "Why, Mr. O'Brien. What a delight to see you so early this morning. Have you had breakfast?"

Patrick rose to his feet. "Yes, ma'am, I have. I'm here to see Miss Sarah."

"You come to see me?" asked Sarah.

Startled, Patrick turned to face her. His heart skipped a beat and he found it hard to breath.

Spellbound by her appearance, her fawn-colored dress covered with beads, shells and colorful quills sewn in a swirling design held his attention as she approached the sofa. Sarah's smoothed, braided hair rested on her bodice. She was beautiful, a haloed vision he had chased these many years.

He couldn't take his eyes off her. He wanted to reach out and take her into his arms. Instead, he shifted his weight from foot to foot, rotating the hat brim in his hands. "I promised to take you for a ride. Would you like to go this morning, say around eleven o'clock?"

Sarah gazed into his face for a moment. "Yes. It would please me."

He gave a small sigh of relief. Stumbling over his words, he said, "Fine. Well, I have to open up the stables. See you at eleven." He backed toward the door and left.

"I do believe that young man cares for you," Jane said peeking out the curtain as he made his way down the stairs. He's extremely nice."

"Yes. It seems that way." A bit embarrassed, she smiled and lowered her eyes.

"I looks after Sugarberry while you's ridin'," Ladesha said.

Jane shot Ladesha a look. "Ah, Sarah, would you be so kind and go to the Post's store? I need a few things. You might enjoy the fresh air."

She nodded. "That would be good."

"Ladesha, there's a list on the table. Please get it for me." Jane turned to face Sarah. "You can add the items to our tally. I'm sure Mr. Tutt will allow that." She read over each printed item before handing the young girl the list.

Once Sarah stepped outside and shut the door behind her, Ladesha waltzed into the room and stood next to her mistress. "They's strange ones, those two. Neither one sayin' much, only their eyes doin' the talkin'."

"Maybe Mr. O'Brien is the solution to our problem with Miss Sarah's leaving."

Ladesha grinned wide, showing her big white teeth. "He surely might be."

Jane sat at the dining room table sipping her tea. She stared out the window trying to think of a plan of escape for the young girl. Nothing seemed to fit right. There was so much to put together: supplies, bedrolls, horses, and a willing companion in Patrick. Then there was the job of convincing Sarah that she must leave before her mother arrived. Jane set down her cup and sighed. All this intrigue made her tired.

"You looks all wrung out, Missus. Don't you fret none. Ladesha will help Miss Sarah get away from this here fort."

"Come sit down by me. I am going to need all the help you can muster. First, in my closet are two saddlebags tucked in the back. We need to get those out and put them in the kitchen. Pack them with food supplies that will keep on the trail."

"Yes ma'am."

"Then there is the question of making two bedrolls from any extra blankets we have. Ones that the commander won't miss."

"Hmm. Lets me see." Ladesha bit her lip as she contemplated this problem. "I could gives one of my blankets and Miss Sarah has two on her bed."

"We need to leave one on her bed so that when Richard discovers her missing, he won't have an excuse to chase after her for stealing. He wouldn't notice one missing cover, but two would be too obvious."

"Well, we's got two to start with."

Jane smiled. "Yes, we do. Patrick probably has a bedroll. We will ask him. Now, is there any extra rope around?"

"Yes, ma'am. There's extra clothesline out back that we can use."

"Very good. We need to keep all of this hidden from my husband's prying eyes. Our next job is how to get Sarah out of the house. We can't use the back entrance. The door is right outside our bedroom window."

Ladesha rose from the chair and strolled into the parlor. Placing her hands on wide hips, she scanned the room, as she shuffled back and forth, mumbling to herself. Suddenly, she turned to face her mistress with a wide grin. Cocking her head from side to side, she said, "We's got a plan."

Jane scooted forward in her chair. "What is it?"

"After the commander goes to sleep, I opens the door and helps Miss Sarah with her baggage."

"Oh, no. That door squeaks too much and the latch is terribly noisy. I've been trying to get someone to fix that door for over a month."

"Hmmm." Ladesha crossed her arms, narrowed her eyes, and stared at the door.

Twirling around to face her mistress, she grinned. "What if I moves the little table from in front of the window and pulls the curtain to one side. Then I raises the window slowly so as not to wake you-know-who. Everything will be ready. The food bag's packed and the bedroll's tied tight. Mmmm, mmm. Then, all I has to do is slip everything out the window onto the veranda. *That man* can be waiting to help Miss Sarah and my Sugarberry outside. Once they's gone, I moves everything back in order. Now that's a plan if I does say so myself."

"Oh, Ladesha. You are a dream. I knew if we put our heads together, we'd find a way to help our Sarah. That way, I won't be part of her escape, because I'll be asleep next to my husband. Oh, it's perfect, absolutely perfect."

"Well, we still has to get *that man* to help."

"Yes, we'll do that tonight. I know just the person to help us out with that."

"You's don't mean that old scruffy scout he's been hangin' around with?"

Jane nodded. "I certainly do. You let me know when the patrol comes back. Then I'll slip out and talk with Mr. Jim Castor."

"Don't you go sittin' in that there bar with him. I don't trust him none. I won't have them men lookin' at you funny. No, siree."

"Now, don't you worry about those men. I won't be going

to the bar. As far as Mr. Castor's concerned, he's quite harmless. We definitely need his help." Jane gave Ladesha a small hug. "I believe it's time to start preparing our noon meal. It's almost eleven o'clock. Sarah will be back shortly, and Mr. O'Brien will be coming around to take her for a ride."

Sarah stood in the parlor waiting for Patrick. Her heart beat rapidly as she thought about being outside, away from this white world. She shut her eyes, picturing the freedom of the wide-open prairie with the wind in her face, flying on the back of a horse. Her mind drifted to the open spaces, no wooden walls to hold her captive, no more scornful eyes to judge her. For a little while she could be herself, in a world she understood.

Ladesha clasped Little Feather against her large bosom. His small hands grasped her white apron as the baby nestled his face against her chest and wiped his nose. She looked down and kissed the top of his head. Raising one hand, he touched her face and tried to grasp her lips.

Jane rose quickly from the sofa when she heard approaching footsteps. She jerked the door open, and stepped aside to regain her dignity. "Do come in, Mr. O'Brien. I believe Sarah is ready. What a beautiful day for a ride."

Patrick glanced at the three women facing him, before he entered the parlor. A warning bell went off in his head. Something was afoot. "Yes, ma'am. It is a nice day."

Sarah moved to his side. "We go."

Jane reached down next to the couch to retrieve a small sack. "Here, take this with you. Ladesha packed you some food to eat while you're out." She handed it to Sarah. "Now, you two have a good ride."

After they left, Jane pulled the curtain aside and peeked out the window. "My husband is walking across the parade grounds and will be here any moment. Is the noon meal ready?"

"Yes, ma'am. The table's all set and the soup is warmin'. We's all ready, aren't we, sweetums?" Ladesha gave the baby boy a gentle hug.

"Good. So far, everything is going as planned. This afternoon, we will pack the saddle bags." Jane dropped the curtain and faced Ladesha. "Take the baby into the kitchen. The commander eats better when the child isn't around."

Hearing her husband's voice in conversation with another man, Jane whispered, "Now remember, when the patrol returns, I will sneak out and visit with Mr. Castor. You stay here and keep everything going as planned. I'm not sure when the wagon train is leaving, but the sooner we get Sarah and Mr. O'Brien on the trail, the better."

Ladesha headed for the kitchen with the baby. "I has my little Sugarberry to help me pack them old bags."

"This evening we will have a quiet meal. We can only hope that the commander will want to retire early."

Yes, everything is going so smoothly. Pleased with herself, Jane sat down on the sofa and fluffed her skirt. She loved it when it was quiet and peaceful.

Bang! The lieutenant threw the door open. Jane startled by the rough entrance, jumped up from the sofa and placed her hand in front of her mouth. "Oh, Richard, you scared me out of six-year's growth."

A foul expression blanketed his face. Taking off his jacket, he flung it over a peg along with his hat. Dropping his gloves on the side table, he stomped into the dining room and plopped into his chair.

Jane joined him, taking her seat. "Well, my dear, you're

home right on time. Ladesha, please serve the commander his meal."

"Yes, ma'am," came the answer from the other room.

Garnett sat, elbows on the table, resting his head in both hands.

"Richard, whatever is the matter."

Sitting up in his chair, he reached both arms forward and grasped the sides of the table. "I received my orders today. They have extended my service at Fort Laramie until May of next year." He shook his head. "Can you believe that?"

Ladesha set the soup tureen on the table and disappeared quickly into the next room.

Jane sat up straight in her chair. Her appetite vanished. All her dreams of spending Christmas in Washington City disappeared like wisps of smoke twirling up a chimney. She'd looked forward to having tea with Mary Fillmore, the President's daughter. Many of the gala affairs began in early November, especially the ball at the White House. This was President Fillmore's last few months of his term. Jane knew how extravagant the events would be. Her imagination envisioned the afternoon teas with the Virginia Senators' wives, the marvelous receptions with the Russian Baron, Alexandre de Bodisc, dinners with her cousin, the Honorable W. R. W. Cobb. Most of all, she would miss driving the length of Pennsylvania Avenue, shopping for fashionable dresses to attend all the functions. Now they wouldn't be back East until another whole year.

Jane grasped her napkin and spread it across her lap, trying not to show her disappointment. "At least we will be back in Virginia in time to celebrate your mother's birthday," she said.

Richard glared at her. "How thrilling."

Jane forced a smile for her husband. "Let's eat and enjoy our meal. We can talk about this later."

Chapter Fifteen

P atrick's heart beat wildly as he rode next to Sarah, following the dirt road from the fort toward the mountains. A dust devil twirled in the far distance. He watched her scan the horizon, taking in everything around her.

Glancing at him sideways, she closed her mouth and inhaled deeply, breathing in as much fresh air as possible. Then she exhaled. "It is beautiful. So free." She shut her eyes and lifted her face to the sun's warm rays.

"Yes," was the only answer he could manage, as his horse trotted beside hers. Staring at the stark treeless prairie, he found the openness a joy to his heart, but he wouldn't have called it beautiful. The rolling green hills in Missoura were beautiful. She was beautiful. But not this god-forsaken, brown-barren land.

"Does riding make you feel better?"

"Yes." Sarah gave him a childish grin. "It makes my heart sing to see the sky as it touches mother earth. My spirit is free. Look, see how the birds glide on the fingers of the wind. I would like that. To go where I want. It would be good."

Patrick tuned his head. Her words pained him. He wanted to give her the freedom she deserved but she constantly put a wall between them.

"Sarah."

"Do not speak to me now. Let us ride." Leaning forward, she pushed her horse into a gallop, her head high, and her bottom barely touching the saddle. Braids flapping against her shoulders, her body moved with the rhythm of the horse.

He watched her dress ride up, exposing a shapely leg gripping the animal's side. God help him, he loved her.

It took all of his horsemanship to keep up with her, as her body blended with the magnificent steed. He knew at that moment he would wait patiently for her to decide when to speak of the future...*their* future together.

After riding for half an hour, Patrick whistled. She stopped, waiting for him to catch up.

"We need to walk the horses. The sun's hot. We don't want to wear them out," he said.

They strolled along side-by-side, her scent arousing his senses. He wanted to touch her, hold her. The thought excited him. Instead, he tried to direct his mind to a question to ask her, but couldn't think of anything to say. Finally, he pointed. "There's a creek up ahead where we can water the horses."

"It would be good," she said.

When they reached the spot, they dropped the reins and let the horses drink freely. Sarah knelt by the shallow stream. Using both hands, she scooped up the clear water and splashed her face. He heard a soft sigh as she found relief from the oppressing noon heat.

"We should have started earlier on a day like this."

"Do not think bad about yourself," she said, glancing

sideways at him. "It is good to be free, to feel the sun on my face."

Patrick removed his hat, dunked it into the water and then doused his head. Next, he dipped his bandana into the water and handed it to Sarah. "Here, wipe your arms and neck. It will cool you down faster."

Doing as he suggested, she wrung out the cloth, sliding it over her arms, across her neck, and on her face. She dunked the bandana again. Without squeezing it out, she tossed it at Patrick. Splat. The handkerchief caught him squarely in the chest.

He grabbed it before it hit the ground.

Sarah giggled and held her hands up. "I am sorry."

Patrick raised one eyebrow, squeezing the cloth with one hand, while flipping his other wet hand at her.

Jumping to her feet, Sarah giggled at his clumsy gesture. She bent over and scooped a handful of water, and flung it in his direction.

He quickly moved, avoiding her attempt to splatter him. "You think your little prank can get me, do you?" He grasped the cloth between his hands, stretching and twirling it, before he flicked the end toward her bottom.

She sidestepped, trying to avoid his direct aim, without success. "Ow," she yelled. "You are a brave warrior with that in your hands." She picked up his hat, dunked it, filling it to the brim.

He rushed toward her, trying to grab his hat, but failed. His shirt took the full direct hit. Grabbing her wrist, he twirled her around with her back toward him, and encircled his arms across her chest, lifting her off the ground, as he stepped backwards into the stream.

"Let me go," she hollered, laughing at his antics. "We're going to fall."

"Hold still, then we won't," he said, gripping her tighter as she squirmed in his arms. Trying to keep his balance, Patrick slipped on the small river rocks in the stream. He keeled over, landing on his behind with Sarah in his lap. She pushed him aside and tried to stand. As she scrambled to regain her footing, she slipped and fell face forward.

Patrick roared, "Now you're good and wet."

He saw her eyes flash, a determined look on her face. Sarah threw herself across his chest, laying him flat out in the water.

"Maybe your mischief will float away."

She got to her feet and strolled toward the horses, his gaze following her every step. Sarah's dress stuck to her behind like a second skin. The view of her bottom swaying from side to side drove him crazy. Feeling the crotch of his trousers tightening, he was glad for the cold-water bath.

She turned and gave him a mischievous grin. "You sit staring. Maybe the cold water is good."

He only shook his head. Finally able to stand, he grabbed his hat and sauntered her way.

"You are an armful and wiggle like a pig."

"A pig? You think me a pig?"

Raising his hands in front of him, he exclaimed, "No. No, that's not what I meant."

She crossed her arms and raised an eyebrow. "What did you mean?"

"I meant, you fight strong."

"Humph. Strong, like a pig." Suddenly, she burst into sidesplitting laughter.

Totally embarrassed, his face reddened. He called her a pig. How stupid could he be? He couldn't think of anything to say when she was around. The words just fell out of his mouth.

"You are a brave man to insult me." She pulled her

knife from the back of her waistband sheath. As she flourished it, the blade gleamed in the sunlight. "I could have cut your neck."

"For getting you wet?"

"No, for the pig. You insulted me."

"Oh." He bit his lip and opened his eyes wide. "I apologize for that. Please believe me, I never meant, that is—"

"A fish is better." She gave him a mischievous grin.

"A fish? A slimy fish?" He narrowed his eyes and gritted his teeth, regretting his last statement. "Maybe we should eat before I get myself into more trouble." He retrieved the food sack from her saddle and found a small shaded spot under one of the few cottonwood trees in the area.

As they ate, he tried to make small talk. His sentences and replies were short. He had no idea how to talk to a woman. What would interest her? He wished his sister, Elizabeth, had taught him a little more about conversation and decorum. He knew how to talk to men and horses, but women were a whole different world. One he wasn't familiar with at all.

Patrick's thoughts drifted to Sarah's past. How to gain her confidence was the biggest problem. How to prove to her that he cared for her? Taking another bite from his biscuit, he followed her every move. He remembered Castor's words to take it slow, but hurry. All these years he waited. Now he knew he would wait until she either joined him or rebuffed him totally.

Rising to her feet, she brushed off her dress and pulled her braids forward to rest on her chest.

Patrick joined her. "You have dirt on your...backside." He reached out to brush it off, but thought better of himself, pulling his hand back.

She eyed him cautiously. "I brush. You watch."

"I can do that. The view's nice." He plopped his hat on his head and strolled toward his horse. "We better get back."

"Yes, it is time." Grabbing the leather food sack, she mounted her horse and sat waiting for him. "It was a good day. Thank you."

"You're welcome. We'll do this again soon, I promise."

As they headed back toward the fort, Patrick thought about what they had shared this day. Her smiles, her funny sayings, his stupidity, they all made him realize how much he cared for Sarah. He loved her sense of humor. It was free and honest. Her laugher was like a bubbling brook trickling across rocks. It was infectious. His mind drifted as they rode side by side.

Sarah's heart was heavy, her mind mixed with thoughts that confused her. She was loyal to her dead husband, but she would never be able to go back to the Arapaho life she shared with Running Swift. The Indian way of life was her past. Her future was the white world and she must decide how to travel this bumpy road, learning again the ways of the white man.

Glancing at Patrick, she knew that in her heart she'd grow to love him more each day. He was a gentle man, kind and honest. Something pulled her to him. Today, she had fun sharing and experiencing the ride into a world she missed.

"It was good to be free today."

He smiled at her and nodded. "Glad you enjoyed yourself."

"Did you?"

"Yes, very much."

"There are things I must think about. It is difficult."

"I understand. I need to mull over a few things myself."

. "I will pray to the Great Spirit. I need to seek answers. My heart is confused for much has changed in my life. I must also think about what is good for my son."

"Yes. Maybe we could sit and talk about both of our worlds so that we have a better understanding."

"I must have time."

Patrick cocked his head to one side and smiled. "I'll wait." Then he rode silently next to her as they approached the fort in the distance.

One day, thought Sarah, *I will be yours. This I know, for it is destined to be.* She laid her hand on her chest, above her heart. *Life is so full of changes.* She glanced at Patrick one more time. Pictures of his arms around her at the stream flitted across her mind. Every part of her body felt alive to his touch. It wasn't until she fell on top of him in the water that she knew she wanted him. His solid chest, strong arms, and masculine smell haunted her. The touch of his hand made her feel alive again. Wild thoughts entered her mind as she envisioned sleeping next to this man.

Would Running Swift's image gradually blur with each passing day, replaced by this tall, handsome white man who loved her? *Oh, my husband, I will not forget you. I will cherish the time we had together. I will teach Little Feather the ways of The People. But, my life must go on for our child.*

Soon she would know what to do. Soon.

Chapter Sixteen

Jane paced the parlor floor, wringing her hands, frustrated over her husband's announcement from earlier that afternoon. Her plans for Sarah were falling apart and she had no idea how to correct the situation. They were to have company for dinner: Mr. and Mrs. Josh Luegge from Alexandria, Virginia. They were old friends of her husband's. The Luegge's surprised Garnett and presented themselves at headquarters this morning.

Ladesha interrupted her thoughts. "We's got the food all ready for the meal and you-know-what-else is packed. How long is these people gonna stay tonight?"

"I have no idea, but I am sure once the men get to drinking and smoking in the parlor, it will be quite late."

"Oh, my. We's got trouble."

"How right you are," said Jane as she peered out the window. The troop was still out on patrol and it was only two hours before the evening meal. "Ladesha, after we eat, you will have to go in search of Jim Castor."

"Oh, no ma'am. I ain't gonna go into that there bar to find that old scruffy man. No, siree, not me. Why's those white men would rather steal me away than let me sit in their drinkin' room. Hmmm, hmm, hmm." She stood shaking her head.

"You want to help Sarah, don't you?"

Ladesha looked down at her feet. "Yes, ma'am, I does."

Jane put her arm around her shoulders. "So do I. Now let's put our heads together. Instead of seeing Mr. Castor, maybe you can locate Mr. O'Brien this evening and tell him our plans?"

"Is the lieutenant needin' my services this evenin' after supper?"

Jane exhaled deeply. "I don't know. We will have to play that one as we go along. Oh, this is all so impossible."

"Now, don't you go givin' up. We'll do it."

"Is something not right?" asked Sarah. She walked into the parlor and joined Jane near the window.

"No, my dear. However, we do need to talk. I guess now is as good a time as any to have a little discussion. Come sit by me on the sofa. Ladesha will fix us some tea."

Sarah relaxed on the seat next to Jane. "My sweet Sarah. So much has taken place these last few days. I know you are struggling with transitioning from—"

"What does that mean?"

Jane smiled. "It means to come from the Indian village to live at the Fort. Anyway, there is something I need to talk over with you."

Sarah stared at her and waited for an explanation.

Jane sat patting Sarah's hand, trying to figure out how to tell her she must leave, immediately, tonight or at least by tomorrow evening. Jane cleared her throat. "Let me explain. Please don't think harshly of us. You must understand Richard isn't a mean man. He is extremely stubborn at times and hasty in his decisions, but he is a good man. Sometimes he worries me to death."

Sarah nodded her head.

"Lieutenant Garnett believes that for your safety, you and your baby should leave the fort."

"You throw me out." Sarah jumped to her feet. "Ask me to leave. That is what you are saying?"

"No. No, it isn't like that. It is because more and more people are visiting the fort and because you are a white woman with..."

"...an Indian baby." Sarah finished the sentence. She turned and stared at Ladesha. "I do not want tea."

Jane grabbed her arm. "Sarah, please sit with me and let us at least talk this over."

Sarah sat stiff and straight as a board. "I will go, if you wish."

"No, it is not my wish. You see my husband believes you will have trouble with people who are staying at the fort. They are building all around us. More and more civilians are setting up jobs and businesses here, now that the Army is better established."

Sarah bit her lip. Ladesha stood in the doorway.

"Ladesha and I have a plan to help you leave late one night."

"You want me to leave like a thief?"

"Please listen to me," said Jane. "This is very hard for me as well. My husband purchased a seat for you and your baby on a wagon train heading east to Independence in a few days. He feels you would do better in a big city where you could get a job."

Sarah watched the Negro woman roll her eyes.

"I understand. I must leave. I will go." She stood up.

"Wait, that isn't exactly what Ladesha and I had planned. At least give us a chance to tell you something else. Something much more important."

Sarah crossed her arms and stared at Jane.

"We have a plan to help you leave your way, with Mr. O'Brien."

"With Patrick?"

"Yes," replied Jane.

Sarah returned to the sofa.

Jane scooted closer. "We have two saddle bags packed with food for you, Little Feather, and Mr. O'Brien."

"Yes, we does," said Ladesha with a nod of her head.

"What we plan on doing is talking with Mr. Castor to see if he will help us. Unfortunately, my husband has invited guests for supper this evening, and I cannot hold up my end of the plan. Ladesha, however, is going to take my place. Isn't that right?"

The servant hesitated and then said, "Yes, ma'am."

"But one thing," Jane whispered, "you cannot reveal that you know about what I have told you so far. It is for your best interest. Do you understand?"

"Yes," answered Sarah.

"Now here is what we plan to do."

After the evening meal at Bedlam house, Ladesha straightened up the kitchen and waited while the Garnetts settled in the parlor with their company. She moved to her room and listened to their conversation, not to eavesdrop, but to see how the visit was progressing. She paced back and forth in the small room, then opened the window and looked out. "Now I can do this. All's I got to do is find Mr. O'Brien and talk with him." The inky black sky held a few stars in a palette and a sliver of a moon.

When the clock struck nine, the lieutenant and Mr. Luegge were laughing and telling stories about times when they grew up together. "That's gonna be a long-winded story. They probably won't leave until midnight from the way those two are drinkin' and fibbin'." She grabbed her shawl, opened her door and took the back stairs.

Sticking close to the building in the shadows, Ladesha edged along the side of the house, stopping at the corner. She canvassed the area, looking to see if anyone was about. No one was out in the backyard area. Suddenly, she heard a noise to her right. Chills danced down her spine, her mouth got dry as she plastered herself to the siding. She turned her head and whispered, "Who's that there?" Shaking like a leaf, she pulled her shawl up around her neck and waited. No answer. "Is you a ghost?"

"Meow." The cat brushed up against her leg.

Ladesha jumped five feet away from where she was standing. "You's about scared me out of ten years' growth. Go home and leaves me be. I's got important business to tend to."

She scurried across the open area toward the adobe huts, staying to their rear, in case someone might be wandering around late. As she rounded the fifth building, the shadows were longer and darker. She murmured to herself, "Hmmm, hmmm, hmmm. Don't wants to go pass them, but I needs to get to the last hut."

As she turned down one side, something made her stop in her tracks. It wasn't a noise or a movement. She thought she heard someone breathing. "Who's there? I knows you's there." No one answered.

She took two more steps. A large smelly hand clamped

over her mouth and a strong arm grabbed her around the chest, jerking her into the shadows. She tried to scream. Flailing her arms and twisting her body from side to side, she tried to get loose. Pushing all of her weight into the man, she backed her assailant into the wall with a thud, knocking the wind out of him. Free from his grip, she gasped for air.

With a raspy voice, she said, "You let's me go, you devil, or I'll squash you like a bug."

Scared to death but angry, she grabbed the man by his hair with both hands and twirled him in circles.

The shadow man managed to encircle her waist with his arms. Breathing heavily, Ladesha threw her weight backwards against him, falling to the ground.

As she landed on top of him, she heard the man moan, "Ohhhh, Lordy!"

He grabbed her by the bodice as she tried to get up.

"Ladesha. Wait."

"Who's you?"

"It's Jim Castor." He let go of her and crawled to the side of the hut, slumping against wall.

She stood up and dusted off her dress. "Why's you grabbin' me at night from the shadows, you...you dried up old man? I's feelin' almighty sore all over from you squeezin' on me. You got nothin' better to do than to roll around the dirty old ground with a full-blown woman. Where's your manners?"

"Have to say this much about you. You got grit, woman."

"I's got more than grit. If I'd leaned harder, your chest would have been as flat as a board. Land sakes, what's you want with me anyway, you old scruffy man?"

Castor got to his feet and felt his ribs. Nothing was broken, but he'd feel sore tomorrow. "I saw you walkin' outside, hidin' in the shadows. It's too late for a good-lookin' woman like you to be out here without some kind of escort."

"Don't you try to sweet talk me, you good for nothin'."

"You might not know this, but there's still a few men all liquored up tonight, lookin' for trouble, not to mention the Indians. Didn't want anyone to find you alone. What in Sam Hill are you doin' out here, anyway?"

"Don't you be cussin' at me. I's on a mission, lookin' for Mr. O'Brien. Needs to talk with him in private."

"Well, he's sleepin'."

"I needs to talk with him tonight. It's all fired important, about Miss Sarah."

"What's wrong with Miss Sarah?"

"Can't tell you."

"What do you mean you can't tell me?" He grabbed her arm. "Follow me. We'll go somewhere safer to talk. These walls have ears." He dragged her along behind the buildings until he reached the stone magazine.

"You sure is fired up and in a hurry. Draggin' me like an old wet sack."

He turned to face her, placed his hands on his hips and narrowed his eyes. "Now you tell me what's goin' on with Miss Sarah."

Ladesha returned to the house tired and dusty, but satisfied. She had accomplished her mission. She peeked around the dining room doorway before disappearing into her room. The Garnetts stood at the front door saying goodnight to their company as the clock struck eleven.

She snuck off to her bedroom, pleased with herself. "That old scruffy man ain't as bad as I thought. Miss Jane is gonna be happy in the mornin' with the news I'm gonna tell her."

Chapter Seventeen

Ladesha bustled about the breakfast table, humming and bobbing her head.

Jane ate quietly, bursting inside, anxious to hear what she had to say.

Lieutenant Garnett smiled at her. "You're mighty chipper this morning, Ladesha."

"Yes, sir. It's a beautiful mornin', sun's shinin' and everythin'."

He turned to his wife. "So, are plans ready for our guest to head east?"

"Yes dear. We're ready."

"Good. I talked with Mr. Schultz yesterday. He will be leaving in three days. I plan to talk with Sarah tomorrow evening after supper. That will give you women one day to pack up her things. I don't want to see her moping around here for several days."

He took a couple more sips from his coffee cup, pushed back out of his chair, and kissed his wife's cheek before leaving the room.

As the door closed behind him, Jane twirled around. "Now, come sit down and tell me what happened last night."

"Well, first I sneaks."

"Get to the point, Ladesha. Did you talk with Mr. O'Brien?"

"No ma'am, I talks with Mr. Castor."

"With Castor? How did you find him?"

"In the shadows. He grabs me and—"

"Ladesha!"

"Anyways, that old scruffy man forced me to tell him our plan. Oh, he got all mad about Miss Sarah having to leave."

"And?"

"He's gonna help us. He plans on talkin' with Mr. O'Brien today. Says to be ready tonight for a window knockin'."

"Tonight? Then we must talk with Sarah and be sure she's ready."

"What do you want to talk to me about?" asked Sarah, as she strolled through the doorway.

Pressing her hand to her heart, Jane started when she heard the girl's voice. "Oh, my. I didn't hear you come in. Please sit with us. There is so much to tell you, and I'm not exactly sure where to begin."

Sarah sat stiffly in the chair and looked at Jane.

Mrs. Garnett leaned closer to Sarah. "Ladesha and I have a plan, so listen very carefully. We want to help you and Little Feather to leave on your own accord with Mr. O'Brien."

"Did Patrick agree to this?"

"Wait. Wait until I tell you everything. Then you can ask questions. Last night, Ladesha went to find Mr. O'Brien. But instead, she found Mr. Castor. After she told him that my husband was about to send you back East, he is going to help us." She touched Sarah's arm. "Now this is what we have planned."

After a rather lengthy explanation, Jane took a deep breath and exhaled. "You'll be leaving this evening. Free to live your life the way you want, you and your baby."

Tears came to Sarah's eyes. "Thank you. Your kindness flows like a brook in my heart."

"I sure is gonna miss my Sugarberry," said Ladesha. She stood up and wiped her eyes. "I'll get Miss Sarah some breakfast."

Jane's eyes followed her as she disappeared into the kitchen. "Both of us love your sweet baby. Now you sit and eat your breakfast. Don't worry about anything."

Jim Castor leaned against the wall of the stable, waiting for Patrick to arrive. Finally, he caught sight of him cutting in front of Bedlam House, heading in his direction. Castor mulled over the speech he was about to give Patrick. *Maybe after a few stiff drinks, this information would settle better. Nah, no matter how I tell him, he's gonna get fightin' mad, and I don't blame him.*

"Mornin'. Once you open up, can you get one of your helpers to stay put while we talk? Got somethin' real important to tell ya."

Patrick looked at Castor for a moment. "All right. I have a few minutes."

"It'll take more than a few minutes. I'll meet you at the bar."

"Isn't it a little early to be drinking that hard stuff?"

"Not for what I have to tell ya. See you over there." Castor moseyed down the road in no hurry. He knew he had time to get where he was going, and he didn't relish what he had to do. *I think I'm gonna need the whole blasted bottle for this job. Hope this works out for Miss Sarah. It's gonna be tricky.*

Patrick entered the bar, the smell of sour liquor, stale smoke, and dust took his breath away. The only light streamed through the small window and door. He waited for his eyes to adjust to the dark shadows that filled the room.

"You're here mighty early this morning," shouted Murphy from behind the counter. Then he pointed across the room. "Castor's already got a bottle."

Taking a seat opposite his friend, Patrick scooted close to the table. "So, what's so darn important that we have to meet here?"

"Have a drink first," as he pushed a glass to Patrick. They both downed their drinks. "Now, you got to promise me you'll keep your voice down."

"What for? Only Murphy's here."

"He won't be for long. The early crowd will be comin' in. Besides, I have something to tell you about Miss Sarah and you need to stay calm."

Patrick froze. "Well?"

Castor wiped his mouth with the back of his hand. "Last night I ran into Ladesha. She's like a brick wall. My chest still hurts." He placed his hands on his ribs. "Anyway, seems that she and Mrs. Garnett have devised a plan to help Miss Sarah and her baby leave the fort."

Patrick gave Castor a puzzled expression. "Why does she have to leave? I don't understand."

Castor picked up the bottle ready to pour. "Why don't we have another drink?"

Patrick clapped his hand over his glass. "No! I want to know why Sarah has to leave the fort."

Castor poured himself a drink and then set the bottle on the table. "Seems that the lieutenant's got a burr up his ass about Miss Sarah. He's purchased a spot for her on the next wagon train east."

Patrick jumped to his feet and shouted, "Hell, you say." He jostled the small table and spilled the drink. "That sonofabitch."

Castor grabbed Patrick's arm. "Sit down, boy. You're drawin' attention you don't want."

Two customers now lounged at the bar and looked their way.

Red in the face and clenching his fists at his sides, Patrick kicked the fallen chair

"Sit down, I say, so that we can talk this out proper like. Flying off the handle won't help either of you."

Patrick picked up his chair, righted it, and plopped into the seat.

"Now, you listen to me," whispered Castor. "If you want to save Sarah from embarrassment and have her safe under your protection, you need to pay attention and be quiet."

As Castor slowly related the concocted plan Ladesha told him, Patrick's mind wandered. He could not believe the commander could be so underhanded, so blatantly cruel. His idea of shipping Sarah and her baby back east before her mother even arrived was cold blooded and evil.

Narrowing his eyes, he caught Castor's words, "...that is if you still want to be with Sarah? Are you listening to me? Jeez, you're off in a fog. Stick with me boy. Now, as I was sayin', I can round up a couple of extra horses from an Indian friend of mine who owes me a favor or two. You have your own bay to ride. Right?"

Patrick nodded.

Castor continued. "Mrs. Garnett and Ladesha are puttin'

together some vittles for your trip. You need to gather your personal gear and bedroll, and be ready to leave tonight. The hard part is gonna be on your shoulders. That is, convincin' that little gal that she needs to leave with you before she's sent away."

Patrick leaned forward and crossed his arms on the table. "I can't believe this is happening."

"Can you get close to her without Lieutenant Garnett suspectin' you?"

Patrick sat there, gritting his teeth. "Yes."

"Boy, you get your act together. You only got today to be ready. Meet me tonight down by the river where the old fort once stood. Say about eleven o'clock."

"I'll be there." Patrick stared at his open hands, palms up. With a more subdued tone, he said. "You're a good friend, Castor. Hope this doesn't get you into trouble."

"Heck, what are they gonna do? Fire me from my high payin' job. I've just been waitin' for an excuse to leave. I've had my fill of this Army and their rules and regulations. Can't even take a leak in peace without someone documentin' it."

Castor poured each of them a drink. "Here, have one for the road."

Patrick downed the drink and stood up. "I need to get back. You riding out today?"

"Nah. Got some important stuff to do. You just watch out for the commander. The troops are drillin' most of the day. They'll be churnin' up the dust in the parade ground, while others work on the new officers' quarters. So he'll be in and out of his office most of the day."

Patrick touched the brim of his hat and left.

He stood outside in front of the barroom door, looking down the dirt road toward Bedlam house. Seeing no one in sight, except for a few soldiers milling around by the flagpole, he headed over to see Sarah.

He knocked twice before Ladesha opened the door.

"Well, look who's come to visit," she announced, smiling wide and showing her beautiful white teeth.

Patrick didn't expect that cheery of a reception from Ladesha. He gave her a quirky suspicious smile.

Mrs. Garnett swept across the parlor floor and extended her hand. "Come in, Mr. O'Brien. We were just talking about you."

Sarah strolled in from the dining room.

"I have to talk with Sarah. It's important."

"Oh, I believe we will need to talk together. However, maybe a little privacy is in order first. Ladesha, come join me in Sarah's room. We need to look in on Little Feather."

"Yes, ma'am. As long as I gets to hold my Sugarberry."

Patrick removed his hat. "How are you, Sarah?"

"I am fine." She walked closer.

"Castor told me Commander Garnett's plans. I wanted you to know that, well, darn that man." He beat his hat against his pants legs."

Silence surrounded them for a minute. Finally, Patrick asked, "Sarah, will you come with me? I'm heading to the Kansas territory where the land is wide open and free. We could build a life together: you, me, and Little Feather. I'd be proud if you'd join me. Doesn't mean you have to marry me." He smiled, "Although that would be pleasing."

"Are you asking me to be your wife?"

"Yes, I guess I am. Hadn't given that much thought. I'm trying to get you to safety."

She smiled. "I would like that."

"What? Going to the territory with me or being my wife?"

"Both."

He stood there dumbfounded, with his mouth open. "You're saying, 'yes'?"

She nodded her head.

He took two steps toward her. Cupping her face with both hands, he caressed her cheeks with his thumbs. Then gently, he kissed her forehead, her nose, and then her lips. He moved back and grinned.

"Would you marry me, Sarah, Vision Seeker, and be my wife?"

"I thought you already asked me?"

"I decided to do it properly this time."

She encircled her arms around his waist and leaned into his body. "Yes, Patrick, I want to be your wife, if you will have *both* of us."

He wrapped his arms around her and held her tight, snuggling his face into her hair. "I wouldn't have it any other way. But you will have to teach me to be a father." Lifting her chin with one hand, he raised her face and kissed her deeply. Then he placed small kisses to her neck, ears, and shoulders.

"Stop," she said, giggling. "Jane and Ladesha will be back."

Jane cleared her throat as she entered the parlor. "Excuse me, but we were wondering if the two of you were ready to discuss the important part of this meeting. We need to get the three of you out of this fort before my husband discovers our plan."

She took a seat on the sofa. "Please sit down. We have exactly four hours before my husband returns."

With a sheepish grin, Patrick released Sarah. "Why, Mrs. Garnett, we are more than ready."

"So I see. Ladesha, set the baby down and join us."

As Jane talked about the plan they had developed, the baby crawled on the floor toward Patrick. Little Feather grabbed his trouser leg and tried to pull himself to his feet, but rolled over onto his back. The baby gurgled and stared up at Patrick with his deep black eyes.

He picked up Little Feather and sat him on his knee. Feeling a bit awkward, he held him with both hands.

Jabbering softly, the baby reached for Patrick's shirt, wiggled closer into his lap, and then laid his head against Patrick's broad chest.

Patrick cradled the baby in his arm, as he sat listening to the women talk.

Chapter Eighteen

After supper, Jane sat in the parlor, embroidering a piece of handiwork. She glanced at the clock several times as she watched her husband, who was busy at his desk doing paperwork.

When the clock struck ten, she set her sewing aside and yawned. "Don't you think it's time for bed, dear?"

"Uh-huh" was the only answer she received.

"Richard."

Without turning to face her, he answered, "I heard you. I still have more paperwork to do. Why don't you go on to bed? I'll be there soon."

"Why must you finish that tonight?"

Annoyed with her question, he twisted around and glared at her. "Why are you in such a huff? Go on to bed. I need to get this written."

She saw her maid peeking around the kitchen doorframe. "Ladesha, will you help me prepare for bed?"

"Yes, ma'am," she said, entering the parlor to follow her mistress.

Once inside the bedroom, Ladesha whispered, "What's we to do? Him staying up late like this."

"We'll both have to go to bed and hope he'll be finished soon. My only wish is that we could have used the backstairs." Jane wrung her hands, then took two long breaths.

Giving Ladesha a pleading look, Jane said, "Watch for the light to go out. After that, give him about twenty minutes before you start moving the parlor table. Now help me with my dress before he gets suspicious."

Ladesha lay wide-awake in her room, waiting to hear the desk chair scrape against the floor or footsteps in the hall. When the clock struck eleven o'clock, she awoke with a jolt. Jumping out of bed, she opened her door an inch and heard the commander's door squeak shut.

She tiptoed into the parlor and sat in a chair near the door, waiting and listening for the usual snoring that resounded through the rooms at night.

Dozing every once in a while, her head bobbed as she tried to stay awake. Finally, she moved to the window and picked up the small table. A set of keys slid off the table and hit the floor.

"What was that?" shouted the commander from inside his room.

"Nothing dear. Go back to sleep," came the muffled reply from Jane.

Quickly, Ladesha set the table down and scurried to hide in the dining area.

The door jerked open as Lieutenant Garnett stepped into the hallway. "I think I'll take a look." Carrying a candle, he trudged down the hallway and looked around the parlor. Seeing no one about, he returned to his room, closing the door behind him.

Ladesha hurried into the room where Sarah stood in the shadows holding the baby and a bedroll. Shaking her head 'no', the maid raised her palms, halting Sarah. Dropping to her hands and knees, Ladesha felt around the floor for the keys. Gripping them tightly in her hand, she stuck them into the pocket of her gown. She moved one curtain aside and saw Patrick crouched down beside the windowsill. She put her finger to her lips.

Again, she tried to move the table, inching it away from the window. Clearing the area, she spread the curtains apart and gradually tugged the window open. Stopping briefly, Ladesha listened for the commander's snoring. Satisfied he was fast asleep, she left to retrieve the two saddlebags.

Sarah made her way to the window. She handed Patrick the cradleboard with Little Feather fast asleep. Slowly, she climbed through the opening.

Ladesha passed the bags to her and quietly slid the window closed. She pulled the curtains together, moved the table back into place, put the keys on the doily, and went to bed.

Waiting in the dark down by the river, Castor held the reins to three horses. Only a few people were out. They didn't seem to notice him. He strained his eyes to see through the inky night for the moon was only a quarter full. "They should have been here by now. How in tarnation are we gonna pull this off if'n they don't hurry? I wonder if they ran into trouble." Then he spied a couple walking fast toward him.

"It's about time you two showed up. What took ya so long?"

"You don't want to know, and we don't have time to tell you. Hurry Sarah, mount and let's get across the river. We've got to be as far as possible down the trail before first light."

Patrick threw the saddlebags over the back of the supply horse and secured them with their bedrolls. Then he tied Sarah's parfleche on top.

Sarah handed Castor the cradleboard. Then she climbed into the saddle and put her moccasin feet in the stirrups. She reached for her son and secured the board on the horn, before she took the lead for the supply horse.

"You take it easy on that man in front of you," said Castor. "He'll take good care of you and that baby."

Sarah smiled. "I know he will."

He walked over to Patrick. "You better get going before the lieutenant wakes up. He ain't gonna be happy when he finds both of you gone."

Patrick bent over and shook Castor's hand. "Wish you were coming with us. We could use your knowledge of scouting out the trail."

"Ah, you'll do fine. Follow your instincts. By the way, where ya headed?"

"Kansas territory, down around the Smoky Hill River. Heard the land there is good. Not many people."

"Well, take it easy and be safe. Watch your scalp. I hear they're having a bit of Indian trouble out that way."

With that said, Castor turned and headed back toward his barracks. He stopped once to look for them, but they had already crossed the river and disappeared into the night.

The next morning, Lieutenant Garnett ate his breakfast as usual then left at his standard time to review the soldiers.

Jane sat nervously, wringing her hands at the table.

"You's got to drink your tea, Miz Jane. There's no reason to worry none. He don't s'pect a thing. The time to worry is this evening when he notices she ain't eatin' supper."

"Oh, I feel awful knowing I helped her leave against his wishes. But, I couldn't let him send her off by herself without someone to look out for her and that beautiful baby."

"I's gonna miss my Sugarberry. Sho was nice havin' a little one around. Maybe one day our Marissa will come home with a husband and a baby. Hmmm, hmm, hmm. Sho would be nice."

Jane thought about her daughter, Marissa, as she sipped her tea. She was back east at the Oberlin Collegiate Institute in Ohio, much against her father's wishes. "Yes. It certainly would be nice if she found some nice young man to marry. However, I'm afraid all of her time is spent studying right now.

"Ladesha, we are going to invite four officers to dinner this evening. I want you to prepare a wonderful meal that will keep the conversation going until the men leave."

"Yes, ma'am. I's can do that real good."

Rising from her chair, Jane said, "I am going to write each of the soldiers an invitation and you will deliver them this afternoon. Now you go about your work as usual while I work at the desk."

"Who's we invitin'?"

"I believe I will ask Sergeants Williams, Prescott, Morrissey, and Brogan. That should be enough to keep my husband busy. Anything to give Patrick and Sarah time to add miles to their journey."

Ladesha chuckled. "Those four will eat us out of house and home. You sho do know how to fill a table with hungry folks, Miz Jane."

Jane Garnett picked up her cup and saucer and entered the parlor. Setting them on the desktop, she sat down and began to write.

* * *

Later that afternoon, Castor sat in the bar at a small round table, nursing a glass of whiskey. He already missed Patrick. *Sure enjoyed talkin' to the young fella. He was a good drinkin' partner. But, the way things were goin' for Sarah and her son, I'm glad they're gone.*

He glanced up, and saw another scout get up from his chair and stroll toward the doorway.

"Hey, West. Got a minute?"

The scout shrugged his shoulders and joined him.

"Sit a spell and let me buy you a drink," said Castor. "Have something important to tell you." He waived his hand at the barkeep and held up two fingers. Murphy nodded.

"It's like this," said Castor. "My service with the Army is up as of tomorrow morning. I've been givin' a lot of thought about retirin'. Workin' out here reminds me of a circus I saw once back in Indiana when I visited two years ago."

"You drunk or something?" asked West.

"Nope, got tired of watchin' all this drillin' and marchin' around here. Tired of going out on patrols and findin' nothin'. Tired of being shot at for no reason and worryin' about losin' my scalp. And all I get for workin' so hard are blisters on my butt and dry mouth from all the dust I eat."

"What are ya gonna do? Where you gonna go?"

"Thinkin' about headin' to Texas. Hear tell the land is cheap with plenty of wide-open spaces. Maybe I'll round up a few head of longhorns and have me a small ranch."

"You ranchin'?" West laughed. "I can't see that."

"Heck, it beats livin', eatin', and sleepin' on a horse or the hard ground all the time. With winter a comin', I want to be warm. Not as young as I use to be. Besides, I might find me a nice woman to share my bed."

West gulped his drink and stood up. "Dang, Castor. That sounds boring as hell. But, I understand why you want to move on. Wish I was a little older. I'd like to find me a good woman other than that ugly, dirty squaw that shares my bed."

Castor bristled. *You ought to be happy that any woman wants to share your bed, you stupid easterner.* He didn't say anything, only nodded. West wasn't worth wastin' words on.

"Good luck," said West.

"Yep. It's time to think about me for a change, before it's too late." Castor gave him a half salute. "See ya around sometime, maybe in Texas."

He watched the young pup of a scout saunter out of the bar.

Castor smirked. All he had to do now was collect his money due him, pack his stuff, and buy enough supplies to get him to the Kansas territory. He tossed the last few drops of whiskey down, grabbed his hat, waved goodbye to Murphy, and left the bar, smiling to himself.

Chapter Nineteen

After the last soldier left the Garnett's house, Richard shut the door with a thud and spun around to face his wife who sat at the table. He stormed into the dining room, fists clenched at his sides. His face a rich magenta from his collar to his hairline. He gritted his teeth and growled, "Where is she?"

"Who, dear?"

"You know quite well who I mean. Sarah," he shouted.

He paced about the room with his hands clutched behind his back. "I went to the stables this evening before coming home. Patrick O'Brien is gone. Disappeared. From what I hear, he left sometime last night. Then I come home to supper and find invited guests at our table, but no Sarah."

Jane tried to smile. "Well, I just assumed Sarah wasn't interested in eating tonight. She did eat a late meal this afternoon."

Garnet stomped down the hallway to Sarah's room. Everything was in its place. "She's not here," he yelled. Slamming the door behind him, he returned to the parlor.

He walked toward Ladesha. "Did you have anything to do with her leaving?"

"No, sir," she answered. "I's been busy in the kitchen gettin' ready for the company. It's all's I can do to take care of myself and Miss Jane." She twirled around and headed for the kitchen. "I's got dishes to do."

"Jane, did you help her to leave. Tell me the truth. Did you go behind my back and help her?"

"No dear. Remember, last night we ate supper and I did my embroidering until late."

He paced back and forth in front of the desk, mumbling to himself. Suddenly, he stopped dead in his tracks. "Well, I'm not sending a patrol out after her," he announced. "Good riddance. Wait until her mother arrives. It'll give me great pleasure to tell her we found her daughter, and then she up and ran away."

He headed for the front door and yanked it open.

"Richard. Where are you going? It's so late."

"I'm going to take a walk. I might even stop at Murphy's. Don't wait up for me." He hesitated for a moment. "Tomorrow, I'll hunt up Schultz and get my money back, since she and that half-breed won't be traveling with the wagon train." He slammed the door behind him as he left.

Castor strolled into headquarters the next morning. Sergeant Hodges sat at his desk, deeply engrossed in his paperwork.

He flopped into the chair next to the sergeant's desk. "Is the commander in?"

Hodges looked up, scorn on his face. "One of these days, you'll get some manners. You could at least say *good morning*."

"It's a waste of time, and I don't have much of that left, now do I?" He grinned and raised his eyebrows at the sergeant.

"Commander Garnett is in, if you truly want to know. However, he is extremely busy at the moment. Now if you don't mind, I have work to do."

"Well, I'll just sit here until he's not busy." Castor propped his feet up on Hodges' desk. "So, I ain't leavin' until I get to see 'im. Nope, don't have much else to do this mornin'."

Hodges stood up, reached over and shoved his feet off his desk. "If you want to wait, that's fine. Just keep your filthy feet off my desk. Go sit in one of those chairs across the room."

Castor saluted him, got up, and ambled over toward the window. "Might as well. Company here has a smell to it. Sorta like stuffy ass." Taking a seat, he tilted the chair back against the wall. Then he took out an old cigar butt, chewed on it for a moment, and then lit it.

Hodges jumped to his feet and yelled, "You can't smoke that in here. It's against the commander's rules. You know that."

"Then let the *commander* come out and tell me that, you chuckleheaded prairie dog."

Hodges glared at him, turned around and ignored him.

Lieutenant Garnett's door opened "What's all the noise out here?"

Castor rubbed his cigar out on the bottom of the chair and stuffed it back into his shirt pocket.

Spying Castor across the room, Garnett waved him into his office. "Come in and take a seat. Need to talk with you."

The sergeant stiffened as Castor passed by with a sly grin on his face.

Inside Garnett's office, Castor dropped into a chair.

The commander sat down and shuffled a few papers in front of him. Without looking up, he asked, "Did you have anything to do with Patrick O'Brien's leaving?"

"Nope, heard this mornin' that he was gone," said Castor. "Musta left sometime last night. I've been spendin' most of my time over at Murphy's makin' a decision about movin' on. You ask Murphy."

"No, that's fine. I just wanted a straight answer from you. If I find out that O'Brien and that squaw stole any army horses, I'll have both their heads."

Castor sat quiet, hat in hand and didn't comment.

"Now let me see. Where were we?" the commander said lost in thought. He looked up at Castor. "Exactly why are you here, Jim?"

Castor crossed his legs and propped his hat on his knee. "I'm leavin' the Army as a scout this mornin'. Thought I'd drop by and tell you so myself. I'll be collectin' my pay before I head out to the store. Need a few things."

"Sure you want to do this? You're one of my best scouts."

"Yep, it's time to leave."

Sitting back in his high-backed chair, Garnett asked, "You wouldn't consider staying around a few weeks to train West?"

"Nope. Got my heart set on goin'"

"Seems like everybody is abandoning this fort. Lost five soldiers this week. Won't get replacements until spring. Where are you headed?"

"I'm headed to Texas to take up some land and rounding up a couple head of cattle. Thought about ranchin'. Maybe even thinkin' about gettin' married."

"You married? Now that I'd like to see."

Castor looked up and grinned. "Well, you look me up in Texas and you might see that miracle."

Castor rose out of the chair and extended his hand to the lieutenant.

Commander Garnett grasped Castor's hand in a firm grip. "Good luck, Castor. If you get the itch to work with the Army again, come on back and see me."

"Don't think so, but thanks." Castor plopped his hat on his head and headed out the door.

Outside, he took a deep breath, stretched his arms and did a little jig. "Feel like a load of horse manure's been lifted from my life. Maybe the stink will eventually blow away."

With his personal gear and bedroll packed, he purchased necessary supplies from the post store to last him several weeks. No telling how long it was going to take him to find those kids. He loaded everything on his mule, Matter, and said his goodbyes to many of his friends as he headed toward Murphy's.

Entering the room with a light heart and anxious to hit the trail, Castor leaned against the bar. "Murphy, give this here civilian a two-fingered glass of your best whiskey and set one up for yourself."

"Civilian, huh?" Murphy poured two drinks and set the bottle aside. Clinking their glasses together, he said, "May you be in heaven before the devil finds you missing." Then he tossed his drink down.

Castor nodded. "Here's to you, my friend."

"So you're leaving. Hear tell you're headed to Texas."

"Yep, as soon as I have one more for the road."

Murphy poured two more drinks. "You really gonna get married?"

Castor chuckled, "Hell, can't tell what I'm liable to do. Haven't met her yet, have I?"

Murphy smiled. "Well, here's to ya." He raised his glass, gulped down the second drink, then wiped his mouth with the back of his hand. "Hate to see ya go, but good luck and take your time getting that woman."

"Not in any hurry. Me and Matter's headin' south."

"How come you call that old mule of yours, Matter?"

"Funny thing you should ask. She's a stubborn four-legged critter. Sometimes she just won't move. Sits her butt right down in the middle of the trail. I'm always hollering 'What's the matter with you?' She got so use to me sayin' that, when I call her Matter, she knows it's time to move along. So the name stuck."

Murphy roared with laughter. "That's one smart mule you got there, Castor."

"Yep. Well, gotta go. Burnin' daylight. Good knowin' ya, Murphy." Castor plunked down a few coins on the counter, touched the brim of his hat as he nodded to his friend, and headed out the door.

"You take care and keep your scalp," Murphy hollered after him.

Outside, Castor mounted his horse and took up the lead rope from his mule. "Come on Matter. We're free to move out. Got a lot of travelin' to do."

He rode down the road parallel to the parade ground and nodded to people who greeted him, wishing him good luck. When he reached the river, he crossed it with ease and headed east on the trail. "Now to find those two pups headin' for Kansas. Might take us a while, Matter, but we'll find 'em." He knew he wouldn't have trouble tracking them. He could find a wood tick on solid rock.

Patrick rode south along the Laramie River, heading east, followed closely by Sarah and the supply horse. The going was slow, for the night was extremely dark and the trail was hard to follow. Finally, they reached the junction of the Platte

River. One mile west of Bordeaux's Station, he pulled up his horse. "That trading post up ahead will be too busy. We don't want anyone catching a glimpse of us. We'll let the horses rest and catch some sleep ourselves."

He found a level spot near the river but off to one side away from the trail. He tethered the horses and unsaddled them.

Sarah spread out their bedrolls and saw to her son's needs. Reaching into the saddlebags, she brought out some food to eat before they bedded down.

"We won't make a fire. Try to sleep if you can. I'll wake you in a few hours," said Patrick.

At first light, Sarah broke out some meat and biscuits to eat on the way while Patrick saddled their horses. In the dark gray hours, she nursed Little Feather. Then she fastened her son's cradleboard to the saddle and mounted her horse. Patrick led out with Sarah and the supply horse behind him.

When they reached the post, he skirted the store and outhouses where the half-breeds slept. From the distance, he saw many wagons in the area and tents pitched by travelers. He was glad to get an early start. The sky was still dark enough to hide their moving down the trail.

The morning was cool but as the sun rose higher into the sky and hovered overhead, the heat pressed heavily on them. They halted for a short time at Cold Springs, and Sarah filled their canteens and water bags. Then she took her son from his cradleboard and let him crawl around, giving him the freedom he enjoyed so much.

"Won't be long and he'll be trying to walk. Soon we'll have to get him a horse," Patrick said with a chuckle.

Sarah started. "He's too young. I'll weave him a riding basket."

Patrick laughed at her. "I'm only joking with you. He is

getting bigger and stronger. Soon he won't fit in that cradleboard. Maybe it's good we're going to the Kansas territory. He's going to need room to grow and move around in."

Patrick clasped his hands around the boy's midriff and picked him up. He tossed Little Feather into the air several times and listened to him squeal with laughter. Then he held the child close to his chest with one arm and cupped his bottom with his other hand, swinging him from side to side.

The baby jabbered, grasping Patrick's shirt tightly with one tiny fist while he tried to pluck at the long brown strands of hair.

"Be careful," warned Sarah. "If he gets a handful of hair you'll be sorry."

"Whoa, little fella," shouted Patrick. "Help me. He's got a fist full of my hair twisted in his fingers."

Sarah bent over in laughter as he tried to extricate himself from her son's grip, without dropping the child on the ground. As the boy's hand yanked on the dark tresses, Patrick's head bent with each tug. Sarah finally took pity on him and opened Little Feather's hand, releasing the long hair.

"Here," said Patrick, as he handed the child to his mother. "He's all yours. I think I'll tie my hair back, before he gets anymore ideas of relieving me of my scalp."

She hugged the small boy and kissed his forehead. "You did good, little one. Maybe the big man will not tease you anymore."

"The big man lost a few strands of hair." Patrick pulled the strands from the child's grip. "I could have a bald spot."

Sarah made a hissing noise and latched her son in his cradleboard. Then she rolled up the bedding, securing it on the supply horse, making ready to leave.

As they rode the trail along the Platte River, she watched

the endless stream of animals, wagons, and people moving slowly in unison. The dust rose from the wheels, sending up a thick billowing screen, obscuring the scenery behind them. "Many wagons are still going west," she said.

Patrick took off his hat, removed the bandana from inside, and wiped the sweat from his forehead. "They're all looking for a new future. Sad as it may seem, they'd probably be better off staying where they came from."

"They look tired and unhappy."

"They are, and they still have miles to go." Patrick felt sorry for the travelers and their burdens. Many of them would never reach their destination.

Toward late afternoon, after they veered south from the river, he searched for a place to spend the night. With no wagons in sight, all was quiet except for a few birds overhead, searching for an evening's resting place. The depressing trail held many unidentified graves by the wayside. One was marked 'Henry Hill, died 1850, RIP'.

He wondered how many other gravesites they'd find along the trail without stones or crosses to mark their final resting place. How sad for the families who left their comfortable homes back east with high hopes, only to lose their loved ones on a dusty trail. Seeing Henry's worn small head stone inscription reminded him of his own father's death, far from his beloved North Carolina, with rolling green mountains filled with laurel and dogwood trees.

"Why do people leave all their furniture and belongings behind?" asked Sarah, bringing him back to reality.

"People pack their wagons too heavy and their animals languish. They'd die if people didn't lighten their load. They throw out food, chairs, and clothing, whatever is necessary to continue their trip. Don't you remember your family discarding items along the way?"

Sarah dodged a large trunk and chair. "I don't believe we reached that part of our journey back then. My thoughts of the wagon trip are a bit foggy, but, maybe."

She rode toward a pile of food. "Look, there's flour and bacon. We could use that."

"Don't, Sarah," shouted Patrick. "Some people poison the food they leave. Their greed will kill others instead of sharing what they can't take or use. Stay over here. We'll be stopping soon. Up ahead is Horse Creek Crossing. We'll camp about two miles west of it. This is Sioux territory. I don't want to encounter any braves looking for trouble."

Sarah's hair bristled on the back of her neck. Sioux! They were strong warriors whose hatred for the white man was unwavering. They didn't particularly like Arapahos either. "It would be best not to meet with them."

Patrick followed the trail into the gorgeous valley, lightly covered in timber. The steep walls of the hills shadowed the valley as the sun declined into the western sky. "We'll camp over there. It will give us protection until we get into the deeper section of the valley."

After their evening meal, sleep came easy as they settled into their bedrolls.

Sarah woke to the snap of a branch. Sitting up she saw five Indians with their faces painted, standing over Patrick, a spear to his throat. He lay very still. She knew if he moved, he would die. Raising her hands slowly, she made signs to explain that they were traveling east to escape the Army.

One Indian grunted and walked toward her. Pulling Sarah to her feet so he could examine her more closely, he flipped her braids and tugged at her dress. Saying something to his braves, they all laughed.

With talking hands, the leaders said, "We want bacon, coffee, and sugar for your safe journey through our lands."

Sarah signed, "We only have a small amount of meat, a few biscuits, and some beef jerky. We are traveling light."

The leader narrowed his eyes. "Then we take your horses."

"No, that is too high a price for going across your lands."

"You pay or your man dies."

Sarah reached behind her and held up her knife. "Trade."

The leader grabbed the knife and threw it to the ground. "Not knife. Want horses," he demanded.

"Here, take my gun," shouted Patrick.

"No want gun. Have plenty guns," said a brave, brandishing his rifle over his head. Sarah interpreted his message to Patrick.

"You no trade horses, you die." The leader waved his hand and two of the braves raised their ready bows.

"Wait," shouted Sarah. She reached into her parfleche, waited a few minutes, and brought out Running Swift's bear claw necklace. She had saved this precious memento to give her son when he was much older. It was his honor to wear his father's necklace and have its protective power.

She stretched her hand toward the leader and handed it to him. "This belonged to my husband. He was a brave warrior who fought the white man and led his people well. Take this in exchange for my man's life and our safe journey to the east."

Two braves advanced to look the claws over, poking it with their fingers. They smiled and nodded their heads as they talked among themselves, trying to decide if this was a good trade.

"Did your husband die wearing his necklace?" asked one brave.

They stared at her, waiting for her answer.

"No. If he had worn this, he would be alive today for its magic is strong."

They nodded in agreement with her answer and mumbled among themselves.

The leader clasped his hands in front of him, hand-signing peace. "Go, but be swift. Your presence here is not wanted. You and your man will not be harmed, but do not return." He slipped the necklace over his head and proceeded to prance about the area, pointing at his chest, shouting to his friends as the other braves congratulated him on his trade.

The spear drawn away from his neck, Patrick got to his feet and saddled the horses while Sarah rolled up their bedding and packed it away. Then she fastened Little Feather to the saddle and mounted her horse.

"We go," she signed. The Sioux stood and watched them leave, following behind them at a short distance.

When they reached Horse Creek Crossing, the water was shallow. The sandy bottom made crossing easy as they threaded through the driftwood that lined the shore. Sarah looked back over her shoulder several times to be sure the Sioux were not following them, to get more payment for crossing their lands. She did not trust them and hoped the neckpiece brought them bad luck for their insolence.

"I'm sorry you had to part with your husband's necklace."

Sarah shrugged. "Our lives are more important. My husband died wearing it. I stole it the night before I was rescued. It will bring evil spirits to the Sioux for their greed."

Time past without anymore incidents. Patrick led his little group through Robidoux Pass, Ash Hollow, and then climbed

Windless Hill. Finally, he turned south, heading for the Kansas territory. When he reached the high plains of the Territory seven days later, he sat on his horse overlooking the plateau ahead.

"Home is somewhere south of here. Freedom from prejudice and a place we can live together the way we want." Patrick reached over, touched her cheek, and then ran one finger along the outline of her jaw.

"We have to be married by a preacher so no one can—"

Patrick interrupted her. "Don't worry about that. I'll round one up. I'm sure we'll come across one heading south. Could be a preacher at the next fort."

"No fort," she shouted. "Lieutenant Garnett might have sent a message already."

"Not enough time. The rider would have had to pass us. Anyway, don't worry, we'll find someone to marry us." He wanted to kiss her, hold her in his arms and lay by her side naked on a buffalo robe. Right now wasn't the time for that. Kissing her from his horse proved to be an obstacle course with the cradleboard hanging from the side of her saddle.

"We'll be stopping soon. Sun's sliding toward the horizon. We need to find a good place to camp. Let's move on while we still have some light."

Chapter Twenty

Following John and the packhorses' lead across the grassy knolls, Caroline Anderson arched her back and rotated her shoulders, trying to work out the stiffness as her horse plodded along in an even gait. Nothing seemed to help. She mumbled to herself, "My bottom's tired and rubbed sore from riding all day. Maybe I'm getting too old for this gypsy life."

Behind her rode the rest of the cavalcade: John's mulatto son, Micah; the Sioux Indian boy, Standing Tall; Sadie Tedder, an elderly woman who once ran a hotel in Hangtown, California; and Ben Wilson, an old reprobate frontiersman who had saved her life when she lost everything on the Oregon Trail. Caroline smiled, "What a strange, mismatched band of companions."

With all the twists and turns her life had taken in the past, she wondered if the future held any normalcy at all. Three years ago, she and her family lived in a comfortable cabin between the cozy green hills of Virginia that surrounded the family farm. It was a good living and peaceful. She understood that way of life and the day-to-day routine.

Looking across the open prairie that stretched for miles, she wished for the comforts of a home, a warm bed, and a secure family life. Many times in the last few months, she asked herself, *why and how did all of this meandering from place to place come about? Why did we ever leave Virginia and take that wagon cross-country?* The only answer that came to mind was a small bag of gold and the cruel hand of fate that had dealt her an evil blow.

Her heart grew heavy as she recalled the loss of her husband and two children. Caroline realized she could never recapture the past, but the loss of her children, James and Sarah, ripped her heart apart. What did the future hold for her? If she did find Sarah, how was she to tell her daughter her father was her Uncle John and not Alexander? Would her daughter understand a young girl's mistake? Would she realize that a pregnant girl accepted any proposal to cover her shame? It wasn't that she didn't come to love Alexander. He wasn't her first love. Her husband had tried so hard and failed miserably. Now he was dead and she was at the mercy of trying to survive with his brother, John

John's basic shortcoming was he never totally understood responsibility, neither to her nor to Micah's mother, D'Alene. It took Micah and Standing Tall to make him face reality to some degree, but he would never change completely.

The short undulating blanket of grass, mixed with blowing dust, stretched as far as the eye could see. The few cottonwood trees, sprinkled here and there, soothed her anxiety. Yet, exhaustion crept into her very soul as she swayed with the horse's rhythmic gait. The sun slid to rest on top of the mountains, closing out another day.

Caroline glanced over her shoulder at the boys behind her. Even though they weren't related and they picked at each other most of the time, no one dared come between them. She could tell they were tired.

"Are we gonna stop and eat?" asked Micah

"We'll be at the fort soon," answered Caroline

At the rear of the caravan, Ben and Sadie rode with their heads bent and shoulders hunched. Following the trail all day was taking a toll on them. Caroline knew they were getting too old to travel across desolate terrain, never knowing where their next bed would be.

Ben kept falling asleep. He never fell out of the saddle, but as he leaned from one side to the other, Sadie shoved him upright.

"Woman, what do ya want?" he shouted.

With the jerk of her head, Sadie's stern expression shut him up quickly.

"John, are we going to spend a few days at the fort?" Caroline's only thoughts were to wash off the dusty trail grime, put on fresh clothes, and wash her hair.

Her brother-in-law turned to face her. "I'm sure it'll take that long to buy provisions, have some repairs made to our equipment, and check with headquarters about Sarah."

"I'm worried about Sadie and Ben. This trip's been hard on them."

Pulling his horse to a halt, John pointed. "We're almost there. Ahead lays the Laramie River. Looks a little high."

"On the other side is the road to Fort Laramie," shouted Micah from behind him.

"Good," said Standing Tall. "I want place to sleep. Bones speak to me. Say, 'get off horse and lay down'."

"I can't wait to sink my teeth into a piece of tasty prairie chicken or rabbit. Anything would taste good right now. My stomach's been speaking to me for four hours." Micah smacked his lips together. "I'm so hungry I could eat my boots."

"Snake taste better," said Standing Tall.

"You and snakes. One day I want to see you eat one."

"Ha. You catch one. I eat it."

"Humph. Sure you will," muttered Micah.

"Settle down back there," yelled John. "I thought by age thirteen you two boys would be more grown-up. Three years of this grumbling is just two too many."

"You ought to marry them off to some ugly old women. They'd both stop complaining real quick," said Ben.

"They're fagged," said Sadie. "We're all wayworn of dust and constant jostlin'. My bones hurt as well as my butt. Sittin' in this saddle can sure scrabble your brains."

Ben grinned. "Ain't your brains you're sittin' on, me sweets."

"Hush. Don't need your comments right now." Then she leaned over and whispered to Ben. "Sugar, you think we could get a good glass of whiskey at this fort? I'm a tiny bit thirsty."

Ben gave her his best impish grin. "Now, woman. Whiskey's bad for ya."

She reached over and slapped his arm. "You old coot. I'm bad for you if I don't get that drink you promised me a couple days ago. You had to go and finish off that bottle all by yourself."

"Well, how was I ta know you wanted a sip?"

"Sip? See if I warm your backside, you miserable little toad."

"Ah, come on, Sadie, don't get mad. I'm only a teasin' ya."

"Ben," said John. "I think we'll cross the river up ahead, north of the fort. The banks aren't as steep, but we'll still need to be careful. They're probably slippery and the water's rough.

"Micah, you and Standing Tall take those two supply mules behind Caroline and cross the river, after the women reach the other side. Give them plenty of lead rope. Ben, you and I'll take the two supply horses over first. Sadie, stay close to Caroline and follow us."

As John and Ben descended the steep bank, the rapid water surged over their saddles, pushing at the riders, almost unseating Ben. The bank proved quite steep. After the two men scrambled out of the water, guiding the two supply horses, John dismounted and stood at the river's edge.

"Caroline, start across, but hang on tight. The current's swift. Keep angling this way," he yelled, moving his arms to his right. After a struggle, the women reached the opposite side. John and Ben grabbed the reins from the women, pulling the horses up the slippery bank.

Finally the two boys edged into the turbulent water. One of the mules lost its footing and drifted to one side. Micah yanked on the rope.

"Pull, Micah, and then give her some rope length," yelled Ben. "You're losin' her. Damnation, son, pull."

Standing Tall moved to block the little mule's drifting. Once righted, they made the bank and dry ground.

"Thought you were gonna lose my sweet Sassafras." Ben patted the small mule's muzzle. He faced Sadie. "You okay?"

"Humph. Now you ask after sweet-talkin' to that mule. You think more of that animal than me."

Ben reached up to appease her. "Now, Sadie."

She shoved his hand away. "Don't you 'now Sadie' me, you old shaggy goat." Turning her head, she eased her horse forward out of his reach.

"Women. Ya can never please 'em."

John shook his head. He didn't know which was worse, the two boys or Ben and Sadie. "Let's go. We need to make camp before nightfall and get into some dry clothes."

The stark, treeless complex of Fort Laramie did not

impress John with its open-air compound. He wondered how the soldiers survived the loneliness in these bleak surroundings, especially during the winter months. The mountains to the west and a curving river that hugged the banks were the only things of beauty.

Following the dusty trail into Fort Laramie, John had counted approximately twelve or more adobe shanties on the outlying boundaries. "Looks like they have a lot more civilians working here now. Won't be long and there'll be a hotel added to the string of buildings."

As he rounded the sutler's store, he dodged children running around and slowly made his way through the small groups of people. Farmers and Indians mingled across the parade ground to the store, crowding the area, even this late in the evening. "Ben, you, me and the boys will walk to the stables. You women stay mounted. We'll lead the way." He shook his head. "Where did all these people come from?"

Micah pointed toward the other side of the open area. "I'll bet there's a hundred wagons over there. They're still headin' west."

Standing Tall's eyes narrowed. He said nothing as he glared at the white people and their canvassed wagons camped on both sides of the river.

John dismounted. "After the horses are settled in, we'll make camp over on the east side, away from the Indians. Not much wind there and we can see the sun come up in the morning. Once we get things settled, we'll grab some food."

"Food," said Micah, mimicking a starving person by grabbing his belly and staggering about. "I can smell it. Lead me to it."

Micah leaned into Standing Tall. The Indian dodged to one side. Both boys started laughing.

Ben grasped Micah by the neck. "You two keep fooling around these horses and one of ya's gonna get hurt."

"Ah, Ben, we're just havin' fun."

"Fun. Ain't no time for that right now. We need to see to these animals and set up camp. Then you two can have fun."

Both boys frowned and ducked their heads.

Sadie perked up. "Goodness gracious, me. Did ya see that new stone addition to the post store, Caroline? Why they've gone and doubled their space. We shouldn't have any trouble gettin' the supplies we need this time around."

"I'd like to buy a new hat."

John lifted one eyebrow at Caroline. "Are you going to throw that old felt one away?"

"No, it belonged to my son, James. I need a bigger one to keep the rain off the back of my neck. This one's seen better days. Besides, one day I might find him to give it back to him."

John lowered his head and kept his mouth shut. The dream of finding her son pained him.

Ben piped up, "Well, now, I think a new hat is a good idea. A woman needs to buy herself some pretties, don't she, Sadie?"

"Now, how would you be knowin' that, you shortsighted fool? Ever buy a woman a pretty?"

He stuck his chin out. "Nope, and don't plan on doing it now either."

"Didn't think so." Sadie patted her hair. "A pretty blue ribbon would be nice."

Ben turned his head and ignored the statement, but a mischievous smile crept across his lips.

"See what I mean. His ears sorta lose their hearing when I mention *buying a pretty*." Sadie's voice grew louder on the last three words as she directed them toward Ben.

He followed behind John, leading his horse away from the crowd.

"I can't believe the changes the army has made around here. Why, I can scarcely recognize the old fort." Caroline turned and pointed toward the crumbling fortress behind her. "I guess that's not much use anymore. There's only two sides to the old adobe fort still standing."

As John and Ben approached the stables, they waited for the two boys and the women to catch up with them. When Caroline reached his side, John grabbed her reins. "I'll take care of your horse. You see to getting those boys to set up camp and store our supplies away safely."

"Here, Sadie," said Ben, walking over to her horse. He reached up and pushed on her behind. "Let me help ya down, my sweet thing."

"You push my rear end again like that and I'll poke you one, Ben Wilson."

"I'm only tryin' to help ya down. You sure are sassy, woman."

Caroline walked around her horse toward Ben. "Sadie, do you need help? Maybe we should invest in a horse-drawn wagon."

Sadie slowly threw her leg over the horse's rump and lowered herself to the ground. "Sure would be a better comfort to my bottom than this here saddle." She staggered a little, trying to regain her balance, and rubbed her rump.

Ben gave her one of his mischievous grins. "Ya want me to give ya a hand with that rubbin'?"

Sadie crossed her arms and stood her ground. "Touch me and you'll lose an arm. I still haven't forgiven you for drinkin' up all that liquor. Sometimes you're one ornery polecat." Turning away from him, she placed her hands on the small of her back as she arched backward. "And then other times, you're as cuddly as a kitten."

Ben beamed from ear to ear. Poking out his chest, he strutted behind her. "I heerd that. Cuddly, huh."

"Don't let it go to your head."

Caroline listened to the two of them. They argued and fumed at each other, but under all of their outlandish behavior, she knew their caring ran deep. Spying the boys, she said, "You two take those supplies up on the other side over there and find a campsite. After you set up the tents, John wants those furs put away properly. Then bring the pack animals back. You can leave your horses here. Sadie and I'll take care of them."

Micah nodded.

"Ben will help you set up camp," said Sadie. "Just make sure those tents are sturdy this time. Don't cotton to having it fall on me again. Gave me a good knock on my noggin last time."

Micah and Standing Tall grinned as they recalled the chaos. They could still picture Sadie screaming bloody murder under the fallen tent, flapping the canvas around. Meanwhile, Ben was lifting the material, trying to find the opening, all the while yelling, "Be quiet, woman. You'll wake the dead."

"Scared us half to death," said Micah.

Sadie pursed her lips together and raised one eyebrow. "If'n I didn't know better, I'd swear you did that on purpose."

"Oh, Sadie, we wouldn't do that to ya. We just didn't fasten it down tight enough."

She crossed her arms and watched the two boys head toward the camping area with Ben.

John walked two horses into the stable. "Hello," he shouted, "anybody here?" He unsaddled one horse and put the animal into a stall.

A young man emerged from behind the back stall, a pitchfork in his hand. "Hi. You want to board your horse?"

"Yes, I have a couple more animals coming in. I need to leave them for a few days." As he unbuckled the cinch, he made idle conversation. "Anything exciting happen around here lately? Any Indian trouble?"

"No Indian trouble, though they aren't too happy with the last treaty. We did have one thing happen, though. An Army patrol brought in a white girl from an Arapaho Indian village about a month ago."

John froze. He stared out the wide wooden doors at Caroline who smiled at him and waved as she talked to Sadie.

"Is that right," he managed to say, pulling the saddle off the horse. He placed it on a stall rail and then turned to face the man. "That must have been interesting. What was her name?"

"Ah, Sarah something." He smiled at John.

"Anderson?" He held his breath.

"Yes. That was it. Sarah Anderson. Young. Redheaded. Good looker, too."

"Where is she now?" John removed the bridle from his horse and hung it up on a peg.

"Oh, she's not here anymore. She and a man named Brady, I think, lit out of here late one evening after everyone was asleep. Darnedest thing, too. The commander was really mad about that."

"Why would he be upset?"

"Well, she was staying with the commander and his wife over at Bedlam House. Don't rightly know the whole story. But, a private told me the next morning, Lieutenant Garnett came into headquarters, stomping around and grumbling to himself. That stuffy old sergeant that works there didn't have much to say that day, either."

"Do you know where this Brady and Sarah were headed?"

"Nope. No one does. Castor might, but he's gone, too."

John gave the young man a questioning look. "Who's Castor?"

"An old scout. He and Brady were kinda friendly. One morning, Castor just up and left the Army. Said he was gonna head south to Texas to raise cattle. Sure wish I could have joined him."

John thanked the young man and headed outside. *How am I going to break this news to Caroline? After all these years of waiting and watching for Sarah, only to find that now she left and we've missed her. I'll never hear the end of taking that mountain pass. If I'd only started back earlier like she wanted to and taken the valley trail along the river, we probably would have been here in time. Well, at least she's alive.*

He stood in the doorway for a moment, hands limp at his sides. *How do I begin telling her?*

As he strolled up to Sadie and Caroline, the women were discussing what to have for supper. The look on his face stopped their conversation immediately.

"What's wrong? They shaved you for more money than you got to stable those horses?" asked Sadie.

"No. Just heard some interesting news." He pursed his lips together and placed one hand on Caroline's shoulder. Then he cupped her face between his large hands, tilting her face upward, tying to speak the words that failed him. "Our daughter was found by an Army patrol."

Caroline jerked away from him and inhaled as her mouth fell open. She emitted a long moan. Reaching her hands out toward him, she grasped his buckskin shirt in her fists. Her knees buckled and he caught her before she hit the ground.

She lifted her face to the sky. "Oh, God, thank you."

Then she threw her arms around his neck and began sobbing. "My daughter, my daughter."

Standing behind them, Sadie whispered, "Lord have mercy."

John clasped Caroline to his chest, his arms gripping her tightly as tears flowed down her cheeks.

She pushed away from him. "Where is she? Is she all right? I want to see her." Then she walked in front of John and Sadie, swinging her arms. "No, I have to clean up first. I need to comb my hair, change my clothes, and clean my nails."

Caroline looked down at her pants. "Oh, my goodness. I need to buy a new outfit. This old thing..." she babbled on, not seeing the expression on John's face.

He stood motionless, staring at Caroline, not saying a word. *Was she losing her mind?*

She glanced at him and stopped talking. "What's wrong? I can tell by the look on your face there's something else. Isn't there?"

He grasped her by the shoulders. "Sarah was here, but for some reason she and a man named Brady left in the dark of night. Do you know a man by that name?"

Caroline dropped her hands. "What?" The color drained from her face. Her jaw went slack as she stared up into his face in disbelief. "No," was all she could choke out.

She shoved John aside and headed toward the stables. "I want to talk with that young man."

He grabbed her by the arm and pulled her back then stepped in front of her. "Wait. We'll get some answers in the morning. We'll find her. Haven't come this far to lose track of her now." He gave Sadie a pleading look and then a slight nod.

Sadie scurried off to tell the others, leaving the couple standing by themselves in their grief.

"What do ya mean, she's gone?" asked Ben. "She was here and the Army lost her? And, who's this Brady fella, anyway?"

"I don't know. John doesn't have all the information yet. And, quit yellin' at me. It's not as though I sent her away, you trudgy little meadow muffin."

"Ain't gettin' after you, Sadie. It just makes me mad to think we missed that sweet gal."

"Poor, Caroline. The news broke her heart. Let's get those boys to finish settin' up these tents. You go stable the rest of the animals, and I'll see to gettin' supper started. Maybe tomorrow we can straighten all this out."

"Yep, no use in tryin' to get any answers this late. But I'll bet your drawers, Caroline'll be up at headquarters when the commander steps his foot out on that porch of his."

Chapter Twenty-One

Early the next morning, Caroline stormed toward headquarters, stirring up dust with her quick, pounding steps. John pushed himself to keep up with her. Reaching the door, she shoved it open. The room was vacant. Not a stitch of furniture, only paper fragments scattered about the floor. A small mouse scurried out of sight through a hole in the floor.

She threw up her arms. "Where are they?"

John stepped inside. "They've probably moved to better quarters. Let's ask around. Now stay calm."

"Calm," Caroline screeched, reaching the point of hysterics. "How do you expect me to stay calm? First, they find Sarah and then she's gone. To make matters worse, no one knows anything about this Brady fella she left with."

He put his arm around her shoulders and kissed the top of her head. "Now simmer down. We'll find her."

They left the door open and made their way into the center of the parade ground.

"Sergeant, can I have a word with you?"

The soldier hurried over toward John. "Yes, Sir. How can I help you?"

"Where is headquarters these days?"

The sergeant pointed across the way. "They moved over to Bedlam House. Bottom floor. First door on your left."

While John was thanking the soldier, Caroline dashed past the men in a near run. When she got to the door, she grasped the knob and abruptly froze. Wringing her hands, Caroline paced back and forth on the porch

As John stepped onto the porch behind her, he watched until he couldn't handle her hesitation anymore. "Woman, you won't get anything accomplished out here on the porch. This is no time to wait to be invited in."

She placed her hands on her hips and faced him, a challenging expression on her face. "What if—"

"What if? After three years you stand here and ask *what if*, knowing our daughter is out there with a stranger." He grabbed her shoulders with large callused hands. "It'll be okay."

She laid her head against his buckskin shirt. "I'm afraid we'll never find her. If the Army doesn't know where she went or how to find this Castor fella, our daughter will be lost forever."

Pushing away, she stepped back. "Besides, if we did find her, look at me," she said, flinging her arms out to her sides. "I look twenty years older than my age. My hands are rough and my nails are ragged. I look more like a miner than a woman. My clothes smell of animals, sweat, and dust, yet they're clean." She bent her head, tears rolling off the tip of her nose.

"Caroline, Sarah has been living with Indians. Do you think she is dressed in silks and satins?" He waved his hand about the area. "Look around. Most people here are barely surviving. Woman, you've come this far, now get inside and find out exactly what the Army knows about your daughter and where we can find Sarah."

She bit her lip and then patted her hair.

John threw open the door and shoved Caroline inside the room. Then he entered behind her.

As she approached the desk, hat in hand, she hesitated for a moment and then said, "Excuse me."

Sergeant Hodges, startled by the sudden intrusion, asked in an indignant tone, "May I help you?"

The soldier was agitated, but John didn't care. Nothing was important except his woman's state of mind and finding their daughter. "The lady is looking for Sarah Anderson," he said. "We heard that the Army found her. Can you tell us about where she might possibly be right now?"

Hodges lifted one eyebrow and his lips curled. "And who are you, sir?"

"Who the hell do you think I am? I'm her father."

Caroline placed her hand on John's arm to placate him. "My name is Caroline Anderson and I believe—"

"Look, sergeant," said John. "Mrs. Anderson and I have been here before and we've talked with you, so don't try to act stupid. I'm not in the mood. Where is our daughter?"

Hodges filed two more papers, closed the drawer, and faced them. Clearing his throat, he drew himself up and gave them a pompous stare. "The Indian squaw lived upstairs with Lieutenant Garnett and his wife, where she was housed for protection. I would suggest that you leave your names with me and I will give the information to my commander, when he returns."

"The hell we will." John grabbed a fist full of Caroline's jacket shoulder and dragged her out the door.

"Wait," shouted Hodges, "you can't go upstairs unannounced."

"Try and stop us," John yelled over his shoulder, as he pulled Caroline up the newly refurbished staircase toward the Garnett's quarters.

Standing in front of the door to the commander's living quarters, he removed Caroline's hat. "Stand still." He beat the dust off her jacket and handed the floppy covering back to her. He grasped the stray hairs from around her face and tucked them behind her ears. Using the sleeve of his buckskin, he wiped the dirt off the tip of her nose and from her cheek. "There, you look presentable. Now let's see if we can get someone to answer some questions. Are you ready?"

He smiled at her and then pounded on the door with his fist until it swung open.

A Negro woman's wide girth filled the doorway. "Whats you want? You belong downstairs with the rest of your kind. This is no place for the likes of you."

John shoved his way into the room, pushing the woman aside, pulling Caroline in behind him.

"Our daughter was housed here and we want to know where she is." He turned and glared at the woman. "What's your name?"

"Ladesha. Now what was you saying about your daughter?" Shutting the door behind her, the Negress cautiously stepped around the rough looking couple.

"My daughter is Sarah Anderson," said Caroline. "We were told that she lived here with Lieutenant Garnett's family."

Ladesha's mouth fell open and her saucer eyes gave the appearance of seeing a ghost. "You don't say. Well, you just waits here till I get Miz Jane. Don't you two move and don't you go sittin' on the furniture." She shuffled away down the hallway. In a few minutes, she returned following a woman dressed in a blue cotton dress with a wide white collar, not a hair out of place.

"Hello, my name is Jane Garnett." She extended her pale delicate hand and limply clasped Caroline's. "You're Sarah's mother?"

"Yes. My name is Caroline Anderson."

"Oh, my goodness. Mrs. Anderson, won't you sit down. I am so pleased to meet you. I didn't recognize you. Last year I briefly caught a glimpse as you rode by." Seated next to Caroline on the sofa, Jane Garnett asked, "And who are you, sir?"

Sitting gingerly on the delicate velour chair, John answered, "I'm Sarah's father."

"Well, before we begin, would you like some refreshment?"

"Please, water would be nice," replied Caroline.

"Ladesha, get these kind people some water while I try to explain all that has happened in the last few months." She turned to Caroline. "I'm not sure where to begin. There is so much to tell you about your daughter's rescue.

"First of all, there are two things you must know. Your daughter's Indian name is Vision Seeker. I'm sure there is a story behind it, but we never asked any questions."

Ladesha returned and handed John a cup.

"Vision Seeker", repeated Caroline, taking a cup from the servant.

"Secondly...well, this is a little delicate to tell you."

"What?" asked Caroline, moving to the edge of the sofa.

Jane patted her hand. "When your daughter came to live with us, she brought her son with her. His name is Little Feather."

Caroline jerked around to stare at John, his face registering shock. "She has a son?"

"Yes, and he is a lovely child."

Caroline shut her eyes for a moment, placing one hand

over her mouth, trying to digest the thought of her baby having a child. Why, she was only a child herself. She took a sip from her cup. "I'm a grandmother."

"Yez, ma'am," piped in Ladesha, "and my Sugarberry is the sweetest little baby. Big black eyes. Coal black hair. Hmmm, hmm, hmm. He is indeed my Sugarberry."

Jane folded her hands in her lap. "Your daughter is a very lovely young lady. I am sure her life in the Indian village was not easy or pleasant."

Caroline asked, "Do you know where she is now? Please tell me, for my heart suffers so."

Ladesha gave Jane Garnett an 'I told you so' look and shook her head from side to side. She whispered, "Here's we go."

"I must swear you to secrecy. My husband must never know what transpired here. Do you promise? You must promise not to be angry with Lieutenant Garnett."

John sat back and stretched his legs out in front of him. "Don't hurt me none in keeping your secret."

Caroline grasped Jane's arm. "Please, I promise."

Jane looked up at Ladesha, who stood with her arms folded across her ample bosom. "I love my husband dearly, but sometimes he can be such an intolerable fool."

She took a deep breath and folded her hands in her lap. "My dear husband arranged to send Sarah back east on a wagon train."

"He what?" shouted John, jumping up.

"Please be seated and let me finish." Jane went on to tell about the plan she and Ladesha hatched.

Caroline interrupted her and asked, "Who is Mr. Brady?"

"Brady? My dear, I have no idea who he is. Sarah left with Patrick O'Brien."

"Patrick O'Brien. Oh, good heavens." Caroline dropped her cup onto the floor, spilling her water.

Ladesha quickly took off her apron and began moping up the water.

"Are you sure?" asked Caroline. "We traveled with his family from the Gap to St. Charles, Missouri. You mean to tell me he was here."

"Yes. He was waiting for Sarah. From what I've been told by a sergeant, who will remain nameless, they are on their way to Kansas along the Smokey Hill River.

"You see, my dear, she is in good hands, she and Little Feather. I'm so sorry she had to leave the way she did. Sarah wanted to see you and now I am sure you will be on the trail again, searching for her."

John rose out of the chair, grabbed Caroline by the arm to help her up, and handed his cup to Ladesha. "Yes, ma'am. As soon as we can get our supplies together, we'll be heading out."

They said their goodbyes and thanked Mrs. Garnett for her kindness.

Heading away from Bedlam House, John said, "You go on back to the campsite. I have a few errands to do. I'll ask around and see if I can't get a little more information."

As John and Caroline descended the staircase, Jane peeked out the curtain and watched them. Ladesha stood behind her, peering over her shoulder.

"I sure does hope they finds them young'uns. That land east of here is full of Indians," she said.

"With the trail cold and no one knowing where they went, only God will be able to help them." Jane let the curtain fall back into place. "We need to keep them in our prayers, but first we have to get the commander's noon meal ready. He'll be climbing those steps any time now. I saw his horse trotting across the open ground."

"We was lucky he was out riding when they come visitin'."

Jane smiled and put her arm around Ladesha. "Yes, we were. I do believe everything has worked out perfectly." Ladesha gave her a gentle hug. "It sure does."

Chapter Twenty-Two

As Castor reached Horse Creek Crossing, seven painted Sioux warriors carrying weapons immediately surrounded him.

"You must pay to travel through our land, white man. We want coffee, sugar, and rifle."

He looked at the Indians from under the brim of his hat. *From the looks of them, they're as dangerous as standin' bare-assed in a nest of rattlers.* He recognized the leader, Sharp Knife, and smiled. Speaking their Sioux dialect, he said, "I see you are brave warriors protecting your land. I come from Fort Laramie."

The leader grunted and narrowed his eyes.

Castor continued, "I greet you and come in peace. Me and your chief, Four Fingers are good friends from the old days. I wish to talk with your chief. Make some smoke."

The braves talked among themselves while one Indian kept his arrow notched and aimed at Castor.

He sat there smiling and nodding to the Indians. *Yes, I recognize you, Shape Knife. You arrived at the fort with Four*

Fingers back in fifty-one. The treaty the Indians signed with the Army was as worthless as a bucket full of piss.

"We take you to village. See if chief talk with you. If not, you die."

Oh, well, this start is a little different than I expected.

"You lead. I follow." Immediately, the riders surrounded him. "I guess I'll just ride along with you all," he mumbled.

Following the creek bed along the sandy bank, Castor kept a sharp eye on his companions. He entered the village amidst yelling children and screeching women who pushed their way to get close to the stranger. Hands reached up, pulling at his shirt and pants legs. One woman yanked on the lead rope to dislodge it from his hands, others were rifling through his supplies until a man stepped out of his teepee and raised his arm. Then the noise quieted down and the crowd moved back.

"We bring a white man who claims to know Four Fingers," said the leader as he dismounted.

"Bring him closer so that I may look upon his face."

Two Braves pulled Castor off his horse and dropped him on the ground. "You stand," one brave said, prodding him with his moccasined foot.

Castor rose to his feet and dusted off his clothing. "Hate to say you're not hospitable, but..." he mumbled. Then he raised one hand.

"I am Castor, one called White Hunter. I come in peace to smoke with Four Fingers, my friend."

The Chief studied Castor. He walked around him, picking up his hat and then tossing it on the ground. The villagers laughed. The Chief sniffed about Castor's ears, his back, and his hair. Coming full circle to face the white man, the chief put his lips together and nodded. "Him White Hunter. Still smell the same."

"Yep, and you're still missing a thumb. Sure hated to cut that off back then, but it was infected and didn't want to see you die."

Four Fingers held up his hand. Then he smiled. "Come. We smoke."

The drums rumbled and whistles shrilled as men and women hurriedly made their way toward the center of camp, vying for a good seat. When the chief and Castor entered the circle, the Indians quieted down. The ceremony was about to begin.

Castor took a puff and passed the pipe. Once the pipe was slid into the sacred pouch, the stories about the wars and hunts of the Sioux began. He relived the tale about Four Fingers and several braves caught in a snow storm up in the mountains where Castor found them half frozen, and how he saved them from death. When the chief came to the part of his losing his thumb by Castor's knife, the crowd of listeners turned to acknowledge him for his bravery. Minutes turned into hours. There was no rushing the Indians. They prepared food and presented to their guest first. Everyone ate, laughed, and ate more.

When the sun slept and the sky became dark, the Indians built a huge fire. Dancers appeared with their spears and animal skins. Their feet lent rhythm to the drumbeat. Bells jingled and voices echoed through the village as the night wore on.

Finally, Chief Four Fingers rose and the ceremony was over. People made their way to their teepees. "You take Shining Star. She is Red Horse's daughter."

"I see. Ah, my friend..." Castor stared into the stern face of his old friend. "All right. That's fine with me."

A smile crested the old chief's face. "Good. Follow me and bring your woman."

Castor motioned with his head and the young girl followed the two men. Romping all night was not his idea of getting a good night's sleep and Indian women were sexually active to well into the morning. He looked her over. She wasn't half bad. Probably about fifteen. There was an inch scar on her forehead and she was a little plump around the middle, but she was still pleasing.

Inside the teepee, Four Fingers took the side pallet with his wife, giving Castor the place of honor to sleep, against the back wall. Across the teepee, sat a young buck and another smaller boy.

Castor slid off his boots. Then he unbuckled his belt and slid his trousers down to his feet as he mumbled to himself, "This is gonna prove to be an interestin' night." He wasn't wearing any drawers. Naked, he sat down and leaned against the backrest. The Indian woman bent over and pulled off his socks, placing them to one side of the bed. She reached down and grabbed the hem of his shirt, pulling it over his head. Picking up his hat, she tossed it on the heap of clothing.

Slightly embarrassed, he pulled up the covers, undid the backrest, and moved it to one side before lying down.

Shining Star stood, disrobed down to her skin, and slid in next to him. "Now hold on for a moment," he whispered as she squirmed deeper into the covers. "Wait a minute. Ah...let me...ohhhh...damn," he moaned.

In the morning, Castor dressed quickly and headed to the creek to clean up. Laying his shirt over some low-lying brush, he bent over the water and splashed some over his head and chest, trying not to get his buckskin pants wet. Nothing like ice-cold water to wake a man up. He swiped armpits with his wet hands, then stood arching his back and moving his shoulders back and forth to work out the kinks. "This nighttime activity's gonna kill me. Too old to hold my own with anything under thirty. I'm more tired now than when I got here."

Returning to the camp, Four Fingers signaled him. "Come, we eat."

The men sat down cross-legged on the grass near the teepee. Shining Star stepped through the opening with food prepared for his breakfast and a tin cup of coffee. Castor stared into the cup. Something was floating in the liquid. At least it wasn't moving on its own accord.

The chief's wife brought out food and drink for Four Fingers, and then the two women disappeared into the lodge.

"Eat. Makes you strong for more women."

"Right now I don't think I could stand more women."

The chief laughed. "You old?"

"The way I feel this mornin', yep. Ain't had that much exercise since Little Bird."

"Your woman?"

"Yes."

The chief gave him a questionable look.

Castor swallowed hard and pointed west. "She and my son are with the Great Spirit."

Four Fingers grunted, nodded, then continued to eat.

The meal was tasty. Castor wasn't sure what he was eating, some kind of meat and thick, gooey stuff. He gulped it down. Flipping the floating item from his cup, he took a drink. The liquid was so strong that it coated the back of his throat. He set his cup and bowl aside.

"I better be goin'. Need to make a few miles today."

"You not leave yet. Make more smoke and then talk."

"Oh, I'd like to do that, but I have to catch up with some people."

"You stay another night." With that said, the chief pushed up and disappeared into the teepee to retrieve his pipe bag.

"Keerist, I'll never get out of here. These Indians spend too much time smoking and having a good time." He was worried about his supplies and his animals.

Shining Star strolled by.

"Wait. You go check on my gear and animals for me."

She stared at him and nodded her head several times, but never moved.

He tried again. "Go look after supplies and animals," he said slowly, moving his hands away from him to shoo her in that direction.

She nodded again. "Fine."

"What's fine?"

"Bags in teepee," she pointed to another lodge. Then she patted her chest and giggled, "Mine."

"Good grief," was Castor's only comment.

"Animals eat. Safe."

Kneeling down in front of him, she wrapped her arms around Castor. "I take care of man."

"Not now. Man can take care of himself. Woman, there's people starin'."

She laughed, then playfully poked his stomach. Taking off his hat, she ran her hand through his hair. Then she brushed the dirt from his buckskin shirt.

His only thought was to escape fast before she became a permanent fixture. What he didn't need right now was a woman tagging along on this journey. He wasn't ready for that kind of permanent situation. Castor leaned forward, pushed her gently backward, and rested his elbows on his knees. This was going to be a long day.

In the late afternoon, the drums called everyone together. Castor watched the children arrive first with their wild, playful antics. Their wrestling, shoving, and scuffling in the dirt attracted no attention from the parents. Men and women scurried into the area and quickly sat in a circle to enjoy the day's activities.

Today would be another day of smoking, laughter, and stories. When would it all end? He looked at Four Fingers who sat down beside him. He couldn't just walk away from the village and insult the chief. It might mean his scalp. You could only be so unfriendly to an Indian. They never forgive or forget an insult.

The events started with hunting stories of bravery and feats of strength. Castor listened to each man's experience as he took his turn, one outdoing the other. The afternoon dragged on with small breaks and more eating. When nightfall arrived and the big fire was ignited, drumbeats reverberated through the valley. Shrilling whistles and shaking rattles reached deep into the soul of all the participants. First, the men performed the antelope hunt dance. Strength in number grew when the women joined the frolicking. Soon people of all ages were twisting and turning. They circled the fire to the beat of the drums in frenzied gyrations.

Exhausted, Castor's eyes shut and his head drooped. An elbow nudged him in the side. Waking with a start, he grinned at his old friend.

Four Fingers stood and the activities ceased.

Castor pushed up and struggled to his feet. Both legs were asleep and pained him. He shook out one then the other. Shining Star remained on the edge of the great circle across from him, waiting for her man. She beckoned him with a wave.

"Go. She waits for you. Sleep her teepee tonight." Then the chief disappeared into his lodge.

Castor brooded. Tomorrow he was leaving no matter

what. Matter. He wondered how his sweet mule was getting along, penned up with the horses. He could relate to the mule's confinement.

As he strolled up to Shining Star, she tittered and walked in front of him, showing the way to her teepee. Holding up the flap, he stepped into the lodge to discover her mother and father lying together under their robes. They stared at the white man's abrupt appearance.

He felt uncomfortable, a stranger in someone's home. Taking off his hat, he nodded to them. Indifferent, they cuddled closer and pulled their cover over their bodies, turning their attention to each other. *With Little Bird, at least we were married. Don't think I will ever get right with all this freedom.* He dropped his trousers, showing his white backside and pulled off his shirt, before crawling under the covers.

Shining Star undressed and joined him, snuggling close. She ran her fingers along his rib cage and up across his chest.

Castor closed his eyes, experiencing a warm glow inside his body that grew into a flickering flame.

"Oh, Jeez," whimpered Castor. He clutched her shoulders and arched his back, knowing she had total control over his body.

Later, Castor lay still listening to the woman at his side soft breathing. Everyone in the teepee was asleep. Slowly, he moved from under the robe, picked up his clothes, and rolled them into a ball. Naked as a Blue Jay, he made his way to the teepee opening and stepped outside. A quick brisk breeze chilled him, causing him to shake.

Stars still littered in the sky. Silence settled over the village. He dressed hurriedly. The morning was cool but he sweated. The chief ordered Castor to stay in camp, and his sneaking away was a grave insult to Four Fingers' hospitality. If caught leaving without a formal goodbye to the chief, his life could be in danger, as well as his scalp.

While most of his belongings hung over the pole racks outside, the rest of his trappings, including his saddlebags, lay on a skin next to the teepee where he stood. Grabbing up his personal items, he cautiously made his way to the pen to locate his horse and mule. Once he saddled Daisy and loaded the supplies on Matter, he led them both out, skirting the village. At a safe distance, he mounted Daisy and made tracks toward the east. He needed to put some distance between him and the Indians. Since he took nothing other than his own things, they wouldn't follow him, but he wanted to be on the safe side.

By the afternoon of the next day, he made his way through Robidoux Pass. He was three days behind Patrick and had no idea where in Kansas the two pups headed. All Castor could do was head south after Windless Hill and hope to locate their trail.

As he rode each day, his mind flitted back to Shining Star, remembering how agile her hands were in rousing him. The smell of her skin still filled his nostrils. It wasn't until he reached the border plateaus that he realized how much he missed the warm body of a female. The more he thought about the native woman, the more he wanted to turn back to get her. It wasn't love, it was purely need. The very thought of her caused his buckskin pants to tighten in his groin.

As he stared up at the sun, warm hazy memories of his wife drifted through his mind, as a gentle breeze licked his face. What would his life have been like if Little Bird and their son had lived? Would he have spent so many years as a scout for the Army or would he have settled down in Texas, bought some land, and raised cattle? Loneliness filled his heart.

Isolation from all other humans took a toll on him as the heat of the day beat down upon his shoulders. Sticky perspiration covered his body. His legs and butt chafed as the wet buckskin rubbed against his skin with each slap of the saddle. His life was changing and he had no idea where it was headed. He knew one thing for sure, he wasn't going back to work for the Army.

He yanked on the lead rope to his mule. "Come on, Matter, we've got some adventures to share. Just you, me, and Daisy." He patted his sorrel. His two best dependable friends. What else could a man ask for?

Shining Star?

Chapter Twenty-Three

Heading eastward, Patrick led Sarah though the rugged, western Kansas, following the plateau's uneven rocky ground, until the landscape began to flatten out slowly, one mile at a time. Along the north edge of the riverbank, they stopped every so often to water the horses.

Pulling the brim of his hat down to shade his eyes, he scanned the horizon. "I see a few buildings up ahead," he said. "Some type of settlement. We'll stop and ask questions."

As they rode into the camp of sod huts, two soldiers eyed them suspiciously. Dismounting, from his horse, Patrick hailed a man, "Can you tell me where we are?"

"This God forsaken place is military camp number 39. You crossed Lost Creek a-ways back."

Patrick looked around. The men were loading furniture, papers and other items onto the back of wagons.

"You moving out?"

"Yes. They're closing us down."

"Who's in charge here?"

"Captain Benjamin Norris. He's down there," pointed the private.

"Thanks." He turned to Sarah. "Follow me."

She rode behind him as he walked through the thick dust, leading his horse.

The captain stood outside a wider hut that probably housed two rooms, his arms loaded with papers. His head jerked up when he spied Patrick heading his way. He squinted into the sun. "Hello. What can we do for you?"

"I'm Patrick O'Brien and this here is my woman, Sarah. We were looking for a minister. Thought maybe we could find one here, but looks like you're moving on."

"The Army decided to close down this camp. We're to report to Fort Leavenworth before the end of the week. As far as I'm concerned, the field mice and prairie dogs can have this place"

He dropped the papers into a box on the back of the wagon, and brushed his hands together knocking off the dust. "The traveling preacher left here yesterday, heading south toward a little place called Yostville. Nothing much there except a few squatters. However, Reverend Pattywacker is always saving souls. If you ride on out, you'll be able to catch him." The captain chuckled, looking over the couple. "He'd be happy to see the likes of you two."

"It's getting kinda late to hit the trail again. Could we spend the night in one of your buildings?"

"Sure. You can bed down in the last hut on the far end. Would you like to join me for supper? Nothing fancy, but it's filling and warm. Mostly beans."

"We'd like that."

"Good. Sergeant, show these people to the last soddy down there on the right."

"Do you think the Reverend will stay at Yostville?"

"He won't leave there until he visits every last squatter. You have plenty of time."

Patrick thanked the captain, touched the brim of his hat, and followed the sergeant.

Before daylight gave way to the gray blanket of night, Patrick and Sarah joined the captain. Three seven-foot tables and benches were set up outside on the scruffy grass to accommodate the small group of soldiers. A private built a large fire to take the chill away from the cool night air coming across the prairie.

Under the scrutiny of several soldiers, Sarah propped her son's cradleboard against one table leg. No one mentioned the baby, but the look on every face expressed disdain toward her. She lowered her eyes and took a spoonful of beans.

A soldier placed a plate of beans and cornbread in front of Patrick. His belly growled. The heavenly smell of warm food made him hungry to look at it. He dug in as though he hadn't eaten in a week.

"There's more from where that came from," said the captain. "We may not have much of a selection, but we have plenty of beans and cornbread."

"Yep, everyday," piped up a sergeant. "Every stinking day."

Patrick watched Sarah suppress a grin. She didn't say a word, but he knew she was listening.

The captain talked about how dismal his camp was and how hard it was to get provisions delivered. "I submit requisitions and it takes nine months to a year to get the supplies filled and out this far. Here we are protecting the western border, watching over the squatters, keeping peace among the natives, and all headquarters can do is push our list to the back of their files. And when they're finally delivered, we don't get everything we order. Take the cats, for instance. This place is overrun with field mice. You can't even sleep in peace without one of them bedding down with you. Requested cats six months ago and we're still waiting. We won't be needing them now.

"I am glad to be heading back to civilization. We've only been here two years, and it was a worthless assignment." He grumbled some more, as each man at the table put in his two cents, nodding his head or making small mumbling comments.

When the meal was over and everyone had eaten their fill, the captain pulled out a cigar and lit it.

Sarah decided to leave the men to their smoking and probably more serious discussion about the conditions in Kansas. She strolled over to the fire, picked up a flaming stick to light her way, and headed into the pitch-black night toward their quarters. She carried Little Feather, who slept soundly, but he'd be awake soon. It was past his feeding time.

When she was well out of sounds reach, Captain Norris leaned forward. "You really going to marry her?"

"It's none of your business," growled Patrick, "but yes, I am, as soon as we catch up with Reverend Pattywacker. She fell on some hard times, not of her own doing, and I plan on being with her as her husband."

The captain nodded. "Well, head east toward the settlement. About a good two-day's ride, you'll come across the Hopkins place first. Nice enough fellow. Has his family with him." The captain took a puff off his cigar. "Not much out there in this Godforsaken prairie except Indians, rats, and snakes. Watch out for the Arapahos. They're teaming up with the Sioux and several other tribes. They aren't mean yet, but there's war in the air and when the Indians aren't happy, the white man suffers."

Patrick perked up at the mention of the Arapahos. He needed to avoid them at any cost, if for no other reason than for Sarah's safety. "Thanks for the information."

"I thought I'd warn you, what with that healthy head of hair you're carrying around and being white, you'd be the first candidate for a scalping. Those long locks would look good on some brave's shield."

The men talked and smoked a while longer.

As Patrick listened to the conversation, he knew what he had to do. *At first light, we'll leave for Yostville and the good Reverend Pattywacker.*

As she approached the hut, Sarah thought about the lonely prairie and what life would be like. The land was close to what the Indians camped on and faces of people from her past haunted her. Dark Moon...Plenty Hoops Woman...Running Swift.

Reaching the soddy, she ducked through the opening and felt her way into the room, holding the stick out in front of her. The musty smell filled her nostrils. Stumbling against a tiny side table, she found two candle stubs and lit them. Dark shadows danced about the room as the flames flickered, then she jabbed the handle of the lighted stick into the dirt floor for more light. Slowly, she looked around and extended her arms shoulder height. The room measured the length of four arms by four arms. A cot barely fit against the length of one bare wall. There were no windows and the floors were hard-packed dirt.

Slipping the cradleboard from her back, she hugged it to her chest. Her son opened his eyes and smiled. She placed him on the cot and undid the lacings to get free him. Slipping her dress up, she began to feed him. When he finished, she snuffed out one candle and lay down next to him, her back to the wall, clutching him to her side. "The mice may be free at night to run across the floor, my sweet one. But they will not be sleeping with you."

Memories of her youth invaded her thoughts, keeping her from sleep. "My son," she whispered. "Let me tell you of a time long ago. I remember a cabin, comfortable and warm. Behind it, ran a shallow cool creek that came from the springs in the mountains. My little brother and I played in the water, splashing with our bare feet over the rocky bottom. It was nothing like this flat brown prairie where you will grow up. Green covered mountains grew tall and surrounded the valley, like the protective arms of a mother. Trees reached to the sky and filled the slopes like warriors, standing shoulder to shoulder. Flowers nestled on the ground and blanketed the valley floor, their fragrance riding with the breeze. When the mountain laurel was in bloom, it was as though angels brushed your nose with their sweet scent." Tears slid down her cheeks.

She brushed her wet lips on his forehead. One small hand rested under her chin. Looking at him reminded her of a young boy from her past. "My brother ran through the fields chasing butterflies and rabbits. I would join him, thrashing through the woods after imaginary enemies. Now he is gone." She swallowed hard. "He drowned in a river on the trail, east of here. I loved him."

She clenched her jaws. Tears trickled from her closed eyes, down across her cheek. A slight moaning sound escaped her lips, as the heart rendering memories filled the shadows of her mind.

"And my mother...chases shadows, searching for me."

She glanced up.

Patrick's frame filled the doorway. He had been watching and listening to her. He strolled to the cot, knelt down and wiped the tears from her face with the sleeve of his soft buckskin shirt. "I promise we will find your mother. And, I vow, I will spend the rest of my life making you and Little Feather happy." The he leaned over and kissed her.

He sat on the edge of the cot, took off his boots. Wedging in next to her, he laid his arm across her shoulder, trying not to crush the baby. Rubbing the top of her shoulders, he said, "Now sleep, we have to leave before first light."

Toward mid-morning, three days later, Patrick sighted wisps of smoke lazily rising from the chimney of a lone soddy. As they rode closer, a couple of chickens pecked at the ground. A cow was staked a small distance from the house and two horses penned in a makeshift corral. The outbuildings consisted of a lean-to built off to one side of the soddy and a makeshift building that probably served as a barn.

A woman worked on a patch of dirt in a small fenced-in area, scratching at the ground with a hoe. By the time Patrick and Sarah arrived at the house, the entire family stood ready to greet them.

"Howdy, friends. Come on in and sit a spell. Are ya thirsty? Want somethin' to eat?"

After dismounting, Patrick shook hands with the man. "I'm Patrick O'Brien and this here's my woman, Sarah. We wouldn't mind some sweet water."

The woman hustled into the house with her two girls, while the boys stood next to their father, watching the strangers.

"You young'uns take care of those horses for these nice folks." Turning back toward Patrick, he said, "My name's Hopkins. Peter Hopkins and my wife Serelda. My first-born, over there, is Thomas and that other one is Sheldon. The two girls helping their mama are Missoura and Illina. The one on the way we haven't named yet."

Pulling up a chair in the shade of the overhang attached to the soddy, Hopkins motioned for Sarah to sit. "This here is the best chair we got. You rest a spell. Mama will be out soon. Missoura, you bringin' out those drinks for our guest?" he hollered.

Sarah took a seat and relished the cooler shade. Her face felt red. She wiped her forehead with her arm. Perspiration trickled down the back of her neck. The heat was oppressive and it wasn't even noon. She released Little Feather from his cradleboard and put him down in the dirt.

After corralling the animals, Thomas and Sheldon returned, playfully shoving each other.

"Quit, Thomas. Stop that pushin'. You two go drag out a bench so as we can sit."

The boys disappeared inside and returned, struggling with the bench through the doorway, hitting the doorjamb.

"Turn it this way," yelled Thomas.

"Quit telling me what to do," replied Sheldon. "You're the one that's causin' the trouble."

Patrick walked over and gave them a hand. He picked up the bench by himself and carried it out to find what shade he could.

Sheldon shoved Thomas'shoulder. Thomas stuck his foot out and tripped his brother.

Hopkins raised his hand and pointed to a spot on the ground. "You two boys sit down right there and behave yourselves. Always a pokin' and shovin' at each other."

Patrick laughed. "I have a younger brother, Joshua, who enjoys wrestling all the time."

"Well, then you understand children. These two constantly have to be a doin' somethin', especially when there's work to be done.

Hopkins and Patrick took a seat.

"Missoura!" her father called.

"Comin', Pa." The young girl returned with two tin cups of water for their guests, and then ducked behind her father, peeking from around his shoulder.

Illina stuck her head around the doorframe, sucking her thumb. She spied the baby and ran to him. Crouching down to face him, she tried to pick him up by grasping him around the middle. He squealed and grabbed her hair with both fists.

"Let go," she yelled. She fell onto the ground with Little Feather hanging on to her hair. She tried to release his fingers as she squealed in pain.

Sarah jumped up and managed to open his hands. "I am sorry. He loves to pull hair. Are you all right

"Yes, ma'am," she sniffled. She ran to her father.

Hopkins picked her up and gave her a kiss on the forehead. "She'll be fine."

"Pa," said Missoura. "Mama wants to know if you want another chair."

"No, it's broken. She can have the bench."

Sarah stood up. "I'll take the bench. The girls can join me."

Hopkins motioned to Patrick. "You want to join me on that stack of sod. It's better than sittin' in the dirt. Besides, it's the only shade you'll find around here." He sat down and leaned against the wall of the soddy.

Serelda Hopkins appeared carrying two more water cups and handed one to her husband before she waddled over to the chair and took a seat

"When is your baby due?" asked Sarah.

"Very soon."

"Who will be here to help you?"

Ms. Hopkins turned to her husband. "He helped birth the last two, but they didn't live."

"I am sorry."

"Life is hard out here. But, now the boys are bigger, they'll be helping their pa."

"There's a widow woman a couple miles east of here who'll come over when my wife's due," piped in Hopkins.

Missoura looked up. "I'll help."

"Me, too," said Illina, proud to be part of the conversation.

"Well, you are big girls and I'm sure your ma appreciates your help," said Sarah, bouncing her son on her knee as he wiggled to extricate himself from his mother's grip.

"Excuse me," said Patrick, "but have you seen Reverend Pattywacker?"

"Oh, he rode through here real fast about four days ago. Didn't stay long. Thought our kids needed savin'. I think after seeing this bunch, he decided to try elsewhere. Guess he is over at Grizzlies' about ten miles due northeast of here. They got seven kids. But I wouldn't stop there. Not what you would consider friendly folks."

With his question answered, Patrick changed the subject to homesteading and squatters claiming rights.

Hopkins became very excited and animate in his gestures as he described the possibility of getting a land grant. "The news is, they're gonna open this land up for homesteading next year. Hear tell, a man can claim a hundred and sixty acres. We've already got ours staked out. I mean, we have squatter's rights here where our soddy's built and all the improvements we've made."

Hopkins continued his story about the land.

Finally, Patrick stood up and shook Hopkins' hand. "Thank you for the hospitality. We need to be pushing off. Would you boys be kind enough to get our horses?" He nodded to Serelda and touched the brim of his hat. "Ma'am."

"Come on back and visit any time," said Serelda.

Once mounted, he asked Hopkins, "Is there a place to stay in Yostville?"

"You can ask for the Hendricks place. They're located further east of the settlement. You can't miss it. There's only a general store with a bar in the back room, and a hut that serves as a jail and meeting place. Not much else, yet. But it's a growin'."

Patrick thanked him, and then headed east. He wanted to reach Hendricks' cabin before dark.

As the sun slipped into the western horizon and the shadows became long, Patrick rode through Yostville, passing the two small buildings. In the distance, he spotted the Hendricks' house.

Dismounting in front of the cabin, he laid his reins over the rail and strolled toward the open door. As he approached the doorway, a woman inside shouted, "What do you want?"

Patrick answered, "We're looking for the Hendricks' place. Peter Hopkins told us that we could possibly get a room for the night."

"Ya found it. Come on in."

Standing in the doorway, Patrick waved for Sarah to join him.

A young girl sided up to Patrick. "Who are you? You're dressed funny."

"We don't see many people dressed in buckskin around here. It's mostly homespun." Mrs. Hendricks stared at Sarah. "Is your woman an Indian? Never saw one with red hair before."

"No, she's not a native. Do you have a room for the night?"

"Yes. You pay up front. A dollar a night and no paper money." With that said, she stuck out her hand, palm up, waiting for her payment.

Patrick reached into his shirt and pulled out a small pouch.

After he put several coins into her palm, she said, "Now you come sit on this bench. I have to get your room ready." She disappeared into the back area.

Several minutes later, she reappeared. "Follow me. My daughter will take care of your horses. We have a small corral out back. That'll cost you more. This room is small but adequate. If you're looking for meals, that'll cost, too."

"We would appreciate at least breakfast in the morning."

"Will you be staying long?"

"Don't know," answered Patrick. "We'll let you know tomorrow."

She lit the lantern on the table and turned to leave. "You'll have to see to your personal belongings and other supplies. My girls only take care of the animals. By the way, I don't want to hear that baby crying all night." Then she shut the door behind her.

Sarah looked about the room.

"I know it's cramped," said Patrick, "but at least there's a large enough bed for a good night's sleep," he reached up and touched the ceiling, "with a roof over our heads."

The bed almost reached from wall to wall, leaving very little walking space. One small table was the only other piece of furniture in the room.

"There are no dirt floors." Sarah laid the cradleboard on the bed and untied the lacings, freeing Little Feather. She sat him on the floor. He immediately rolled onto his stomach, got up on his hands and knees, and began to rock back and forth. "He is getting too big for his cradleboard," she said, placing it against the wall. "We need to make a travel basket for him."

"Tomorrow we will figure something out. Right now I have to see to our things."

Later that night as they lay in bed together, Sarah nestled her head against his chest, her arm thrown across him.

"Sarah, I've been thinking. We could stay right here near Yostville. I know there isn't much to see, but the land will be opening up next year. We could stake out some land east of here and build us a soddy with two rooms. People around here are friendly enough and they don't seem to mind that we are a different couple."

She didn't answer.

"Maybe by the time Little Feather is ready for book learning, this will be a town with a church and a school. Why, you could teach the children to read and write at our home. There is so much we can do out here without prejudice, restrictions, and hatred."

"And the Indians?" she asked.

"That's one thing we can't control. We'll have to depend on our luck and my rifle."

"Let us speak of it again tomorrow. I am tired and there is much to think on."

"Tomorrow, then." He shut his eyes and immediately began snoring.

Sarah understood why he was excited. It was the land...his land. Maybe this would be a good place to settle down. She would give it more thought tomorrow after they found the minister. But, tonight she needed sleep.

Chapter Twenty-Four

Mrs. Hendricks place a platter of eggs and meat on the table, one of her daughters brought in the fried potatoes and the other one set down two tin cups of coffee. Patrick paid Mrs. Hendricks and then dug into the vittles.

They didn't talk much. Little Feather crawled about the room seeing what he could get into until the two little girls spied him. They collapsed on the floor near him and began to play.

"Don't let him get close to your hair," Sarah said. "He'll pull it."

Mrs. Hendricks returned from the kitchen with cup in hand and joined them at the table.

"So what have you two decided to do? You gonna travel on or try your hand here? Sure could use the company of another woman around."

"I do believe we are going to look a little east of here and stay around." Patrick shoved in another fork full of food into his mouth.

"Good. My name's Pleasant."

"Nice to meet you. I'm Sarah."

"I'm Patrick." He extended his hand. "Glad to meet you ma'am."

"My man's name is Annanias, but he answers to Nat. He's out right now but he'll be back tomorrow."

"Do you know if Reverend Pattywacker will be back around soon?"

"Oh, yes. He only left because Nat was gone. Been after my husband for months, trying to talk him into accepting the Lord. That's a waste of time if I do say so myself."

She took a swig of coffee. "You two gonna get yourselves hitched?"

"Yes."

"Well, sho' fly, if that ain't the best news I heerd lately. A wedding right here. Can you beat that, girls. We'll have to get that roaming minister back. He'll be tickled pink to have something to do."

The two girls joined their mother on the bench.

"This here's my oldest, Charity. And the youngest is named Sophia after my ma."

Charity slid off the bench and joined Sarah. "Are you an Indian?"

"Charity, don't ask any questions."

"That's all right. No, I was on a wagon train a long time ago and was kidnapped by Indians."

"Ya don't say," said Pleasant. "Now that's something to think about."

Charity peeked around Sarah. "Is he an Indian?"

"No," answered Patrick, "I'm just a man in buckskin."

"Oh," She quickly lost interest and slipped off the bench. She straddled Little Feather and pulled him away from the doorway. Her sister, Sophia jumped off the bench and joined her sister on the floor.

"Those two surely do love babies. We had one about two years ago, but he died of consumption. Terrible time for all of us. Nat was really sad to lose that young'un."

Mrs. Hendricks continued to talk while Sarah and Patrick settled back drinking their coffee. She told them all the gossip about each of the six families living around the area.

Two weeks later, the minister returned and stopped in at the Hendricks.

"Hello, ma'am. Has your husband returned?"

"Yep, he's out back cuttin' wood. I wouldn't go bothering him while he has an ax in his hand. You sure do rile him up."

"Oh, yes. Never bother a man working. Might I rent a room from you for a few days?"

"The room is rented, but you can sleep in the barn out back. It's comfortable and safe. Course, the price will be the same since you'll be taking meals."

"You're quite right. The barn will be adequate."

"By the way, we have a young couple staying here. They want to get hitched."

"My goodness. What wonderful news. Where might they be now?"

"They're out lookin' over some land. They'll be back soon. Sit yourself down and I'll get you some coffee."

The reverend took a seat on the bench, placing his hat next to him.

"Won't this be a great event? Our first wedding in Yostville. Why, I think it's about time we start thinking about building a church here."

Pleasant almost dropped the coffee pot at that statement. "I do believe you have to wait until the homestead sets in.

We don't want the army dropping by to run us all off. There's only a few families within fifteen miles around here and we're all trying to stay low."

She set the cup on the table and placed a piece of bread on a plate for the minister.

"Thank you that's mighty nice. I did miss breakfast. You're right about staying low. I almost forgot."

Annanias Hendricks stuck his head in the back door. His wife quickly waved him away.

Charity ran inside to announce that Patrick and Sarah could be seen riding in.

Reverend Pattywacker gulped his coffee down, picked up the last half of the bread, and grabbed his hat. He hotfooted it out the door to wait for the young couple.

Sarah's hand shook as she unbraided her hair. This was her wedding day and she was as nervous as a scared rabbit. As she reached for the comb, she knocked it off the bed. She bent over to retrieve it.

"Well, I see you're almost ready," said Mrs. Hendricks, standing in the doorway.

Sarah straightened up quickly.

"I didn't mean to startle you. People are coming in from all over to witness this event. We don't have many exciting times around here, mostly births and deaths. Here, let me help you. You're as nervous as a cat."

"Where is Patrick?" asked Sarah.

"He's outside with my Nat, setting up benches and chairs for people to sit on. I saw Serelda Hopkins outback, resting in the shade. I'm surprised she's here with that baby due any day now. That wagon trip musta jostled her from kingdom come."

"She's here? I'm surprised, too."

"You know, we women have a harder time here than the men, but we're sturdy. Maybe she's prayin' the birthin' will happen while she's in town. There's enough women here to help out."

"Pleasant, how did you come by your name? I noticed you hesitated when you introduced yourself."

"Well, my pa was happy when I arrived. I had seven brothers. When he saw I was a girl, he said 'what a pleasant surprise.' So, the name stuck. Do you need any help getting dressed?"

"I am going to wear this doeskin dress." Sarah reached into her parfleche and retrieved a turquoise hairclip.

"My goodness, what a lovely hairclip. Where did you ever get it?"

Sarah turned the clip over in her hand. "From a very kind lady."

"Here, sit down and let me fasten it for you. This is going to look beautiful in your auburn hair." Pleasant snapped it into place and fluffed Sarah's hair across her shoulders. "What is that grass doing on the bed?"

Pleasant reached for the offending item, but Sarah grabbed her hand. "Don't. It was a cross before someone ruined it."

"Who ruined what?" asked Patrick. He stood in the doorway, blocking the light. "Let me see that."

Sarah rose and handed the mangled cross to him as he entered the room

Sensing the young couple needed privacy, Pleasant excused herself. "I do believe I need to peek in on my girls to be sure they're watching your son. You won't have to worry about him. He'll be in good hands."

Patrick nodded and then turned to Sarah, holding the

grassy item in his large hand. "You kept this with you all these years."

"Yes. You gave it to me back in Missoura and told me one day you would come for me. You kept your promise."

He closed his hand and stuck the cross in his pocket. Then he turned on his heels and headed for the door. "I'll be back in time for the ceremony. Meet me outside by the reverend."

Sarah took a deep breath, patted her hair one more time, and strolled outside. She made her way among the benches and chairs, hoping to find some shade.

Having heard the news about a wedding, people arrived by horseback and wagons, bringing baskets of food. Others mingled and chatted with each other as the tables filled with goodies to eat. All were strangers, dressed in their Sunday best, who came to party and celebrate her marrying Patrick. Many nodded and smiled as they passed her, but no one stopped to talk. She felt alone and lost in a world she was trying to recapture.

Next to the log cabin walls, she found some shade and leaned against the building, waiting for Patrick. Tapping her foot to the tune of 'Whiskey in the Jar', Michael O'Brien came to mind with his squeezebox. Patrick's father was a loud boisterous man who loved his music.

Nervously, she twisted the fringe on the sleeve of her dress. A dog meandered up to her, sniffed her left leg and trotted off. On the other side of the tables, the minister stood talking with a couple, all the while patting their young son's head.

Her life was about to take a different road and she was uncertain where it would lead. As she stood there, she tried to remember Running Swift's face, but all she could see were shadows. Time had taken its toll on her life as a warrior's wife.

The oldest Hendricks' girl ran up to Sarah. Charity shyly handed her a hair wreath made of braided flowers. "This is for you to wear. My sister and I made it."

"Thank you." She placed the wreath on her head and smiled at the young girl. "The gift is perfect. It makes me feel special."

The girl grinned and then dashed away.

Sarah spied Patrick briskly rounding the corner of the cabin. "Don't you look pretty? Flowers and everything."

"Are you two ready," shouted Reverend Pattywacker, pulling at his collar. "It's getting a mite warm standing here waiting on you, young man. The sun's straight up."

"I'm sorry to keep everyone waiting. Had something to do," Patrick said.

"Well, I wouldn't think there was anything more important than your own wedding. Let's get started."

Looking down at her upturned face, he raised one eyebrow and grinned. "I believe everyone is waiting for us."

She nodded.

He grasped her hand and headed toward the minister. "We're ready."

"Good. Now come stand over here and face me. All right, everyone, gather round and let's get started before the heat finds us. Where are the witnesses?"

Pleasant and Annanias Hendricks walked forward.

"Let's begin." Reverend Pattywacker opened his Bible and nodded to Jimmy John.

The old man pulled his harmonica from his pocket. "Well, don't be making any long winded speeches."

"You play that mouthpiece of yours, Jimmy John and leave the preaching to me."

Jimmy John joined the other two musicians and played his harmonica with the only song he knew, *Nelly was a Lady.*

The minister squinted his eyes at the old man and made a face, before he opened his Bible. After reading a verse, he spoke a few words.

Patrick looked at Sarah and winked.

Finally, the minister asked for the ring.

"I don't have one, but I do have this. He pulled a leather thong threaded through the loop of a tiny gold cross from his pocket. Slipping it over Sarah's head, he said, "This will have to do until I can get you a ring."

Folding her hands, she rested her chin on her thumbs. "Oh, it is beautiful." Tears filled her eyes.

"I brought it all the way from Missoura for you. It took me a while to find it in the saddlebag."

"That will do just fine." Reverend Pattywacker cleared his throat and asked, "Wilt thou, Sarah Anne Anderson, take this man to—"

"Yes," she whispered.

"It's *I do*," he reminded her. "Now you two seem to be in an all-fire hurry."

"I do," she repeated.

Patrick turned toward their friends who stood around silently watching them. Taking Sarah's hand, he covered it with both of his. "I, Patrick Michael O'Brien, take this woman, Sarah Anne Anderson, to be my lawful wife from this day forward. I give her this cross in token of my love and devotion, for she is a good and honest person who I have loved for many years. I also take Little Feather as my son and will raise him the best that I can." Then he looked into her eyes. "And I will call him *son*."

"Well, there isn't much more for me to say, except, I pronounce you man and wife." The minister closed his Bible. "I believe we are quite finished."

The fiddler took his cue and played *The Wild Rover*, as people clapped their hands, keeping time to the music.

Patrick bent his head, cupped her face within his hands and gently kissed her on the lips. "Welcome to my world, Mrs. O'Brien." Then he wrapped his arms around her and clasped her tightly to his chest, kissing her deeply.

When he released her, she whispered, "I love you."

Pleasant Hendricks banged a spoon against a pot. "Okay everybody. We've set out a few eats. There's prairie chicken, relishes, wild plum sauce, and bread. We also have three cakes. So, come help yourselves. I could use some assistance from the women to get these drinks out to the tables. And, don't anyone touch that whiskey until later."

"Did I hear whiskey?" Jimmy John rubbed his hand across his mouth and dashed toward the tables to be first in line.

Someone shouted, "Pass the hat. This young couple needs a start. Don't be shy now. Every little bit helps. If ya don't have any coins, potatoes and onions will do." Everyone laughed as the hat passed through the crowd.

"Don't forget. After you eat, we've lots of dancing to do."

"And whiskey to drink," shouted Jimmy John.

People stepped up and shook Patrick's hand.

"Congratulations."

"Good luck."

"Hope your years ahead are good."

As they spoke to Sarah, she shyly nodded and said, "Thank you."

After the last person moved away, Patrick placed an arm across her shoulder. "I think we should rescue our son from those four lovely girls over there. He looks to be more than the Hendricks and Hopkins girls can handle."

Sarah giggled. "Yes, I do believe our small brave has them looking for help."

Patrick strolled over and picked the boy up. Tossing him in the air, Little Feather squealed. Holding the child in his arms, he smiled down at Sarah. "We're a family now. I've acquired a wife and a son, all in one day."

"I need help here," shouted Pleasant. "Someone get this woman into the house. You two women, get the water boiling at my fireplace. I need some of you men to get four of these chairs back into the house and get some boards to lay across them. Hurry, we have a baby that's impatient to be born."

Annanias Hendricks picked up Serelda while Peter Hopkins hurried into the house with two chairs. Several women rushed behind him. Jimmy John grabbed a handful of food, stepped back against the logs, and watched all the activity.

"Sarah, have my girls show you where some rags and cloths are. You children, stay outside." Then Pleasant shouted at a man shouldering a board, "Take it inside, you loggerhead. Can't wait all day for you to decide what to do with that."

In the cabin, Mrs. Hendricks still shouted orders. "No, no, not there. Push those chairs together more and lay the lady down. All right, all you men out, scoot. We women can do the rest of this here birthing without you getting in the way."

Patrick held onto Little Feather as he watched the door shut.

Annanias Hendricks patted him on the back. "Give that little fellow to the girls over there and join us behind the store for a drink of whiskey. Got a couple of jugs in the back room just waiting for an occasion like this. The young'un will be okay. This might be a long night."

Jimmy John hotfooted down the dirt road.

"Whiskey's the key word for Jimmy John and he doesn't care how far he has to go for a drink. He's always the first to show up. That old coot's gonna die one of these days drinking all that rotgut." Nat waved. "Come on Pete, join us. You should know by now how long it's gonna take this baby to appear, this being your seventh and all."

Then he whispered to Patrick, "He's nervous. They already lost two at birth."

"I know." Patrick pursed his lips together. His thoughts flitted to Sarah. *Will she be able to handle having a baby out in this desolate area?* His mind eased as he watched Little Feather crawl in the dirt.

Peter Hopkins trudged toward the two men, hands in his pockets. "Hate to leave her. She's getting' too old for bearin' kids."

Annanias chuckled. "Then you better start sleeping in that shed you built or add a lean-to onto your cabin. And quit pokin' her."

"Come on, let's get us a drink before it's all gone." Patrick strolled down the dusty road toward the store.

Hours later, Pleasant opened the cabin door and yelled, "Annanias Hendricks, get yourself over here and say hello to your new son. You men can quit your drinking now." She wiped her hands on her bloody apron, untied the sash in the back, and stepped back inside.

Sarah took the last of the dirty towels and rags out the backdoor. A few stars overhead beckoned her into cool evening breeze that tickled the waving grasses. Night crept in as the gray sky hugged the land on the western horizon.

Her wedding day...she wanted to cry. It was nothing like she dreamed of as a little girl. Where were the pretty flowers, the strong man who would ride up and carry her away in his decorated buggy? No one she knew attended the ceremony: no parents, no brother, no neighbors. All were strangers in a strange land, and she married a man she hardly knew, but one who never forgot her.

Looking down at her chest, she grasped the cross between her thumb and finger. "Now I have a real cross to wear instead of the grass one he made me."

Smiling, she brought the necklace up to her lips and kissed the cross. "Forever," she whispered.

Chapter Twenty-Five

Castor followed the narrow beaten trail north of the Smoky Hill River, through the Kansas plateaus and into the flat prairie lands. After his meeting with the Sioux at Horse Creek Crossing, he was cautious, constantly looking over his shoulder and across the horizon in front of him. He was in Arapaho territory and didn't want anyone sneaking up on him. His wares weren't gold or silver, but he knew the Indians could use the coffee, sugar, salt, and blankets he had packed on his mule.

"You know, Matter, the darn sun baring down on a man sure makes a body mighty uncomfortable. August is always hot here. Think I prefer the mountains any day."

To his right, he caught a glimpse of a movement in the tall grasses. He slipped his rifle from its sheath, laid it across his lap, and kept moving, all the while keeping a good eye in that general direction. What he didn't need was any surprises. Keeping his horse at a good trot, he glanced sideways without moving his head. There it was again.

He patted his horse. "Daisy, we could be in for a challenge here real soon. Can't make out what that is. But, I swear I saw an arm."

Suddenly, the mule stopped dead in his tracks. "Matter, now isn't the time to be contrary. Come on, girl," he coaxed, pulling on the lead rope. "Let's get out of here before you're soup and I'm dead."

As he talked to the mule, he saw a head rise above the grass tops and bob back down. Raising his rifle to his shoulder, he searched the horizon and took careful aim. He sat there ready, waiting for a clean shot.

Not seeing any more action, Castor slipped from his saddle, rifle in hand. Crouching low, he made his way circling the spot he had seen movement. As he got closer, he heard a soft noise, as though someone was in pain. Dashing forward, he raised his rifle ready to shoot, brushing the waist high grasses aside with his body. He waved his rifle from side to side covering as much area as possible looking for any assailants that might pop up. As he turned to his left, he tripped over a dark rock in front of him. His rifle fired and he landed on his back. The rock moved.

Jumping to his feet, he grabbed a handful of garment. An Indian woman curled in a ball, raised her head. Her face was bloody, her hair matted with dirt and debris, and her body shook.

She mumbled and touched her parched lips. Raising one arm, she wrapped it around his calf. "Ah," she groaned, and then doubled over onto the ground.

Picking up his rifle, he ran back to his horse, grabbed a canteen, and returned to the squaw. Hunkering down beside her, he lifted her head and let her drink small sips. Then he helped her to sit. Holding her up, he gently used one hand to brush the hair from around her face.

Speaking Sioux, he asked her name. No response. Then he tried Arapaho. She nodded. *Well, at least she understands me.* He asked again, this time in Arapaho.

"Plenty..." she said, coughing between words, "Hoops... Woman."

"Why are you out here by yourself? Where are your people?"

"Husband dead. Baby dead. I die."

He stared at her once pretty face and realized that many years ago, he felt that terrible pain and anxiety when Little Bird and his son died. His heart turned cold, a little each day without them.

"Well, we can't have none of this." He lifted her into his arms and carried her and the canteen back to his horse. Putting her on the ground, he hung the canteen on Matter. Then he hoisted the woman onto his saddle and mounted behind her.

Castor continued following along the river on an easterly path. After an hour of riding, the woman's moaning got louder. He decided to stop and make camp. He searched for a place along the river by a clump of trees.

Dismounting, he found an even spot and stomped some of the grasses down to make a bed for her. Then he gently pulled her off his horse and laid her down. He took the saddle from his horse and placed it under her head to make her comfortable. She gave him a weak smile.

"Sleep, I'll be back soon." He followed the river and found dried buffalo chips he needed. He returned and dug up the grass in order to bare the ground for a small fire. He added the dried twigs he had gathered from around the few trees that shaded the area to the buffalo chips. The Indian woman was fast asleep.

Pulling some of the hot coals to one side, he set the coffee pot to heat. Castor laid out his bedroll, and then grabbed some jerky. "Not much to eat. Maybe I need to shoot me something fresh."

Grabbing his rifle, he headed back into the grassy area, taking his time to trudge through the hip-high growth. In front of him was an area of low growing vegetation. He spied an unlucky rabbit and fired.

Back behind him, the woman screamed and screamed. Grabbing the dead rabbit by the ears, he dashed back to the campsite. He raised his rifle, ready for an attack. Plenty was on her hands and knees, wild eyed, rocking back and forth, and chanting. Seeing him with the weapon, she raised her hands in front of her face. "No kill me. No kill me," she screamed at him.

Putting his gun and rabbit down, he approached her, saying, "Friend. Help you. Food. I hunt."

She clasped her hands to her chest. "`*Oo.* `*Oo.* Yes. Yes."

He sat down next to her and enclosed her in his arms. She tried to pull away, but he was persistent by patting her head and speaking low. "Friend. I won't hurt you. Friend."

She laid her head against his chest, tears streaming down her face.

"I will not harm you, Plenty Hoops Woman." He pulled her into his lap, cradling her in his arms.

When his arms fell asleep, he laid her down on the grass mat and covered her with his blanket. He sat there watching her breathe evenly, wondering what terrible events caused her to be out on the prairie by herself.

Finally, he decided he better attend to his animals. He led his horse and mule to a small stream for water. Then, he tethered them in the tall grass, close to the campsite. He removed the coffee pot and laid the meat on the hot coals, turning them ever so often.

Later after Plenty woke, he dusted the ash off the food and fed her. Then she fell back to sleep.

Castor sat by the fire, wondering if her loneliness and heartbreak would ever go away. He poured himself another cup of coffee.

As he watched the fire flicker in the soft breeze, his mind went over the last few days of his marriage to Little Bird. How happy she was to be pregnant. She was so sure they were to have a son. At first, the delivery went well, then complications set in and the midwife in the village could do nothing to save his wife. When they brought out his son, tears filled his eyes. He raised his son to the heavens. "I will protect this small one, Little Bird." But, he could not even keep that promise. By morning, his son had also passed away. He burned them both on a tree scaffold together according to her belief. Even now, the pain in his heart was deep and lasting. Downing the last of the dregs from his cup, he banked the fire, lay down, and pulled a blanket over his shoulders.

When he woke in the morning, Plenty sat cross-legged on her bedding, staring at him, hands in her lap.

"You been up long?"

She nodded.

"Hungry?"

He stirred up the fire, added a couple of chips, a few pieces of dried wood. Once the coals were hot, he set the filled coffee pot on them to heat while he made ashcakes.

She crawled into the high grass to relieve herself. Back on the blanket, she stared across the prairie. "Nothing left. Look to Great Spirit to take me. He never come."

He nodded. After pouring a cup of coffee and dusting the ashes off the cake, he handed them to her, along with a handful of cold rabbit. "Eat. You will feel better."

"Not better, ever." She took the food and drink, only nibbling at the rabbit.

"Eat. You will travel with me and we need to leave soon."

Her head jerked up, mouth open. "Why you want me?"

He only shook his head as he ate. The only answer he could give her was destiny. She might understand that answer, but he didn't feel like sharing it with her. No matter how he looked at it, she was here.

After eating, Plenty went to the river to wash. She sat in the grasses next to the bank and ran her fingers through the coal-black tresses that fell to her waistline. Carefully she parted her hair with her fingernails and skillfully braided each section.

Castor packed the supplies on the mule. As he saddled Daisy, he kept a constant eye on the woman. He admired her strength and her ability to bounce back from the state she was in last night. She was a beautiful woman, filled out in all the right places. Her deep brown eyes, saddened with pain, haunted him. She had asked him 'why do you want me?' Why was he taking her along with him? He told himself he couldn't think of leaving her to die a lonely death in the prairie. Was that the real reason?

With great effort, Plenty got to her feet, and made her way back toward Castor. As she grew closer, she stared into his face. It was as though her eyes could see into his heart. Not watching where she was walking, she stumbled. He rushed to her side and lifted her to her feet. She raised her head. Placing one finger on his top lip, she drew along the edge, resting the tip of it on the bottom lip. He licked her finger.

"You are a good man."

He raised his hand and cupped her cheek. "Thank you. You are a beautiful woman."

She backed away from him, pushing against his chest.

He smiled. "I'll do you no harm." Then he flicked a stray grass from her braid. "Come. We need to ride." He climbed into the saddle and then extended his hand to help her up.

Castor rode with the Indian woman behind him for the next two days. On the third day, a small settlement appeared on the horizon.

"Looks like civilization to me. Maybe we can buy some supplies." He noticed Plenty was a bit edgy, but she didn't say a word.

A farmer driving his team and wagon toward them, hailed Castor. "Where ya from?" the man asked.

"Fort Laramie. What's the name of this here place?"

"Yostville. Not much right now, but when the land opens up soon, it'll become a town."

"You wouldn't have heard of a Patrick O'Brien coming through here, would ya?"

"Sure enough. He and his woman got married a little over a month ago. They live on the other side, about ten miles east. You a friend?"

"Yes. Thank you." Castor tipped his hat and rode on. As he approached the general store, he remarked to Plenty, "Not much here. It needs a lot of growing. I'm gonna stop and you can join me inside if you want."

She shook her head and pointed. "I sit." An old chair was propped up against the store wall in the only shade around.

Once the supplies were packed on Matter, Plenty and Castor rode on east, heading away from the settlement. They traveled about five miles out. Night was coming up quickly so he selected a spot down by the river, off the road.

She gathered wood and buffalo chips, while he prepared supper. After eating, they sat around the fire drinking their coffee. She extended her cup. "Sugar."

He reached into the bag and gave her another pinch.

"Why you take me with you?"

"Well, you asked me that before. I don't have an honest answer except I couldn't leave you behind." He took a sip from his cup. "I could feel your pain and it brought back memories I buried many years ago."

She sat silently, waiting for him to tell his story.

"My wife and son both died. She was Shoshoni. They are buried in the mountains where we lived."

"My heart is sad for you. Deer Hunter was my husband. Pawnee come, raid village. He and baby son die." Her eyes filled with tears and she lifted her chin. "My heart cries for them."

"Yes, the pain remains for a long time, but eventually the memories fade. We need to get some sleep. Tomorrow we ride out early to visit my friends."

As they approached the soddy, Castor hollered, "Hello. Anybody home." He dismounted and helped Plenty down.

Patrick threw open the door and stepped out. "I can't believe my eyes. Castor, you old scoundrel. Whatever in the world are you doing here? Sarah, come on out and see who's here to visit us."

He grabbed the scout's hand and pumped it. Then he spied Plenty. "Who you got traveling with you? Didn't know you had a woman." He nodded to her. "Glad to meet you."

Sarah stepped through the doorway and stopped short. Shock registered on her face. "Plenty Hoops Woman," she shouted.

Plenty ran to her and embraced her, crying in Arapaho. "My sister."

"Well, I'll be darned," said Castor. "They know each other."

"Sure seems that way. Come on in. We were just sitting down to eat breakfast. Better yet, help me move the table outside. Sarah, can you and your friend manage to get the benches out here?"

After Plenty and Sarah served the food and brought the drinks to the men, they sat down to listen to the conversation.

"All this as far as the eye can see will one day be ours. I plan on filing a homestead claim against it when they open it up to settlers. In the meantime, we got a soddy built to protect us right now. But, I'll be hauling in some logs from east of here to raise a cabin probably next spring. Don't think I can do it before winter sets in."

"What's your hurry? Looks like your home is comfortable and room enough for the two of you."

Sarah smiled and placed her hand on her stomach. Plenty understood and grinned. Then she hugged Sarah.

"Oh, I see. When is the baby due?"

Patrick smiled sheepishly, "You'll have to ask Sarah that question."

"Late spring," replied Sarah.

"I guess I'll stay around to help you build that cabin. Then if you don't mind, Plenty and I will share your soddy."

"Better, yet," said Patrick. "I'll help you build a dugout in the bluff north of here."

"Suits me fine," replied Castor.

Plenty looked at Castor and then to Sarah, who explained what the men were saying.

"He wants me for his woman?" she asked.

"I don't know," said Sarah. "He said you would share our soddy with him."

Castor glanced at Plenty. "I will protect and care for you as long as you want to live with me."

Sarah translated Castor's statement.

Plenty stared straight ahead for a moment and then nodded once.

"Does Lieutenant Garnett know you were headed to Kansas?" asked Patrick.

"Nope." Castor smiled at Plenty and then turned to face Patrick. "Everybody back at the fort thinks I'm headed to Texas to start a cattle ranch."

Patrick glanced at his wife. "Did Mrs. Anderson ever show up?"

"Nah." Castor paused a moment. "Sorry Sarah. I couldn't stay around there anymore. Left the Army and now I'm a free man."

Patrick looked at his wife. "Don't worry. One day your mother will find us or we'll find her. Until that time, Castor has come our way with his woman. Glad to have you stay, my friend."

Chapter Twenty-Six

The night showed no stars and the moon hid behind the clouds as thunder rumbled in the mountains west of the campsite.

Ben sat in front of the blazing fire, watching Caroline and John, waiting to hear what the Garnett's had said about Sarah. He took another piece of rabbit from the skewer and chewed the meat off the bone.

"These rabbits you boys caught this afternoon are mighty tasty."

"Standing Tall shot one of them with his bow. I got the other two with my rifle. His almost got away, hopping with that arrow stuck in its butt."

"No, I hit target."

"You had to club that poor thing to put it out of its misery."

Standing Tall gave a backhanded swing at Micah. "You lie. You tell them truth."

Micah ducked.

Ben threw the bone at the boys. "Next time it'll be a

bucket of water I toss at ya. You two are worse than a couple of girls."

The boys stopped and glared at Ben.

Micah shouted, "We are not—"

"Girls?" finished Standing Tall, jumping to his feet. "I am not a girl." He pounded his chest. "I am a brave." Then he stalked off.

"Well, now you've gone and done it," piped in Sadie.

"What? I only told the truth. These two pups are always a-fightin' and carryin' on. Young whippersnappers. Can't wait 'til they grow up. One of these days, one of 'em is gonna get hurt and I don't want to see that."

"Why you miserable old gopher. You got a soft spot in your heart after all."

"Humph, ain't neither. There's nothin' soft about me."

"How about your ass?" Sadie said, poking his bottom.

John roared. "She's got you there, Ben."

"I've been sittin' in front of this here fire all night awaitin' ta hear what you learned about Sarah, all the while my *ass* is falling asleep. So," Ben propped his hands on his crossed legs, leaned forward and stuck his chin out, "I'm awaitin'."

John glanced at Caroline.

She nodded. "We first went to headquarters and they told us that Sarah had been living with Lieutenant Garnett and his wife. So we went to visit them."

John picked up the rest of the story. "Mrs. Garnett told us that the commander had planned to send Sarah back east on a wagon train before we got here. Mrs. Garnett was upset over that, so she helped Sarah leave with a young man she knew."

"What?" shouted Ben. "You mean to tell me the commander... Why that sonofabitch."

"Ben, watch your language," chided Sadie, feigning innocence. "There are two ladies present."

Ben placed the side of his hand on his forehead, above his eyebrows and looked around. "Where?" he murmured.

"You old duffer." Sadie jabbed him with her elbow. "You're sittin' next to one."

He smirked, but didn't say a word.

She turned to Caroline. "Did she go off with that Brady fella?"

Caroline tried to explain the mix-up in the names. "It wasn't Brady, but O'Brien." She told about her trip west with the O'Brien family, the death of the father in St. Charles, Missouri, and Patrick staying behind to care for his mother and siblings.

"So," she continued, "Patrick came out here and stayed a whole year, waiting to find Sarah."

"Now, isn't that sweet," said Sadie.

"Have to say, he sure is a determined young buck." Ben reached for the last piece of rabbit. He looked up to see if anyone objected. When no one looked his way, he bit into it.

"So, what happened?" asked Sadie.

"Yes, what happened?" Micah leaned forward.

John spoke up, "O'Brien left late at night with our daughter and her son."

Ben choked on the meat he was chewing.

Sadie pounded his back. "Well, what do ya know? Sarah's a mother. That makes you grandparents. Congratulations."

Caroline beamed and nodded.

John sat silent, smiling.

"When are we gonna head out and find them?" asked Ben. "Where are they headed? Does anybody know?"

John poured himself a cup of coffee. "Talked with a couple of soldiers who heard that they're headed to the Kansas territory along the Smoky Hill River area. It's a bit rough on

the western border, from what they said. Seems the Army
sent a couple of patrols out that way a few months ago to
settle some Indian troubles. The sutler told me the land is
pretty rugged there, but further east, it's more fertile. I think
Patrick is headed in that direction." He glanced around for
Standing Tall.

"Look. Caroline and I talked this over. The trip might
get a little rough and we'll be on the road for several weeks.
We thought maybe you and Sadie might want to stay here at
Fort Laramie."

"What?" shouted Ben. "Why, you young whiffet. You
want to leave us behind."

"After all we've been through together," finished Sadie.

"You're not leaving them, are you?" asked Micah.

"We go together," said Standing Tall, who returned to
the group circle.

"Yes, we all go together." Micah got to his feet and stood
next to his friend. "Ben and Sadie are family."

John held up his hands for silence. "Enough! I didn't
say we were *leaving* them behind. I asked if they wanted to
stay here. This traveling is rough on them."

"Young man," said Sadie, shaking her finger at him, "you
let us decide when we've had enough. It's not the travelin'
that bothers me, it's this old man that drives me to drink."
She leaned over and whispered in Ben's ear. "By the way,
where's that bottle you promised me."

Ben gave her one of his sly grins and threw her a couple
of smacky kisses.

"If that's all you want, you little piece of chicken
droppings, the whiskey is cheap."

Ben cackled, "I guess I should've asked for more."

John took a drink and set his cup down. "Here's the
plan. We'll spend tomorrow getting all of our gear mended,

supplies purchased, and anything else that needs tended to. We have one day to get our business straightened away. Then, the following morning, we'll follow the Oregon Trail east. Once we get far enough out, we'll turn south toward territorial Kansas and the Smoky River. No way should any of us breathe a word of where we're going or who we're looking for."

"Everybody will know who we're lookin' for," replied Micah.

"That doesn't mean we have to agree to what they think they know. There's one more thing. We were told an Army scout helped Patrick and Sarah in their escape. I believe his name is Castor. Jim Castor."

"Jeez, I know him," Ben shouted. "He's a right sorta fella. I beat him in a card game right here at Fort Laramie. Had a winnin' hand and no money to cover the bet. Remember, Caroline, you staked me with a watch."

"Yes, I remember. He wasn't too happy to lose to you."

"You play your cards the way they fall. That's the way it is. Not my fault he had a losin' hand."

"The rumor is, this Castor fella is headed to Texas. It's a shame he didn't stay around so that we could talk with him." John pushed up from the ground and dusted off his trousers. "We need to bed down. Tomorrow's going to be a grueling day. Micah, you bank the fire. Standing Tall, go check on the animals."

He extended his hand to Caroline and pulled her to her feet. "The rest of you get some sleep."

Two days later, before the sun rose to kiss the prairie good morning, John and his fellow travelers crossed the Laramie River and headed east on the Oregon Trail. He led the group past wagons circled for protection, all waiting for the day to push west over the mountains. No one stirred, for the morning was still young. He was happy to think they were leaving the fort behind, before anyone noticed they were gone.

He glanced over his shoulder to check on the supply horse behind him. In the moonlight, he could make out the rest of his group. Heads bobbed and bodies swayed to the rhythm of each horse footfall. The trail would be easy for the first half, so he hoped to make twenty miles today. The only stops he wanted to make during the day were for water and the noon meal.

When they reached Horse Creek, blood-curdling yelps greeted them as they approached the west side bank. John started to ease his rife from its sheath.

"No," shouted Ben. "Let's see what they want first."

"I thought the Indians were friendly. Well, they ain't gettin' my hair," said Sadie, pulling her hat down to cover her ears.

Seven Sioux braves surrounded the travelers, making John a little nervous. Ben held up his hand as he made his way to the front.

"How. We come in peace," he said in their language. "We wish you no harm, only to pass through the water and travel on."

"You speak truth?" asked the head warrior.

Ben held up his hands, "I raise no weapon to you. We have our women with us."

The Indian looked at the two women, then spied the Indian boy in back. "He prisoner?"

"No. He is his son," Ben said, pointing to John.

The Indian squinted his eyes and looked suspiciously first at John and then at Standing Tall.

"You," said the brave, nodding to Standing, "you his son?"

"Yes," answered the boy. He walked his horse up next to John. He sat tall in the saddle to prove he was an equal.

"Hmm." Ignoring Standing Tall, the warrior rode forward to Caroline. "Red hair like sun. See other woman with red color."

Ben's ears perked up. "You saw another woman with hair like that."

The Indian nodded. "In moon of red cherries."

"What's he saying?" asked John.

"He told me that he saw another woman with red hair like Caroline about two months ago, about mid July."

"Ask him if a man was with her, tall fella with long, dark brown hair."

Ben relayed the question.

The Indian nodded and smiled. Pointing east, he said, "Go that way."

"He said..."

John stopped him short, "I understood that answer. Is he going to let us pass?"

Ben talked with the brave. "He wants coffee, blankets, sugar, and a new shirt."

"John, it's worth the information he gave us. We now know that Sarah and Patrick passed this way."

Ben and John dismounted. Reaching up into the pack animals, they unloaded a small portion of everything the Indians had requested, including one of John's shirts. They handed the goods to three smiling braves who eagerly received the bounty, while the other four stood guard.

When they were allowed to leave, Sadie exclaimed, "I really thought we were gonna die back there. Them Indians weren't at all friendly lookin'."

"Sioux strong warriors. They fight mean," said Standing Tall.

"But they told us about Sarah, and I, for one, feel they earned the items we gave them." Caroline was happy and now anxious to push forward. "How much further until we turn south into territorial Kansas?"

"Many miles," answered John. Turning to Ben, he said, "Women. First you're traveling too fast, then not fast enough."

"I think you need to look back this way," piped up Micah.

John turned around. "Ben. Without turning around, look behind us, about a quarter mile back. We've got some Sioux braves tracking us."

"Oh, my. Maybe they want all of our supplies." Sadie glanced back, and then turned to Caroline. "Honey, don't you worry. We'll get where we're goin'."

Ben adjusted his hat. "This here gray hair is mine and I aim to keep it."

John stared straight ahead. "Keep on riding. Maybe they'll give up and return to their camp."

"Do you think they want to go with us or ambush us?" asked Micah.

"No ambush," replied Standing Tall. "They watch us. Want horses."

As night fell and the campsite was established, John sat drinking his coffee and talking with Ben. "The women are tired."

Ben glanced sideways at Sadie. "She's already asleep."

"So is Caroline."

"Where're the boys?"

"They're checking on our shadows. I hope they're careful."

Micah and Standing Tall appeared out of the darkness and hunkered down by the fire next to John. They poured themselves a cup of coffee.

"Well?" Ben asked.

Micah took a sip from his cup. "They're still out there. They didn't build a fire and tethered their horses west of the campsite."

John dumped out his cup. "Tonight we sleep light. We'll set up a watch. I'll be first. Standing Tall, you relieve me once the moon gets high. When you get tired, wake Micah. We need to keep a close guard on our horses and be vigilant to any movement or sound we hear."

Ben drew up his chest. "What about me?"

"You need to get everyone up in the morning and watch over the women. Now, everyone get a good night sleep while you can."

Chapter Twenty-Seven

Ben crawled over and shook John. "Wake up," he whispered. We got company about 300 feet out. There's two in the bushes to your right and two to your left, a-creepin' up on us."

The sky still held the stars and the sliver of a moon, but a soft rose hue spread across the eastern horizon.

John yawned. "Where are the boys?"

"Lying over there in the tall grass with rifles ready.

"Don't wake the women just yet."

"We're awake," said Caroline in a hushed tone. She lay behind him, holding a revolver, ready for action.

"Then you and Sadie take cover behind those two trees over there and stay put."

He crawled toward the boys. "What's going on?"

"I spied them," said Micah. "They've been watchin' us for about a half an hour. Now they're movin' closer a little at a time. They know we saw them." He tapped Standing Tall on his shoulder and pointed to his left.

"I see," he whispered. "They want horses."

"Well, they ain't a-gettin' them." Ben stumbled to his feet to retrieve his rifle from behind him.

A shot rang out.

Ben tumbled backwards about four feet. He dropped his rifle and grabbed his right shoulder. "Keerist. I'm hit."

Sadie screamed and scrambled to him. "Oh my precious man. Don't you dare die on me. Ain't come this far to lose you now."

"You women take care of Ben. Boys, hold your fire until you can get a good shot, but keep your heads down."

Micah fired. A yelp followed the blast. "Got one."

As Ben lay in Sadie's arms, he spied a movement in the grass. "To your left, Standing Tall."

Before the Indian boy could fire his rifle, another Sioux warrior gave a war cry, leaped into the area, and tackled John. He tried to reach his weapon, but the Indian held him by the throat and a tomahawk in his hand. Quickly, John grabbed both of the brave's wrists. They fought hand to hand, rolling on the ground and across the dying embers of their fire.

When the warrior eased back and raised his weapon, Caroline took careful aim and fired her revolver. The warrior looked surprised and then fell face forward on top of John.

He shoved the dead man off to one side and gave Caroline a half smile. "Good shot."

She tried to smile. The gun shook in her hand.

He crawled over toward the boys. "We have two more to worry about. Now, stay down. Do either of you see them?"

"One was to my right," said Micah, "but I don't see him anymore."

"Stay put. He'll show himself soon."

John's head jerked up when he heard the whinny of horses in the distance. "Hold your positions. They're leaving."

He lay there a few more minutes. Nothing. "Everybody up, we need to pack up and get out of here. They'll be back to collect their dead and we don't want to be here." He turned to face Ben. "Can you ride?"

"Yep. A small scratch."

"Small scratch, my ass," retorted Sadie. "Let me take a look at that arm. Now, lie still and quit movin' around, you hairy gopher."

She removed his jacket and shirt from the injured arm, much to his chagrin. "There's no hole in back so the bullet must still be in there. The bone seems to be intact."

Sadie placed her hand over the area to apply pressure. "He's got some bleeding, but I'm gonna pack the wound. Now hold still, you ornery old polecat." She ripped several pieces from her petticoat and bandaged Ben's arm tightly.

John nodded toward Standing Tall. "Get Ben's hat and take out the bandana. We'll make a sling for him."

Ben grimaced as she tied the sling around his neck, pulling the arm upward and across his chest.

John picked up Ben's rifle. "We gotta get moving." He turned to Ben. "We'll make a stop further down the line and remove the bullet."

"No use in doin' that. I can ride."

Sadie glared at him. "You want to die of blood poisonin', you contrary ole fool?"

"What's the sense of diggin' it out? It doesn't hurt much."

She gripped his wounded arm.

"Ow! Dang-nabit, Sadie. Did ya have to do that?"

"Humph. Don't hurt much, huh? At the next stop, we're takin' that bullet out, with or without your help. And, I ain't wastin' anymore breath on ya."

They mounted their horses quickly. Sadie climbed into the saddle behind Ben.

"Why do we have to ride double? I'm fine, woman."

"Move up, give me a little more space, and quit flappin' your gums."

An hour later, John called a halt. "Standing Tall, take care of the horses. You have first watch. If you see anything, let me know. Micah, go get some water. Caroline, start a fire so that we can sterilize my knife."

John walked toward Sadie. "How's he doing?"

Sadie slipped off the saddle while John held Ben upright. "It's a good thing I rode with him. He passed out right after we hit the trail."

"We can only make a short stop so let's get that bullet out. We need to put more miles between us and those Indians, in case they change their minds."

John tugged on Ben. He fell off the horse and into John's arms. "Set up a place for him, Sadie."

She got a blanket and spread it on the ground.

John laid him down. "Goodness. He weighs more than I thought."

Sadie shook him. "Ben, wake up. I'm gonna need that whiskey bottle you keep hidden. Where is it, Ben? "

He opened one eye. "Whiskey? You ain't usin' good whiskey on this arm. No sirree."

Sadie stuck her face right up to his, nose to nose. "Ben Wilson, you tell me where that bottle is or I'll rip off your arm. Then you won't have to worry about a little old bullet."

He gulped. "It's in Micah's saddlebags."

Micah retrieved the bottle and handed it to Sadie. She gave the boy the evil eye.

"I didn't know it was there," he protested.

When the small fire blazed, John put his knife into the red coals. "Boys, we might need your help. Hold him down so he doesn't move. We don't want Sadie doing something other than removing a bullet."

She held the bottle to Ben's lips, pausing ever so often to let him come up for air. As the liquor trickled down his chin, she wiped away the drops. When he got close to the bottom, she removed the bottle.

He gave her one of his charming grins. With his speech slurred, he asked, "Ya got anymore?"

"Enough to clean your wound and a swallow for me to steady my nerves."

She leaned over and whispered into Ben's ear. "I'm tellin' you one thing, old man. This swallow of whiskey isn't gonna save your hide. You still owe me a full bottle of the good stuff."

He smiled and then burped. "Sure, Sadie girl. Soon." Then he passed out.

She took a deep breath, lowered his head to the blanket, and reached toward John for the hot knife.

John opened Ben's mouth and stuck a leather sheath between his teeth for something to bite on.

The boys knelt down next to Ben and pinned his legs and arms down, giving Sadie plenty of room to work.

She looked at each one of them and nodded.

Sadie cleansed the area around the entry wound with whiskey, and then she gulped the last swallow for herself.

"Ready," she said, leaning over Ben to retrieve the bullet.

After she was finished, Sadie looked at his sleeping face and ran her a finger across his chin. Tears trickled down her cheeks. "Can we rest here a spell?" She looked up at John. "Maybe an hour?"

"Good idea. Why don't you women pull out some food? We can eat while we wait."

Caroline sat with her knees up to her chest, her arms hugging them. She rested her head and closed her eyes.

John strolled over behind her. "We'll make it and find Sarah."

Her head jerked up. "I'm not worried."

"Yes you are." He sat down beside her. "And, I don't blame you."

"I was thinking back to everything that has happened since we left California. It's been one experience after another. Sometimes it's been good, other times it's been bad. It's never an even, happy line. When will we settle down?"

He rubbed her shoulder. "I promise, when we find Sarah, we will settle down near her and—"

"And what?"

He took a deep breath. "Maybe even get married."

"Is that a proposal, John Anderson?"

"Ah," he nodded his head gently several times. "I think so."

"You think so?"

"Well, it's probably the best that I can do. Never proposed to a woman before. Darn, never took a woman serious before. When I watched you shoot that Indian back there, I realized I didn't want to lose you. You might have been killed. It scared the jeezus out of me." He looked down at his boots. "You know I, well..."

"Having trouble saying what you want to say, John?"

He gave a funny, embarrassed laugh. "Yes." He touched her face and then cupped her chin. "I love you, Caroline. Will you marry me?"

She grinned, reached up and pulled his face toward her. Then she kissed him. "I've waited a long time for that proposal. Didn't think you had it in you."

"Neither did I."

"What proposal?" Micah asked. He stood straddle-legged in front of them, hands on his hips.

John chuckled. "He doesn't miss much does he? I asked Caroline to be my wife."

"Hey, everybody, I'm gonna have a ma," Micah shouted as he did a shuffle, swinging his arms about

Standing Tall's face turned to stone.

"You, too, snake lover. We're gettin' a mother."

The Indian boy smiled. "We need a woman."

Offended, Sadie asked, "What do you boys think I am, cow dung? I'm a woman."

"Nope," said Micah, "you're our grandmother."

"Oh." She grinned from ear to ear. "You hear that. I'm the grandmother." Her eyes welled up with tears. "I've never been a grandmother before, or even a mother."

"Don't cry, Sadie. We didn't mean to hurt your feelings," said Micah.

John laid his head in Caroline's lap. "Sadie is just happy, boys. I think you touched a soft spot in her heart she didn't know she had."

"What's Sadie cryin' about?" asked Ben. He tried to sit up but pain caused him to moan.

"I ain't cryin', I'm happy. Now lie down, you drunken sot."

"Oh, you sound real happy."

"I'll have you know, John just proposed to Caroline."

"Well, I'll be," replied Ben. "I must be drunk."

"When are you gonna make me an honest woman, you bundle of sweetness?" Sadie gave him one of her come-hither smiles and fluttered her eyelashes at him.

"You got something in your eye, woman."

"No, I'm waitin' for an answer," she replied, briskly.

"Ah, Sadie. I'm happy the way things are."

"Don't *ah Sadie* me. I've been carin' for you, cookin' your meals, doin' your wash. At least you could give me your name."

Caroline egged Ben on. "Why don't you tell us your full name, Ben?"

John sat up. "I guess Ben is short for Benjamin, right?"

"I don't think so," said Caroline.

"Woman, I'm sorry we ever had that talk on the trail to Californy." He gave her the evil eye. Three years ago, he made the mistake of telling Caroline his full name and swore her to secrecy. Now she was stepping over the line. He rose up on his good elbow and glared at her. "Remember, I rescued you and got you out to John as you asked me to."

"Ha! I had to bribe you with my dead husband's watch, you miserable vagabond."

Micah said, "Now you sound like Sadie."

"Well, we're all waitin', you adorable little rascal." Sadie tickled him under his chin.

"This is gonna be good," whispered Micah to Standing Tall. "He ain't likin' to tell us so it's got to be bad."

Ben cleared his throat and mumbled his name.

"What, I didn't catch that," said Caroline.

"Neither did I and I'm sittin' right next to him. Spit it out, you chawed piece of tobacco."

"Alluissius Nebednego Potter Wilson," he shouted. "Are ya happy, woman?"

Sadie's mouth gaped open. "Ya don't say." Then she reached over, patted his cheek, and kissed the top of his head. "That's quite a name you got there, Bennie. I'd feel real important wearin' that name."

"Ya would?" A sheepish grin spread across his face. "How about that?"

"Darn," said Micah. "And I thought mine was bad."

"What is your full name?" asked John.

"Micah D'Lafayette Pere de Sauze Anderson."

"I always wondered what your mother named you. I'm only sorry I didn't know about you before I left St. Louis."

"She named me after my grandfather in New Orleans."

Caroline put her arm around the boy. "Micah, she loved you enough to give you her father's name. That should mean something to you."

"Someday I'd like to meet him and tell him what a wonderful person my *maman* was."

John placed his hands on his hips and stared at Micah. "I think that's a great idea, son."

Standing Tall tossed a clump of dirt in the direction of the warm embers. "Where is mother now?"

"She died about five years ago. She's a star in the sky like your ancestors."

Both boys smiled.

John stood up and brushed the dirt off his pants. "Enough talk. We need to be heading out since Ben is awake. You boys get the horses ready. I'll take care of Ben, while you women gather our things together."

Caroline saw the pain in John's eyes. She knew he felt remorse for not shouldering the responsibility of raising Micah. But his mother wasn't the only woman that John had left behind. She was a casualty, too. How was she going to explain to Sarah that John was her father and not Alexander? She took a deep breath. *I'll cross that bridge when I get there.*

Chapter Twenty-Eight

Patrick heard horses approaching behind him. He smiled knowing it was probably Hendricks and a few men coming to help him build one of his outbuildings. He set down his saw and turned around to face a ragtag group of dusty travelers riding from the direction of the settlement. They were too far away to make out their faces, but he knew they weren't his neighbors. He shielded his eyes from the sun with his hand, then looked to be sure his gun rested on a log two feet behind him.

A woman dismounted and strolled toward him. She smiled. When she removed her hat, red hair tumbled to her shoulders. "Hello, Patrick."

Startled by the voice, he stared at her. "Can it be? God, Almighty, it's Mrs. Anderson. How in the world did you ever find us? Where did you come from?"

He took three giant steps toward her, wiped his hand on his trousers, and extended it.

She grasped his hand, shook it, then threw her arms around his neck. "How are you, Patrick?"

"Caroline," said John, embarrassed for the lad. "Don't smother him."

She released him and stepped back, wiping the tears from her face with the sleeve of her shirt.

"I'm fine ma'am," he replied. "How about you?"

"Right now I'm tired, hungry and happy to see you."

"Forgive me for my bad manners. Won't you all come on in? Sarah isn't home right now, but she'll be back soon."

"How is my daughter?"

"She's fine Mrs. Anderson. I'm sure she's gonna want to see you. Sarah has suffered a lot, her ordeal with the Indians and the people at the fort. I've never seen her happier since we left the fort," he looked at Caroline from under his eyebrows, "even with the baby and all."

She gently placed her hand on his arm. "Rest easy, Patrick. I know about her son."

"His Indian name was Little Feather. But we've changed it to James Alexander.

Caroline beamed. "That's a lovely name."

Patrick continued, grinning from ear to ear. "He's smart, too."

"I see that you've settle into fatherhood quickly."

"Wait till you see him. He's starting to crawl. What a handful. You have to be careful, he eats everything off our dirt floor. That's why I've got to get a cabin built in the spring."

John slipped from his horse and laid the reins over the small hitching post. Then he sauntered over to Ben and helped him down.

Ben stood mumbling to himself. "Darn horse, stumbled every which way. Didn't miss one hole in the trail." He spied a chair leaning against the soddy and ambled toward it.

Caroline introduced everyone. "That's Ben Wilson staggering toward the chair and over there is Sadie Tedder."

Ben only mumbled, but Sadie waved.

Patrick nodded.

"This is John Anderson, my late husband's brother."

John reached forward and shook Patrick's hand.

Patrick frowned. "I'm most grievous about your husband, ma'am. How did it happen?"

"We'll talk later. Those two boys over there are Micah and Standing Tall, John's sons."

Patrick eyed the two boys, one was a mulatto and the other an Indian. "Quite a group you have here, Mrs. Anderson. Let me get the other chair for Miz Tedder."

"Sadie, honey," she corrected him. "The name's Sadie."

He grinned at her and turned on his heels, disappearing inside the soddy. When he returned, he set the chair up against the wall. Then he took Sadie's arm. "Here, ma'am, let me help you to a little more comfort than a saddle."

"Humph," Ben grunted.

Caroline sat on an old stump while John and the boys relaxed on the ground.

"Can I get all of you some water? If you'd like, there's leftover biscuits and beans inside."

The two boys jumped to their feet. "We'll help."

John smirked. "I believe they're hungry."

Caroline got up and made her way toward the door. "Let me get the food ready. You boys can bring out the drinks. But first, get the extra cups from our supply pouch." She disappeared inside.

"Where do you get your water from?" asked John. "Don't see a well."

"Have to haul it in from about six miles north of here. We keep it in a big barrel inside. That way the dust doesn't settle on it."

"You have much in the way of bad weather around here?"

"The neighbors say the winters are harsh with heavy blizzards and blowing snows for days on end. The area in the low lands down by the river flood when we get heavy rains. But most the time, it's the dust and wind that's bothersome. One other thing that worries me is the spring tornadoes. The neighbors say that they sorta crop up all of a sudden like. Haven't seen one yet, but I hear they tear up everything."

Caroline stood in the doorway and stared at him. "We rode one out somewhere on the Oregon Trail, west of Independence. Lost many wagons and animals. We had to bury several people. They're nasty storms." She shook her head and returned inside.

Micah carried out two tin cups and handed them to Sadie and Ben. Then he returned to get more.

Standing Tall brought out biscuits in a large bowl and passed them around. Caroline carried a pot of beans and set it on the ground.

Patrick pointed at the boys. "You two—"

"Micah. Standing Tall," came the boys' answer in unison.

"Right. Micah and Standing Tall," he repeated. "Go inside and bring out two benches so that we'll have a place to sit. John, would you help me carry out the table."

Once everyone was comfortable and the table was set, Patrick asked, "How did you find us? Where did you come from? Were you at Fort Laramie?"

"Whoa, son, one question at a time."

Ben spoke up before scooping up a spoonful of beans. "I'd say he's a mite impatient."

Caroline told of their travels, meeting with Jane Garnett. She explained how they followed the trail from the Fort Laramie to Yostville. "The rest was simple. Seems everyone around this area has heard of you and Sarah."

"Did they tell you we were married?" asked Patrick.

Surprised, Caroline exclaimed, "No. My goodness. A son-in-law."

Sadie slapped her spoon onto the table. "Where's this minister. We need to get him back out here to do a little more work." She elbowed Ben. "Right, Bennie?"

Patrick shook his head. "He won't be back until spring."

Ben glanced at her sideways. "Ah, shucks. Now ain't that a shame?"

"Don't you *shame* me, you ornery old goat. Humph. Think you've gotten lucky, huh? Well, you got another think coming. I ain't leavin', so you just pray that spring comes early and that minister returns on time. I could get real ornery."

"Sadie, why do ya gotta be so mean?"

"You ain't seen mean yet."

Caroline laughed. "Don't mind them, Patrick. He's sweet on her."

"What?" Ben jumped out of the chair, knocking it over. He stared at Caroline. "Whatever put that idea in your head?"

Sadie grabbed his arm. "Oh, Bennie."

"Don't Bennie me." He moved his chair and sat down. "Women! There's a conspiracy here and it's all against *Bennie*. I need a good drink. You got any whiskey."

"No, sir," answered Patrick. "Only water."

"Pshaw. There's not even a saloon in that settlement back there. How far is the next town?"

Patrick tried not to smile. "I'd say probably a little over four hundred miles due east, as the crow flies."

Ben sat with his mouth open not able to say a word.

"Four hundred miles, huh," said Sadie.

"Yes, ma'am. Near Kansas City and Westport."

She slapped his right arm. "And we had to go and use up all that good whiskey because you went and got yourself shot."

He squealed in pain. "Sadie, you're one cantankerous woman. That's my sore arm."

Patrick gave them a puzzled expression. "Are they always like this?"

"Always," came the answer from the boys in unison.

"Sometimes worse," added John, chuckling. "But we wouldn't have them any other way."

Caroline collected all the bowls and cups, taking them inside the soddy. Then she returned and slipped onto the bench next to John. The cooler afternoon breeze was delightful. Waning sun, in hues of bright orange and gold, hung above the green-gold prairie grasses, like a big eye watching her.

Micah and Standing Tall slipped away, heading into the open field, shoving and pushing each other.

Sadie and Ben sat on their chairs, satisfied to lean back and shut their eyes.

John and Patrick talked about farming the land, how to build a soddy, and what the requirements were for homesteading.

Finally, Patrick got to his feet and scanned the horizon. "Sarah should be home by now. She never stays very long, especially when she has Jamie with her. Our neighbor's wife has been sick and she has five little ones to care for. Sarah's been helping out twice a week."

"Hey," shouted Micah, as he ran toward the soddy. "There's a horse heading this way without a rider."

Patrick jumped to his feet and made his way toward the galloping animal, waving his hat. He halted the horse and managed to grab the loose reins.

John was right behind him. "Whose horse?" he asked.

"Sarah's. I'm heading over to the Johnson's cabin." Patrick led the tired horse toward the corral.

"Wait, we'll go with you." John sprinted toward the corral, shouting, "Micah! Standing Tall! Get our horses ready. Grab the rifles. Let's go boys. We gotta ride."

The boys dashed for their rifles and John's, then rushed toward the corral to saddle their animals.

Patrick mounted his horse and shouted, "Hurry, we have a ways to go." He stood ready to ride.

"What's going on? John, where are you going?" asked Caroline. She grabbed his shoulder.

"Sarah's horse came home empty. Gotta go. I'll explain later." He jumped into the saddle and galloped after Patrick, the boys following closely behind.

She stood frozen to the spot as she watched the four riders disappear into the horizon.

Sadie strolled out to her side. "Where are they off to so fast?"

Her voice shook. "I'm not sure. Something's wrong. Sarah's horse came back riderless."

"What are you women jabberin' about now?" Ben yelled from his chair, stretching his neck to see what caused all the sudden activity. "Where did John and the boys take off to in such a big Goldern hurry?"

Sadie yelled and waved her hand at him. "Just sit there and be quiet, you noisy magpie. I'll tell you in a minute." She touched Caroline's elbow. "Come on honey, let's go back and get things ready for when they return. There's no use standin' out here."

"How far is it to their neighbor's place?"

"I don't know."

Caroline scanned the horizon for some form of life, but with the sun setting, the eastern portion was already turning hazy blue-gray.

Sadie meandered over to Ben and explained about the horse.

"Maybe what we oughta do is light a lantern so they'll be able to find us on their return," said Ben. "Ain't nothin' we can do sittin' out here. Let's go in."

Sadie picked up a chair and disappeared inside. Once she lit the lantern, she reappeared in the doorway. "Come on in, honey. We'll all wait together and put this lantern in the window so they'll be sure to find us. Maybe the horse just got loose."

Caroline started into the horizon. "I'm going to wipe Sarah's horse down and feed her. You go on in. Be joining you in a little while." She looked over her shoulder before strolling toward the stable.

Oh, dear Lord, I'm so close to seeing my daughter after all these years. Please don't let me lose her now.

Chapter Twenty-Nine

John, Patrick and the boys galloped toward the Johnson's cabin. As they drew closer, they could see that the house was dark. Suddenly, a bullet whizzed over Micah's head.

"Hey, watch who you're shooting at," he yelled. "We're friendly."

"Johnson. Is everyone okay in there? It's Patrick O'Brien."

"Dang," came an answer inside the house. "I didn't know it was you, O'Brien. I thought it was those Indians coming back again. Wait a minute until we get the barricade from in front of this door."

Johnson's gruff voice drifted outside. "Somebody light a lantern so I can see to move this stuff."

Finally, the door opened and Sarah dashed out to greet her husband.

Patrick quickly dismounted. The force of his wife's running into his arms almost knocked him off his feet.

"I'm so glad you're here," Sarah said.

"What happened?" he asked. "I got worried when you weren't home before dark. Then your horse came galloping back without you and Jamie."

Johnson stood to one side with his rifle in his hand. "We had visitors this afternoon. A few Indians stuck their heads through the windows, and then they walked right into the house. They poked their noses into everything, picking up stuff and trying on my hat. I was waiting for them to lie in my bed."

"We gave them food," said Sarah, "and coffee with sugar. Made them happy for a while. But they watched Jamie and me all the time." She stood back and hugged herself. "They were no-good Pawnees."

"I think they wanted to kidnap your wife and child once they got their bellies full." Johnson laid his rifle across one arm. "Anyway, they disappeared outside and milled around looking about the area. Then all of a sudden, one Indian stormed into the house with his raised tomahawk, shouting and carrying on. I grabbed my rifle and shot him. We shoved his body outside and barricaded the door. They hid over by the shed. Damn if they didn't start firing arrows and bullets at us. When all the firing calmed down, they snuck in and collected the dead brave before taking off. Wasn't sure how long they'd be gone or if they'd even return."

"My horse ran off when the first guns were fired," said Sarah.

"Is anybody hurt?" asked John.

"Nope, a little shook up, that's all." Johnson jerked his head toward the cabin. "My wife and babies are fine. You want to come in and sit a spell?"

"No, thank you. Need to get back. We have company anxiously waiting for us back home," replied Patrick. "I do have a favor to ask of you, though. Can you loan me a horse? We left Sarah's at the cabin. He was all lathered up."

"Sure, go saddle up one. I don't think the Indians took the horses." Johnson scratched his head. "That's the strange part. After a while, those braves just up and left without taking a thing. Really thought we were goners this time, me with only one rifle."

"Micah. Standing Tall," said Patrick. "Go get a horse for Sarah."

"I need to get Jamie and see to Mrs. Johnson before I leave." Sarah headed toward the doorway, calling over her shoulder, "I'll be right back."

With the moon full, the trail was easy to follow. Sarah rode close to her husband with her son in the saddle in front of her. Whispering, she asked, "Who are these people? The man looks familiar." She glanced around at John again.

"I'll explain when we get home. You won't believe the story."

"Wait, I know him. That's my Uncle John behind us, isn't it?"

"Yes."

She jerked around in her saddle and looked him over. "With all the excitement, I didn't recognize you."

"I didn't recognize you either." John nodded. "Good to see you again, Sarah."

She turned to Patrick. "Is my mother with him?"

Patrick smiled at her, teasingly. "Now, let me see. I do believe there is a woman with him. John," he shouted. "That woman that's with you?"

"Yes," came a reply.

"Is that Sarah's mother?"

John, teasingly asked, "Boys, would you say that was Sarah's mother back at the soddy?"

Frustrated, Sarah yelled, "Quit. Give me a straight answer. My mind is worried, but my heart knows the answer. She's at our soddy. Right?"

"Let me think."

She raised her voice two decibels. "Patrick!" Jamie jumped, hearing his mother's voice. She kissed the top of his head and patted his stomach with the fingers of her hand that held him tight to her body.

"I guess that woman waiting at our place is your mother."

Sarah stared ahead, tears welling up in her eyes. She was unable to speak for a moment. Her lips quivered. "My mother is here," she whispered. "I cannot believe she has found me after all these years."

She choked back the sobs that rose in her throat. Her hands shook. Feeling dizzy from the exciting news, she grabbed the saddle horn with her left hand to keep from falling out of the saddle, gripping the reins between her fingers.

Arriving at the soddy, Sarah handed Jamie to Patrick. She dismounted and stood holding the reins in her hands, staring at the house. Her hands trembled and her knees felt weak. *Inside is my mother. How I have prayed these many years for this day.*

Suddenly, she was afraid her mother would reject her because of the life she had been forced to live with the Arapahos, and for bearing a half-breed.

She dropped the reins and quickly turned to her husband. "Patrick, what if my mother doesn't like what she sees? Look at me. I'm more native than white. My skin is dark. And, what of my son?"

"My sweet Sarah. She is your mother, not one of the neighboring women."

Embarrassed, Micah and Standing Tall stayed in the background and tried to look busy with the horses until John said, "Come on. Let's see if there is any food left."

Holding the baby in one arm, Patrick grasped Sarah's elbow and led her toward the cabin.

When she heard the horses approach the soddy, Caroline threw open the door and dashed outside. Stopping short a few feet from her daughter, she looked at Sarah. The little girl she once knew was now a beautiful woman.

John strolled over and stood by Caroline's side.

She stepped forward. Her voice shook. "Sarah? Do you remember me?"

"Yes," replied Sarah. She tried to control her emotions but her lips quivered and her body shook.

"Are you well?" asked Caroline, awkwardly.

"Yes." Sarah hesitated for a moment. "Much time has passed between us. I am not the same person you remember. My life has changed. The road has been hard." She looked down at her moccasined feet. "Can you accept me the way I am?"

Caroline reached her hand out and touched her daughter's arm. Tears filled her eyes. "You are my Sarah and always will be. It is not how we look on the outside. It is what we have within our hearts. I loved you as a child. I love you more as a woman."

She choked back a sob. "Look at me, Sarah. Do I look the same? I wear dusty pants, beat-up boots, and a buckskin jacket. My hands are rough, my face is lined from the weather, and I have gray in my hair."

Caroline wiped the tears with the back of her hand. "My life has been different than what you remembered. I travel from one location to another." She gestured her hand toward John. "We have no home, only the trail and the horses that get us from place to place. My clothes may appear rough, but my heart is soft and still holds you dear."

Sarah held her head high, but tears trickled down her face. "So much has happened since we last saw each other."

"I know that. It doesn't mean we cannot love each other more. We are still the same person inside." Caroline stared at her daughter, dressed in a buckskin dress.

"Please," she pleaded, grasping Sarah's hand, "take me into your heart again. Don't shut me out. Give me a chance to start over. I have waited and searched so long to find you."

"Mother!" Sarah rushed into her mother's arms and sobbed like a small child.

Caroline held her close and patted her daughter's head resting on her shoulder. Tears flowed down her cheeks as she comforted Sarah.

"I love you mother. I have missed you so. Please don't ever leave me. Please," she pleaded. She looked up and entwined her fingers in her mother's hair.

"You use to do that when you were a child." Caroline kissed her forehead. "I've missed you, too. My heart has pained me so much these last few years. I promise I will never leave you again."

Sarah stood back and took her son into her arms. "Mother, this is my son. We call him Jamie."

"Yes, I know, Patrick told me."

"His father is dead. He is all that I have of my life with the Arapaho. Together we survived." She looked at Patrick. "This wonderful man came looking for me. He is now my husband who cares for us."

"Of course I remember Patrick." Caroline touched the baby's cheek. "What a beautiful grandson." She took the baby into her arms and hugged him. "He's a sturdy child."

Jamie grabbed a handful of hair and laughed. Extricating herself, she handed the baby to John.

Sarah glanced at him. "I see that Uncle John hasn't changed too much."

"Only more handsome," came John's reply.

"Looks like you're settling in territorial Kansas, Uncle John," remarked Patrick.

"Looks that way," replied John, struggling to hold onto the baby.

Sadie and Ben stood in the doorway watching the reunion between mother and daughter.

"Well, I'll be. I do believe we're stayin' in one place for a while, Sadie."

"Oh, Bennie." She blew her nose in a bandana. "We're gonna have a home." She reached over and gave him a peck on the cheek.

"Now, don't go and get all mushy on me, woman." He sounded gruff, but a smirk played across his face.

Pulling Patrick to one side, John asked, "Do you have any whiskey hidden away?"

"In the stable," replied Patrick. "I'll go get the bottle."

"That'll make Ben and Sadie happy." John chucked the baby under his chin. Jamie grabbed two of his fingers and bit down hard. "Ahhh. I think he brought blood. Maybe we should go inside and feed this little one."

"I think that's a good idea," replied Sarah.

Looking over her mother's shoulder, Sarah spied Standing Tall. His eyes narrowed as he stared at her. A Sioux warrior. She knew there was no love lost between the Arapahos and his tribe. *Who is this Indian boy? Her mother called him Uncle John's son. How long will he stay in my home?*

Chapter Thirty

Caroline jolted awake to fists pounding on the door. She rubbed her eyes and stretched her arms over head. "Good gracious, what now?"

Sarah slipped from her bedroll on the floor. "Who's there?" She wrapped a cover around her and trudged slowly toward the door. "Can't believe we'd have company this early in the morning," she mumbled.

"Wake up and open the door. Got something to tell you," came a man's voice.

Sadie sat up in the bed she was sharing with Caroline and then fell back against the pillow. "I wonder if he's at least single." She rolled over and shut her eyes.

Caroline elbowed her. "Sadie!"

Sarah opened the door. Castor stood in the doorway, glum faced and breathing hard. "Well, good morning, Castor. Come in."

"Can't right now, no time to talk."

"What's wrong?"

He scanned the room behind her. Only seeing three women, he asked, "Where's Patrick? Need to see him."

"We moved him out to the stable with the rest of the men, last night. But with all that pounding, I'm sure he's awake now."

Castor turned on his heels and hotfooted toward the large building across from the soddy.

"I wonder what he's all fired up about," exclaimed Caroline. She sat on the edge of the bed, slipping her legs into her trousers.

Sadie rolled over and leaned on her elbow to stare out the door. "You two gonna make breakfast? If so, give me a minute and I'll join you."

Jamie escaped from his mother's bedroll and crawled toward her. She quickly shut the door and picked him up. When she cradled him in her arms, swinging him back and forth, he twisted and wiggled to escape. "And I suppose you're hungry?"

"I do believe he wants down." Sadie laughed as she watched the child grip his mother's hair, pulling himself up her chest and over her shoulder. "He sure is strong for a small one. Like a yearlin'. Listen to him jabber away."

Caroline dipped some water into a bowl, set it on a small table and splashed her face. "It won't be long and he'll be walking. Then we'll all have trouble keeping up with him." Toweling her face dry, she pulled on her shirt and combed her hair.

Sarah sat her son on the bed with Sadie. "That will be the time I have to watch for the bull snakes. He'll want to play with them."

"Bull snakes?" Sadie's eyes grew large as silver dollars. "You don't say. You got things like that around here?"

Sarah stirred up the fire and laid two logs on the glowing embers.

"When the rains come, the snakes hide in the grass roof. Once the roof weakens, the snakes fall through. That's what Serelda Hopkins told me. You have to watch for them."

"Oh, now, isn't that a nice kettle of fish." Sadie grasped the toddler's hands while he pulled himself to his feet. "Look, he's trying to walk." He collapsed onto the bed, giggling. Turning over quickly, he crawled to the edge of the bed. "No, you don't, my sweet dumplin'. You'll bust your head open, sure as shootin'." She held onto one foot, dragging him back from the edge.

Caroline looked out the window into the dark. "I wonder what's going on over there in the stable."

Sarah filled the coffee pot with water, pulled a few hot coals to one side, and sat the pot down on top of them. "I don't know, but something isn't right. Can't imagine, Castor banging on the door this early."

Caroline strolled over to the table and picked up a large bowl to stir up some biscuits. "Sarah, why don't you go on out and see what the men are up to?"

Sarah glanced out the window. "They're talking up a storm over by the stable doors. Ben's swinging his arms and Castor's pointing to the west of here. Haven't seen him that excited in a long time. He sure is stirred up about something and it looks like John and Patrick aren't too happy either."

"Well, go on out there and find out what the problem is," suggested Sadie. "Those men get riled up real easy like. Probably somebody's cow died or maybe a wife ran off with that minister."

Sarah laughed and shook her head. "I doubt that. Reverend Pattywacker wouldn't—"

"Pattywacker?" Sadie asked. "What kind of a name is that? Is he the one gonna marry me and Ben?" She sat there with her mouth open. "Pattywacker," she repeated, "Lord have mercy."

Sadie picked up Jamie and joined the other two women. "Castor. Isn't that the man that Ben whooped at poker back at Fort Laramie?"

"Yes," replied Caroline. "You should have seen the expression on his face when Ben won. He threw his cards across the table and called him an old duffer. Ben almost jumped across the table and punched Castor in the nose."

"Here they come. They look all fired up," Sadie said. She scrambled across the room, away from the window. "We'll know in a few minutes what's goin' on."

Caroline placed the biscuits in the large Dutch oven, covered the pot with a flat lid, then shoveled hot coals on top.

Sarah sliced some beef and gathered the tin plates.

Patrick pushed open the door and everyone filed in behind him.

"Castor, you having breakfast with us?" asked Sarah. "There's plenty for everyone."

"Speaking of Plenty. She's riding up right now." He edged toward the doorway and waited for the Indian woman to join him.

Micah and Standing Tall lounged on a bench, while John and Patrick stood in the middle of the room.

"Castor just told us some bad news," said Patrick. "Seems sometime last night, a few Pawnee braves murdered the Gisslies, west of town. Killed everybody including the children."

The women gasped.

"In all my born days. Everybody?" asked Sadie.

"White man take Indian land and kill game. Indians cannot survive without the buffalo. Army raids villages and murders our people. The treaties are no good. Nothing is the same," replied Standing Tall. "Fighting gets worse. Soon, big war party come."

Plenty moved to Sarah's side and hugged her. Looking over her shoulder, she spied the two boys on the bench. She narrowed her eyes and glared at the Indian boy. "Sioux brave. Not good," she said, in Arapaho.

"What did she say?" asked Caroline.

"She is happy to be here," lied Sarah.

Ben eyed the Indian woman and Standing Tall. He strolled over to sit next to the boy. "Seems you got that woman all stirred up. Must be that native instinct you have or that outdoorsy smell that captivates 'em."

"Humph. Sioux not like Arapahos. Not trust them."

"Well you better get that out of your head, young fella." Ben pointed across the room toward Castor. "You see that big man over there? Well, that's his woman and I know for a fact that he ain't nice when he gets a burr under his saddle. So a word of warnin', we're all family here and we plan to stay that way. Now smile," said Ben.

Standing Tall glared at him and then forced a grin.

"That looks more like a sneer to me." Ben gave him a what-for look.

The Indian boy jumped to his feet. "I go see horses," he announced and hightailed it out of the room, slamming the door behind him

"Yep, you do that and stay out of trouble," Ben shouted after him.

John watched Standing Tall disappear into the early morning mist that cloaked the open fields. He moseyed over toward Ben. "What's going on with Standing Tall? He looks like he ate a green apple."

"Seems that he and our Indian lady don't see eye to eye with each other. Like two ornery bears tryin' to hole up in the same cave. Don't think he's too crazy about Sarah either."

As the men sat at the table and ate, Sarah poured more coffee. "What is everyone going to do about the Gisslies?"

"Hopkins and a few other men from town are gonna meet here," said Patrick. "Micah, after breakfast, you and Standing Tall go over to the Johnson's. Tell him to bring his rifle. From what Castor says, the Pawnees didn't leave the area and will be back. We need to hunt them before they come after us."

Sarah stood white knuckling the handle of the hot coffee pot. "They are dangerous to fight. Many times they attacked our village. They kill for pleasure."

"Yep, they sure do," agreed Ben. "Got cornered one time up at Green Mountain after the rendezvous in '36. Me and Schmidt just built a shelter for the night, when out of nowhere these three braves show up. Seemed friendly at first, then they turned ugly. Whupped my weight in wild cats that day. Barely escaped with my scalp."

"You and your stories," said Sadie, jabbing him in the ribs.

Patrick motioned Ben to shut up.

Ben ducked his head and drank his coffee.

"Sarah, I want you to take the women and Jamie into the settlement to the Hendricks. You'll be safe there. The Hendricks' house is a strong fortress and all the women have rifles. Besides, Pleasant would be happy to have you visit." Patrick walked over to his wife, and took the coffee pot from her hands. "Does anyone else want more coffee?"

Sarah nodded as her eyes glided to Plenty.

After the sun stretched above the horizon, the women packed saddlebags with food and clothing, taking as much as they could load on two mules and two extra horses.

Sarah led her horse out of the gate. Holding her son in her arms, she sided up to Patrick. "You will be careful? Beware of the quiet, for the birds will tell of their coming. The tall grasses will be your only cover."

"I'll be fine. You stay away until I come for you. Take

care of our son and Sadie. Your mother and Plenty will help you." He kissed her on the nose, then cupped her face, devouring her lips.

"Be safe," she whispered. After she climbed into the saddle, he handed the small boy up to her. She secured him in front of her and rode to join the other women.

Patrick watched her ride west, heading down the trail to follow along the river.

"They'll be fine," said John, standing behind him. "Those three know the land and will care for Sadie. They'll be safe. Now, let's get ready. The others will be here soon. Grab your rifle."

Chapter Thirty-One

Sarah rode west toward the Hendricks cabin, scanning the flat prairie and rising knolls. In front of her, on the far horizon, rose the plateaus in a golden blanket. She enjoyed the freedom the prairie offered her and had come to love the way the hip-high grasses moved, swaying in unison as a breath of the wind danced across the tops. Miles upon miles of graceful waves of beauty surrounded her, except when a rocky knoll or bluff cropped up.

She glanced to her right and smiled at Plenty who rode silently, a grim expression on her face. "What's wrong?"

Plenty looked at the ground and leaned forward. "Many signs here not good. See, much broken grass. Goes off from trail."

"Could be a large animal."

"No, several horses follow." Plenty made hand movements to show what she meant.

"Pawnee?" asked Sarah.

Plenty nodded.

"What's she talking about?" asked Caroline, riding up closer to her daughter. "She seems to be upset with something."

"Plenty says that the line of broken grass over there, leading toward the north is a trail left by Indian horses following single file."

"Do you think we need to turn back and get the men?"

"No. If the signs are true, they're headed north toward the spring, about six miles from here."

Caroline turned in her saddle to check on Sadie. The older woman swayed with her horse. She slumped over the horn, her eyes closed. "Sadie! Wake up before you fall off and hit the ground."

Sadie jerked awake, pulling on the reins. "What? I didn't say anything."

The women all laughed.

"I didn't say you were talking. I said you were gonna fall off your horse."

"Men come." Plenty pointed to a few riders approaching them from the east.

"That's probably Mr. Hendricks and a few neighbors headed out to our place."

As the riders drew closer, Sarah waved.

Once Hendricks reached the women, he pulled up to talk. "You better get going. Make sure you stop at my place. Pleasant's waiting for you."

"Tell Patrick, there's a trail of unshod ponies headed toward the springs north of here. Plenty thinks its Pawnees."

Hendricks touched the brim of his hat, then he and the rest of the men galloped west toward the O'Brien homestead.

The dusty trail dipped down toward the Smoky Hill River. With the sun rising high in the sky, perspiration trickled down Sarah's neck. "We'll stop up ahead for a quick break and water the horses."

She hugged Jamie who had both hands full of horse mane. He pulled and yanked the hair, while he slapped his heels against the bottom edge of the saddle. "If your legs were any longer, my poor horse would be confused by all that heel pounding."

Her son let go of the mane, leaned forward and grasped the horn, chewing on the leather. "I believe he's getting hungry."

Plenty reached into a small pouch at her side. She pulled out a tiny piece of jerky and gave it to him. He dove sideways for the tidbit, sliding cockeyed in the saddle.

"Wait," shouted Sarah. She grasped the boy with one arm, pulling him to her stomach to keep him from falling off her horse.

"There's a nice level place just ahead by the river where we can stop and water the horses," Caroline pointed. "It'll give my squirmy grandson a place to release some of that energy."

Halting their horses, the four women dismounted and stretched their legs. Sarah placed Jamie on the ground some distance from the horses, and he immediately crawled toward the water.

"You need a rope on that one," said Sadie, as she watched Sarah dash to catch her son. Sadie leaned back and placed her hands on her lower back. Then she grabbed her canteen and took a swallow.

Caroline's horse raised his head and whickered. "I wonder what brought that on."

Plenty, squatting by the water's edge, jumped to her feet. "We go, now."

"Why is she so nervous? I wished she spoke English," said Caroline.

"We need to get moving." Sarah picked up her son and handed him to Sadie. She placed her foot in the stirrup and threw her leg over the saddle. Sadie handed her son up to her.

The women walked their horses, two by two, back onto

the trail, heading west, toward a small bluff. As they crested the top, five yelling Pawnee surprised them. The braves sprung from the tall grass and dashed forward with raised tomahawks and clubs. The scared horses whinnied loudly and rose up on their hindquarters, while the riders tried to control their mounts and avoid the braves.

Caroline pulled her rifle from its boot. She was able to get off one shot, missing her target, before a Pawnee knocked her off her horse. The warrior grabbed a handful of hair ready to slash her throat, when she wiggled around, reached forward, and grabbed his testicles, twisting hard. He dropped his knife, bending over, holding himself. Quickly, she picked up the knife and holding it with both hands, buried it into his back. On hands and knees, she searched for her rifle in the tall grasses.

One brave grabbed Sarah's reins, yanking them out of her hands, while another brave clutched Jamie by the throat and tossed him some distance into the grass. She screamed, pulled her knife from her waistband, and fell off her saddle onto the Pawnee. She wrestled him on the ground, rolling over and over. With one hand free, she quickly raised it and shoved her knife into his throat. A third warrior, seeing his friend fall forward, blood gushing from his wound, rushed toward Sarah. A rifle shot sounded and a surprised expression flashed across his face before he hit the ground. A fourth brave let go of Sadie and dashed toward Sarah, swinging his club. He brought it down across her blocking arm full force, knocking her off her feet, face forward in the deep grass. As he raised the club one more time over his head, another rifle shot rang out. The Pawnee fell dead beside her.

The last brave pinned Plenty on her back, both arms stretched over her head, while he straddled her chest. She bucked and screamed at him all the while trying on release his grip on her wrists. Sadie picked up a club and swung it, catching him squarely across the side of his face. Plenty squirmed out from underneath him, as he lay dazed. She picked up her knife and slit his throat.

Sarah lay curled in pain. "Find Jamie," she screamed. "My son. Find my son."

Caroline dropped to her knees to examine Sarah's arm. "Lie still and let me see how badly you're hurt."

Plenty shuffled through the grass, following the cries of the infant. Finding him, she picked him up and cradled him in her arms. "I find. He is good," she said in Arapaho. She handed Jamie to Sadie.

Sadie didn't understand the words, but she knew what the Indian woman meant. Looking over the small boy, only his dignity seemed to be hurt.

Plenty grabbed the reins of her horse and climbed onto his back.

"I get horses," she announced to no one in particular. She took off at a trot into the high grasses, following the trail left by the animals.

"Sadie," shouted Caroline. "Can you find my hat? Get me the bandana from inside it. Need to make a sling for Sarah's arm."

Plenty returned with the horses in tow. She dismounted. "We go now. We lost much time. Need to make settlement soon.

Caroline helped her daughter mount her horse. Then she gave Sadie a leg up.

Plenty stepped around the dead warriors and mounted her horse, carrying Jamie.

Throwing her leg over the saddle, Caroline looked back at the three women. "We don't have time to head to the Hendricks' place. We need to get back to the soddy and report to the men. Let's ride."

* * *

Patrick watched the riders approach. "The men are here," he yelled at John.

Ben rose from the chair and strolled over to stand with Patrick. "Where are the boys? Every time ya need 'em, they're off somewheres."

"They're in the stable getting some of the animals saddled."

Hendricks rode up and quickly dismounted. "Saw the women. They're on their way."

A rifle shot sounded from the west, and another.

"Dang, the women are in trouble," yelled Patrick.

Hendricks jumped back into the saddle and galloped off with the other men.

"Get your horses saddled and let's ride. We need to catch up with Hendricks and his men," shouted Patrick, as he ran toward the stable.

A bullet whizzed past him and struck the stable door. Ducking behind the water trough, he spied two Pawnees on the side of his soddy and three lay on top of his roof. Several others rode in from the east, firing their rifles.

John took cover back inside the soddy. "Ben, get in here."

Ben turned toward John and sunk to his knees, falling forward, as a bullet caught him in the head.

Micah and Standing Tall dashed to the opening in the stable with their rifles in hand. They fired at the braves on the roof, killing one, hitting another. The other Indian slid off the back. More Pawnees rode in from the north, circling the soddy and stable, firing their rifles.

Patrick scrunched low in the dirt without a weapon.

"Got another one," yelled Micah as bullets zipped passed Patrick's head.

"Keep firing and stop counting."

Standing Tall fired at a rider.

John yelled, "Hey, you boys in the stable, be careful. You almost got me. When you shoot, don't aim near the door or the two windows."

"Pa, do you think Ben's dead?" asked Micah, firing several times.

"I'm afraid so." Suddenly, Patrick yelled, "Sonofabitch, I'm hit in the leg. Keep firing. We need to keep them busy until Hendricks and the others get back."

Sarah slumped forward and used her good hand to grip the horn of the saddle to keep her balance. She swayed dangerously with each step the horse took. Her head felt light, her left arm was painful. The world around her was off balance. She knew she needed to stay in the saddle and hang onto the horn.

Caroline held onto her reins, leading Sarah's horse behind her. "Sadie, fire my rifle again. The men should be coming to meet us."

Plenty pointed into the eastern horizon. She hand signed *horses.*

"What's she saying?" asked Sadie.

"I'm not sure but I think there's a couple of riders coming." Caroline squinted. "Yes, the men are coming."

When Hendricks and the men rode up, the women greeted them with shouts of joy.

"Glad to see you men. Had a run in with a few Pawnee braves. They're about a quarter of a mile behind us," said Caroline.

"Saw them heading over the bluff as we rode toward you." said Hendricks.

"We took care of them. Thought they were gonna get my scalp." Sadie was indignant.

"I believe they broke my daughter's arm and possibly her shoulder," said Caroline. "We need to turn around and make it back to the men."

Plenty sat listening to the conversation, glancing at each speaker. Every time Jamie tried to squirm out of her grip, she shoved him back into place.

Sadie looked from each man's face. "Where's my Bennie? Ya didn't bring him out.

"He always comes and greets me, 'cause he's afraid of losing me." She chuckled at her joke. "I thought he'd rescue me, the old goat."

"Ah, he's not with us, Sadie," one of the riders replied. "We heard your rifle shots and galloped out here fast. But, about a mile out, we could hear gunshots back at the O'Brien place. Maybe you women need to stay here. You'll be safer."

'Ain't no way we're not goin' with you," Sadie said as she mounted her horse.

"All right. If you're ready, we need to get back. You women stay behind us in case we run into any trouble. Let's ride."

As they neared the O'Brien homestead, the place looked quiet. "Let's not ride all the way in. Looks a little suspicious. Too quiet." Hendricks pulled his rifle from it sheath, as did the rest of the men.

Plenty dismounted and handed Jamie to Sadie. Then she walked several horses over to the side and looped their reins together. Caroline jumped from her saddle and quickly moved to help a man get Sarah off her horse

As the men approached the soddy, Hendricks shouted, "Hello, O'Brien. You still here?"

"Is that you, Hendricks?"

"Yes, we got the women out here and your wife is hurt."

Patrick threw open the door and hobbled outside. He searched the area and spied the women back behind a small knoll down the road a bit. He limped toward them, dragging a bandaged left leg. "Sarah. Is she all right?"

He found her lying on the ground. He collapsed next to her, leaning on his right side. "What happened to her," he asked, looking up at Caroline.

"We were attacked by some Pawnee braves about three miles out."

"Anybody else hurt?" He looked from face to face.

"No."

Patrick got to his feet and scanned the horizon. "Are the warriors following you?"

"No, those five won't be following anybody."

Sadie sauntered toward the Soddy. "Bennie, where are you, you sweet thing. Come see your sugarplum. I got a story to tell you about how I whopped—" She stopped in mid-sentence. "What's wrong?"

John took her by the shoulders. "Sadie, I've got some bad news for you."

She stared at him.

He ducked his head for a moment, and then looked into her eyes.

"No, not my Bennie," she wailed. "Not my lovin' man."

John held her up as she began to collapse.

"How? Why?" she screamed, tears streaming down her face.

"Some Indians rode in and shot up the place. Ben tried to get back to the soddy. He caught a bullet in the head and died instantly."

She pounded her fists against John's chest. "No, no, why my Bennie? What am I gonna do without my sweet, honey man."

John encircled his arms around her, hugging her close to his chest as she cried, her shoulders shaking.

Sarah looked up. "Is it true that Ben is dead?"

Patrick stood above her. "I'm afraid so."

She noticed the wrapping around his right leg. "What happened to your leg?"

"I got hit. One of the Pawnee bullets found its mark."

She gasped, "Are you okay?"

"I'm fine. You're the one I'm worried about. We need to get you inside so that your arm can be tended to."

Hendricks strolled up. "I sent a man over to get Johnson. He does a good mending job." He nodded to Patrick, "I think we ought to get both of you inside."

"Where are the boys?" asked John.

Micah stepped out from behind Hendricks. "I'm here and Standing Tall's in the stable taking care of the horses."

"Let's go, Miz Sarah." Hendricks picked her up and headed toward the soddy. Patrick hobbled after him.

Plenty held Jamie and waited. She spied Castor standing near the doorway.

John strolled along, his arms around Sadie. "We'll bury him right over there in that nice level spot. That way you can see him whenever you want. He'll always be with us."

Sadie started to cry again. "That wonderful old man. Gone. Gone forever."

Micah stood watching the group disappear inside. Sadness filled his heart as he looked around at the tall grass. "Why did I ever leave St. Louis? I didn't have much of a home there. Had to sleep on the streets, but at least I knew what to expect each day. Here it's always a surprise."

"You lost? Sun take your mind?"

He turned to face Standing Tall. "No, just asking myself why I'm here in godforsaken land and not back where I belong."

"You belong here with me, my brother. If you leave, I have no one."

Micah slipped his arm across Standing Tall's shoulder. "Brothers forever."

Taking one last glance toward the soddy, the boys headed to the stable.

Chapter Thirty-Two

Through flowing tears and heavy hearts, Caroline and Plenty washed Ben's body and dressed him in his best clothes. Patrick could not scrounge up enough lumber to make a coffin, so they sewed him up in the canvas cloth that John had stuck away in his traveling bags.

It was mid-fall and the heat was still stifling. Micah and Standing Tall worked hard, shoveling the grave until the hole was wide and deep enough. Sweating profusely under the hot sun, they stuck their shovels into the dirt. Wiping the dust from their arms and hands, they sat down in the shade near the stable to wait.

Later, Castor and Patrick stepped outside carrying Ben, followed closely by John supporting Sadie. Her steps were lumbered and unsteady as she clung to his arm. Head bent and leaning into him, she sobbed with each step. Closely behind them, Sarah walked with her broken arm now securely bandaged. Carolyn followed her daughter while Plenty carried Jamie. The procession advanced around to the back of the stable to a piece of land facing a small grassy knoll that would now become a family cemetery.

John and Castor lowered Ben into the freshly dug grave.

Sadie stopped at the gravesite, while the others gathered close to her. "I'm gonna miss you, you ornery old man. Yes, I am. Drinkin' partner and all."

Tears streamed down Sadie's cheeks. "Why'd you have to go and get yourself shot, Bennie? What am I gonna do without you? Who's gonna keep my backside warm this winter."

Sarah put her good arm around her shoulder. "You'll always have a place with us. We love you Sadie."

"I know. It's just, I was lookin' forward to seein' that Pattywacker minister, and me and Ben tyin' the knot this spring. It's not fair." She covered her face with her hands and broke down into heart-rending sobs.

Patrick cleared the lump from his throat and began reading from the Bible.

Later in the afternoon as Plenty and Caroline cleaned up the dishes, the ground vibrated beneath their feet and a bowl danced across a shelf.

"What in the world is that?" asked Caroline, grabbing her son up into her arms. "It feels like the earth will split wide open."

Plenty and Sarah smiled at each other. "Buffalo," they shouted in Arapaho.

"What?" asked Caroline. "Speak so I can understand you."

"Buffalo, mother. The winter herds are coming through. We are going to have fresh meat." Sarah whirled around the dirt floor with excitement.

Micah ran inside, followed by Standing Tall. "Can you feel the ground shake? The buffalo are coming."

"Much work, but plenty meat for eating," said the Indian boy, patting his stomach.

"Buffalo, never ate that before. Guess it's better than snake or some other critter I've tried," said Sadie. "Don't know nothin' about them."

"Don't worry, Sadie," replied Sarah. "You can stay here with me and Jamie. He needs someone to love him while they're gone."

John rushed into the room, grabbing his gun and ammunition. He turned and ran into Patrick, almost knocking him over as he crossed the threshold with Castor right behind him.

"Looks like we'll have plenty of meat for the winter," said Castor. He smiled at his woman and spoke to her in Arapaho, "The buffalo finally came and there's much work ahead. Are you ready?"

"Yes," said Plenty. "I will make you a warm robe to cover your body. Good strong moccasins to protect your feet from the snow."

Castor sided up her. "You are a great comfort, woman."

She smiled and looked down at the dirt floor, embarrassed by his kind, loving words.

A sneer crossed Standing Tall' lips as he glared at the Arapaho women. "Sioux women make better moccasins."

Raising one eyebrow, Castor glared at him. "Enough. You will have respect for these two women."

Avoiding the confrontation, Standing Tall raised his head in defiance and stepped outside.

"Mother, you must go with them. Grab your knife and saddlebags. Make sure they're empty," Sarah said.

"I don't believe we've ever hunted buffalo, have we John?"

With excitement in his voice, John answered, "Nope. But, there's always a first time for everything. A buffalo hunt. This is great."

Sarah smiled. "Plenty will show you, mother. She has much experience with the buffalo. Here, take this old buffalo robe."

"Are we gonna cover the buffalo after we kill him," Caroline asked.

"No, you'll need this to haul the meat back. You'll butcher out in the grass."

Castor announced to the men, "We have to stop by my place on the way. Need to get some of our equipment and more ammunition."

"Micah, where's your rifle?" asked Patrick

"In the stable. I'll get it as I leave."

"Is everybody ready?" shouted Castor. "Daylight's burnin'. We sure as hell don't want to miss this hunt. Standing Tall, come in here."

The young brave sauntered into the doorway, crossed his arms, and took an arrogant stance. His eyes narrowed as he glared at Castor

"We're putting you in charge of this hunting expedition. Your skills for killing buffalo are better than anyone's here. Do you think you can handle that?"

Standing Tall's mouth fell open. Surprised, he asked, "I take charge?"

"Yep, that's what I said. You don't want me to repeat myself, do you?" replied Castor. "Are you ready?"

The Indian boy nodded as he looked from Patrick to John.

Castor patted the boy's shoulder as he walked passed him. "Well, let's go. You better get your weapon."

"How about that?" said Micah. "And you stomped out of here, all mad a few minutes ago. Come on, let's get our stuff."

"I not stomp, leave quietly." A puzzled expression crept across his face, then he smiled. "I'm in charge!"

"Well, you won't be if you stand there all day," said Micah.

Sarah leaned against the doorframe. Sadie stood beside her with the baby in her arms. They watched the hunters saddle their horses and head out to hunt.

Jamie squirmed to get down, arms over his head as he tried to slip from her clutches.

"Here," said Sadie, passing the small boy to his mother. "Why don't you take this one outside?"

Sarah grasped her son with one arm and headed outdoors. "You and I have some waiting to do, son," said Sarah. "Why don't we go and enjoy the day. You can crawl in the dirt all you want and maybe I'll sit and talk to Ben."

The hunting party lay on top of a small hill, overlooking a moving black mass of wooly backs that covered the area for many dusty miles.

Plenty's mind drifted back to the days in Arapaho camp and the comfort of her teepee. She reached her hands into the grass as she imagined touching her beloved things. The excitement in the village when buffalo appeared. *Buffalo, buffalo* the shout went up from her people. Her heart skipped a beat as she remembered the thrill of watching her man skillfully ride among the hairy beasts. Hands So High held his head erect, the pride and honor of downing a buffalo. She could almost smell the fresh kill and taste the buffalo hump soup. If only she could go back to the days of The People.

Tears filled her eyes for the memory hurt. She remembered her dead husband and child, and life in the Indian village. Turning to Caroline, she wanted to tell her what was in her heart, only the white woman would not understand.

Plenty knew those days were never more. She must accept the changes that are part of her life now. There was no going back, ever.

Standing Tall whispered to the men as he outlined his plan, pointing to various points where they were to ride into the herd.

The two women listened, knowing they needed to stay behind until several of the bison were killed.

"We ride," whispered Standing Tall.

Mounting their horses, the men galloped down the small slope and into the herd, scattering most of the huge beasts, cutting off a small group. Shots rang out and thunderous hooves bit into the grass, stirring up huge clouds of dust, throwing dirt and clumps of grass into the air. It looked like a large black ocean wave moving across the prairie as the bison moved in unison, escaping to the south.

Caroline watched the skill of the Indian boy and Castor as they drove the small buffalo group back toward the women. The dust billowed upward creating a huge screen.

Plenty grabbed Caroline's arm and pointed, before jumping to her feet. She motioned 'Come.' Then she took her knife out and made several swipes.

Caroline nodded.

The women rode toward two dead buffalo.

Reaching the first animal, they worked feverishly skinning, cutting the meat into large chunks. Plenty was the most skilled and directed Caroline on how to do the work. They cut the legs whole, tied two together, and slung them over the horses' rumps. They bagged entrails and hung them from the saddle horn. They worked feverously until the entire buffalo was dissected and ready to take back to the soddy.

As they made their way toward the next bison, Plenty watched Standing Tall ride toward the other men. Suddenly, his horse stepped into a gopher hole, threw him to the ground, and then galloped away. A stray buffalo turned, pawed the ground, and charged toward the Indian boy. Standing Tall stood with his back to the bison. Hearing the pounding hooves, he turned and faced the charging bull. Plenty watched in horror as the huge bison closed the distance. She shouted, but her words were lost in the noise that surrounded the hunting party. Racing to her horse, she jumped into the saddle as Standing Tall managed to avoid the first charge. Pushing her horse into a gallop, Plenty rode like the wind shouting and waving one hand to ward off the bison. Reaching Standing Tall's side, she grasped his hand, swung him up behind her, and rode off. Veering her horse to one side, she outmaneuvered the bison, barely escaping the deadly thrust of his horns.

A shot rang out and the bison crashed to his knees, slid forward and fell on its side, dead.

Castor rode up behind them. "Looks like the women are doing more than skinning the kill. You okay, son."

"I am fine," he replied as he slid off Plenty's horse. He stood there, head bent. Then he looked up at her and signed, "The Great Spirit is with us today. I am grateful for my life you have given me. You are now my sister."

Plenty nodded, rode off to continue her work.

"Not bad for an Arapaho, huh? This must be your lucky day. By the way, John's got your horse. She's limping a bit, but her leg isn't broken. You'll have to ride double with Micah."

"Hey," yelled Micah, as he rode up to Castor. "We only needed three buffalo, not four. I thought Indians could count."

"I count. With your belly always hungry, we need more meat. Need more robes for winter."

"Let's quit sparring, boys. We need to help these women get this meat back."

"That's women's work," said Standing Tall. "I kill buffalo, not clean."

"Listen, you young scallywag. Work is work out here. You are one arrogant sonofabitch," sputtered Castor. "Everybody pitches in to get it done. I don't ever want to hear either of you boys ever say *It's women's work*. Now get over there and wrap that meat." He rode off in a huff.

"Standing Tall, can't you ever be quiet and listen? Every time you open your mouth around him, we're in trouble. I didn't say a thing and I get my butt screwed."

"Skinning buffalo is women's work."

"He didn't ask us to skin it. He only wanted us to wrap it up and haul it back. Maybe in an Indian village you don't do that. But out here...oh, just keep quiet around Castor. You surely do set him off."

"Him old man."

"Yep, and that old man can be mean, too. I'll bet he can whip both of us with one arm tied behind his back. I ain't gonna test him. If you're riding with me, let's go." Micah offered Standing Tall his hand.

Sarah sat next to Ben's small cross talking to him, all the while watching Jamie. The toddler crawled over the dirt mound and rolled onto his back, giggling. She couldn't help but smile at his antics.

"Oh, Ben. You should see this little one. He is so cute and gets into everything. Why, he's here right now playing next to you. Yes, he's a handful to care for, but I'll bet by Christmas, he'll be jabbering and walking." She paused for a moment. "I'm so thankful that you found my mother and guided her to California. I know I didn't thank you properly but you did a grand thing. Thank you for being there for her. Just think, if you hadn't helped my mother, you never would have met Sadie."

She looked up in time to see her son choking. She struggled to her knees, pulled him to her, and dug the grass and dirt from his mouth with her fingers. He chomped down on one. "Ow, you little rascal. Here I am saving you and you have to bite your mother. Maybe we need to get you something to eat besides me."

Glancing to her right, she made out figures of the hunting party riding over a knoll toward her. "My goodness, they're back already. I need to get you cleaned up before your father sees what you've been up to." She tucked Jamie under one arm like a sack of flour, and made tracks toward the riders. He grasped the side of her doeskin dress with both hands and squealed as she jostled him with each step in her crushing grip.

John and Castor arrived first, each with large hunks of meat wrapped and tied to the backs of their horses.

Sadie wiped her hands on a cloth as she stared at massive bundles of Buffalo meat. "My, oh, my," was all she could say.

Sarah passed Jamie to Sadie. "I'd say the hunt was a success."

"We shot four buffalo. We're all hauling it in. Can't waste this precious meat," said John.

"How are we gonna work all this today?" asked Sadie.

"We can keep some of the meat bundled up and put it inside so it doesn't draw any wild animals," Sarah replied.

"Much of the meat will be dried for winter use," replied Castor

Patrick rode in and slid gently from his saddle. He hobbled toward a chair that leaned against the soddy and stretched out his bandaged leg. "Ah, that's better."

"Where are the boys?" asked Sarah and Sadie in unison.

Castor shaded his eyes as he looked into the horizon. "They'll be coming in soon. You know how those two are, slow as molasses."

As Plenty and Caroline rode in behind the men, Castor and John started unloading the buffalo bundles.

"Here come the boys now," said Sarah. "What in the world are they trailing behind them?"

The boys approached dragging four skinny trees and leading Standing Tall's horse.

"We thought you might need these to make a drying rack for the meat strips. At least, that's what Standing Tall says."

The Indian boy jumped off the back of Micah's horse and tied his horse up at the post. Taking out his knife, he began slicing off small branches from the spindly tree.

"This is all we could find. Not many trees around here," said Micah.

"No, you have to travel farther east to find trees," said Patrick. "These will have to do."

Several nights later, Micah returned from the stables. "Has anyone seen Standing Tall? I can't find him anywhere."

"Saw him heading west on his horse," replied John.

Micah dashed outside to his horse. As he rode across the prairie, his thoughts were troubled. *Darn that stubborn Indian. He's been acting funny for days, now. I wonder what's bothering him.*

Five miles from the soddy, Micah spied Standing Tall sitting on top of a small hill. He joined his brother and sat down beside him, Indian style. "So, what are you thinking about?"

"I hear the wind call from the north. It is time to go home to see grandfather."

"Why? Aren't you happy here? I thought we were brothers?"

"We are, but spirits speak to me. They say it is time."

"Time, phooey." Micah paused for a moment. "Don't talk to me about spirits. You're just mad because Castor's always telling you what to do. Besides, you're not happy with his Indian woman."

"No, peace is between us. She saved my life." Standing Tall ran one hand across the matted grass at his side. "I must go back home to Lakota country." He stopped for a moment seeing the puzzled look on Micah's face. "We do not call ourselves Sioux. That is white man's word. We are Lakota."

Micah nodded.

Standing Tall pulled several pieces of tall grass and twisted them together. "You may come with me if you want, but it will hurt your father's heart if you do."

Micah bit his lip, took in a deep breath and then exhaled. "Darn, you're making this hard." He plucked a long piece of grass and stuck the stem end into his mouth and leaned back onto his elbows. Twirling the grass with his tongue, he thought about the trip north. It would be an adventure, but leaving his father and friends pained him.

"I guess I'll be staying behind. But you will come back, right?"

"Only time will tell."

"What does that mean?"

"Great Spirit will guide me. When it is time to come back, I will return." Standing Tall opened the medicine bag that hung around his neck. He reached inside. He extended his fist to Micah. Unclenching his hand, a red stone lay on his palm.

"I give this to you for protection while I am gone. It has magical powers. Keep it close to your heart. Do you remember when Mary at Fort Bridger gave the bags to us?"

Micah sat up and picked the stone from the Indian's hand. He rolled it between his fingers, and then he dropped it into the pouch that rested on his chest. "Yes, I remember."

Getting to his feet, Micah headed toward his horse. "I have something for you." He poked around his saddlebag, grabbed something, stood there for a moment, and then sat down next to Standing Tall. In his hand was an eagle feather.

"My father gave this to me at Fort Laramie, the night before we met. He told me he found it in the mountains a long time ago. Here, take this and wear it proudly for you're now a strong warrior. That's why my father named you Standing Tall."

The Indian lad reached slowly with both hands. An eagle feather, a prized possession among warriors. The glint in his eyes danced and a smile spread across his face. "This is a great honor to receive this gift from my brother. I will wear it with much pride." He stuck the tip into his braid behind his ear with the feather pointing downward.

"Oh, you got a lot of pride. Ask Castor."

The boys laughed.

Standing Tall grew serious once more. "Listen to the wind. It whispers its secrets and carries messages from those that love you."

Micah closed his eyes. Maybe his *maman* would call his name or he might hear Black Annie, his old nanny whisper to him. His heart yearned to feel their arms around him, to hear their words, to feel their love. He wished he lived in the past just for a moment to tell them both he loved them.

The two boys sat together watching the sky turn from rosy pink to shades of blue-gray as they shared their last night together. When the stars appeared, they climbed back onto their horses and headed toward the stable.

"You must promise not to tell others until I am gone."

"I promise," said Micah

Chapter Thirty-Three

For three weeks, Micah moped around the stable caring for the horses and doing odd jobs at a snails pace. When he told his father that Standing Tall had left to return to his village in the north, John wasn't surprised. With his brother gone, there was no one to share his secrets with. He lived in a house full of adults who didn't have time for him. His spirits dipped low.

As the days grew shorter and colder, his morale hit rock bottom and he spent a lot of time daydreaming. Occasionally he would take Jamie with him as he walked across the prairie or down to the river. But other days, he rode north over the hill and returned later, never an explanation as to where he had been.

Early one morning, before Micah could escape, John grabbed his son by the shoulder. "We're cutting sod today and need your help. So don't disappear. Saddle up your horse. We're leaving soon."

Micah bit his lip, swallowed a smart remark, and strolled toward the stable.

Caroline glanced over Patrick and John's shoulders, watching the boy trudge away. "He sure is lost without Standing Tall."

John glanced sideways at her, surprised to see her standing there. "He'll get over it. Besides, our young brave will be back one of these days. Standing Tall doesn't fit in either world now. But he's always welcome here."

Caroline smiled, strolled over, and picked up the baby. "Is Hendricks coming out to help you cut the sod?"

"Yes. He's supposed to be bringing a couple of other men with him. Making bricks to build us a soddy takes more than a few people, especially if we want to be in before the snow flies."

Sarah covered her hand with her apron, grabbed the coffee pot handle, and poured cups of the hot brew for everyone. "Pleasant said we probably have another month or so before the first snow hit. Might get a few flurries between now and then."

Patrick sat nursing his steaming cup. "We're working as fast as we can. John and I been working on that acre of buffalo grasses. No way to plow strips when it's that high. It took most of the day. Good thing we sharpened those two scythes. That's the toughest stuff I've ever worked through. Roots have to be a foot deep."

John grinned. "Or deeper. Glad we've got Hendricks' plow instead of having to use shovels."

"Yes, me, too. Drink up," Patrick said. "We need to get out to that field."

As Micah daydreamed, he leaned on his shovel stuck in the ground. Far into the horizon, the land rose up and touched the sky, blending into one. Sometimes the puffy clouds lay across the sky like a white blanket, almost smothering him. It was beautiful but never seemed to change unless a storm was brewing. The bleakness didn't do much for his enthusiasm. "When are the others coming?"

"Soon," replied his father. "Help me hitch these two horses to the plow."

Castor rode into the field and dismounted. "Mornin'. Is Hendricks comin' out today?"

"Yes, he should be here any minute," answered Patrick. "Looks like him riding in now, with his wagon. Seems he's got Hopkins and another fella with him."

Hendricks halted the wagon on the edge of the cut grass and jumped down to join the men. "Ya think we weren't comin'? Brought Jed Thompson with me. He's an old hand at building with sod. We'll leave him in charge."

"Okay with me," replied Patrick

"What do you think, Jed?" asked Hendricks. "You ready to get us working?"

"Yep, let's get going. Hendricks, you run that plow of yours two feet wide," said Thompson. He turned to Patrick. "Grab yourself a shovel and cut those strips into three foot lengths. You there." He pointed at John.

"Anderson," he replied.

"Anderson, when the boy loads them onto the wagon, I need you to stack them, nice and tight. Move the wagon as we go. Hopkins, you help the boy load the strips."

Hopkins nodded, acknowledging he understood.

"What can I do?" asked Castor.

"Grab a shovel or a corn knife. You and I are gonna cut the strips. The more bricks we get cut the faster we get done. By the way, once we get this here wagon loaded, do you have the ground ready to build your place?"

"John's staked off a level piece of ground south of my place. The grass is already cleared off," said Patrick. "The women are over there right now smoothing and pounding the dirt with spades."

"Sounds like we need to get to work then. The way we're moving, the women folk will be sitting around waiting on us."

Hendricks stirred up the horses and the plow dug into the thick matted grass.

Work progressed hour after hour, strip after strip. Micah's shirt and arms were dirty from hands to shoulder. His back ached from bending and lifting, but he knew if he complained the men would rib him. He stood up and rolled his shoulders, before taking off his hat and wiping the sweat from his forehead with the back of his dirty sleeve. The bricks were stacked five feet high from front to back on the wagon. It would take three or four trips to get enough sod over to the building site. Gazing across the prairie, he watched dark clouds gathering in the west. Another one of those boisterous rainstorms. He hated them.

"A storm's brewin'," he announced.

John placed a sod brick on top and looked up. "Sure looks bad. It's coming this way and fast." He stepped down on the wagon seat and then jumped to the ground. "What do you think Hendricks?"

The wind was already gusting and suddenly whipped the back of Patrick's jacket over his head as he turned away from the blowing wind. "I think we got us a granddaddy of a storm coming straight at us."

A deluge of rain fell from the sky, dousing the men as they ran for cover under the wagon. Lightening cracked across the sky. Fiery fingers jutted and danced toward the ground in a spectacular light show. Micah stood mesmerized as a dozen spears of light flashed in the sky. Thunder resounded across the prairie, repeatedly, creating its own kettledrum music.

"Get down, Micah." Hopkins grabbed the boy's pants leg and yanked him onto the ground, pulling him under the wagon. "You want to get killed out there."

"Damn, this might be bad," said Hopkins. "The last time we had this much lightening, there was a huge grass fire. Spread almost to the settlement."

"With the weather this cool, you'd think these storms would be over with by now." Jed covered his head with his arms as a loud clap of thunder sounded above.

"Somebody grab the horses before we're run over or they bolt. Dumb animals," shouted Hendricks.

John crawled out from under the wagon. Hunched over, keeping low and next to the animals, he made his way to the front. Grabbing the bridles of both horses, he wedged himself close. "If I get hit, so do you my lovelies. Easy now. It'll be over soon, I hope."

The back of his shirt stuck to his skin, chilling him to the bone as he stood with his hands above his shoulders. Rain trickled into his sleeves, down his arms to his armpits. His boots were soaked as he stood in a mud puddle. All he could think of was a warm fire, a comfortable chair, and a bowl of hot soup.

As quickly, as the storm raced in, the black clouds traveled on eastward. The area was now muddier, cooler, and glistened with diamond water drops. Slowly the sun peeked out as the storm clouds gave way to a few white billowy clouds. The men crawled from under the wagon.

Mud splotched Micah's face, his hands caked with the gooey gunk. His temperament was at its lowest peak. Water laden trousers clung to his legs, causing him to walk bowlegged.

Patrick rolled out, grabbed the wheel and pulled himself up. "We should get started back with this load."

"I agree. Grab the shovels and we'll head to where you want this dropped," said Jed. "We might even get some of these bricks laid before dark. We'll bring the rest of the sod over tomorrow."

"I'm sure there'll be eats waiting for us at Patrick's. Sadie and the women were cooking all day yesterday. Come on," said Castor. "My belly's a-growlin'."

Hendricks climbed onto the seat, Jed next to him. "I'll get my plow tomorrow. Micah, why don't you ride up on top?"

A large grin plastered on his face, Micah made his way to the top of the sod. "You can see a long way from here. There's Castor and Patrick's soddy's way over there."

John, Patrick, and Castor gathered a few shovels and handed them to Micah. Then they mounted their horses and headed toward home, followed by Hopkins who rode Micah's horse.

Two weeks later, Sadie carried a bucket of water from inside the O'Brien soddy. It was washday and there were several loads. She struggled across to the open area where she had built a fire to heat the water. After it was boiling, Micah helped her by pouring it into the big kettle. She had a pile of clothes on a square table ready to wash.

"I'm gonna need one more for washing and another for rinsing."

"Ah, Sadie. Do I have to get them now?"

She placed her hands on her hips and bobbed her head from side to side. "Micah Anderson, it won't hurt you one..."

She paused as she peered over his shoulder and saw riders coming toward them.

"Oh, Lordy, help us. Indians! And they're movin' in fast." She gathered her skirt up over her knees and high stepped it toward the soddy, shouting over her shoulder, "Get your rifle, Micah. Hurry."

Dashing through the doorway, she all but collapsed into Sarah's arms, out of breath. "Indians...here...look." She pointed toward the door.

Patrick grabbed his rifle, followed closely by John. Dashing outside, they loaded their weapons and made ready in one smooth motion.

"Where's Castor?" yelled John.

"In the stable," answered Micah, standing behind the men.

Plenty dropped her work and ran outside after the men.

"Sadie, you stay in and watch after Jamie," said Sarah. She ran to join Plenty.

"You women stay inside," commanded Patrick. "Don't know what they want, but it doesn't look pretty from here."

The Indians rode straight toward the soddy, whooping and howling, their rifles and spears raised in the air. They were dressed for war with their faces painted.

Sarah quickly glanced at Plenty. The two women pushed the men aside and stepped forward.

John whispered, "Looks like they know those braves."

"Micah, lower your rifle, but stand ready. We don't want to spook them," said John. "And smile. Our throats aren't cut yet."

The men slowly lowered their rifles, but were ready to fire at the least sign of hostility.

Sarah dashed out in front waving one arm and shouting in Arapaho. "Stop! We are friends. Sisters of the Long Beaver Band. I am Vision Seeker."

Standing beside her, Plenty yelled, "I am Plenty Hoops Woman, wife of Hands So High. We are Arapaho."

The on-coming Indians slowed their pace, halting their horses a few feet from the women. Their faces showed no quarter and their body movements emanated their hatred and desire to attack.

One warrior yelled, "We come for scalps. Step aside and let us show these white devils that we are true warriors. We do not hide behind our women."

"No," pleaded Sarah. "These are good people. Hear our words."

The leader held up his hand for silence. He mumbled to the others and lifted his head, eyeing the women. His spear carried a blonde scalp still bloody from a fresh kill.

"You say you are Arapaho, yet you live with a white man in his house. Why are you not with your people?"

"Our husbands were killed and our village raided. Many of our people are now with the Great Spirit." Sarah pointed to the men behind her. "These people saved us and fed us."

The brave to the left of the leader, leaned over and spoke to him. Both men nodded their heads. "We of the Greasy Face Band, brothers of The People, greet you. Our hearts are open and offer you protection. You may ride with us. We go to our winter quarters where our families now camp. Get your horses. We must leave."

Plenty gave Sarah a sideways glance. She spied Castor standing over by the stable. She wished with all her heart that he wasn't so near right now.

He stared at her. She knew he understood the conversation. He didn't flinch a muscle or blink an eye. A blank expression hid his feelings. He stood holding his rifle in his arms and watching her wrestle with a decision that would change both their lives.

Sarah whispered, keeping her head bent. "You're not thinking about going back with them, are you?"

Plenty hesitated, a puzzled expression on her face. "I thought maybe—"

"Think what will happen to you when you go with them. They will marry you to the first warrior that steps up and claims you. You will have no say in the matter. Aren't you happy here? What about Castor?"

Plenty turned once more toward the man who saved her from death. A man whose kindness had no end, but he was white. She closed her eyes. Maybe a vision would touch her and give the answer she could follow. She mumbled, "Oh, Great Spirit, help me. I am confused and saddened. I miss my teepee and the old way of life."

Sarah touched Plenty's shoulder. "That is no more, my sister. Not for us. Stay here where we can be together."

The Indian leader gave her a questionable look. "Speak louder for I cannot hear what you say. You must decide now, for we cannot wait."

A warrior from the back rode forward, toward the women with a raised hand in peace.

Sarah and Plenty stared at him, their mouths opened in surprise.

"I am Strong Bow. Remember me?"

"Yes," answered Sarah. "You brought the body of my husband back to me. Your kindness is well remembered."

"My brother, Cut Nose, lost his wife several months ago. He needs a wife. You both can live together with him for I know he would keep you well."

"So it will be," said the leader.

Plenty glanced at Sarah.

Sarah tried not to look appalled. "I remember Cut Nose. He always beat his poor wife. This is not good, Plenty. I will not go. Patrick is kind to me and I love him. I carry his child."

She looked at Strong Bow and smiled. "You do me a great honor to offer the place of wife for your brother. I am sure he would be a good husband. But I must stay here for now my life has changed."

Strong Bow lifted his chin, his nostrils flared. He pointed to Plenty. "And you?"

"I remember Cut Nose. He is a great warrior and hunter. My heart is filled with sorrow for the loss of his wife, but I, too, must stay." She bowed her head to Strong Bow to show him respect.

He only glared at her, one eyebrow lifted to show his indignation. "Humph. My brother can find better. Good *Indian* wives among our people than the two of you." He yanked the horse's reins and returned to the back of the group.

Patrick and John watched as the tall Indian talked to the two women. He pointed toward the men. Suddenly the Indian sat up straight and stiff, scorn on his face.

John whispered. "We might have trouble here. Don't like the way they're looking at Sarah and Plenty."

Patrick glanced sideways at Castor who stood transfixed watching Plenty. "He understands what they're saying and I'm not sure I like his expression."

Sarah shook her head and made hands signs, as did Plenty, while they talked. Finally, the lead warrior nodded, turned his horse and rode off with the group in tow.

Caroline rushed to her daughter's side. "What did you tell them? I thought for sure some of us were going to lose our scalps."

"I told them I was Vision Seeker of the Arapaho tribe, the wife of dead Running Swift."

Patrick moved to his wife's side. "Did they want you to join them?"

"Yes," she answered. "But life for us with The People is no more." She leaned into her husband's arms and laid her head on his chest. "I am happy where I am and with my husband." She patted her belly. "Our child will have a good father."

Patrick kissed the top of her head and wrapped his arms around her. "You had me worried there for a minute. But, I'll never doubt you again."

Castor propped his rifle against the stable door and strolled over to stand in front of Plenty. "You were offered a husband in their village. You could have gone with them."

"Yes, it is true."

"Why didn't you go?"

Plenty lowered her eyes. "I thought about what he said. I was confused. I dream of the old ways, the Arapaho life, but they are no more. My road has been long and hard since my husband and child died. Nothing is the same. There is so much to learn in your world."

She looked up and searched his face. "I do not speak your language and cannot understand always when the others speak. I am a lost soul in the wind and sometimes my heart hurts. Even birds rest in their flight. Sometimes I feel I am falling and there is no end to reach."

Castor moved a stray hair from her forehead. "Would you feel more secure if you called me husband and we spoke our vows?"

Her eyes widened. "You do not have to marry me, for your life is different from mine."

"I've never had to do anything I didn't want to do. That you must believe."

He cupped her face between his large hands and kissed her nose. "I love you, Plenty Hoops Woman. As God is my witness, you fill my heart and life with meaning. Will you be my wife?"

She grinned. "I do not have a father or a brother for you to bring horses to."

"Your worth is greater than any amount of horses." He swooped her up into his arms and twirled around. "You are my woman, forever."

Then he shouted to the wind, "Do you hear me world? This woman is to be my wife."

"What a marvelous day this is," shouted Caroline.

Sadie ran toward them carrying Jamie. "First a war party and now a weddin'? Things sure do change fast around here."

"Yes," answered Sarah. "Castor just asked Plenty to marry him."

"Well, he sure is actin' funny. Never saw him cut up like that. Strange what gettin' married will do to a man," said Sadie.

Castor put Plenty down and then put his arm across her shoulder. "I know it was a hard decision, but I'm real happy you women decided to stay with us."

Sarah looked into Patrick's eyes and smiled. "It was not a hard decision for me. My life is here with my family."

Caroline hugged John. "Your father and I are happy that you didn't go with the Indians."

"My father? He's in the spirit word." She stopped and stared at her mother. Then she looked at her Uncle John.

Dead silence surrounded them as everyone waited for an explanation from Caroline.

"Oops," said Micah, as he sauntered toward the stable.

"What do you mean mother?" Sarah searched Caroline's face for an answer.

Realizing the implication, Sarah's eyes narrowed as she

pursed her lips together. "No, he's not my father. He can't be. My father's dead."

Caroline looked up at John and then back to Sarah. "Let me explain."

Tears welled up in her eyes. "No," she screamed at Caroline. "I don't believe you. How could you? I hate you both."

She took off running passed the soddy and into the high prairie grass.

"Sarah. Wait. Hear me out," pleaded Caroline. "Wait."

Chapter Thirty-Four

John grabbed Caroline's arm before she could dart off after their daughter. "Wait. Maybe Plenty should go to Sarah first. From what I've seen, they're close, like sisters."

Castor nodded in agreement. "John's right."

"She's still my daughter. I need to talk with her, explain why things are the way they are." Tears trickled down Caroline's face.

John put his arms around her, holding her close. He kissed her forehead. "I understand, but let Plenty go. Let her ease the way first."

Caroline looked up into his face. "All right, I'll wait. But there is so much I must tell her."

John brushed her tears away with his thumb, one eye at a time. "Let's take one step at a time right now. Especially since the cat is out of the bag about my being her father."

Castor spoke to Plenty, explaining the situation. Finally, he said, "Go to your sister. She is troubled."

"I will talk with her and comfort her. Sarah is strong, but her heart is sad. Life is not easy. Many hills to climb."

She moved to Caroline's side and patted her arm. Struggling with the white man's language, Plenty said, "I bring her back, mother." She mounted her horse and rode north across the prairie.

Castor relayed Plenty's intent, then said, "Why don't we have somethin' to eat. Sadie, you got anythin' to go with that pot of soup ya got warmin'?"

Sadie switched Jamie to her hip. "Sure do. If you men'll bring the table and chairs outside, I'll have a meal you won't forget."

Micah screwed up his face. "Soup and bread? We had that yesterday."

"Go get the chairs, Micah, and be quiet. If you're hungry, you'll eat," said John.

Plenty decided to go to her dugout knowing Sarah would not go too far on foot.

The door stood open. Dismounting, she tied her horse to the post and stepped inside. Light crept through the two small paper greased windows on each side of the door. The men had dug one large room out of the side of the hill with a thick grassy roof supported by several beams. A meager selection of furniture consisted of a bed in the corner, a small table and two chairs.

Sarah lay curled in a ball, facing the wall, with the blanket clutched in her tight fists as she cried.

Plenty stood in the doorway, blocking the light behind her. "Is your heart so broken that love has left you."

Sarah sat up and stared at her friend and sister. "Did you not hear what my mother said? My Uncle John is my father. My real father!"

"People of our tribe believe that a good husband should

take many wives. They ask the Great Spirit to watch over them and bring forth children. Sometimes it does not happen. Death waits in the shadows of childbirth. You should know. Many women leave their families to walk the path with our ancestors. Maybe women take many men."

"But he's my uncle. You don't understand. He is a coward."

"No, he is brave. Did he not guide her here for her to find you? Did he not keep his son and Standing Tall with him, and protect them? He is a man, strong but soft of heart."

"You make it sound so right."

"My father, Big Elk, married his brother's wife. Two Eyes did not want her anymore. He beat her." Narrowing her eyes, Plenty sat on the bed next to Sarah. "He cast her from his first wife's teepee without a robe when the snow flies. She was my mother. Big Elk took her in. She was not pretty, but he did not care. She was a good woman. He loved her. Now, they are stars that fill the heaven and guide my path. One day, I will join them."

Sarah reached over and touched Plenty's arm.

Plenty turned and looked straight into Sarah's eyes. "There is no shame in what has happened between your mother and uncle. Their life was before your other father. The only shame is yours for not giving them your love. Our journey has many rough trails. We must be strong."

Sarah hung her head. "I guess I should be ashamed of myself for being so childish. My anger is how Uncle John arrived at the cabin back in Virginia. He spread that small bag of gold in front of my father. That's all it took to get my pa to head west. Mother didn't want to go and leave all of her treasures. Now that I think about it, my mother suffered more than anyone. She lost her comfortable home, her daughter, my brother James, and my father on that terrible journey. I look at her now and see a different woman"

Sarah thought for a moment. "I should have waited for my mother to explain. But, the news was so sudden, it shocked me."

"Yes. Words hurt you. Now, you must open your heart. Let it guide you. Go to her. Love her. You do not have to understand the past. One day she will ride the wind with the Great Spirit above. You will not see her beautiful face again until you join her."

"You are so wise," said Sarah.

"There has been much sadness in my life. Now I smile, for Castor loves me. It is hard to think of him as a white man. He is a warrior of my soul. Soon we marry."

"I will be there with you." Sarah jumped to her feet and hugged Plenty. "My sister, always."

"Come, we ride back together. You must talk with your mother. There is much to share. Listen to her story. Then you must tell her of Running Swift."

Sarah wiped her eyes with her fingers. Then she patted her hair and straightened her dress. "I will go to hear what she has to say." She lifted her chin, "But, I don't have to agree with it."

Outside, Plenty said, "Let her thoughts travel to your mind. Take them to your heart and know she is a woman who loved two men. You loved two men. Is it so difficult to understand?"

Sarah thought for a moment. *What Plenty says is true. I have loved two men.*

"No." Her expression softened as a smile crept across her face. "For I know it can be so."

"Listen carefully. Then you will understand the words. We go."

* * *

Caroline leaned against the doorframe, munching on a piece of Sadie's delicious bread. Hearing a horse approach, she strolled outside and rounded the corner.

Plenty jumped from her horse and stood holding the reins.

Sarah sat tall, staring at her mother. She hesitated for a moment and then slid over the horse's rump.

"Please talk with me. I have not done a terrible thing. Let me explain," pleaded Caroline.

"Mother, I will listen, but not here. Come. Walk with me to the river where we can sit and share where our lives have taken us."

The two women headed across the prairie grass. Plenty watched them for a few minutes. From behind, she heard a small sound. Smiling, she said, "You are a noisy white man. If I were a warrior, your throat would be cut."

Castor put his arms around her, hugged her tight, and rested his chin on her head. "I am glad you are not a warrior for I would have nothing to offer you in my bed."

She giggled. Wiggling out of his grip, she jumped into his arms, wrapping her legs around his waist, nibbling on his earlobe. "We go now," she whispered. Disentangling herself, Plenty climbed into the saddle and galloped toward their dugout.

"I love a wild woman." He hustled toward the stable to get his horse.

When the two women reached the river, Sarah sat in the grass watching the slow current bubble over the rocky bottom. "The river is low. We need more rain."

Caroline paced back and forth. "Yes, I can see that."

For a moment neither spoke. The silence seemed to stretch forever

"I cannot call him father," Sarah blurted out.

"I don't expect you to."

"Mother, how could you? Did my father know?"

"No one knew, only my mother." Caroline stopped for a moment, crossing her arms. "Sarah, many changes take place in a woman's life. At first, they're insignificant ones. Bit by bit, they attach themselves to each other. When I was young, about your age, I was wild and free, living in Pennsylvania. I thought life was wonderful. I gave my love to an adventurer whose first love was taming the next mountain."

Sarah stared at her mother, not saying a word. She scrunched her brows as to question the line of conversation, but not a word escaped her lips.

"I thought I loved John. I was so careful except once when..."

Caroline lowered herself next to her daughter. "We were so young. When he went away, I found that I was pregnant. There was no way I could live without shame. I was unmarried and having a baby. Alexander came into my life. He was handsome and kind, on the quiet side. He asked for my hand in marriage. I was thrilled. After we were married, we moved to Virginia. You see, little changes already taking place in my life. I didn't notice them, they were everyday happenings."

"Did you love my father or did you marry him because you were pregnant?"

"I cared for Alexander and grew to love him deeply. He was a wonderful man. When he proposed to me, I accepted to save my good name. I came to realize how kind and loving he was. Alexander was responsible, unlike your Uncle John."

"Uncle John, my real father. I hate him for this. Why did he have to come back into our lives?"

"Sarah. If you must hate someone, hate me. I gave into him. It was my fault. Changes, Sarah, that is what life is all

about. Changes that you don't see at first. Changes that creep
up on you and manifest into a large obstacle. Changes ride
the tails of a breeze, traveling erratically. I look back on my
life from where I stand now and see that everything had
clumped together. I have asked myself, why? How did I
arrive where I am now? What did I do to reach here or what
would I have done to change the direction of my life?"

Sarah rested her chin on her clasped knees.

Caroline scooted closer to her daughter and hugged her.
"Please forgive us, Sarah. Your Uncle John is a changed man.
He cares about people and works hard."

"I don't care what he does. If it wasn't for him, we would
still be back in Virginia. Pa and James would be alive."

"Sarah, we can't go back to the way things were. Think.
One day you will have to explain to Jamie about his father.
By Indian law, you were married. By white man's law, you
weren't. Think about how you will handle that. What will
you say to him?"

Sarah lifted her head and glanced at her mother.

"You see, nothing in this world is guaranteed or easy,"
continued Caroline. "We plan our lives one way. Living
them is a whole different story. My mother told me that a
long time ago. I laughed at her. When I was younger than
you, I announced that I would marry a rich man who owned
acres of land and had a big house with fancy furniture."

Caroline stretched her legs forward. "Look at me, Sarah.
I am an older woman, bronzed and hardened, traveling with
a group of misfits who I dearly love. I know that I wouldn't
change my life now for anything only because I feel
comfortable in my skin. I have made a decision as to where
I will live and with whom. I don't own land, I roam it. My
house most of the time is under the heaven's stars. Yet, I am
happy to be with John Anderson. His gentle ways make me
happy. That is worth more than money."

"Do you really love him, mother?"

Caroline smiled. "Yes, he grows on me day by day. I owe him my life many times over. Please try to understand. Forgive my youthful daydreams, the frivolous ways I had as a young girl. I made a mistake a long time ago, yet I received a beautiful daughter that I love very much."

Sarah threw her arms around her mother. Caught by surprise, they both fell back into the grass. "I love you, mother. I don't know if I understand all of it, but I forgive you. I just can't call him father."

"You don't have to. I understand. Micah felt the same way once. So did Standing Tall."

"That's another thing I don't understand."

Caroline raised her eyebrows, a smirk on her face. "One day I'll explain about the boys. Right now, let's take one situation at a time."

She reached over and kissed her daughter's forehead. "I love you, Sarah."

"Yes mother, I know. I love you, too."

Staring into the sky, Caroline watched a hawk circle and glide ever so gracefully. She took several deep breaths. "Life is like the winds of change that glide over the wings of a bird, wild and free."

Sarah shut her eyes. She could smell the greenness of grass as she listened to the birds above. Slowly, she sat up and faced her mother. "I must tell you about Running Swift."

She watched the expression on her mother's face.

"Go on," said Caroline. "I'm listening."

"It was a Crow brave who kidnapped me from our wagon and later traded me to the Arapaho. At first, life was hard, but later I learned to live like an Indian woman."

Caroline sat listening to her daughter's story. She didn't interrupt, but her soul cried for a young girl who had her childhood stolen from her. Now barely a woman, she carried a load far too heavy for her age. Sadness overwhelmed Caroline as tears slid down her face. She reached out and touched her daughter's shoulder.

Sarah choked. A lump wedged in her throat as she spoke about Running Swift. "He gave me a beautiful son. My husband was killed in a wagon raid one day. My heart hurt and life did not seem worthwhile. I kept going only because of my son. My husband's mother was hateful. When the Army rode into our village in retaliation for the raid, a soldier shot her. Jim Castor rescued me and took me to Fort Laramie. He is a kind man and loves my sister, Plenty."

When Sarah finished her story, she leaned into her mother's arms to be comforted. She sat there, eyes closed, allowing the love she craved for so long to seep into her heart, mind, and body. A calm came over her.

"We should be heading back," said Caroline. "I am sure everyone is waiting and wondering what happened to us."

"I was thinking, mother. Like you, my whole life is so different from what I thought it would be. When we lived back in Virginia, I imagined a man kneeling before me, asking for my hand in marriage. There would be a big gathering at the church, friends and neighbors from all around would come. We'd build a cabin near you and father."

She paused for a moment. "But, here I am. I live on a prairie in a grass soddy with a dirt floor. I have slept with an Indian and gave birth to his son. I have experienced wars and witnessed death. When the soldiers came to rescue me, I saw the disrespect and hatred in their eyes. Now I am married to another man and I'm not yet twenty."

Caroline raised her daughter's hand to her mouth, kissing each finger. "I know what you mean. I'm much older than twenty and I still don't understand all that has happened to our family." Caroline looked around. "If only your brother, James, could have seen this land."

"Do you think he really drowned in the Kansas River?" Caroline sighed. "No, there is a place in my being that tells me he is still alive. My heart cannot turn him loose. I keep praying and hoping one day he will show up. But, until that time, I have a wonderful son-in-law, a mischievous grandson," Caroline patted Sarah's belly, "and a soon-to-be grand baby."

"Life is strange."

"Have you picked a name for this child you carry?"

"Caleb Michael"

"What, no girl names?"

Sarah laughed. "We only have one, Caroline Ann."

John and Patrick stood vigilant as their eyes searched for their women.

"Should we go after them?" asked Patrick.

"No. Give them a bit more time. They'll be back."

"Here they come now," announced Micah, jumping off the fence railing.

The two women strolled arm in arm through the tall grass. Neither seemed to be in any hurry.

Reaching the soddy, Caroline faced John. "Maybe you and Sarah need to talk."

Sarah bit her lip as her mother pushed her forward.

"I think that's a good idea," said Patrick. "It's gonna be a while before Sadie gets that meal warmed up."

John nodded, offering his arm to Sarah. "Let's go visit Ben."

Sarah pushed passed him, walking ten paces ahead.

Reaching the gravesite, he rested on the ground, picked a long piece of grass, and stuck it between his teeth. "I don't know what your mother told you, but do you have any questions?"

Grasping her hands behind her back, Sarah paced back and forth. "She told me about your love affair before she married my father."

She turned to watch his reaction when she spoke the word 'father' to see if he would cringe. The muscles in his face never moved, a blank expression was all she saw.

"I'm glad she shared that with you. You do understand that I never came between them. I respected their marriage."

Sarah found it hard to hate this man, her natural father, who sat unemotionally at her feet. "I understand that. I want *you* to know that I cannot call you father."

"I don't expect to take Alexander's place in your life. I only hope that one day I can earn your respect. I love your mother very much. She is a wonderful lady."

John rose to his feet.

Sarah backed up. "Why did you come to Virginia? We were happy back there. If you had stayed in California, none of this would ever have happened."

John thought for a moment. "I don't know. Maybe I wanted your mother closer to me. I still cared for her. Honestly, I missed having family around. Life in California, panning for gold, is a lonely, cold life. Most of the men that look for the yellow dust die within three months of their arrival. No one truly gets rich prospecting. I missed talking to my brother and sharing my life with him."

"And his wife," was Sarah's caustic remark.

"Yes and his wife. I'll admit to that. I needed to see her again. My life had no purpose. I drifted from spot to spot, dreading each day as the sun came up. When your mother showed up in Hangtown alone, I hated what I had done. It's hard to live with yourself when you know you have caused harm to those you love."

Sarah stared at the man whose hair was beginning to gray at the temples. Lines creased his forehead and around his mouth. He looked older, more haggard than she remembered. Maybe it was time to forgive and forget.

"Uncle John, I am glad that you are there for my mother, that you care for her and protect her. However, someday, you need to explain about Micah and Standing Tall. For now I am part of their lives."

"Yes. I owe you that much."

Walking over to him, she put her arm around his waist. She saw his mouth quiver and tears well up in his eyes. He didn't speak only nodded his head and patted her on the back.

"Let's head back," she said. "I am tired and hungry. My feet are swollen and my body says it's time to sit down and rest."

Smiling, he placed his arm across his daughter's shoulder.

Epilogue

For over a month, Micah sat cross-legged on a grassy knoll each evening staring into the western horizon. In the last few days, the weather had turned colder, the snow flurries still held off. Trying to stay warm, he pulled his hat down over his ears and raised the collar of his heavy wool jacket to cover the back of his neck. The brisk cold wind whipped around him. He tucked his hands into the sleeves of his coat.

Tonight, his mind wandered on no particular thought. The quiet gave him peace, but the loneliness ate at his heart. This night was no different from any other night he spent dreaming and longing for the Indian.

"Somewhere out there, my brother, you are seeking answers to your life. Come back, Standing Tall. I miss you."

He watched the sun slip to the earth, kissing the ground as it disappeared. The late fall sky was cloudy, but the rose and pink reflections hung heavy above the prairie. He would wait until the last bit of light passed to the other side of the world before he would head home.

Finally, he pushed up from the ground and stood. He glanced north one more time. His eye caught a movement in the distance, but the gray sky hindered his vision. He held his breath. Was that a rider coming his way? The horse had a familiar gait.

A smile crested his face. He wanted to shout, cry out, but instead he crossed his arms and waited.

Standing Tall was returning home.

~The End~

About the Author

A native of Missouri, Gwyn Ramsey spent many hours at the library, reading Nancy Drew, Little Women, Treasure Island, Anne of Green Gables, and many others. Stories were important to her, but it wasn't until she was in high school that she tried her hand at writing. She took journalism and wrote for the school paper. When she finished high school, she went out into the work world and eventually married.

She attended the Florissant Valley Community College in Missouri and pursued a Computer Applications Associates Degree. When Gwyn and her husband retired to Florida, she decided to try writing again. As her stories evolved, the characters came alive.

Writing is now an important part of her life. She has traveled across the United States with her characters through undeveloped territories, seen the wonders of the west in its magnificence, and eaten the dust from the covered wagons as she walked the Oregon Trail. What an adventure her characters have taken.

Gwyn's historical family saga, *Journey to Tracer's Point*, was released in July 2008, published by Sundowners, a division of Treble Heart Books. Her second book in this series and newest release is *Winds of Change*. Come join her in an adventurous ride of Americana stories that will thrill you.